Also by Jeanne Kalogridis

COVENANT WITH THE VAMPIRE

CHILDREN OF THE VAMPIRE

LORD OF THE VAMPIRES

THE
BURNING
TIMES

A Novel of Medieval France

Jeanne Kalogridis

SCRIBNER PAPERBACK FICTION

PUBLISHED BY SIMON & SCHUSTER

NEW YORK   LONDON   TORONTO   SYDNEY   SINGAPORE

SCRIBNER PAPERBACK FICTION
Simon & Schuster, Inc.
Rockefeller Center
1230 Avenue of the Americas
New York, NY 10020

First Scribner Paperback Fiction edition 2002
SCRIBNER PAPERBACK FICTION and design are trademarks of Macmillan Library Reference USA, Inc., used under license by Simon & Schuster, the publisher of this work.

For information regarding special discounts for bulk purchases, please contact Simon & Schuster Special Sales at 1-800-456-6798 or *business@simonandschuster.com*

Designed by Charles B. Hames
Manufactured in the United States of America

1   3   5   7   9   10   8   6   4   2

The Library of Congress has cataloged the original Simon & Schuster edition as follows:
Kalogridis, Jeanne.
The burning times : a novel / Jeanne Kalogridis.
p. cm.
1. France—History—14th century—Fiction. 2. Carcassone (France)—Fiction.
3. Abbesses, Christian—Fiction. 4. Goddess religion—Fiction. 5. Witchcraft—Fiction.
6. Confession—Fiction. 7. Monks—Fiction. I. Title.

PS3561.A41675 B87 2001
813'.54—dc21   00-046326

ISBN 0-684-86923-3
0-684-86924-1 (Pbk)

ACKNOWLEDGMENTS

For one who makes her living with words, I now find myself at a dreadful loss for them. This book haunted me, first as an idea, then as an unfinished manuscript, for over twelve years. How can I possibly convey the depth of my gratitude to the many who suffered with me throughout its creation and/or offered their sage advice during the countless rewrites?

By all rights, thanks must go first to the man who listened to my bare-bones idea and suggested that I put it on paper: my agent, Russell Galen. Without his encouragement and belief in my abilities, this book would not be. Thanks likewise go to my international agent, Danny Baror.

I am likewise indebted to my editor at HarperCollins UK, the very talented Jane Johnson, who showed such enthusiasm for *The Burning Times* that she bought it not once, but twice; to my U.S. editor at Simon & Schuster, Denise Roy, who brought her wonderful historical expertise to the project; and to my German publisher, Doris Janhsen of

List Verlag, and editor, Caroline Draeger, who both demonstrated great patience and faith.

A special thanks must go to my readers, who freely gave their time, and whose comments had enormous impact on the book: to my cousin Laeta, an uncanny writer and editor, who saw the manuscript in its many incarnations; to my dear friend Lauren Hoey, one of the most thoughtful readers I have ever met; and to George and Beverly and Sharon.

Last of all, I must thank two people who indirectly contributed to this project: Jan and David, whose small act of kindness brought such peace of mind.

For my

Beloved

'Tis the heretic that makes the fire
Not she which burns in't.

—THE WINTER'S TALE

There is no fear in love;
but perfect love casteth out fear.

—JOHN 4:18

PROLOGUE

Sybille

I

It is a hard, deafening rain.

Fast, malignant clouds shroud the moon and stars, and the softer velvet black of the night sky; profound darkness veils all, save for those instants when lightning illuminates the distant mountains, and I see:

My galloping mount's coat gleaming like onyx, his wet mane whipping like a Medusa's crown in the angry wind; see, too, the road to Carcassonne before us, studded with stones, brambles of wild rose, and bushes of rosemary that yield their astringent fragrance as they are crushed beneath the horse's hooves.

Rosemary brings memories; roses are not without thorns; stones are hard.

Hard as the rain: in the flash, it appears long, jagged, crystalline—a hail of icicles, of small, frozen lightning bolts. They pierce and sting, and though it seems right that this moment should be physically painful, I feel a welling of pity for the stallion. He is exhausted, gasping from the long, strenuous run; even so, when at last I rein him in, he fights me, rearing his head.

As he slows reluctantly, lifting strong, graceful legs to pace side-long, I put one palm flat against his shoulders and feel the muscles straining there.

He is sensitive, my steed, in the way most animals are, though he does not possess the Sight: he cannot see those pursuing us, but he can sense the Evil residing in one particular heart. He shivers, but not from the autumn chill, and rolls his great dark eyes to look questioningly back at me; I can see terror in the whites.

We have fled our enemies this long; why, now, do we wait for them?

"They will not hurt you," I tell him softly, and stroke his neck as he whinnies in protest. His coat is cold and soaked from sweat and rain, but underneath, the muscles emanate heat. "You are a fine horse, and they will take you where it is warm and dry, and feed you. You will be treated kindly."

Would that I should encounter the same.

In that instant, I want to weep, hard and bitter as the rain; hard, so very hard. The stallion senses this and, distressed, increases his pacing. I collect myself and give his wet neck another stroke. My pursuers would say I was casting a spell on the poor animal; but I know it is only the opening of one's heart to another creature, the unspoken sharing of calm—a true calm I must look deep within myself to find. One cannot lie to animals.

I am almost near the end of my journey, but the Goddess has spoken: there is no further use in running. Should I continue to flee and my Enemy to chase, none of it will save my poor Beloved. Surrender provides my only chance—a slender one, fraught with risk, and my Sight will not reveal the outcome. I shall live, or I shall die.

Soon the horse and I fall silent and still. The rain has eased, and in the absence of one noise, I hear another.

Thunder, but there is no lightning in the sky.

No; not thunder. Hoofbeats—not one pair, but several. We wait, my steed and I, until they come closer, closer, closer. . . .

And out of the darkness appear four, seven, ten cloaked men on horse-back—the very ones I have Seen in my mind's eye all the dark hours of my flight now materialized in the flesh. A black cloud slips to reveal a slice of new moon, and the glint of metal: nine of these men are gendarmes from Avignon, from the pope's personal cadre. I am encircled. They close in, drawing the noose tighter, and lift their swords.

New moons are for beginnings; this one bodes an end.

I and my stallion remain perfectly composed, perfectly still.

Suspicious, some of the gendarmes face outward: where are my protectors? Certainly, they lie in wait nearby, ready to spring on my captors; certainly, they would not have simply abandoned me, a small and unarmed woman, their supposed witch-queen.

Ah, no; 'twas I who tried to make my escape without them—but so loyal were they that they soon found and joined me. And when the Goddess demanded my surrender—mine, not theirs, for She had need of their service elsewhere—I sent them away. At first they refused to leave me; indeed, Edouard swore he would die first. I could only close my eyes and open my mind, my heart to theirs, that they might hear the Goddess as I did.

Edouard sobbed as though his heart would break; the others' faces were obscured by their hoods, but I sensed the silent tears streaming down their cheeks. We said no more; needed say no more, for all was known. Thus my brave knights rode away.

And now I watch three of the Enemy's men leap from their horses to plunge swords into sparkling blackberry brambles, into thick, tall foliage, blades whistling as bits of leaf and stem go flying. One man climbs up into a nearby olive tree and hacks off branches until he is satisfied no one waits in ambush.

Mystified, they return to their mounts' sides and stare at me as I continue to sit, calm and quiet as my stallion. Darkness or no, I see fear upon the gendarmes' faces. They wonder why I do not simply bewitch them—turn them into swine, perhaps, and escape.

All of them, that is, except the tenth man, who feels quite certain this capture is his doing. This is the cardinal Domenico Chrétien. Unlike the others, who are cloaked in somber black, he wears upon his back and head the color of blood. His countenance is broad and plump, with upper and lower lips of crude thickness, and eyes hidden in deep folds. His body is likewise soft, belying the heart within.

Commandingly, he calls: "The Abbess Mother Marie Françoise?"

This is the Enemy. We have met only once upon this earthly plane, though on another we are old acquaintances. It is difficult not to look upon him with familiar contempt. So filled with self-loathing is he that he would kill anyone who reminded him of what he is. There is only one alive capable of greater harm to my people—the one I have come to stop, lest I and my Race be obliterated from the face of this world.

"The same," I reply to his question. I struggle, and manage to conquer my hate; to do otherwise would make my soul as closed as his.

"You are under arrest on the charge of heresy, witchcraft, and maleficium *directed at the Holy Father himself. What say you?"*

"That you know better than I of what I am guilty."

A humble admission on the face of it, but my Enemy understands this veiled rebuke, and his expression subtly darkens, though he dare say nothing in front of his men—his men, who have no idea what is actually happening here, who would not believe if they were told. "You will come with us, Abbess."

I do not resist; indeed, I give a nod of compliance. Even so, I am pulled roughly off the horse, who rears, knocking down one of the guards and causing minor alarm until he is at last subdued. As I had told him, he is a fine mount; the gendarmes appreciate this, and one of them takes hold of his reins and speaks soothingly until the animal is reassured.

As for me, I am stripped of the cloak that hides my dark habit, veil, and wimple, and my arms are bound behind my back; then I am flung facedown over the back of a different horse and tied to the saddle. One man murmurs: "Now there's the perfect position for a highborn lady."

The others snort faintly at this, but no one laughs, even though I am bound, outnumbered, and apparently at their mercy. In the silence that quickly follows, I hear their fear.

It is a difficult ride home. My face slaps against wet horseflesh, and when the rain begins again in earnest the back of my habit is quickly soaked through, leaving my spine aching with cold. Water runs down my arms and legs and neck. Inverted, my veil grows heavy with rain and soon falls; my wimple slips, leaving my shorn head exposed, letting the rain spill into my ears and nose and eyes.

I try to comfort myself: it is the Goddess's will. It is my life's mission, foretold from my birth.

On the way to my destiny, the horse from time to time steps upon and crushes pungent herb; I close my stinging eyes in pain at its perfume.

Rosemary brings memories.

PART I

Michel

CARCASSONNE, FRANCE

FRANCE

October 1357

II

In the vast rectangle of shade cast by the centuries-old and barely completed Basilica Saint-Nazaire, the scribe Brother Michel slowed to glance at the activity across from the cathedral's entrance—and quickly clamped his tongue between upper and lower front teeth, that the pain might distract him from a rush of anger.

On top of a berm, workmen swung mallets above their heads and brought them down, ringing, on four-foot-high stakes. The autumn sun was unusually strong that day; heat waves roiled up from the pierced earth, shimmering darkly about the men's ankles and lower legs, as if the fires had already been set. The stakes formed the traditional half-circle that opened onto the basilica's great doors. The cathedral itself was in the style of the eleventh century, a Heaven-tall Gothic box with vast high windows, arched like hands pressed together in prayer.

Those elbowing past each other on the narrow cobblestone streets— merchants, peasant mothers and children, beggars, horse-borne noblemen, brown-robed monks, and black-frocked nuns—stared with frank curiosity at the scene. People plodded along grimly, mouths downturned as if melting away in the unexpected heat—but at the sight of the workmen, faces, speech, and gestures grew abruptly animated.

A hesitant merchant to his fellow, yellow felt circles pinned to their chests, to warn others of what the famed inquisitor Bernard Gui called "the vomit of Judaism": *A burning, then . . . has it been decided already?*

A black-wimpled widow of the lower nobility, eyes narrowed with indignation, to her basket-bearing maid: *They mean to martyr her; and she a saint already. Just because she is from Toulouse, you know. . . .*

Two monks upon a donkey: *Good riddance, and Devil take her.*

We could bring a nice picnic, then, and the children. This last from a white-turbaned, slightly cross-eyed peasant matron, smiling at her surly husband to reveal three front teeth broken off at a neat diagonal.

Impossible not to hear every word, indeed, not to feel the breath on which each was uttered, so narrow was the street. As the sweating bodies of men, women, and animals brushed against his own, Brother Michel instinctively put a hand on the ivory inkhorn belted at his hip—fearful not so much that it might be the target of pickpockets, but that it might be torn from him by the fierce tide of traffic. At his waist was tied a large black bundle containing writing tablet, quill, and scrolled parchment; for this reason, he maintained half an arm's distance between himself and his master, the Dominican priest and inquisitor Charles Donjon, who confidently led the way through the chaos.

Michel forced his gaze away from the sight of the workmen and the stakes, for this particular trial prompted within him a rage beyond the norm. *I thought the point was to save them, not kill them!* he had once cried out to his adoptive father—the head of the French Inquisition, Cardinal Chrétien—in one similar instance, furious at the civil authorities' assumption there would be any executions at all. He still felt anger, even more so now because he believed, along with the widow, that the accused abbess was indeed a saint, wrongfully accused; indeed, in his home city of Avignon, he had seen her heal a wounded man with a mere touch of her hands.

Thus, Michel now considered each distant blow of the hammer a challenge. *God, may that be one stake that goes unused,* he prayed silently; *and there, another . . .*

By all appearances, the secular arm of the law had apparently already decided that there would be a large number of executions. *None has been offered the chance at salvation, yet they cannot wait to light the fires,* Michel thought. He chafed at his mission—only his second inquisition, and the first still left him with nightmares.

The milkmaid behind him gave him a strong, carefully balanced push with her knee without spilling a drop from the buckets suspended from her shoulders; the quarters were too cramped for him to turn far enough to see her properly, but he heard the gentle slosh of the liquid and smelled it just starting to sour in the unexpected heat. The people ahead did not budge—entranced as they were by the notion of coming executions—and he was instead forced tightly against Father Charles's back; the crackle of delicate parchment between them made Michel wince.

Despite the milkmaid's jostling, Charles remained steady on his feet; indeed, his very wake emanated calm and dignity. He was a small man, a full head shorter than his protégé, but his posture was straight and sure, his torso broad and solid beneath his frock—simple and black, in an age when clergy of his noble breeding and stature within the Church dressed in bright-colored silks, satins, and furs. He and Michel had been invited to stay at the bishop's luxurious palace near the basilica and built directly into the city's ancient fortifications. Father Charles had found a diplomatic way both to accept and decline: he and Michel would stay very nearby—at the Dominican cloister adjoining Saint-Nazaire. The two had risen well before the sun for lauds—this even though they had not entered Carcassonne's gates until dusk the night before, and had attended matins with the inmates at midnight. At prime, they shared refection with the brothers (barley and cabbage soup); when the sun was finally up, they paid their respects to the bishop, who insisted on feeding them again—this time on rich pastries and sausage.

Bishop Bernard Rigaud was a strange, surly old man, with a pate as pink and downy as a newborn's peeping out from under his skullcap; his blue eyes protruded so alarmingly, Michel had trouble looking away from them . . . and from the bishop's plate, upon which the pastries and sausage had been milled into an unrecognizable mush.

"For the good of the Church, and His Supreme Holiness, Abbess Marie Françoise must be made an example of: no one can be permitted to commit an atrocity against the pope—outside his own palace, no less—and live." Rigaud leaned forward and lowered his voice, as if fearful of being overheard. "But we must be swift—as swift as possible—and discreet. Many of the locals have already taken offense at the arrests."

The last was not surprising; the populace in the South, especially here in the region of Languedoc, still remembered the slaughter that had occurred here and in the nearby metropolis of Toulouse. Tens of thousands had been massacred by northern knights in the name of God and the Parisian king. No matter that the victims had been heretics—the Albigensians, who believed in two gods, one evil and one good, and that radical offshoot of the Franciscans, the Fraticelli, who claimed that Christ had held no property and therefore neither should the Church.

But the very thought of condemning the abbess to death without a proper interrogation and trial brought a stunned protest to Michel's lips. He dared not say the first words that came to his mind—*But she is a true saint, sent by God on an errand of mercy*—for they were more than impolitic. Before her arrest, the Church's official attitude toward Mother Marie Françoise had been one of decided skepticism, and Michel had kept his beliefs to himself, to spare himself and his mentor not only embarrassment but suspicion.

Before he could utter the less incriminating *But, Holiness, how shall we be certain of her guilt without a proper interrogation?* Father Charles spoke.

"Your Holiness," the diminutive priest responded, his tone one of utmost respect, "I certainly understand your concerns. But I can only do as God and Church law—"

"You shall do as Cardinal Chrétien has ordered," Rigaud said firmly. "Let us say that he is . . . concerned by the low number of convictions on your account, Father, and your reluctance to properly utilize torture. The Abbess Marie Françoise represents a chance for you to . . . redeem yourself."

"Redeem?" Michel asked, forgetting, in his haste to defend his mentor, to mimic the deference of Father Charles's tone. "But, Holiness, we came from Cardinal Chrétien's side ourselves not two days ago, and he gave no such order. And if he had aught to say to Charles, he could have easily said so then. Besides, there is no enmity between His Eminence and Father Charles—far from it."

As he spoke, Charles put a restraining hand upon his young charge's shoulder, to no avail.

At Michel's impudence, the bishop had drawn back his head and puffed out his chest like an adder ready to strike. "You would call me a liar, boy?"

Then, as a realization occurred to him, he deflated and smiled. "Ah, yes, you are his adopted son, aren't you, Michel? Well, then, surely your father has trained you in the workings of politics. He has pointed out to me that the abbess had certainly been a Christian when she first joined the nunnery. Thus, when she turned to witchcraft, she became *relapsa.*" And with vicious swiftness, he thrust a spoonful of mashed pastry into his mouth, and savored it between tongue and palate a moment before swallowing.

Relapsa, a fatal word. It meant a soul who had accepted Christ, only later to reject Him—the abominable "sin against the Holy Spirit," which neither God nor the Church could ever forgive. Once the word *relapsa* was uttered, an execution soon followed.

Michel had expected Father Charles to rush to the abbess's defense at once; but the priest remained silent, which prompted the young monk to counter:

"Begging your pardon, Holiness, but how can we be sure she is *relapsa* before hearing her testimony?"

With only a slight movement of his head and shoulders, the bishop managed the effect of lunging forward; the bulging blue eyes, clouded with age, regarded Michel with veiled fury. "Do you wish to put both yourself and the good father here in further disfavor? Do you?"

"He does not," Charles interjected swiftly. "He is a good soul, and simply wishes to see all brought to Christ. As do I, Holiness."

"A noble goal," the bishop allowed, leaning back, slightly mollified, "but one that is not always attainable. You are young yet, Brother Michel; in time you will come to see that there are souls whose folly is so great, whose hearts are so filled with vileness, even God cannot save them."

"But if," the scribe asked humbly, without meeting the bishop's gaze, "if perhaps it could be proven that Mother Marie is *not relapsa* . . . and that her actions were inspired by God, not the Devil . . ."

"Most rhetorical," Rigaud answered, becoming annoyed again. "She is guilty: there are witnesses. If I am not mistaken, *you* were one of them."

At this, Michel bowed his head meekly, though his heart was in turmoil. How could the bishop, a Dominican, accuse the abbess of being evil? Dominicans held special devotion in their hearts for Christ's mother, who had given the rosary to Saint Dominic; and it was said that Mother Marie communed directly with the Virgin and was her representative on earth. The reports of miraculous healings grew daily.

Obviously, His Holiness was old and confused; certainly Chrétien had never said such a thing concerning the abbess. In fact, it would have required a messenger from Avignon to ride at top speed through the night in order to bring a letter to Rigaud before Michel and Charles themselves arrived in Carcassonne.

Beside Michel, Father Charles sat—calm, silent, implacable.

Rigaud permitted a small smile to play upon his thin, blue-tinged lips; surprisingly, he still possessed most of his front teeth, stained the color of oak bark. "I know that I can trust you, Father, and the young brother, to do what is right. The crime committed against the Holy Father is enough to merit the harshest sentence; but there is also the issue of the abbess's untoward influence upon the people. If she survives, even in a state of excommunication, there remains the chance of a popular uprising against the Church—and even the danger that she may secure political backing from certain . . . misguided superiors."

Superiors within the Church, Michel knew: Rigaud was right that, because of her reputation as a saint, the abbess possessed great political power—so much so that, prior to her arrest, she had wielded far more influence upon the Toulouse archbishop than the bishop of Carcassonne himself. So that was it, then: Rigaud, frightened and jealous, was determined to see the abbess dead.

At once, Michel heard in his mind Father Charles's familiar admonition: *You are too hotheaded, my son; you must learn to respect your superiors. God has placed them above you in order that you may learn humility.*

Humility. It was difficult to remember the need for humility when kneeling beside the pyre of one writhing, screeching in the flames. After being required to witness the burning of the first man condemned with his help as scribe, Michel had staggered back to his cell at the monastery and vomited until there was no more bile; and then had continued to retch for the space of an hour or more. Chrétien had followed after him and held his head; and afterward, as Michel lay gasping on the grand inquisitor's brocade-covered lap, had smoothed his forehead with a cool cloth, saying: *It is hard, I know, my son; it is very hard.*

Michel had insisted he was leaving, that he could never continue such a gruesome calling, but Chrétien had wisely explained it thus:

First, the weight of their deaths rests upon my shoulders alone. Do not be proud, Michel, but remember that you are only a scribe.

Second, God has given us the most difficult task of all, one that tests our courage daily; and were I one of the accused, I would want one as devoted and caring as you in attendance. For I know your good heart, and how you pray unceasingly for sinners; and I know God hears you. I saw you at the side of the condemned as he perished by fire, and I firmly believe that your prayers there brought his soul to Christ in the hour of his death. God has given you a special cross to bear in this life—would you prefer that one callous and uncaring take your place? Or will you accept your burden cheerfully, and in so doing, bring about the greatest possible good for those who most need it?

The day you were left as a babe outside the papal palace, Michel, God sent me a dream: a dream that you were to become the greatest of all inquisitors, the one who would unite the Church again in the one true faith. God has chosen you for a great mission: be brave, and pray to Him for strength.

The memory merged with that of Rigaud, rising from his well-cushioned throne, a shuffling, stoop-shouldered skeleton draped in skin and scarlet satin. "Three days," he said. "Three days to obtain confessions from the women, and to turn them over to the secular arm for execution."

"Three *days* . . ." Charles breathed, stunned, before Michel managed to echo the same words. This was certainly not Chrétien's order.

"It will be sufficient for you," the bishop stated flatly.

"But Your Holiness," Charles interjected, "there are six women involved, and often it takes days to elicit a single confession—and with only myself and Father Thomas, I don't—"

"It will be sufficient," Rigaud repeated, this time in a tone that indicated all discussion was over. Without further words, he raised his bowed arms, palms extended and slightly cupped—to bless the two younger men and send them on their way, Michel presumed. Following Father Charles's example, he slid off his stool and knelt.

Something bright and shining slipped from between the old man's fingers and fell an inch, two, three—then dangled in the air. A golden crucifix on a chain—no, two; one in each hand. The bishop went first to Charles, then to Michel, solemnly placing them around each man's neck. The cross was twice the width of Michel's thumb, almost twice as long, and thick; its edges were not square, but ornately scalloped filigree, and the golden Christ that hung upon it was so painstakingly rendered, one could see each separate thorn in his crown, see the pupils in his eyes. Above him was nailed a scroll: *I.N.R.I., Jesus of Nazareth, King of the Jews,* and above that was inscribed the six-pointed Star of David—an unusual addition. The worth of so much gold was enormous.

The bishop, hand trembling slightly with age, made the sign of the cross over the two kneeling men, saying: "These have been purified and blessed by the pope himself; wear these at all times during your mission, for she is a dangerous woman, and these will protect you from her power." Rigaud began to turn away, then paused and added, smiling faintly: "You shall need such protection, for Chrétien's spies are everywhere; you will be watched closely. Beware that you do not disappoint him, Father: the penalty for your failure will be severe."

By the time the meeting with the bishop ended, it was the hour of terce, almost mid-morning; out in the street, the sun, painfully bright after the dimness of the palace, had begun to heat the cobblestones. The two of them walked in silence for a time; then Michel said:

"Father, tell me that I have misunderstood my own ears. Tell me that Rigaud is not threatening us if we do not find the abbess guilty."

Charles stopped in mid-stride and turned to face his scribe.

"In the first place, Michel, *we* shall not be the ones to find her guilty or innocent. *I* shall, and so it is no concern of yours."

Humbled, Michel bowed his head in acknowledgment.

More gently, Charles asked, "You believe she is a saint, do you not?"

Michel hesitated. At last, in a low voice, he replied, "I do."

"Then I understand your dismay," Charles said, his tone matter-of-fact. "Even so, it is not your place to judge the innocence or guilt of prisoners: it is mine. You know that Chrétien and I quite disagree with your opinion, and that we are your superiors. As far as the bishop—he may threaten all he wishes, but I shall send a dispatch to the cardinal this evening advising him of Rigaud's inappropriate comments. You need have no fear of him."

Despite Father Charles's words concerning the abbess, Michel trusted the priest to do what was right before God, for he had always done so in the past. Mother Marie Françoise was a saint (in fact, Michel secretly prayed to her); Charles would realize it when he met her in the flesh and heard her testimony, and would render a just verdict.

And Michel would pray unceasingly for God to change the cardinal's heart.

Traffic finally began to move again, with the gentle sloshing sound and the faintly sour smell of warm milk. The pace increased, and soon the two men were walking briskly down the narrow road of brick, past tall, narrow shops with their wooden display cases opening out directly onto the street, so close that Michel's sleeve brushed against fragrant, cooling loaves of bread, over sharply aromatic wheels of cheese and newly cobbled slippers. Overhead, the top floors of the wooden structures, where the merchants and their families lived, leaned alarmingly forward; in some instances, the homes on opposite sides of the street actually touched, shading the passersby below. Michel glanced up at the sound of laughter, and saw the baker's wife reach out from her third-story window to jokingly slap the arm of her neighbor, the winemaker's wife, who stood smiling in her own home across the street.

After a time, the shops grew fewer and farther apart as the road widened; at its intersection with another broad avenue stood the prison, a great square of stone a fraction the width and height of a cathedral, and distinctly unremarkable in design. Michel was in step with the priest as the two of them ascended the timeworn, sloping steps leading up to the heavy wooden double doors, passing lawyers and argumentative clients. A sentry, his sweat-gleaming forehead puckered in a perpetual scowl, stood just outside, and gestured at the one open door without a word as the Dominicans approached.

Michel stepped inside and blinked as his eyes adjusted to the abrupt dimness. In the long, narrow entryway, there were no windows; the only light source was a burning rag torch ensconced in the mildew-covered wall.

"Jailer!" the priest called, then delicately withdrew a white kerchief from his sleeve and cupped it over his nose, covering his black moustache and most of his thin strip of beard. It was cooler here than outside, certainly, but just as certainly not more pleasant: the fragrance of rose and lavender coupled with the underlying smell of human shit, blood-infused urine, and misery. Every prison smelled the same; and each visit evoked in Michel the same terrifying childhood memory: of a pig whose execution had been botched by the monastery's cook. The animal's throat had been only partially cut, so that it escaped and dashed screaming about the barnyard, leaving blood and excrement in its wake—as well as an even more horrid, pungent smell that the cook had later explained was the smell of fear.

Human torture produced an eerily similar stench, one that lingered long after the suffering ceased.

A moment's silence passed, followed by uneven approaching footfall and the jingling of metal. From the darkness appeared the jailer, a short, broad, thick-limbed man with a slight clubfoot. At first it appeared the crown of his head was shaven in the monk's tonsure, but closer inspection revealed it to be the work of time and nature.

"Ah, Father!" he cried, smiling, revealing both front teeth and a canine missing. "Father Charles, isn't it? Welcome, welcome! We have been eagerly awaiting you! It's not often we're graced with such an expert as yourself." His sibilants whistled sharply.

Behind his white kerchief, the priest's expression warmed slightly, but he did not smile; the work at hand was far too somber. Instead, he gave a gracious nod as he replied, words slightly muffled,

"Can you tell me whether Father Thomas and his assistant have arrived yet?"

The jailer shook his head. "The torturers are here—but no word from Father Thomas."

As part of the inquisitional tribunal, Thomas had been supposed to make the journey from Avignon with Charles and Michel, but had been detained a few hours by "personal business." Had it been another priest, Michel might have worried about brigands on the road—but he had heard the rumors; from Charles's taut silence regarding the matter, Thomas's tardiness probably had to do with his mistress. But as one of Chrétien's favorite protégés (a greater favorite, Michel sometimes suspected, than the cardinal's own son), Thomas was allowed special lenience.

"May we see the prisoner, then?" Charles asked their host politely. "The abbess, Mother Marie Françoise?"

"Ah, yes . . ." The jailer rolled his dark eyes, which were so deeply set and narrow that the whites never showed. "The Great Whore of Carcassonne, some call her; but you should know that some of the locals here still consider her a saint, and are not so pleased about a trial. Not that I'm one of them." He paused; a faint lasciviousness crept into his tone. "Father, is it all true? What they say she did in the papal palace?"

Michel felt his lips twist in disgust: he had heard the rumor that the abbess had performed an obscene sexual act, a magical act, its aim to harm Pope Innocent. She had committed no such crime; indeed, she had done quite the opposite. She had healed a wounded man with no more than a touch.

As Rigaud had pointed out, Michel had been a witness—and he had thought at first (though he had told no one) that he looked upon the Holy Mother herself, radiant from within. Then the image had faded, and he had realized that he looked upon a mere woman in Franciscan garb; yet he was no less convinced that he looked upon an emissary from

God, for when she glanced up from her astounded victim, her face shone no less with holy light.

How could sinners speak so vilely of such a saint?

Now, in the jail's antechamber, Father Charles's face grew stern, his gaze pointed; he lowered his kerchief so that his full, magnificently regal face, with its gaunt cheeks and thick, coal-colored brows, might be seen. "We will see the abbess now," he told the jailer softly.

"Of course." The man sighed, turned smartly so that the large ring of keys at his hip clinked together, and made his way slowly—one shoulder dipping low as he stepped on his misshapen foot, the other rising as he stepped on the good. Charles and Michel followed him down the corridor to a stone staircase. Coiling like a snail's shell, the stairwell was even narrower than the city streets, permitting the men to proceed only in single file.

From below came a woman's unrestrained screams. Automatically, Michel fought to control the feeling of pity and began to pray:

Hail Mary, full of grace; the Lord is with thee. Blessed art thou among women, and blessed is the fruit of thy womb, Jesus. Holy Mary, Mother of God, pray for us sinners now, and at the hour of our deaths. . . .

At the sound of the screaming, Father Charles clutched the jailer's shoulder in a hawklike grasp. "Have you other prisoners besides the Franciscan sisters here?"

The jailer hesitated just reluctantly and long enough that Charles understood his unspoken answer at once, and continued: "What are the torturers doing with my prisoners already? They have no right to act without my orders!"

Michel gasped, outraged.

The jailer ducked his head and studied Charles's slippers. "They came in from Paris an hour ago, *monseigneur,* and demanded I bring them the nuns. I thought—truly I did, *seigneur*—that they were acting on your instruction."

"They are *not.*"

The man looked up, suddenly eager to accuse. "So I understand now, good Father; and now that you speak of them, it seems to me that they were quite drunk when they made the demand. I suspect they came straight from a tavern and brothel, sir, and never slept the night. . . ."

"Take me to them at once." Father Charles waved his black-sleeved arm in a short, fierce gesture indicating that the jailer should fall silent and continue moving—which the man did, with no little alacrity.

At last they arrived at the bottom of the staircase, which opened onto a vast cellar. To the right was a great communal cell; to the left, a number of smaller, private ones, as well as a pair of large double doors partially ajar. The air was chillier here, and far more foul.

Red-faced and huffing, the jailer led the two men into the corridor between the private cells and the large communal one, which consisted of nothing but stone floor strewn with straw and surrounded by iron bars. Inside, a group of six nuns—all defrocked, in their undershifts—huddled together, furtive and forlorn. All appeared to be French noble-women: long-nosed and soft-fleshed, their cropped hair accentuating necks white and sweeping. They had been born into wealth, donated young to a convent, and knew nothing of life save needlework, reading, and contemplation. They should have been in leg irons, but instead sat unshackled on the straw—a sign, perhaps, of the jailer's disavowed sympathy.

As Father Charles and Brother Michel passed, the nuns' collective gaze followed them; the women turned their heads in unison. Two of the sisters—one fair, one dark-haired—wept frankly as they murmured prayers, their eyelids newborn pink and swollen; the rest bore the expression of mute shock Michel had seen so often.

The jailer paused at the doors of the torture chamber; from within emanated the sound of guttural laughter. Michel could restrain himself no longer; knowing he risked his master's reprimand, he bolted forward and flung open one of the doors. At once he caught sight of a pale form suspended half a foot above the ground by a pulley and chains that bound each wrist, pulling the arms up and back. This was the strappado, which used the victim's own weight to pull the shoulders from the socket; not only was the device efficient, causing dislocation and agony within minutes, but after torture ceased, the pain continued to intensify until the victim surrendered and confessed.

The woman hanging from it was apparently unconscious: her head had fallen forward, chin resting on her collarbone; beneath small, scallop-shell breasts stretched a pronounced rib cage, a long, flat white belly, and prominent hipbones above a delta of golden hair. Her legs were thin, gangly, slightly bowed. On the stone wall behind her, her silhouette—a feminine messiah suspended upon an invisible crucifix—wavered in the rag torches' glow.

One of the torturers stood in front of her, on tiptoe so that he could grope her breasts; the second, almost too drunk to maintain his balance, nonetheless was dragging a box behind her even as he fumbled to free himself from his leggings.

"Let her down!" Michel shouted, running into the chamber, and, with a grace and strength that surprised him, knocked the box dragger off his feet. The other torturer, eyes glazed by drink, let loose his prey and turned belligerently toward her would-be rescuer. Michel was a tall man, but the second torturer was taller and heavily muscled. For the space of a heartbeat, the two glared at each other. Michel prepared himself for the charge.

"Let her *down*," Charles thundered in the doorway, with the ferocity of Christ expelling the moneychangers from the Temple.

The standing torturer angled his great beet-colored jaw in the priest's direction. "But we were told—"

"I care not what you were told by others. From now on, you listen only to *me*."

"But you—"

Father Charles lifted his hand in a menacing call for silence.

Common sense won over drink and temperament, and the torturer, judging Charles to be a dangerous foe in ways other than physical, sighed and took hold of the strappado's pulley. The woman sank to the ground like an abandoned marionette; Michel gathered her—a heap of skin and long bones—into his arms while the second released her wrists from the chains. The situation precluded any false modesty: Michel felt no embarrassment, only horror at her bruises and misplaced bones, and the indignity done her. He used the sleeves of his robe to shield her body as best he could and carried her past Father Charles into the corridor.

Inquisitional law forbade jailers, torturers, or inquisitors to beat or rape inmates, though such crimes happened all too often. Charles and Michel often uncovered such abuses, as well as ignorance or outright disdain for prisoners' rights. Established practice forbade torture without either the inquisitor's presence or permission; the *Practica Officii Inquisitionis Heretice Pravitatis,* published three decades earlier by Bernard Gui, was extremely specific in this regard and granted the accused certain rights. One was that they were given the opportunity to confess *before* torture was applied; another was that torture was never to be applied gratuitously, but judiciously, always with the aim of generating a confession.

"I should report you now," the priest told the two men with mournful rage, "and have you charged not only with breaking the rules, but with the crime you so nearly committed here. However, I have little time; and so I offer you another chance to abide by the law. See that you do . . . or I shall make it a point to interrogate you myself. And I am sure you can imagine the creativity with which one torturer might ply his trade upon another."

With that, Charles headed back into the corridor, and accompanied Michel—with the help of the jailer's key—into the communal cell. Michel lay the unconscious sister gently upon the straw; immediately, fleas leapt up onto them both. At once the nuns gathered around her, heedless now of the inquisitors; with soft sobs and murmurs, they covered her nakedness with a filthy blanket.

"Sisters," Charles addressed them solemnly from the other side of the bars, "I beg forgiveness for this miscarriage of justice, and remind you that you will all be offered an opportunity to avoid such a fate."

One or two of the nuns glanced up at him with eyes veiled as their heads had once been; impossible to tell whether their solemn expressions signified contrition or repressed hatred. The others remained focused on the injured one in their midst; and none noticed when the two inquisitors retreated and the jailer closed the bars back over them.

Without another word, the chagrined jailer led the two clerics down the corridor, past a second vacant communal cell, then a row of empty private cells, until he came to the very last of the latter. There he stopped at a wooden door bound by rusted iron, with bars set into a window at eye level, and a slot near the floor through which food or water might be pushed. This door he unlocked. It swung open with a groan.

Michel entered behind Charles.

The cell was the same as so many others: a dank straw-strewn earth floor, a latrine bucket full of piss, a small fat-soaked rag torch near the entry that emitted feeble light and smoke that covered everything with fine, black soot.

At the same time, it was somehow different: in a ceramic holder on the floor, a fine white candle burned, causing wavering arcs of light to leap against the walls. The stink had lessened here, to the degree that Charles tucked his kerchief into his sleeve.

A holy place, Michel thought at once, and fancied he detected the faint smell of roses. The memory of the last time he had seen her—in Avignon, amidst a noisy crowd—returned to him with force.

On a slab of wood suspended by chains from the stone, a woman lay on her back with her face turned toward the wall. The instant the two inquisitors stepped between the woman and the candle, their shadows fell across her and onto the wall above, with the eerie silhouette of dark smoke swirling about their shoulders.

Even in the dimness, Michel could clearly see that, emerging from her thick cap of nape-short glossy black hair, the line of her cheekbone was swollen, perhaps broken, and that her breathing was short, sharp, shallow, that of one suffering from broken ribs. The torturers had gotten to her first; instinctively, he thought of his pharmacopoeia at Avignon, and silently prescribed willow bark for the pain, and a paste of comfrey leaf, marigold petals, and olive oil for the bruising. . . .

Father Charles settled upon one of two stools placed there expressly for the inquisitors. Michel did the same, sitting slightly behind the priest, and unlaced the bundle at his belt as Charles gently asked, "Mother Marie Françoise?"

The woman's body tensed slightly.

"I am Father Charles, a Dominican priest sent by the Church to investigate your case. And this"—he indicated his assistant with near-paternal pride—"is my scribe, the foster son of Cardinal Chrétien, the Dominican Brother Michel."

And he held his pose an instant, as if he were waiting for the abbess to turn and acknowledge them both. When she did not, his demeanor turned somber. "But first, Mother, I must beg your forgiveness for the wrong committed against you. Those men had no right to touch you until you had been given an opportunity to confess. It will be reported."

Slowly, the woman turned her face toward them.

Michel repressed a gasp of horror. He had expected the small, veiled woman he had seen so recently in Avignon's public square, cupping her hand to the eye of a kneeling prisoner; a handsome woman, with olive skin, large eyes, a snub of a nose.

Now the abbess regarded them with one normal brown-black eye; the other, half hidden behind the broken, swelling cheekbone, was swollen shut of its own accord and covered with congealing blood from the eyebrow, which had been split open a thumbnail's length at the highest point of its arch. The wound gaped, red and raw, and the blood had spilled down one temple and cheek, as well as down the side of her nose—which itself was bruised and bleeding onto her cut and purple upper lip.

Beneath her wounds, she seemed physically unremarkable. She was small, perhaps twenty years of age—young to have attained the powerful position of abbess and such divergent reputations.

Yet there was beauty in her bearing, her calm dignity in the face of such disastrous fortune. Of the countless prisoners Michel had seen in his years of service alongside Father Charles, she alone bore no fear.

Again memory transported him to Avignon, to the moment she had looked up from the healed man and gazed directly at him, Michel. He had been convinced she knew him utterly, every thought, every intent in his heart; emanating from her was a love especially for him, a love so holy, so pure, so intense he scarce could stand. Yet he had returned her gaze, and her love, with the realization: *God is here.*

At once, lust fiercer than he had ever known consumed him, filling not just his loins but his entire body until even the tips of his fingers ached with desire. Ashamed, stricken that he should feel physical desire for such a saint, he had prayed again, silently: *Get thee behind me, Satan. Hail, Mary, full of grace . . .*

And the latter phrase he had directed toward the abbess.

Father Charles's voice, tinged with outrage, drew Michel back to the present.

"They shall pay for their crime, Mother. In the interim"—the priest's manner turned perfunctory—"let us waste no time. A preliminary list of charges have been compiled against you." Without looking at his assistant, he thrust an upturned palm in the monk's direction.

Michel recovered, opened his bag, and unrolled a thick scroll of several parchments; he chose the appropriate piece and handed it to Charles. Though the older man had long ago come to depend upon Michel to be his reading eyes, he knew the words by heart: "The slaughter of innocent children, intercourse with the Devil, the casting of hexes, *maleficium* against various individuals in Carcassonne, not to mention the most grievous charge: *maleficium* against His Holiness, Pope Innocent...."

Save for the very last charge and the name of the accused, all the parchments in Michel's bag read the same.

Charles trailed off. "Mother, I ask you now: will you confess to the preliminary charges?"

Tears welled suddenly in the abbess's good eye; a drop spilled from the corner and slid down the length of her nose.

Father Charles somberly displayed the parchment to her as Michel reached for the quill and inkhorn. "The document has been prepared; you need only sign it," the priest said. "It is the list of charges I just read to you."

As he handed Charles the quill, Michel saw that the abbess looked not at the parchment, but directly at him and then at Father Charles, and in a moment of astonished and inexplicable revelation, he knew she wept not at the pain inflicted by the torturers or the shame of prison or the fear of a painful death.

She wept out of pity for them, her inquisitors. Out of a depthless compassion; and he felt his throat constrict painfully in reply.

She stared back at Michel, cheeks shining with blood-tinged tears, her expression utterly composed. How innocent she looked—small and wounded in her torn and dirtied white shift, like an androgynous child with her close-cropped hair and large eyes.

None could look upon her thus and fail to see the saint, fail to see God beyond. Despite the grotesquerie of her wounds, her face, her open eye contained the numinous; perhaps, Michel thought, Jesus had appeared thus to his captors on the eve of his crucifixion.

He meant to turn toward Father Charles, to gauge the older man's reaction, but suddenly his head reeled, and he felt himself on the verge of fainting....

.   .   .

And he was no longer himself, the monk Michel, but another man, a stranger, lying on his back, staring up at the sunlit sky. So blue it was, so tranquil, so indifferent and cold, this place of stones and screams—now so quiet, so still. In the blueness above, swirls of darkness shimmered, moving: carrion birds? he wondered, or the approach of Death? He was too weak, too calm, too devastated to care which.

Then the sky and death-birds were replaced by a human face, female and heart-shaped, with eyes shining and black, a dab of a nose, and lips that were truly the shape of a just-opening bud. Indigo brows and lashes; olive skin that had seen the sun. She reached down for him, smiling; he tried to smile back, and could not—there was too much blood everywhere—blood on metal, blood on earth, blood on his tongue, but none of it mattered, for he had at last seen *Her*. . . .

. . . and despite his weakness, he was filled with overwhelming devotion and unbearable physical desire. Yet with the objectivity of the dying, he felt no shame. Such passion seemed sacred, inseparable from the Power that flowed from her into him.

Her voice, low and beautiful—a voice he had known long, long ago; a voice he had always known, but not remembered: The God that you seek is here, don't you see? Your life is *here*. . . .

The words and the warmth evoked such freedom, such deep joy and relief that he let go a rattling breath, and died in peace.

Michel returned to the present with a start. It was as though he had been dreaming but not asleep, for here he had just passed the quill to Father Charles as if nothing had happened—or rather, not dreaming, but swept up in the last memory of a dying man, a stranger he did not know.

It was a vision, God-given, yet its meaning eluded him entirely; at the same time, the element of lust embarrassed him, for that had surely been added by his sinful nature.

Michel's hand moved instinctively to the crucifix hidden at his heart; at the same time, Father Charles gave him a piercing glance before proffering the quill and parchment to the still-prone woman.

The abbess's tears ceased at once; she shook her head. "No."

Surprisingly, Charles did not persist. He lowered his arms and returned the rejected items to Michel, who returned them to the bundle and drew out a tablet of wax and a stylus used for recording additional names, charges, and amendments to confessions.

With the stylus, the scribe wrote in the wax: *In the year 1357, on the 22nd day of October, one Mother Marie Françoise from the Franciscan convent at Carcassonne was formally placed in judgment before the Dominican Father Charles Donjon of Avignon, and did refuse to confess to the crimes with which she has been accused.* And then he waited, stylus poised, for Charles to then ask whether she wished to confess to other crimes or to make a statement.

To Michel's astonishment, Father Charles said to the nun, "Obviously, you have no desire to cooperate with this investigation." Almost at once, he rose and turned to leave; dismayed, Michel hurriedly gathered up his writing implements and did the same.

"But I will confess," the abbess said with sudden strength. "Only not to your document."

Charles swiveled to regard her, the hem of his dark frock swinging, and it seemed to Michel that his voice held the faintest trace of disappointment. "You will . . . ?"

"Confess," she said, but her voice and eyes and face revealed no trace of penitence or regret. "In my own words; and only to him." She pointed at Michel.

The priest's thick dark eyebrows formed a sharp, ominous V; his lips thinned until they paled, and for the space of several seconds, he directed a blazing glare at the reclining abbess. At last he said: "Shall I tell you what you already know? That my assistant is not yet a priest and cannot legally take your confession? That I will never permit him to be alone in your presence?"

"Shall I tell you what *you* already know?" she countered with absolute fearlessness, absolute disrespect. "That you have your orders to find me *relapsa,* condemn me to die no matter what I say?" She paused to indicate Michel with a glance. "*He* is not afraid to hear the truth and record it."

Ashen, Charles turned heavily back toward Michel. "This one cannot be helped. Call for the jailer, Brother."

"But, Father—"

"*Do* it."

It took all of Michel's accumulated years of monastic obedience and loyalty for him to do so, looking out of the small barred window and calling more loudly than necessary, for the jailer had been waiting just outside, and his cheerfulness and alacrity in opening the door failed entirely to cover his embarrassment at being caught spying.

During the course of the day's work—three more unproductive interrogations—Father Charles seemed increasingly subdued, and by its end, as the inquisitors made their way out of the prison into brightness and warm, sweet air, his brow was furrowed and his step slow. Rather than discuss the day's events, as was his wont, he remained silent.

Michel, too, maintained silence, for his disappointment in Father Charles was profound. The law demanded the abbess be given several chances to confess. But Charles had uttered ominous words, words he had never spoken before, words that clearly sounded a death knell for the accused: *This one cannot be helped.*

I am going mad, Michel told himself, for the world and all he believed in had been turned upon its ear. His master was a scrupulously honest man; never would Charles fail to give a prisoner a fair hearing. Yet today he had practically condemned the abbess to die with her scarce uttering a word. And the Church was run by good, saintly men—but today, Rigaud was blackmailing a priest into ignoring inquisitional law.

Father Charles sighed and looked back at the street and the oncoming traffic, which had thinned now that the hour for supper had come. In the late afternoon light, he appeared wan, almost haggard. "Brother Michel," he said, "I believe it would be best to have a different scribe attend me tomorrow morning."

Here it was: Charles would return to the abbess on the morrow and recommend execution. And he did not want his foster nephew present to see his shame.

At the same time, a part of Michel could not quite believe it true.

"But why, Father? For some reason, the abbess trusts me; and if my presence can aid in obtaining a confession—"

"She wants you alone, Michel, but her reasons have nothing to do with trust. I saw the strange expression you wore when she looked at you this morning. You were not yourself. Dare I ask what passed through your thoughts?"

Michel hesitated; a part of him felt the strange vision should remain secret, inviolable . . . yet another part knew that Father Charles wished only to protect him from harm. "I . . . it was like a daydream; I looked through the eyes of a dying man in another time, another place. . . . And she—the abbess—was there." His tone grew forceful. "It was a vision from God, Father. I sensed His presence."

"All this talk about 'sensing God' and having visions; your approach to religion is too emotional. God is in the liturgy, in the breviary, not in flights of fancy." Father Charles shook his head and gave another sigh, this one even more sorrowful. "She bewitched you."

"But the bishop said that the Holy Father himself blessed the crucifix, that it would pro—"

"I understand that, Brother. But the fact remains: she bewitched you. Your 'daydream' was hardly from God." He paused. "My son, why do you think I so quickly removed you from her?" His tone turned ironic. "Or do you think I was simply following Rigaud's orders?"

This last gave Michel pause; so he said meekly, "If that is true, then I will pray for forgiveness. I will perform whatever absolution you deem necessary, Father, but I want to help, to remain at your side. I know God can save her; and I know I can be of service. I *know* it."

"Michel. My son. Can you not understand? She is poison to you."

"How can you know that, Father? You were there, on the dais, watching her, as I was. . . . Is it not important to learn the truth, to save a soul who might possibly be innocent? A soul who might indeed be a *saint?* God was in that cell today—in the crowd on that day of my first execution in Avignon—or do you no longer recognize Him?"

Charles turned from him as if slapped. Michel regretted the pain caused by the question, but persisted. "If she is indeed a witch, why would she want to cast a spell upon *me,* Father? Why not you? I am only a scribe, of little use to her. As you pointed out, I do not decide her fate. I can only pray for her."

The priest's brown eyes filled with tears. He opened his mouth to speak, then closed it again, clearly overtaken by emotion. At last he uttered hoarsely, "I would gladly surrender my life to protect you from harm. Will you not indulge an old man in this? Will you not trust me? I will not see any ill befall you, nor will I see your integrity compromised."

"But no ill—" Michel broke off, suddenly realizing what Charles was saying: that he wished to protect his foster nephew from many things—not only possible bewitchment, but a sense of guilt should the abbess be found guilty with his help.

Humbled, Michel bowed his head. "I must regretfully protest, Father."

"You have no choice, Brother, but to obey your master's order. I began my service as a scribe; and I shall serve this time as my own."

That evening Michel spent in solitary prayer, but his exclusion from the abbess's cell still disturbed him. He wanted to trust Charles to give the accused a fair hearing, even if it meant provoking the bishop's wrath, but the priest's reaction toward Mother Marie in the cell had seemed startlingly genuine.

And so Michel contemplated the path he should take in the event of the abbess's execution, bishop be damned. At the very least, he should publicly denounce the action, perhaps even write a letter to the pope. Rigaud might lobby to have him expelled from the Dominican order—a thought that troubled him little, for Chrétien was far more powerful and would protect him from the bishop's wrath. But upon reflection, Michel decided such an expulsion might be in fact a great relief. Instead of serving God by watching the guilty condemned to die, he could perhaps join the Franciscans, and wander the countryside preaching and saving souls before they angered the Inquisition.

For now, however, loyalty required him to obey orders; and the possibility that Charles's harshness had been feigned, that he might find the abbess innocent and face Rigaud's censure himself, gnawed at Michel. If such a thing occurred, how could he protect his mentor?

A conundrum indeed: either outcome required one whom he revered to suffer.

Thus troubled, he eschewed the evening meal with the monks, and remained in his cell in a state of meditation and prayer.

Save Mother Marie and her sisters, Lord, and I will do whatever You ask. I will pray unceasingly, will flagellate myself each night, prostrate myself in public, fast in the wilderness. . . .

And move Father Charles's, the bishop's, and the cardinal's hearts to charity, Lord. Help them to see that she is Your servant.

As he prayed, the sunlight that streamed through the cell's small, unshuttered window eventually grew feeble, then waned to twilight; and from thence to dark. Through it all, he remained on his knees until some time close to the middle of the night, when he at last rolled onto his side and fell fast asleep upon the cold stone.

He was the stranger again, looking out through another's eyes, listening with another's ears, unable to see the stranger's face, for it was as though his soul had taken residence inside the other man's body, heart, and mind.

In the chill of the morning the stranger rode, thighs and calves gripping the rippling muscles of his mount; his right hand gripped a lance—a heavy weapon, yet his youthful arm was more than strong enough to wield it, and at his hip he wore a sword the length of his own leg.

Upon the sheath was embroidered a single red rose.

In the far distance, the king's crimson banner writhed in the wind—the fork-tongued Oriflamme, embroidered in fiery gold. The rider to his left, an armored knight with silver in his beard, features hidden by his helmet, bore the flag of Our Lady surrounded by stars. The rider on his right, a younger man with red-gold hair, gave him a look of grim encouragement.

He knew these men; knew them intimately, as they knew him. Slowly, slowly they advanced together, and he saw at last that they three were but a single drop in a sea of animals and men. Quiet reigned, save for the cries of a hawk, the rustling of the horses' hooves on fallen leaves, the occasional muffled cough. Through the branches of half-naked trees, he looked down from the mountaintop and, through the parting mists, saw a curve of river below, shining quicksilver in the just-rising sun.

Abrupt trumpets in the distance.

The scene faded at once to *her,* to the abbess, yet she was neither nun nor witch, but woman. A striking woman clad not in a burlap shift, but one gossamer white, luminous as the moon. Upon her perfect shoulders, down her back and arms, blue-black waves spilled. She sat upon the wooden bench in her cell, knees pressed to her chest, arms wrapped tightly about her shins.

Quill and parchment in hand, Michel stood before her, the scribe ready to take her confession; with feeble panic, he saw that he was alone, without Father Michel to distract him from his lust.

Yet his panic faded when he looked into her intense black eyes, at the holy love and desire there. She rose, holding his gaze, and when she stepped toward him, her shift melted into the darkness and she shone before him naked.

He did not resist when she pulled pen and parchment from his hands and cast them down, nor did he protest when she wound her arms about his ribs and pulled him down to press her soft, unbruised lips to his own.

He kissed her, and with a thrill he had never known, pressed his hand to her breast. Ecstasy it was, unsullied by any thought of wickedness, the innocent joy of Adam and Eve coupling in the Garden.

Virgin though he was, he took her there upon the damp cold earth, and she, the wiser, guided him. Instinct consumed him like fire, and he pressed against her, flesh to flesh, face to face, the joy and yearning reaching unbearable intensity until she touched fingertips to his face and whispered: "God is *here,* don't you realize? God is *here. . . ."*

Michel woke at the moment of climax with a deep, rasping intake of breath—and deep pleasure mixed with habitual guilt at the throbbing contraction, the spewing of seed, the contractions again, gradually ebbing with the beating of his heart.

Within a second, full consciousness returned. He was a monk in Carcassonne, on the floor of the cell provided him by fellow Dominicans, embarrassed once again by his evil thoughts concerning the abbess, and confused by his dream about the soldier.

With alacrity born of disgust, he sat up and cleaned himself with one hand, wiping up the semen with the folds of his loose undergarment—brusquely, so there was no chance of deriving pleasure from the contact. A rapid knock sounded at his cell door. Michel let go of the damp fabric in his hand, then struggled to smooth his still-ragged breathing. "Yes?" Certainly it could not be time for matins; they would have rung the bells.

"It is Brother André," came the reply—whispered, so as not to wake the others. "May I enter?"

"Of course."

The thin wooden door opened the span of his forearm, and an elderly hunchbacked monk slipped inside without a sound. The oil lamp in his hand illumined his face with harsh light; shadows deepened the creases around his mouth, beneath his eyes, producing a slightly ghoulish effect.

"Brother Michel," the old man whispered, his tone urgent, secretive. "Father Charles is seriously ill. He has asked for you. . . ."

Michel rose at once and fetched his robe from a peg on the wall, and slipped it on, the memory of the dream quickly replaced by worry. "Ill?"

Brother André crossed himself, then let go a breath upon which rode a single ominous word: "Plague . . ."

III

They had moved the priest from a monk's cell to more comfortable accommodations: a guest room with appointments befitting nobility, and a real featherbed with pillows. Nearby on an ornately carved table, two candles in a six-stemmed candelabra cast flickering light.

Father Charles, however, seemed quite unable to appreciate the change in his surroundings: he thrashed groaning upon the bed, arms and legs flailing, head turning from side to side. At times his eyes were squeezed tightly shut; at others, they opened, wide and horrified at some distant sight only he could perceive.

Next to the bed, another monk—this one also older, perhaps in his fourth decade—sat upon a stool.

As Michel entered (and his guide, Brother André, departed), the Dominican caretaker rose and held his hand up in warning. His voice was low, as if he did not want his patient to hear. "It's plague. Have you—"

"It doesn't matter." Michel stepped up to the bedside. "I will help care for him."

Father Charles let go a strangled, burbling cough; at once, the care-taker lifted Charles's shoulders up and forward, holding a large white kerchief to his lips.

As the monk gently cleaned a foul-smelling mixture of blood and phlegm from Father Charles's beard and mustache, he said softly to Michel: "Then I am even sorrier to tell you: this is the worst sort, the kind that settles in the lungs. Most who catch it die. If God wants him, we'll know in two days, more or less. I've already summoned a priest."

Michel felt no pain at first, only cold and deep surprise; then he remembered to let go his breath, and with its release followed a surge of near-unbearable hurt. Somehow he mastered it and did not weep, but the other monk saw and said apologetically:

"It still breaks out from time to time, especially in the countryside. It's the air, you know, and this strange, sudden heat—"

"Michel?" Charles gasped, his eyes wide and unseeing, his hands groping at the darkness. "Is it Michel?"

Michel moved at once to the priest's side and took one fevered, damp hand. Charles's skin and lips were gray; upon his forehead, in his sil-vered black mustache, beads of sweat caught the candles' flames, a thou-sand glittering, tiny jewels.

"I'm here, Father. I'm here. I'll stay and pray for you tonight."

At the sound of his nephew's voice, the priest stilled. Michel turned to the other monk and said, more softly: "Go to bed, Brother."

The monk nodded and left; Michel settled onto the stool, Charles's hand still in his. "I'm here, Father," he repeated. "I will not—"

"This is my arrogance, don't you see?" the priest rasped, struggling to sit; Michel rose and gently pushed him down. "My arrogance! I trotted you around like a trained pony today, showed you off as if to say, 'He's mine, he's all mine!' May God have mercy on my soul!" He coughed violently; Michel helped him sit, then, one arm around the priest, reached for the kerchief the other monk had left upon the table and held it to the priest's lips.

The coughing continued for some time, and Charles's breathing grew gurgling and stertorous; when it was over, Michel took away the kerchief—saturated a dangerously bright red—and propped him up on the pillows so that the sick man could breathe more easily.

"Bless you, Michel," the father said, for an instant weakly lucid. "You are truly like a son to me. . . ."

Michel straightened, lifting the rosary on his belt, then knelt. "I will pray for you, Father. If you're able, pray with me. . . . Blessed Virgin, intercede on thy servant Charles's behalf, that his suffering may pass and he may be restored to health. O, Holy Mother of God—"

"*She!*" Father Charles reared up in the bed, eyes maniacal. "*She* was the one who did this to me!"

Aghast, Michel crossed himself at the sacrilege.

"This is all her work, don't you see?" Charles continued, with such vehemence that drops of spittle landed on Michel's face. "Part of her sorcery!"

Only then did Michel realize that the priest spoke of the abbess, not of the Holy Mother.

Outwardly, he remained calm as he rose, and firmly but tenderly pressed Charles back against the pillows. "Do not worry, Father. God is stronger than the Devil; He will protect us, and heal you."

"God and the Devil have nothing to do with it!" the priest raved, the muscles in his arms rigid, his eyes wide and glittering. "You don't know how strong *she* is, or how desperate. . . . I was an idiot, I thought I could keep her from seeing. . . . And the bishop, the bishop—you must be careful, you cannot trust—Chrétien would as soon see you dead. I cannot keep— What an arrogant fool I am! Can you forgive me? Can you?"

And he began to weep, so piteously that at last Michel said, "Of course I forgive you. Of course. Now be still. You must not say such things about yourself, or the good cardinal." And he held Charles down, murmuring: "Quiet, Father, quiet . . ." until at last the priest's eyes rolled upward and closed, and his body went limp against the bed.

Abruptly, the father's body jerked; a pungent mixture of black blood and chartreuse bile spilled from his mouth onto his chest. Michel fetched a cloth from beside the washbasin and carefully mopped the liquid up.

For the next hour, he sat upon the stool and wiped away the red froth that bubbled from the sick man's lips while another Dominican came and administered extreme unction. After the priest had left, when Charles did not regain consciousness, Michel sank to his knees and prayed.

In the blessedly cooler morning, Michel headed back to the jail, armed with several clean wax tablets and the remaining unsigned confessions. He had spent the night on the floor beside Father Charles's bed, wrestling with the situation. He was a mere scribe, with no power to free or convict prisoners; nevertheless, Mother Marie Françoise had said she would confess to none but him, and while he was terribly distraught over Charles's illness, the chance existed that God had, in a way, used it to answer his prayer on behalf of the abbess.

For if he, Michel, were granted the power to convict or free her, he would most certainly choose to free her—and to bear the full brunt of Rigaud's wrath.

And Father Charles, should God see fit to raise him from his sickbed, would be free of all responsibility and reprisal.

Thus, when morning came, Michel left the ashen, unresponsive priest in the Dominicans' care. And when he climbed the steps leading to the prison, slowed by weariness, a voice behind him called: "Michel! Brother Michel!"

He turned and saw behind him a clean-shaven, handsome young man with hair, brows, and lashes the color of flax, and pale blue eyes. "Father Thomas!"

"And where is your constant shadow?" Thomas asked with easy good humor—humor, Michel knew, that hid a hardened heart. The grinning young priest was dressed in a navy silk frock edged with satin burgundy piping (sedate garb compared to the embroidered frock of rose-colored satin he often wore in the more decadent ambience of Avignon). In one close-fitting sleeve, he had tucked a small sprig of blooming rosemary from one of the countless wild hedges that grew in Languedoc.

To Michel, Thomas represented the worst of the priesthood: an undisciplined, irreligious bon vivant more interested in women and wine than God. A year earlier, he had appeared from nowhere as one of Chrétien's protégés, and the cardinal so doted on him it was rumored the young man was his illegitimate son. Nothing was known of Thomas's past, except that he had obviously been exquisitely educated and bore the features of the French aristocracy. He had volunteered no details about himself, and none dared ask, for to annoy Thomas was to risk Chrétien's ire.

But the fact existed that, despite the favor the cardinal often showed Thomas, only Michel had been adopted as Chrétien's son, and thus was heir to the cardinal's considerable fortune; and for that, apparently, Thomas had never forgiven the young monk.

"Actually," Michel said, "Father Charles is ill." Merely speaking the words revived his grief; for if Chrétien were his adoptive father, then Charles, an aide to the cardinal, was certainly an uncle and confidant. Chrétien's enormous responsibilities had forced him to leave the raising of his foster son first to nuns, then to the wise and tolerant Charles. Michel was closer to no other man.

Thomas's smile evaporated at once. "Dear Lord, I hope it isn't plague. There's been a small outbreak at the Dominican monastery where my scribe . . ." He narrowed his eyes at Michel. "That's right, you and Father Charles are staying there, aren't you?"

Michel gave a nod, and from that small gesture Thomas understood the severity of Charles's condition. "Poor devil," the young priest murmured, then added emphatically, "I pray *you* are feeling well, Brother Michel."

"I'm fine," Michel said stoutly.

"Good." Thomas gave an approving nod and his tone turned matter-of-fact. "Well, God must have a plan: I lack a scribe, you an inquisitor." He took a step toward the entrance; but when Michel held back, the priest turned toward him. "What is it, Brother?"

"The abbess," Michel said, amazed and concerned by how easily the manipulative words came to him. "She volunteered to confess yesterday—but not to the prepared statement."

"And Father Charles gave her the opportunity to do this, of course," Thomas prompted; it was not a question.

Woefully, Michel shook his head. "She said she would confess only to me—alone. It is improper, I know; I am no priest. But she has not been given the legally required opportunity. . . ."

Father Thomas cocked a pale golden eyebrow. "Quite the dilemma, then," he said quietly, "for the bishop and—may we speak frankly?— your father are in a great hurry to see her convicted. If we say she refused to speak—well, things are bad enough with the people as it is. They'll think we put her to death without a fair trial." After brief consideration, he continued: "Brother. . . . I have heard that you have completed the training to be ordained as a priest and an inquisitor."

"Yes, Chrétien insisted on it."

Michel began to say more, but Thomas waved a hand for silence; and though his gaze turned inward, his eyes remained focused on the monk. "So you are qualified by virtue of study and experience to hear her confession, if not by Church law. . . ." After a time, he emerged from his thoughts and told Michel: "Here is the plan, then; we shall go together to visit the abbess. If she will confess in my presence, all is well and good. And if she will confess only to you, then I will continue with the other prisoners—and I will use the whole of my influence to have you ordained as of this very day. I am the priest, after all; it is far more fitting that I, rather than a monk, make the request of Rigaud."

"Of course," Michel replied, ignoring Thomas's dig and affecting an attitude of somber reluctance. In truth, his heart was filled with gratitude. Never had God so resoundingly answered a prayer.

At the same time, his mind was troubled. Was it true, then? Had his adoptive father—a man he had always believed unquestionably just—given the order, in advance of a fair inquisition, to have the abbess executed?

Father Thomas's rosemary sprig was no match for the stench as they descended into the dungeon; the smell that morning was particularly pungent—as it always was once torture began in earnest. It was the odor of blood: blood in the feces, in the urine, in the vomit; blood drying on skin, in fabric, in hair.

The dungeon was brighter today by virtue of extra torches that had been lit . . . perhaps to accommodate the Parisian torturers, who could be heard talking and laughing beyond the high double doors of their gruesome chamber. Michel kept his eyes downcast but could not help catching a peripheral glimpse of the communal cell, and mounds of reddened linen in the straw.

The jailer once again opened the abbess's private cell—this time not bothering to lock it behind him as he left to fetch stools at Father Thomas's request.

Upon the suspended wooden bench sat Mother Marie Françoise. Yesterday's wounds looked even worse today: the deep cut that had split her eyebrow was crusted red-black, the eyelid beneath it a deep violet and so swollen that in profile it eclipsed the bridge of her nose and only a slit of dark, shining eye was visible. Her upper lip was a mottled and puffy red-violet.

Yet no further physical damage had been done her since the day before: and her voice was strong, though trembling with fury and grief.

"My sisters," she challenged, as the jailer brought two stools for the men. Thomas pulled his fearlessly close to the abbess and sat, his expression utterly calculating and unmoved. Michel settled on the stool beside and not quite behind the priest. Despite the abbess's wounds, the passion of Michel's dream rose in him afresh, in the image of her body, naked and shining, breasts luminous as the moon as she reached for him, enveloped him. . . .

The scribe's ears and cheeks bloomed with sudden heat, and he struggled to master both his lust and his shame. Let Satan attack if he would; he, Michel, would keep his mind focused on God, on the holy task at hand.

"My sisters," Mother Marie repeated, with passion of a different sort. "For two days, I have listened to them scream. Why must they be tormented so, when *I* am the one accused of a crime?" One arm held her ribs; the other gestured at herself with a fierce, stabbing motion. "Yet since the arrival of your inquisitors, no one has touched me. *I* was the one found in the papal palace, not they; *I* was the one who—"

"Let us not posture, Mother Marie," Thomas interrupted with calm directness. "There are only two ways out of your current predicament, and that of your nuns: death and damnation, or confession, which leads to eternal life and ends the need for us to glean information from your cohorts. Unfortunately, the good cardinal has not given us much time.

"Now, Brother Michel"—Thomas continued, nodding at the monk—"has already informed me that you will not sign the confession presented you. Is that true?"

She glanced angrily in Michel's direction, then back at Thomas, and gave a brusque nod. She had seemed so frail and small to Michel the day before; now she seemed well capable of commanding a nunnery—and of frightening a bishop, or advising a pope with authority. *Jesus in the Temple, scattering the Pharisees,* Michel thought admiringly, while Thomas prompted:

"And that you will confess only to him, and no one else."

"Yes, yes, I have said that, but that has nothing to do with the suffering of my nuns!" An anger that was indeed righteous, Michel thought, for it was based solidly in compassion for others, without a tinge of self-interest.

Thomas parted his lips to release a small noise of exasperation. "Your nuns will be dealt with fairly, according to Church law—just as you will, Sister. Now, speak quickly and honestly: will you confess to me?"

"I will say it again: I will confess only to Brother Michel."

"Very well," the priest said curtly. "Because of your stature in the Church, I will accede to your request to have Brother Michel hear your confession. And should you lie, or in any way abuse the privilege we have granted you, you will indeed suffer alongside your sisters." Thomas rose with a rustle of silk and left the room; Michel followed.

Just outside, Thomas hesitated, his gaze distant and unfocused; a burst of raucous laughter from the torturers' chamber echoed down the corridor, but he seemed not to hear it as he drew Michel aside confidentially, his manner as serious as the scribe had ever seen it. "Take her confession, Brother, and I will see it made legal in the eyes of the Church. Only mind that, within the allotted three days, we have sufficient evidence to convict her. Already protestors have assembled outside Rigaud's palace; we had to summon the gendarmes to disperse them. Her death must come quickly."

Thomas held out his hands; Michel passed him the black bundle, and the belt that held quill and inkhorn, keeping the wax tablets and stylus; then the blond priest moved off toward the communal cell.

With an intake of breath and a sense of triumph, Michel stepped back inside the cell and closed the unlocked door behind him.

"Mother Marie Françoise?" he asked respectfully. Now alone with her as he had been in the dream, Michel nonetheless felt capable of controlling his indecent impulses, though they persisted. He wished only to aid her, and treat her with the devotion her saintliness deserved.

She turned her swollen face toward him, and fixed him with a look of emotion so profound he could not interpret it. "Brother." Her voice softened, as though she now addressed a dear friend. "We have so little time. . . . I know what they have planned for me. Will you hear my confession? Will you write it down, as best you can, just as I tell it?"

"I will," he replied gently. A sense of extraordinary holiness, calm, compassion, emanated from her presence, permeating him and every atom of the little cell. How could Father Thomas have failed to sense it? How could Charles—or Chrétien?

Reverently Michel sat, picked up tablet and stylus, and, his heart grateful to God, began to write:

In the year 1357, on the twenty-third day of October, one Mother Marie Françoise, abbess of the Franciscan convent at Carcassonne, was formally placed in judgment before the Dominican—

Here he left a blank large enough to fill in his own name, or another's, then continued.

—inquisitor of heretical depravity, deputed by the Apostolic See to the kingdom of France—having taken oath upon the Holy Gospels of God to speak the whole truth and nothing but the truth about the crimes of heresy and witchcraft, both in respect of herself as a principal and also as a witness in the case of other persons, living or dead, has said and confessed . . .

I V

My name is Marie Sybille de Cavasculle, and I was born in a village outside the walled city of Toulouse with a caul over my face. According to my grandmother, whose strong, beautiful hands delivered me and a hundred others into this world, this marked me as one gifted with the Sight.

According to the priests and inquisitors, this marked me as one in league with the Devil.

I do not worship their Devil. Nor do I worship their other gods—Jesus, Jehovah, the Holy Spirit—but I respect them, for all gods are One. I worship the Great Mother, the one many call Diana, whose secret name the inquisitors shall never know.

If this makes me a witch by their definition—very well, then, I am a witch, just as surely as they are Christians and murderers.

Terrible things have happened in my lifetime. I have known famine and pestilence and war, but the worst suffering was that which was needless—needless, because it was inflicted not by the capriciousness of any god, but by human ignorance, human fear. It is difficult enough to be forced to assume the outer trappings of religion and bow to gods one does not revere. But now many innocents have been tortured, and many have perished in the flames—the servants of the Goddess, by whatever name they know Her, and the Jews, and even devout Christians who made the mistake of annoying those in power. Every woman who dared use the old knowledge of herbs and charms to heal the sick, to bring a child into the world, and was foolish enough to confess it, has met with a fiery fate. So much knowledge, forever lost . . .

Our tormentors have set down many lies about those who serve the Goddess, so that all who hear them are misled. I have come to realize that even the inquisitors themselves have no idea of the scope of their errors. Those who know the truth dare not speak out, for fear of the strappado and the stake; the Inquisition has silenced us all.

And so I tell my story here. Some of it I lived myself; some was told me by others; some I saw with the Sight. I give as full a truth as I know, without fear of reprisal, for I have lived and suffered much, and know what end awaits me.

But I fear for the servants of the Goddess who follow me. Even now I See—with Her eyes, not my own—the flames leaping higher. The worst is coming. They have claimed my Beloved, he who was my destiny; I am but one now, and know with bitterness that my solitary magic is not enough to avert the coming Evil.

Unlike the Christians, I do not pray that my tale survive me in these dangerous times, and find its way into the proper hands. I have taken steps to ensure it; by the Mother's power, I know it will.

V

At her first two sentences, Michel had gasped in shock and stopped writing: Impossible, yet here she was with her own lips proclaiming that she was a witch, a practitioner of magic! But he had sensed within her the presence of *God*. . . .

Lord, help me! I have been foolish and proud, and Father Charles and the bishop are right.

Such was his dismay that he thought to put away his stylus and tablet, to rise and leave the cell, never to return. He had *prayed* to this woman, this witch.

The abbess said nothing, but merely waited patiently until Michel recovered and lifted his stylus again, at which point she continued to speak.

When she was finished, she studied him with, of all things, sympathy.

"Poor Brother Michel," she said kindly. "I have shocked you—and I know how desperately you yearn to save the . . . fallen. In fact, I know the very next question you wish to pose."

"Do you?" he asked warily, unsure how to react to her now. Should he leave and turn her interrogation over to Father Thomas to avoid being further charmed? Should he fulfill his duty to the Church and trust the bishop's crucifix to protect him?

Had he been a fool to think God had answered his prayer to save the abbess? But things had fallen into place so easily with Father Thomas. . . .

She gave a short, grim laugh. "Not because of any magical trick . . . but because I know you are a good soul. You want to ask whether I was ever a Christian—to be sure I am not *relapsa,* so you can rescue my soul."

"*Were* you ever a Christian?"

"Never. But the reality of what I am is not so dreadful as the Church would have you believe." She paused, then stated firmly: "I shall start with the story of my birth now."

"Mother, we haven't time. In fact"—and he drew in a breath that was pure pain, but he could not deny his duty—"whether I take any further confession from you at all depends on your answer to the following. Did you work evil magic against His Holiness? Did you attempt, in any way, to harm him?"

"I cannot—I could not. It is not in my nature to do such a thing; it is like asking a fish whether it flew. You were there, in Avignon; you saw the extent of what I did. Now will you hear my story?"

"I will," he said, relieved. "But we need not begin with your birth."

She gave him a look of sheer disbelief, tinged by a smile. "How else can you prove I am not *relapsa,* Brother, unless you know the whole of it?"

He opened his mouth to disagree—but, finding no suitable argument, closed it again. Indeed, it occurred to him that perhaps God *had* answered his prayer for her. After hearing her confession, he could endeavor to bring her to Christ—for even now, he sensed much that was good emanating from her. And so he settled more firmly on his stool, determined to remain.

Her manner suddenly darkened; candlelight and shadow played upon her wounds, giving a ghastly effect, and her voice dropped to a murmur. "We both know, my friend, that the powers directing you are determined to see me burn, and quickly. Will you indulge me in a small kindness—to record my story ere I die, that something of me might remain at the end of its telling? And in order to know *me,* you must also hear the story of my Beloved, a knight who was destroyed by the evil forces that have brought me here. Without him, there is no longer hope—for me, for my Race; it is in memory of him that I tell our story."

"Mother Marie, I cannot—"

She countered at once: "Together we made one soul; I cannot speak of myself without speaking also of him."

"I may scarcely have the time to record *your* confession," Michel said honestly. "Especially, Mother, if we are to start with the story of your birth. Perhaps you overheard how much time the authorities have allowed us: three days, no more. Beyond that, I must also tell you that I will not be swayed by your spells or arguments, and I will pray unceasingly that your heart be brought to Christ, that you may be saved."

She paused at that to study him intently; at last she gave a nod.

Once again, he lifted his stylus and began to write.

PART II

Sybille

TOULOUSE

August 1335

VI

I was born into fire.

Here is the story as it was told to me:

Late summer it was, and the air was heavy with the coming storm, alive with unhurled lightning. Outside, the villeins who farmed the land were walking home alongside horse-drawn carts, wheels creaking under the weight of this year's heavy wheat harvest. Sweating, my grandmother glanced up through the unshuttered window, hoping to catch a glimpse of her son; but dusk and thunderclouds both were gathering so that she could not tell one shadowy scythe-bearing man from another. Even so, the Sight whispered to her that my father would soon appear in the open doorway. He was a peasant who toiled in the *seigneur*'s fields outside the walled city of Toulouse, born Pietro di Cavascullo in Florence. To avoid the infamous prejudice and suspicion of my native region of Languedoc, he took on the name Pierre de Cavasculle. Noni, on the other hand, steadfastly refused to be known by the appellation *grandmère;* nor would she call my father anything but Pietro.

We were not as poor as some, though poorer than many; being uncorrupted by the luxury of the convent then, and ignorant of Avignon's splendor, I thought we were rich. We possessed a bed, but the mattress was straw, not feather, and my father owned a plow but no horse. Like almost everyone in our little village, our thatched cottage consisted of one room with a straw-strewn earth floor, a hearth, the family bed, and a table for dining. Ventilation was provided by two windows, so we were constantly covered in black soot; I never knew of chimneys, or even that I was dirty, until I entered the convent.

So it was that my mother labored near the hearth of our little cottage; and her anguished screams brought Ana Magdalena's attention back to her duty. Catherine of Narbonne was her name, and she a matron of twenty. Catherine had pitched forward from the birthing chair onto the floor. Now she crouched on all fours, growling like a beast from the pain. *Poor child,* my grandmother thought; the birth pangs had come upon her hours before sunset a full day before, and now she was too spent, too beside herself to do anything but screech like a wild animal and curse anyone, anything, even God and the child within her. Her husband and mother-in-law she had cursed almost from the beginning, Ana Magdalena thought with a glimmer of wry amusement.

She knelt beside the suffering woman. Catherine had slouched forward so that her forearms rested against the earth floor, and upon them, her pale, perspiring brow; with one frail fist, she beat the straw-littered ground. Gently, Ana Magdalena leaned forward and lifted the girl's hair—a waving red-gold veil, beautiful and gleaming despite its dampness—and arranged it upon Catherine's back. Tradition insisted that it was ill luck to bind the hair of a woman in labor, and while Ana Magdalena, the most skilled midwife in all Toulouse, did not believe in that superstition one whit, her daughter-in-law did—and the mother's confidence was of supreme importance at a birthing.

Especially in a first birth, such as this one. Catherine might still seem young—but she was old in terms of childbearing. Almost six years she had been married to Pietro, and six times become pregnant; and six times, Pietro had comforted his grieving wife while Ana Magdalena took the tiny, unborn child to bury it in the olive grove.

Six times, Ana Magdalena had hoped that the vision given her by *la bona Dea,* the good Goddess, would come true: of a girl-child destined to become a great priestess such as had never been seen in centuries, a girl who would grow into a woman and save her people, her Race, with the talents given her. A woman powerfully gifted with the Sight . . .

A father's daughter, the Goddess had said, *and a mother's son . . . Together, they will save their people from the coming danger. And you will be the girl's teacher.*

Danger? Ana Magdalena had asked humbly, suddenly stricken with fear. But there came no reply; it was not given her to know, and so she did not press or permit herself concern—only joy that she would be allowed to know this child, her own grandchild, her beloved son's daughter.

"Catherine," she said sternly, and reached for a rag soaked in water; when the girl's pains eased and she looked up at last from her misery, Ana Magdalena firmly, swiftly swabbed her face and brow with it. Despite the heat, the girl shivered; gooseflesh appeared on her bare arms.

"Mother, help me!" she cried, so pitifully that Ana Magdalena, long inured to the anguish of breeding women, was moved. "I know not whether I am burning hot or freezing cold!"

The older woman pulled the girl back into the birthing chair, and hurried to the cottage's one table, where an earthen pitcher of herbal tea had long since cooled. She returned to Catherine and raised the pitcher to her lips. "Drink, child."

Suddenly suspicious, Catherine turned her face away. "How do I know you have not bewitched it?"

Ana Magdalena permitted herself an audible sigh of exasperation. She was used to the vacillating and inexplicable emotions of breeding women, but not to the mistrust Catherine had shown her throughout this pregnancy. "Mother of God, Catherine! You have drunk another two pitchers of the same tea before this one! It is nothing but willow bark with a calming herb. It will ease the fever and pain. Now, *drink!*"

The last word she uttered with such force that girl submitted with sudden meekness, swallowing such a great gulp that Ana Magdalena warned, "Small sips, small sips, else you—"

Before she could say the words, *Turn your stomach,* Catherine belched, then vomited up a small amount of yellow bile. With instinct born of experience, Ana Magdalena managed to remove the pitcher just in time. The vomit spilled onto the front of Catherine's homespun undershift, streaking the dull fabric from breast to belly with yellow-green. No point in cleaning it off now, Ana Magdalena thought distractedly; the shift was already stained with birth water, blood, and earth from the floor.

Dutifully, she wiped Catherine's face again with the cloth, then said to the moaning girl: "Hold still, my sweet; I will check on the baby."

She crouched down in the blood-scented straw. The birthing chair had been arranged so that Catherine could sit, legs astraddle, with her back, head, and arms fully supported. It was fashioned from cut, bundled hay, one bundle supporting her tailbone; two others, turned lengthwise, supporting either pelvic bone, with an infant-sized gap between them. With a deft hand, Ana Magdalena reached under Catherine's wet, twisted shift and felt her swollen pubis.

The pains were constant now; birth had to come soon, and if it did not, the midwife would practice surgery and free the babe from the womb, if need be. She was skilled enough to do so without losing either mother or child; few midwives were knowledgeable enough to accomplish it anymore, since the city barbers and physicians complained about it, claiming that this was rightly *their* domain, and not that of ignorant peasant women.

Unschooled she was in letters, but far from ignorant of her chosen skill; so she felt with the practiced touch of her long, narrow fingers that yes, the babe had dropped. The head had not crested so that it could be seen, but it was not far from doing so; it could be felt, hard just beneath the girl's swollen womanhood. Ana Magdalena smiled as she brushed a fingertip across the baby's soft crown.

Laughing, she withdrew her hands, wiped them on the damp cloth, then flung it aside. Kneeling on the straw, she cried happily, "The baby is *here,* Catherine, my darling! *Here!* I felt its little head. . . . It will not be long now. . . ."

She had almost said, Her *little head,* which would have been a grave mistake, indeed. Catherine was already suspicious and unsettled by her; the girl knew, with an instinct that must have been the Sight repressed, that the older woman had been taught the wisdom of the Race, and secretly practiced the old religion. Christians rejected the old beliefs and the Sight, claiming both came from their Devil.

Such a one was Catherine. Ana Magdalena had known, years ago, when her son first fell in love with the red-haired beauty, that this girl possessed the Sight almost as strongly as did Ana Magdalena herself. But the tragedy was that Catherine had been reared a strict Christian; not only had she learned to reject her ability, she had come to fear it.

Yet Ana Magdalena had given permission for the two to wed, thinking: *I shall be as a mother to her, and shall take her as the daughter I never had, and school her in the ways of the Wise.* And it seemed to her that the Goddess, too, blessed the union.

But Catherine's fear of the old Wisdom and her own talent had not eased over the years. Ana Magdalena found that she not only could not broach the subject with the girl, she could not even refer, however subtly, to the Wisdom in her own home unless Catherine was absent. Even so, Ana Magdalena loved her, and Catherine had seemed to return that love, and had trusted her mother-in-law for the past six years—until she became pregnant with this particular child. From that moment, her distrust had escalated until it created a barrier around her affections that Ana Magdalena could not breach.

For the older woman to have admitted that she had known since its conception that the child would be a girl might just send Catherine running to the village priest to tattle on her mother-in-law, the sorceress.

Well, let her, Ana Magdalena thought. *Then she will have to confess that when she knew she was pregnant a seventh time, she finally came and asked me for charms.* And so there was a charm of herbs beneath the birthing chair of hay, and another of words uttered over the tea; and there was magical protection cast all over the house, magic too sacred to be represented by herbs or chants.

Deep thunder rolled in the distance; a cool but humid breeze caused the open wooden shutters to clack gently against the earthen wall. The sounds were soon drowned out by the laboring woman's cries.

And despite the important task at hand, the midwife glanced over at the open door, knowing without seeing, without hearing, that her son stood there in his sweat-stained tunic littered with bits of grain and wheat stalks.

Pietro stood, hesitant, sickle still in hand, his large eyes filled with unspeakable weariness. His namesake father's eyes had held that same exhaustion, Ana Magdalena recalled wistfully; a peasant's burden was to toil constantly in the fields he rented from the *grand seigneur,* and in the *seigneur*'s own huge fields, as well. Such a life sapped a man's strength so there was little left for his own family.

His father's eyes he had, and his mother's Sight. But as Pietro grew older and joined his father in the fields, his interest in the old Wisdom lessened. Ana Magdalena did not press; it was not his destiny to use his talent, but to pass it on to his only child.

Ana Magdalena smiled a worn greeting at her son as he entered, then laid down his sickle and slipped his feet out of dirty wooden sabots. "Catherine is well, and about to bear your child."

At this, Pietro's features wreathed themselves in a smile so bright Ana Magdalena caught her breath; it had always been this way with her son, he with an expression so solemn that she never was sure what he was thinking. And then he would smile like the morning sun gliding over the top of a gray mountain, and she would be dazzled. He stepped toward his wife, reaching for her. "Catherine, is it true? Shall we have a son at last?"

"I know not," she groaned. "It is horrible, horrible. . . . I am weary enough to die. . . ." She bared her teeth, face contorting with the effort to hold back a scream.

He crouched down beside her. "Oh, Cat. Please, yell. It is worse for me to see you be brave. . . ."

To oblige him, she let go the building shriek, with such unrestrained ferocity that he shrank back, startled.

Ana Magdalena went to the hearth and fetched him a plate of warm stew, a thick dish of cabbage and leeks, and, in special celebration, a fine whole chicken: he deserved a little meat in his belly—as would Catherine, once she was delivered. Pietro sat at the table and let his mother serve him the stew with a chunk of brown bread. Warmth still emanated from the extinguished hearth, but a cooling breeze sailed through the open door and window, dispersing the hearth smoke. With the breeze came darkness and a clap of thunder that made Catherine jerk her head like a startled doe.

Ana Magdalena lit the oil lamp and carried it over to the birthing chair, then set it carefully to one side on the floor so that she could see the babe as it came, but Catherine, in her travail, could not knock it over. As if cued, the younger woman began to keen; Pietro, looking troubled and somewhat sickly, rose and picked up his dish. "I will eat outside." And he went out to sit in the cooling gloom.

Ana Magdalena knelt and probed once more with careful, efficient fingers. The child's position was as it should be, and the cord well away from the baby's neck. "Daughter, I see the baby's head, and all is well. Now you must use all the strength you have left to push this child into the world."

As she spoke, a violent gust of wind entered the cottage, rattling the open shutters and sending a chill through Ana Magdalena's bones—not because of the cold, but because of the evil that rode in upon it.

Diana, la bona Dea, protect the child, she prayed immediately, and in her mind strengthened the invisible barriers surrounding the little house, but it was too late. Something—a will, a mind, an unholy force—had entered and settled nearby; the older woman sensed its presence as surely as she had felt the wind evaporate the sweat upon her face and arms. But where—and what—was it?

Before Ana Magdalena could form a question in her thoughts, Catherine looked up, and the light from the oil lamp caught her eyes so that they glowed a malevolent yellow-green, like a wolf's when it ventures near a night fire.

Ana Magdalena drew in a breath. These were merely her daughter-in-law's eyes, narrowed in pain, she told herself—yet at the same time, another intelligence resided there, one deadly and smirking.

Impossible for it to have penetrated all of her precautions, all her prayers and charms and the circle of protection about the little cottage. Yet here it was, bold and defiant.

"Be gone with you," Ana Magdalena commanded in a tone of righteous fury, with such force that her voice broke. At once, the sinister gleam in Catherine's eyes turned to innocent puzzlement and misery.

"What?" the girl moaned, to which Ana Magdalena replied kindly: "Nothing, child. Push." And she took Catherine's small, pale hands in her own large, dark ones.

With low, guttural growls and a grip that crushed the bones of Ana Magdalena's fingers, the young mother began to push; soon, a bit more of the babe's crown showed. Yet in the midst of it, Catherine stopped pushing and wailed, "I cannot! I cannot. . . . Mother of God, help me!"

"She hears and will help," Ana Magdalena replied swiftly, her thought only of the child waiting to draw its first breath. "You only need push once more. Only push once more, my daughter." She caught hold again of the girl's hands.

"I am not your daughter!" Catherine shrieked with sudden wildness; her face contorted into that of a snarling beast, her eyes grew narrow, feral. *"You* have done this to me, old witch! You knew I was too weak, that I would die of this, yet you gave me potions and charms to keep this child in me— You want this child for your own wicked purposes!" And she slapped Ana Magdalena's hands away, with such surprising force that the older woman, still on her knees, lost her balance and fell hard onto her side.

The lamp, Ana Magdalena realized, with terror. In the split second before she struck the floor she tried desperately to move, to avoid it, but it was too late. . . .

Her shoulder struck the lamp, knocking it over so that the fragrant olive oil inside spilled out onto the floor as a stream of liquid fire. The oil that was not immediately consumed soaked Ana Magdalena's black skirts. In the time it took her heart to beat once, twice, she watched, horrified, as flames ate at the hem of her garments and leapt across the floor to the hay birthing chair, and the soft nest of straw beneath it, readied for the coming child.

Stamping, slapping at the encroaching fire, Catherine screamed continuously—whether with fear, rage, or the pangs of birth, Ana Magdalena could not say, for she was far too engaged in rolling in the earth, trying to smother the flames that had burned away half of her widow's skirts and now threatened her undershift.

"Pietro!" she screamed. "My son, help!"—while Catherine, who had miraculously thrown herself clear of the flaming birthing chair, lay on her side, bellowing:

"God! God! *God!*"

In the midst of the black smoke and fire, Pietro emerged, his eyes stricken, yet at the same time tempered by that uncommon steadiness he had possessed since childhood. Ana Magdalena slapped at her oil-soaked skirts so that bits of them sailed as glowing ash into the air, and cried out as the heat singed the hair on her legs and arms. The edge of her black wimple began to smolder, and she pulled it from her head and flung it aside.

Then Pietro was upon her, wrapping her swiftly, tightly, in the one wool blanket the family possessed. The instant the flames were smothered, he unwound the blanket and ran toward the fire that threatened his writhing wife.

Ignoring the smarting burns on her shins, Ana Magdalena struggled to her feet and ran to the hearth, where the pail of the day's water sat. She grabbed it and hurled its contents at the bright conflagration that had been the birthing chair. With a sharp hiss, the fire dimmed, and a plume of dark smoke rose from its midst; Pietro put out the remaining flames with the blanket, then cried: "Mother, attend her! The babe is born, but it makes no sound!" Catherine lay at last blessedly silent, save for her exhausted panting. From between her legs dangled a long, bloody cord, and at its end, slipped forward onto the ground, lay the babe: a perfectly formed dark-haired girl, little red fists tightly curled, face veiled by the afterbirth, the bloodstained sac in which it had spent the past nine months. A caul, Ana Magdalena realized, with a thrill that turned the skin on her arms to gooseflesh despite the heat; a very special omen, the Goddess's mark for a child doubly Sighted, doubly destined.

Aloud, she cried, "Not blue, see? She is not yet blue!" She cast aside the pail and rushed to the babe. With a single motion she took from her belt the dagger, used it to cut the cord, then replaced it, and swooped the infant up into her arms and removed the caul. With the tatters of her ruined skirts, she wiped away the red-black blood and ivory birth cheese from the placid little face, then turned the child over and administered a staccato thump between its shoulder blades.

The effect was magical; the baby coughed, then drew in its first breath and began to squawl in earnest.

Catherine stirred. "Is it a boy? A son?"

"A healthy girl," Ana Magdalena announced, and proceeded to weep with happiness while Catherine sobbed—with shame at its sex, or a more sinister regret for its survival? Pietro smiled at the child, but clearly his joy was tempered with disappointment.

"Am I the only one glad to greet this child?" Ana Magdalena snapped. "Thanks be to God"—and in her own mind added, *and to the Goddess*—"for this healthy daughter!" As was her right in the home where she was raised, she proclaimed, "Her name is Sibilla."

There, she had said it: *Sibilla,* a fine pagan name, sent her in dreams. *Sibilla:* the wise woman, priestess and prophetess, the Great Mother's own.

Struggling to sit, Catherine reached for the child, and countered in a tone that was pure defiance, "Marie. Her name is Marie, for the Virgin, and I will not hear otherwise. This is not Italy, with its quaint old customs, and this is not a pagan house."

Ana Magdalena coldly raised one thick black brow. "Call her what you will, my daughter-in-law, but her name before God and His Mother will always be Sibilla."

"Pierre!" Catherine turned her head, red-gold hair fanning across one shoulder, green eyes pleading. Even drenched in blood and sweat, her legs smeared with dark afterbirth, she was beautiful, and her husband would deny her nothing. "Pierre, shall you permit our only child to bear a heathen name? And not even a proper French one?"

Ana Magdalena raised herself to her full height and stared fiercely at her son. She was about the Mother's work, and at such times, she felt the Goddess descend on her with uncanny power. All this, she knew, Pietro could see in her eyes; and she knew she need say nothing, do nothing to press her case. In any matter, her son practiced Christianity only to placate his wife, but Ana Magdalena knew that if he cherished any deity at all in his heart of hearts, it was the Goddess . . . and the gaze of She Who was Mother of all would serve to remind him of his duty.

He looked at her, saw the message there, and understood; yet at the same time, Ana Magdalena knew he could not entirely deny his lovely wife.

So he sighed, ever weary, and said calmly: "I will not hear you women arguing. Fire or no, this is a happy day—a good harvest come just before the rain, and our share of wheat already sheltered in Old Jacques's barn tonight, and the birth of my first child. Her name is Marie Sybille, and that is that."

And he helped his wife onto the bed.

Ana Magdalena continued with her work as if Evil had never entered the cottage, had never claimed Catherine as Its ally. She helped her daughter-in-law out of the birthwater- and blood-stained shift, then bathed her as best she could with the damp cloth—it was too dark now to fetch more water from the well. As it was night, the girl did not dress again; when Catherine's bare skin turned to gooseflesh despite the heat, Ana Magdalena draped the remainder of the scorched blanket around the girl's stooped shoulders.

Then she bound a rag around Catherine's thick, soft waist, and tied to it another rag to catch whatever blood followed the birth, and gave the girl a strong sleeping draught mixed with willow bark. At long last, she cleaned the babe, swaddled it, and presented it to its mother. Despite Catherine's initial disappointment, she cooed with delight at the child, and carefully followed the midwife's instructions on how to suckle it while Ana Magdalena combed and braided her long red hair. And when the child had eaten its fill, the midwife brought Catherine a bowl of the cool stew and the rest of the chicken, which the girl ate hungrily.

Soon Pietro had hung his clothes over the horizontal pole at the head of the bed, and father, mother, and child were all three asleep. Quietly, Ana Magdalena swept the charred remains of the birthing chair and the burnt straw outside. By then, the storm had come—the raindrops fat and few at first, then long and driving and needle-sharp, so much so that when she looked from the window toward the south, she could not make out the olive grove there.

She gathered up the dirtied rags and Catherine's stained undershift, and hung them on the branches of the little olive tree to let the rain wash them clean.

The rain, too, had washed away the danger that had threatened the child; the Evil was gone, fled to some distant place (else she would never have permitted Catherine even to hold the child)—but it had not been destroyed, Ana Magdalena knew, and would soon return again.

Her duty to her son and daughter-in-law was done; and now, at last, it was time to care for the throbbing burns upon her shins. Thanks to *la bona Dea,* they were not so bad as they might have been. Ana Magdalena lifted her scorched undershift and saw that there were not even any blisters, only large patches of smooth, shiny, red flesh where all the fine, dark hairs had been burned away. With the skin unbroken, she need not fear infection; and though it was too dark to gather lavender for a soothing compress, the good Lady had provided the best medicine of all to take away the heat and sting.

Ana Magdalena fetched what was left of the stew and the chicken bones, some of which had some meat left on them. Then she tucked up her skirts to her hips and sat in the doorway, bare legs stretched before her into the cool rain. There she enjoyed her dinner and remained until her legs were covered in gooseflesh and her teeth chattered; after the heat of the day, the cold was a delight.

There she sat for some time, praying and contemplating what she now had to do. Catherine had somehow opened herself to the Evil, which wanted to harm the baby; what was to stop her from opening herself to It again?

But now that Pietro was asleep, Ana Magdalena could flee with the infant and slip unnoticed to another village, another town, another city, and raise the girl as her own. It seemed the safest way: yet her heart was troubled. If she left, would *she* in turn be unconsciously doing the Evil's bidding?

A few hours later, the storm had passed. Outside, the silence was interrupted only by the sweet, high song of crickets and the mournful, muffled hoots of an owl. Catherine lay on her back, snoring softly beside her husband; snuggled between man and wife lay the baby, in the crook of her mother's arm. As always, Pietro slept silent as death, lying on his side with one cheek pressed fast to the mattress. Ana Magdalena knew she could shout into his ear and there would be no waking him, not until the hour before sunrise, but Catherine was a light, anxious sleeper. Certainly, she had had a sleeping potion and was exhausted by her long labor—but the strong link between mother and child was unpredictable.

Even so, Ana Magdalena thought, *I can do only as the Goddess bids.* She rose from the bed with slow, deliberate movements, then turned to face Catherine and the child.

Bathed in a pane of moonlight, the swaddled infant lay quietly; indeed, she had not cried out once since her birth. *Like her father,* Ana Magdalena thought fondly. Pietro had been such a calm, contented child that there were times, shortly after his birth, when Ana Magdalena had forgotten the new babe had come. The redness of Sibilla's little face had eased to a pink glow. Beside her in the shadows, Catherine seemed pale; a miracle, indeed, that such a frail woman had given birth to such a healthy babe.

The midwife leaned forward, stretched out her hands, and slipped them underneath her granddaughter, careful not to brush against the sleeping mother's arm. The child stirred inside her restraints, eyes fast shut, but made no sound; smiling, Ana Magdalena lifted her up, slowly, gingerly.

Catherine stirred suddenly and whimpered with pain in her sleep. The older woman froze, still leaning over the younger, the babe raised less than a foot off the mattress.

After a few thrilling seconds, Catherine settled and went back to her snoring. Ana Magdalena released an inaudible sigh, gathered the child up into her arms, then stole barefoot out into the night.

Diana, protect us tonight, she prayed, feeling the grass cool and damp beneath her callused feet. And as she walked, her way was bathed in a sudden brightness, so that she could see each wildflower, each blade of grass, each herb, even the brown hare that stood on its hind legs, sniffing the air; she gazed upward to see, emerging from the fleeing clouds, the waxing moon, ringed by a faint mist that glowed with hints of rose and azure. At once she was seized by a sense of love and destiny so strong, the moment seemed timeless: she had been born for this, she had done nothing in her life before this nor would do anything after, but walk upon the grass and wildflowers holding this child in her arms.

She lifted the dozing infant to her lips and kissed its impossibly tender forehead. The baby frowned in its sleep like a quizzical little monkey, a crease appearing between its downy eyebrows before its features smoothed themselves. Ana Magdalena laughed softly—

Then immediately fell silent at the sound of wolves howling nearby—in the depths of the olive grove, the very place where the Goddess now directed her feet. For an instant, no more, she halted, and saw in the darkness the green glint of feral eyes, the eyes Catherine had for those few moments possessed, the eyes of the Enemy.

Fear stirred within her; just as swiftly, she banished it. "Be ye of this world or no," she told the creatures, "in the name of the Goddess you must now leave, and stay respectfully clear." Deliberately, swiftly, she began again to move; and the howling and the eyes disappeared at once.

Woman and child encountered not a soul before they arrived at the edge of the sacred olive grove planted by the Roman invaders, where ancient trees—some the height of six men standing upon each other's shoulders—stretched their silvery limbs against the sky. Ana Magdalena stepped beneath the first sheltering branch; immediately, the thick, leaf-covered boughs dimmed the moonlight, which filtered through the breaks in a tiny ray here, a sliver there, illuminating tiny patches of sparse grass and damp-smelling earth. To the midwife, it made no difference. Over the years, she had come here many times at night—drawn at first by instinct and moon-tides, then by camaraderie—and knew her way well.

The trees at the grove's periphery had only recently been stripped bare of their fruit. But as she neared the secluded center, the trees became heavy with unharvested fruit, left there to honor the Queen of Heaven. Ana Magdalena felt the swollen ripe olives beneath her feet and smelled the rich fragrance released as they were crushed. Tomorrow there would be incriminating purple-black stains that she would be wise to hide from Catherine.

At last she arrived at the little clearing, where the life-sized replica of the Mother stood in her guise as Mary. Carved of wood, the statue was very old; the nose had partially rotted away and refused to hold the paint that was lovingly replenished every May festival, and there were scratches and marks on the Mother's feet, as if some wild animal had gnawed there. A fresh rosemary wreath, adorned with glistening rain-drops, had been placed upon the crown of her sky-blue veil, but the rain had ravaged the more delicate garland of wildflowers around her neck. Reverently, Ana Magdalena stepped forward and with her free hand swept away the soggy olive leaves sticking to the Goddess's shoulders, and repaired the garland as best she could.

Then, careful to keep her balance with the bundle in her arms, she knelt upon the wet ground, and whispered: "*La bona Dea*. She is Yours, and I swear upon my spirit that she will always be so. Guide me as her teacher, and protect us from the forces that would take her from You."

And she set the sweet child on the bed of olive leaves and wet flowers at the feet of the statue. From her waist she took her dagger and, with a feather-light touch, traced the symbol of Diana upon the baby's brow. Then she bowed her head, forming in her mind her next request.

"Shall I take the child away from her parents—or shall we all remain together?"

No reply. Ana Magdalena repeated the question, to no avail, which meant that there *was* no definite reply; it mattered not which path was chosen, the outcome would be the same. And so she contemplated for a time, eyes closed, until a more meaningful request came to her.

"Show me the strongest magic, that I may protect her."

Ere her lips formed the question, the Mother replied: *I will show you your choice.*

And the Sight came upon Ana Magdalena swift and strong, stronger than ever it had come her whole life, even when coaxed with herbs or pleasure.

Suddenly she was no longer in the wood, but seated in a fine cottage, one with a fireplace and two rooms, and stools on which to sit, and a large hearth filled with wood and a crackling fire. Beside her sat a lovely young woman: Sibilla, she realized, and at Sibilla's breast was an infant girl; and at Ana Magdalena's feet, a young boy played contentedly with a wooden doll. The older woman's heart overflowed with happiness: these were her great-grandchildren. . . .

At once came an explosion, sharp and crystalline, like the loud shattering of glass—a sound Ana Magdalena had heard only once before in her life, as a bride at the altar when someone had hurled a great rock at the cathedral window, sending shards of sunlit color flying. A bad omen, she had judged it then, cringing beside her groom and the priest: by then they were openly calling her *striga* in the village, and she'd had to come to the city to find a cleric who did not know her to perform her wedding. She and her new husband had moved to another village shortly afterward.

A bad omen, she sensed even now, before she opened her eyes to find herself back in the wood, its great olive trees now ablaze.

Indeed, the flames that sprang from them appeared preternaturally brilliant in autumnal shades of crimson, sunset, ochre; and alive, undulating, serpentine from between the branches toward Ana Magdalena . . . and the precious child. She scrabbled on her knees toward the infant Sibilla, but the fire surged forth, down the trunks of trees and onto the damp leaves and flowers, scurrying over them with the same swiftness with which wind sweeps through grain, and created a wall between woman and babe.

Without thought, Ana Magdalena reached through the flames— magical ones, she was sure these were, for though they burned bright, they consumed neither wood nor leaf—then withdrew her hand with a shrill cry at the pain, staring in astonishment at the red and blistered palm.

"Sibilla!" she cried out, no longer mindful of waking any in the town, and pushed herself to her feet; at once the fire grew taller, and opaque, blocking all sight of the infant, who made not a sound. Ana Magdalena could see nought but the great trees, aflame but untouched, like the bush of Moses.

Terror took her then, for the child's sake and her own; so intense did the heat grow that she felt the exposed flesh on her face, her arms, her legs begin to blister. Even as pain and fear consumed her, she saw beyond the surrounding fire into the darkness—and the glinting green eyes regarding her there.

Lupine they were, yet of an intelligence far greater than animal, and set within a still darker form—human, tall, and gloating. At the sight of them, she heard in her mind the sound of shattering glass.

The Evil had been present since the day she was born; she had grown up aware of Its presence, knew her life was a struggle against It.

"Goddess, help me!" she cried. At once, the flames abated enough to reveal the placid features of the wood statue; Ana Magdalena felt relieved. This was no attack of the Evil, she reminded herself, but a vision she had requested of the Goddess, in order that she might learn the strongest magic.

So she calmed her thoughts. And with the rush of a great wind, the fire swept down out of the trees, leaving them whole and green, and slithered across crackling leaves and earth to condense itself into a ring about Ana Magdalena's feet and legs.

There was still great pain, and for an instant fear fluttered inside her like a bird seeking escape; then it stilled, for between her and her Enemy stood a living woman in the place where the wooden statue had been.

A woman with hair of shining black, and eyes dark as water in a well; young and strong, with her mother's nose and her father's lips and olive skin. . . .

"*Sibilla,*" Ana Magdalena whispered, her voice tremulous with joy. Despite the unremitting agony of the fire, she could feel nought but love and happiness at the sight of her granddaughter, grown and beautiful— and amazement as, before her eyes, the woman's face became beatific, translucent, transformed by internal radiance.

"*La Dea viva,*" Ana Magdalena murmured; *the Goddess lives.* For no human face—or wooden statue—could possibly express such infinite peace, infinite joy, infinite compassion.

She had known her grandchild had been chosen for a great destiny, but she had never known this: that Sybille had been chosen to become a living Vessel.

And at that moment, Ana Magdalena's heart opened utterly to compassion, embracing all: embracing the flames, embracing the pain, embracing whatever destiny the Goddess might choose for her. Embracing even the lurking Enemy, who was most to be pitied.

As she felt her compassion directed toward its distant, glowing eyes, they at once began to shrink, smaller and smaller, as did its dark form, too, until the creature was no longer the size of a man, but that of a small wolf, then a dog. The yellow-green eyes flickered, dimmed, extinguished.

Fear, Ana Magdalena realized; fear was to it like meat to a wolf—feeding it, increasing its strength. At once she understood the wall around her daughter-in-law's heart, and the substance of which it was built. Despite all of Ana Magdalena's magic, all her prayers, Catherine's fear had opened the child to danger.

Of a sudden, Ana Magdalena came to herself, and saw she knelt alone in the dark olive grove, quiet save for the rustling of small creatures: at her knees, her swaddled grandchild slept quietly. She looked somberly up at the familiar wooden statue, its lips curved gently upward in a benign smile.

"You have shown me these things for a reason, *bona Dea*; now let me be Wise."

As she prayed, there came the hooting of an owl as if in reply.

Two paths lay before you, the Goddess said, a voice both unmistakable and silent in Ana Magdalena's heart. *One safe; the other fraught with danger. It is up to you to decide. Only the most extreme magic can transform the child into what she must become. Only the most powerful, which she cannot accomplish alone: thus, of all people in the world, I have entrusted her into your care. This is your destiny, the reason for which you were born. Will you make your decision, for her? For me?*

"I will do this," Ana Magdalena whispered, her eyes filling with tears of love and grief. "I will do this. And may we both make our way safely into Your sheltering arms. . . ."

For a time she knelt with head bowed, overwhelmed, heart open to the Goddess; then at last she rose and gathered up the babe.

She and little Sibilla would continue to live with the child's parents; why create grief for them, when the Enemy would follow the child wherever she went? Besides, Ana Magdalena now knew from which direction the Evil would try to attack.

And I must take great care to allow no fear in my heart; Goddess help me to keep it at bay.

At last Ana Magdalena bowed to the Goddess and began to walk slowly back through the grove.

Catherine tossed restlessly in her sleep, under the spell of a troubling dream: The baby was crying, a sorrowful little owl-hoot, and Catherine felt a stirring in her swollen breasts, a sudden wetness; her milk had come again, and it was time to feed the baby, the baby. . . . Where was the baby?

Somehow, she was no longer in the bed, and the landscape about her was dark, shrouded in mist; no matter how hard she strained to see, she could not find her baby, even though she had placed it right beside her.

She tried to cry out: Marie, my darling. . . . Where have they taken you, little one? Yet her voice died in her throat. She could make no sound, only flail about, blind, helpless, aching with love and fear for her new daughter.

Before her in the writhing mists, a dark form coalesced. Catherine blinked, straining, until at last she recognized her mother-in-law, dressed in her dark skirts, with her blue-black hair streaming free to her waist.

In her arms, Ana Magdalena bore the child.

Catherine reached, grateful, for her daughter. But the older woman pulled the baby beyond her grasp, laughing. And the more Catherine struggled to catch hold of the infant, the more Ana Magdalena pulled it away, taunting her:

The child is mine, Catherine. It was I who ensured her conception and her time in your womb, I who birthed her.

No, no! Catherine screamed. *My baby! Give me Marie!*

Sardonic laughter. *Her name is Sibilla.*

With a start, Catherine woke, one hand fluttering to her breasts, which were indeed leaking milk. Ever since she had conceived this child, wild dreams and horrifying images had haunted her, all of them of her mother-in-law trying to kill the child. For six years, she had lived in peace with Ana Magdalena, and even grown fond of her: now, the very thought of her so terrified Catherine that she thought of running away, of leaving her beloved husband and fleeing with the baby; surely she would have already done so had the labor not left her too weak.

To Avignon, she had decided months ago—though why she should go there eluded her. She knew no one in the city, and had in fact never been; but it was a holy city, a thought that brought comfort.

She turned her face toward her husband in the darkness. Beside her, Pierre slept, his breath coming in slow, deep sighs.

But the baby, which had lain between them, was gone.

The jolt was primal, purely physical; she sat bolt upright, heart pounding, her first thought, swift and horrible, that she or Pierre was lying on top of the child, crushing and smothering it—but no, there was no sign of that. The little one had simply vanished. She turned her head toward the side where her mother-in-law slept, and saw that Ana Magdalena was also gone.

At once she remembered the dream, and felt its mindless panic seize her again. She began to tremble. They were true then, all her wild fears: Ana Magdalena had stolen the child.

She let go a low cry and pushed herself from the bed, grimacing at the fresh stab of pain as her feet reached the floor. As she took a step, she pressed a hand to the rags bound between her legs; the ache there was fierce, and Ana Magdalena had warned her that if she moved overmuch for the next day, she could begin to bleed again.

One hand on her belly—Catherine was surprised to find it still large, but soft and empty now—and the other between her legs, she waddled, hunched over, to her dirty shift and pulled it on, then stumbled to the half-open door.

At the doorway she paused and peered out—searching for the silhouette of a woman cradling a child, and called in a hoarse whisper: "Ana! Ana Magdalena!"

No reply. The moon was bright; she could make out the other villeins' thatch-roofed cottages, their whitewash faded to gray, and the faint outline of the distant olive grove. In the opposite direction, so far away it appeared no larger than her thumbnail, stood the great walled city of Toulouse.

Bent over from the discomfort, she staggered out into the night. And with each step, her anxiety grew. The fire—it had been a bad omen. She would have burned to death, and little Marie, too, if Pierre had not saved them. Catherine had tried since her first day of marriage to trust Ana Magdalena, even to love her as the mother she had never had, since her own had died giving birth to her. Ostensibly, the old woman seemed to care for her daughter-in-law—but there were times Catherine could not help being afraid of her. Ana Magdalena was too knowledgeable of the old pagan ways, and even though she seemed devoted to the Virgin Mary, she never called her by name. *La bona Dea, la bona Dea,* the Italian phrase for the beloved saint; but the term literally meant *the good Goddess,* and the village priest had taught her long ago that Mary was *not* a god in her own right, but a saint. To call her Goddess was sacrilege; and though she had mentioned it long ago to Pierre, he had only said that in Italy, the term was used for Mary, and his mother was a good woman and he would hear no more of it, no matter what the priest said.

And then there was the matter of Ana Magdalena knowing things before it was possible to know them. Oh, the old woman tried to hide it, but Catherine remembered how she had smiled noncommittally when her newly pregnant daughter-in-law had confessed her hopes for a son. She had seen that strange light in the old midwife's eyes and could almost hear her thoughts: *Wish for whatever you want; but it will be a girl.*

And so it had been . . . and Ana Magdalena had named the child Sibilla. *Does she think me slow-witted?* Catherine thought with sudden anger. *Does she think I do not know it means seer, sorceress? And Pierre—*

Pierre, whose mother still insisted on calling him Pietro, after all these years in France. Did she think he still lived in Italy? Catherine had never been to that country, but she imagined it a lawless place where the Devil reigned and all the women practiced witchcraft. *Thank God we have our own papacy now in Avignon, and the Holy Father is French. . . .*

And Pierre, as always, had been too lenient with his mother, and had named the child Marie Sybille.

Catherine paused in her walking. She was at the outskirts of the meadow, facing the harvested wheat fields, without thought as to her destination. Once more, she called out her mother-in-law's name; once more, the reply was silence.

As if guided by an unseen force, her feet turned themselves toward the olive grove. She began, haltingly, to walk again.

As she did, a terrible thought seized her: God was punishing her by taking her child away. She had sinned, had she not? Had allowed the midwife to use charms, to perform whatever sorcery was necessary, so that she, Catherine, might bear a healthy child. She sobbed aloud, remembering how, only two days before, she had watched Ana Magdalena set a small cloth bundle stuffed with herbs at the base of the birthing chair.

And God had sent a holy fire to burn it down, a fire that consumed the sorceress's skirts and even threatened Catherine and the babe. It had been a warning. *God!* she prayed, silent tears streaming, *Only return my child safely to me, and I will see her baptized on the morrow! And I will never let that evil woman touch her again. I will raise her to be a devout Christian. . . .*

All the horror stories she had ever heard about witches flooded her imagination, causing her to sob in earnest: of evil crones stealing babies, quartering them at the Black Sabbath as a bloody sacrifice upon the Devil's altar, then boiling the little dismembered bodies for meat and soap. Of witches stealing babies from the beds and sucking out their blood, leaving their tiny corpses white as a ghoul. Of children bewitched, then returned to their families so that, when the innocents grew old enough, they rose from their beds and slaughtered their sleeping parents on the Devil's behalf. . . .

Catherine remembered how, upon rare occasions, she would wake and find Ana Magdalena gone in the night. When once she had questioned her mother-in-law about it, Ana Magdalena merely smiled ruefully and said, *Now that I am older, I do not sleep as well, and sometimes go walking to tire myself.*

What if all the stories were true?

Fear propelled her. Gasping, hunched over, she made her way slowly toward the distant grove. By day, the site was considered hallowed, blessed by the Virgin—but at night, few dared enter, for it was rumored to be enchanted then. Some said imps worked magic there, desecrating the shrine to Mary, wreaking all sorts of mischief, and if someone found them there, he would be bewitched, doomed to wander lost inside the grove forever.

Soon the ache in Catherine's womb turned into a throb, and between her legs, she felt a sticky wetness. Dizzied, she sank panting to her knees; the grass in front of her began slowly to spin. She squeezed her eyes shut.

And when she opened them again, she saw a figure—half dark, half light—running toward her in the moonlight.

Ana Magdalena, the babe mewling in her arms.

"Catherine!" she called, and the girl, seeing her child alive and well, gave a sigh of utmost relief.

"My baby—" She reached for the child—a mistake, for in her dizziness, she pitched forward and stopped herself from falling face-down only by throwing out her arms.

"Catherine." At last Ana Magdalena knelt beside her, the babe in her arms. "Oh, Catherine, my dear, look at you! Oh, my sweet, you are bleeding, and shivering. . . . Why did you not stay in bed?" She put a cool hand on the girl's forehead, and her voice and gesture were so tender, so full of honest alarm that the girl felt ashamed to have so doubted her. And yet . . .

Catherine looked at her mother-in-law's feet, and the dark purple stains there. Determination eased her dizziness; she pushed herself back on her haunches, and pulled her daughter from the old woman's clutches.

Ana Magdalena did not miss the meaning of either glance or gesture; immediately, she began to explain. "I could not sleep, my darling, and the babe was fretful; lest she wake you or her father, I took her with me, to calm her. . . ."

Catherine pulled down her shift, and after some effort, convinced the child to nurse. The old woman fell silent, and Catherine ignored her coldly; the ache in her womb was eased by a sudden pleasurable contraction. And more: a strange instinct had come over her. At last, she directed her gaze up at Ana Magdalena, and said, with cool determination:

"She will be baptized on the morrow."

"Impossible," Ana Magdalena countered at once. "Tomorrow would be too soon for you to leave your bed, even if you had not started to bleed again. Now, if you have not harmed yourself too seriously, you should remain abed at least a week."

"She will be baptized on the morrow," Catherine repeated calmly. She gazed deep into Ana Magdalena's eyes and knew the old woman understood the meaning buried there—even if Catherine herself did not completely understand it.

You cannot have her, old woman. She is mine, and I will see to it even if I have to send her far away from both of us.

But in Ana Magdalena's eyes there shone a determination as fierce and bright as Catherine's own, one that claimed the baby for a power far older and wilder.

For a moment, the two women faced each other in hard silence. And then Ana Magdalena rose slowly to her feet, and lifted Catherine and the baby up. "Come, child. Put your arm upon my shoulders, so. . . . Slowly, slowly. Let us get you and the baby home."

Catherine felt a pang—not of physical pain, but of regret. She had wanted to love this woman, to trust her, to have a mother of her own at last; but for the good of her child, she dared not. For though Ana Magdalena had only spoken kindly to her and showed concern with these last words, Catherine sensed the meaning behind them, hard and inflexible:

Her name is Sibilla. . . .

VII

That is the story of my birth, said Sybille, as the Goddess revealed it to me. For the next few years, my childhood was unremarkable; but in 1340, the inquisitor Pierre Gui, brother of the better-known Bernard, came to our fair city—and with him came a vision, and my first experience of the Sight.

I tell it as it was given to me, for I recall but one aspect of it, and that I will speak of later. . . .

TOULOUSE

June 1340

VIII

Inside the walled city of Toulouse, the public square in front of the partially built cathedral was filled with throngs of people and the spirit of merrymaking: more people, Ana Magdalena decided, than she had ever before seen gathered in one place. From where she sat, she could see perhaps a hundred other carts come from the villages surrounding the city, each one crowded with villeins and their children; in front of the rows of carts, hundreds more people stood facing a berm where stakes had been erected. Dozens of gendarmes encircled the berm and the scaffolding erected directly behind it.

And those were only the peasants; the cathedral and square were ringed with nobles seated in shaded jousting boxes. Much to the villeins' amusement, after an unseasonably hot two weeks, Toulouse had wakened to a mid-June day that was some twenty degrees colder than expected. With glee, they observed the nobles shivering in the shade each time the cool breeze rustled, while the peasants themselves enjoyed the gentle warmth provided by the sun. A few whispered that the strange weather was the result of witchcraft; but most simply pointed at the shivering nobles and laughed.

At least part of the entertainment was provided by the highborn and their finery: the men in tunics, leggings, and feathered caps in shades of bright yellow, saffron, red; the ladies in silk gowns of ruby, emerald, sapphire, and gold circlets and crowns that anchored sheer veils fluttering in the breeze. Excited, Catherine leaned forward in her seat next to Ana Magdalena, and nudged the older woman, calling attention to this lady or that, and remarking on a new color of dye, or a slightly newer fashion of bodice, or a more elaborate headdress.

In the back of a large straw-strewn wagon, two families—Pietro's and his neighbor Georges's, with his wife, Thérèse, and four sons, aged three months to five years—were enjoying a lively picnic. It was a festive occasion, with all the villeins excused from working in the fields, and all in Georges's wagon were having a grand time, save one. Ana Magdalena forced herself to smile and nod, to drink from the common pitcher of ale and to eat her bread and cheese and fresh-made mustard with apparent relish; but her heart was heavy.

Only one sight eased her sadness: her granddaughter Sybille, the picture of health—at the moment, running around the wagon at full tilt with Thérèse's older boys—sturdy little legs pumping, cheeks red, single dark braid flying behind her.

"Sybille," Catherine called easily. "Time to have something to eat." She did not need to repeat herself; the girl stopped running at once and came obediently to the side of the wagon.

Even at four, nearly five, years of age, Sybille was self-possessed, an adult in a child's body. She had her father's calm steadiness and none of Catherine's fluttery anxiety or quick temper. Indeed, for the past year, she had spoken without any childish impediment, and sounded years older than Thérèse's son Marc, who was six months her senior; but her voice was still high and piping.

When the baby was six months old, Pietro had finally put his foot down, telling both women: *Her name is not Marie, her name is not Sibilla.*

It is Sybille, Catherine—a good French name, my grandmother's name— and for you, too, Mama, her name is Sybille, because she is not Italian, but French. And if I hear either of you women arguing, I will throw you both into the Garonne River and raise the girl myself.

The women had both made an honest effort to use the same name. At any rate, the name stuck, although there were times when Catherine revealed what she *really* felt the girl's full name was, and called her *Marie,* just as Ana Magdalena sometimes slipped and called the girl *Sibilla,* out of fondness, when the two of them were alone.

Since the night of the girl's birth, Ana Magdalena tried to do as the Goddess had taught her in the olive grove: to keep all fear from her own heart, and (magically) from Catherine's, too, to protect the girl. The three females had lived together so harmoniously for the past years that Ana Magdalena had almost forgotten the Evil that threatened her grand-child, that had filled her daughter-in-law with such wild suspicion.

Pietro lifted his daughter into the wagon; Sybille went at once to her grandmother's arms, much to Ana Magdalena's delight. It seemed she had always loved her grandmother best, which guiltily pleased the older woman; she in turn loved her granddaughter fiercely, more even than her own sons, for whom she would gladly have surrendered her life. Catherine watched, smiling wanly, showing no outward trace of jeal-ousy.

Sybille sat in her grandmother's lap—carefully, without plopping down heavily, as an ordinary child was wont—put her arms around Ana Magdalena's neck, and kissed her, whispering: "Why are you sad, Noni?"

Ana Magdalena drew back in surprise to look at her, but there was no time to reply. A hush fell over the crowd; Ana Magdalena looked up, heartbeat quickening, and saw a group of soldiers on the berm. Eight tall stakes were anchored firmly in the earth.

La bona Dea, *help me bear this. . . .*

She pressed her lips to Sybille's hair, and drew in the sweet, sour, uncomplicated scent of a sweaty child.

Whispers passed through the crowd like the breeze as, in the distance, a procession emerged from the cathedral: a group of prisoners, escorted by an unnecessarily large contingent of gendarmes.

Six women and two men, each shorn, dressed in the burlap shift of the penitent, and hobbled by iron shackles, so that they could take only small, mincing steps, even if they had not been beaten too severely to do otherwise.

Six women and two men, nameless faces for the fire, but Ana Magdalena saw each person with the clarity of the Sight:

A defiant fifteen-year-old girl, eyes red-rimmed, but carriage proud; a crone so stooped and frail with age that she could scarcely walk with the heavy chains; two women, handsome and strong, clearly loyal friends who encouraged each other with glances; a graying middle-aged woman, face and eyes somber, turned inward; and a young mother, not two days after the delivery, her belly soft, her hard-swollen breasts full of milk. And the men, one old and weeping, head bowed, the other barely twenty, wild-eyed and muttering. A lunatic, poor man, who had muttered some nonsense about God or the devil, and would pay for it now with his life.

All were bruised about the face, with swollen jaws or lips or eyes. The two friendly women and the younger madman had arms that hung useless from grotesquely dislocated shoulders. The elderly woman, her sparse white hair sticking straight out from her skull, had an enormously swollen forearm, probably broken. The healer's instinct gnawed at Ana Magdalena: she wanted desperately to take the old woman to her home, set the arm with one swift, agonizing motion, then comfort her with poultices and and a strong draught for the pain.

But she could only sit, helpless, silent, as the crone stumbled in the square and collapsed into a heap upon her shackles. A guard hurried to her side and tried to lift her to her feet, but the old woman could not be roused. He carried her off while the others shuffled in their chains until at last they stood before the scaffolding.

As the prisoners and guards stopped, a group processed out onto the high scaffolding: *two crows and two peacocks,* Ana Magdalena thought in disgust. In fact, she knew she looked upon two inquisitors from Paris, and two vicars of the local archbishop.

The head inquisitor—a sharp-featured man with thick black brows and hair short after the Roman fashion—mounted the platform first and stood waiting to address the crowd while the others filed in front of their cushioned seats. Like his tall aide, he was lean and dressed austerely in a plain black cleric's frock—a stark contrast to the well-fed vicars, both of whom were stuffed like sausages into their bright purple silk frocks.

A brief burst of trumpet fanfare followed, then the ascension of Toulouse's *grand seigneur* and his retinue, including his only child, a boy with carrot-colored curls, dressed in a sky-blue tunic with white leggings; he clung fast to his father's hand and stared owlishly at the crowd.

At once, Sybille thrust herself from her grandmother's arms and sat straight, frowning at the little boy. Ana Magdalena watched her; this was more than a child's simple attraction for another. Did she perhaps recognize him from another time?

And as she and Ana Magdalena watched, the seigneur and his entourage took their seats; the crows and peacocks followed suit, with the single exception of the grand inquisitor. He stood, expectant as a coiled viper.

His assistant stepped forward and, with consummate self-possession, began to read the list of names with their corresponding charges.

Anne-Marie de Georgel, for *maleficium* against her neighbors, worship of the Devil, attendance at his sabbath, and sexual congress with him. Catherine Delort, for *maleficium* against her neighbors, worship of the Devil, attendance at his sabbath, and sexual congress with him. Jehan de Guienne, for *maleficium* against his neighbors . . .

Six more times, the same charge; even against the poor crone, who lay off to the side, unmoving upon her shackles. The weeping gray-haired man, upon hearing his name read aloud, fell to his knees and cried out: "I confess! I confess to all charges, and beg forgiveness from the tribunal and God. Only spare me!"

The inquisitor raised his hand for silence. "It grieves this tribunal," he shouted calmly, "that we have failed in our primary mission, which is to bring all heretics back to God. However, the word *heretic* itself means 'choice'; and these unfortunates have chosen to deny God. Therefore, we have surrendered them to your local authorities, who have sentenced them to death for their foul acts. These good gendarmes will see to their execution, and the *grand seigneur* will serve as the government's witness.

"I exhort you, good people of Toulouse, to refrain from showing hostility toward the condemned. Do not curse them, but have pity upon them, and pray that their heresy inspires you to faithfulness. For the agonies they face now are but pale shadows of the eternal torment they shall meet within the hour."

With that, the crow at last took his seat.

At once it seemed to Ana Magdalena that she no longer sat in the hay-filled cart beside her four-year-old granddaughter, but there upon the platform, so close to the *seigneur* that she could touch him—nay, so close that they were face-to-face, nose-to-nose, and she could feel his breath warm upon her cheeks; could see each crease in his forehead and between his dark brows; could see his Adam's apple bob as he swallowed, and the small muscles in his cheek twitch as he clenched his clean-shaven jaw.

So close that she could feel the anguish in his heart, and know it matched her own. Knew, with him, that these were innocents, every one, that the confessions were lies born of the secret dreams of the inquisitors. Knew that some of them—especially the fifteen-year-old girl, and the matron Delort, and the gray-haired, weeping man—were touched by the Sight, and had merely been injudicious in its use or incautious in concealing their talent from others.

And Ana Magdalena looked upon the *seigneur*'s handsome, strong face and into his eyes, then down at her transfixed granddaughter, and realized: *It is no wonder that she stares. For the* seigneur, *he is one of us.*

Her attention was immediately distracted by the closer spectacle of the gendarmes, three of whom dragged the young man toward the first stake. En route he fought as best he could, though shackles bound his ankles and useless arms: with a lunatic's uncanny strength, he drew back and butted first one, then another, with his head. But it was not enough: the third policeman stepped in and delivered a powerful blow to the young man's jaw. His knees buckled at once; as the crowd cheered, the other two gendarmes caught him beneath each shoulder and dragged him to his stake. There they forced him to his knees and bound him, kneeling.

Even then, as they piled kindling about him, he rallied enough to spit in his captors' faces.

Meantime, two other gendarmes had dragged the unconscious crone to the second stake, arranged her in a kneeling position as best they could, and tied her there; her head fell forward, hiding her face, so that only the thin white halo of her shorn hair, with its underlying pink scalp, could be seen.

Two by two, the other women were tied to stakes; and when the gendarmes' work was accomplished, the noonday bells began to toll. With all the prisoners in place, one of the gendarmes scraped two pieces of flint together; a second touched the spark with an oil-soaked rag bound to a poker. The rag caught fire at once, and the gendarme carried it first to the pile of logs and kindling that circled the kneeling young madman to his hips.

Ana Magdalena looked away and covered her face with her hands. Look away she might, but she could not blot out the voice of the madman, howling with vicious fury: "Hell for you all! Hell for you all!"

As the breeze began to carry the scent of smoke and cooking flesh, the resolve that Ana Magdalena had held foremost in her heart for the past five years broke; and she trembled at the memory of the pain she had experienced in the olive grove the night of the babe's birth. A vision though the flames had been, the physical agony they had inflicted was real: and the greater anguish had been the fear in Ana Magdalena's soul. Since her girlhood in Tuscany, her deepest, most secret terror was that her Goddess-given abilities might someday be discovered by the Church, and that her life would end at the stake.

Now that fear, as she recalled her vision, overtook her once more. Her fingers parted slowly as she felt her gaze drawn toward the scaffolding and the men seated there: not to the *seigneur* and his son, or to the peacocks, nor even to the grand inquisitor . . . but to his tall, broad-faced assistant. With preternatural clarity she saw him, and watched, trembling, as he slowly swiveled his head until he faced her, then met her gaze directly, his lips curving upward ever so slightly in triumph.

Sunlight glinted—yellow-green and predatory—in his eyes; at that instant, Ana Magdalena tried, but could not draw a breath.

This was the Evil: but with a sudden sense of revelation, she also knew that this man who embodied It was born on the very same day as she. Had been destined to be her soulmate, the Lord to her Lady, a leader of the Race—but his own self-loathing had transformed him into the opposite of what the Goddess had intended. His inborn magical powers he now used to hunt down his own people, to feed off them. And as he did, each day he grew stronger, so that the danger to them continued to increase. . . .

"*Domenico,*" she whispered, recognizing him as the young man who had hurled the stone through the cathedral glass in protest of her marriage. She had rebuffed him, for he had chosen to refuse the Goddess and his destiny.

And now he had followed her to France—seeking to destroy her grandchild.

She blinked, and in place of the madman, the beautiful young goddess-Sybille of Ana Magdalena's long-ago vision now writhed in misery at the stake, her black hair consumed so that only a charred, oozing scalp remained; the rosebud lips were stretched taut in a perpetual howl.

"Sybille!" Ana Magdalena screamed silently, and in her mind, the Enemy whispered:

Do you wish to know why the fire terrifies you so? Because you have always known this to be your fate; because you have always known it to be hers. You cannot escape me forever. . . .

With a thunderous rushing in her ears, as if she had been swept from her feet by an enormous wind, Ana Magdalena felt herself pulled from the wagon: and when she opened her eyes again, she was in the midst of a great conflagration—herself, and the grown Sybille, and all those suffering ones bound to stakes and crying out in agony at the solid wall of flame that surrounded them. As they shrieked, vapor poured forth from their mouths like smoke and swirled in a long, sinuous vortex toward the scaffolding. . . .

The scaffolding, where the Enemy, safe and distant, smiled. Smiled and drew in the vapors cast off by the suffering as one draws in smoke from a pipe; and savored them, sighing.

Then I shall not scream, Ana Magdalena told herself. *I shall not feed him.* . . . And by an agonizing act of will, the older woman closed her mouth and eyes.

Immediately Ana Magdalena returned to reality—only to find that her granddaughter no longer sat safely on her lap. The girl had risen and stepped forward until she stood—distracted, indeed, entranced—at the cart's shallow edge. "Sybille, sweet," Ana Magdalena said swiftly, fighting a fresh surge of panic, "come back and sit with me before you fall."

Strangely, the child did not move to obey her grandmother's order; instead, she remained motionless with her back to the others, apparently captivated by the spectacle of those burning.

"Marie Sybille!" Catherine snapped, her tone a mixture a surprise and indignation; never, in the child's short life, had she ignored her elders or been slow to comply. "Do you not hear your grandmother? Come!"

Still the girl did not move, but stood, oddly stiff and straight in her homespun dress with her coal-black braid falling in a perfect line down her back. "The flames," she said, in a voice mournful and womanly, to someone distant, invisible. "Mother of God, the flames . . ."

At once, Catherine rose and stumbled across the uneven straw to the child, and as she passed by Ana Magdalena, the older woman saw the strange greenish glint in her daughter-in-law's eyes—the presence of the Enemy.

The older woman lurched forward and caught Catherine by the elbow; the younger woman turned and snarled, but it was too late: with her other arm she swiped at her daughter, in a motion that might have been an attempt to grasp or to push. . . .

Sybille at once lost her balance on the uneven straw; she screamed as she hurtled backward, over the wagon's edge. More screams followed: Catherine's, and the startled one of the mule, and Pietro's, joined by Ana Magdalena's own. . . .

Such are the memories of my grandmother, as she and the Goddess made them known to me. My own recollection of the event is quite different: I remember looking at the flames when the entire sky began to shimmer with the same peculiar roiling motion as the heated air above a fire. And then it began to melt away, to dissolve, gradually revealing a different scene, a different reality. So captivated was I by the sudden shift of scene that I was unaware of my existence separate from the vision; I was absorbed by it.

The Toulouse I knew gave way to a far larger city, with a more magnificent square—one surrounded by a great, glorious cathedral, and a white marble palace grand enough for a king, and other lavish buildings that spoke of great wealth, of Rome in all its glory. For one instant, I marveled at the grandeur; the next, I was thrust into Hell, and the gleaming buildings were obscured by a wall of flame.

Within those flames, dark figures writhed: bodies trapped within, and they cried out to me: *Sister, help us! You are the only one who can save us*. . . .

They reached their dark arms toward me, pleading; and thinking to pull them free, I stretched my hands toward them, but cried out in pain as the fire touched my own flesh: I was not immune. To my shame, I drew back, desperate to ease their suffering while at the same time eager to prevent my own. At that instant, I realized that I was trapped, for the flames—and the shrieking victims within them—now encircled me.

Yet beyond the flames I saw two figures standing: one black and one white. A sudden desperate urge to reach the white one overtook me; I took a step forward into the flames, but at once the agony made me scream in horror, then retreat.

As I watched, trembling with fear, the black figure drew closer and closer to the white one. . . . With terrible certainty, I knew that should the darkness consume the light, it would mean the triumph of Evil. Again I thrust my arm into the fire—and screamed again, in both pain and frustration that my own terror would allow me to advance no further.

Yet I knew that if I did not expose myself to the flames and pass through, all would be lost. And as I watched, the dark figure coiled serpentine about the light, and began to devour it.

Before it was extinguished, the light cried out directly to God—nay, to a Power far older and wiser and mightier than God Himself—and was heard.

I plunged myself into the fire and cried out to that Power too.

At once I was swept into a sweet timeless ecstasy that no words can describe. I communed with a Power so awesome in Its scope, so far beyond the human pale and my poor head's capacity to conceive of the Almighty that I felt humbled in Its presence.

Yet It was nothing like the dour God presented us by the village priest, the Father-God of hellfire and damnation and commandments and purgatory. This Power cared not one whit for convention or rules or the petty politics of prelates or the manner in which It was worshiped, or even if It was worshiped at all. It simply was. It was life itself, joyous and chaotic and all-consuming. It was pure ecstasy.

When at last my mind recovered from the timeless void, I saw myself kneeling in the olive grove, before the statue of the Blessed Virgin—but She was alive, a living woman, the breathing incarnation of the unutterable joy I had experienced. At first Her smiling face was that of my beloved grandmother; and then She became myself as a grown woman, laughing and reaching with welcoming arms to my kneeling child-self. And she would be my daughter, after I was gone, and my daughter's daughter, blooming afresh throughout the generations. . . .

I swooned again, and this time when the blackness cleared, I saw only the thatched roof of our little cottage, and the open window . . . and beyond, the midmorning sun in a bright blue sky. The light pained my eyes and I raised a hand to shade them.

"Are you awake, Sibilla *mia?* Sit up for me, child," my grandmother, Noni, said. She stood before me with a cup. Back then, her hair was still the color of a fat, smooth raven. Like me, she was small, but wiry and strong, and she wore, as always, her widow's black wimple and kirtle. I thought her the wisest woman on earth, for she knew how to set bones and lance boils, how to tell from a woman's week-old urine if she was pregnant, how to make salves for bruises and teas for fever and cough. Sometimes for the family, she made charms, but instructed me never to speak of such things, for the mere mention of them lessened their power.

I ran my hand over my face and caught the scent of smoke. "People," I said, and began to cry. "People died. They burned them."

"Hush, my sweet," she said, and brushed a stray piece of straw from my hair. "Their suffering is over now. Sit up, Sibilla."

I understood then that I was in our cottage home, and that my father had gone already to work in the fields, and my mother to gather water and wash clothes at the river. I remembered, too, the events of the day before in the city square, and realized that my grandmother thought I was referring to those poor victims.

Before I could speak, Noni held the cup to my lips. I knew it was one of her bitter teas, but I opened my mouth without struggle—I had lost this particular battle too many times—and drank it down, grimacing at the astringent taste of willow bark, an ingredient my grandmother favored for treating every ailment. Nonetheless, I swallowed it to the bitter dregs. Noni returned the empty cup to the cupboard, then sat beside me on the straw and laid a hand on my forehead. I closed my eyes in bliss at her touch.

One of the strongest memories of my childhood is that of my grandmother's hands. They were not soft, like my mother's, but weathered, bony and callused. Yet they were always warm, and if I sat quietly and attentively enough, I would feel the special tingling warmth that only Noni's touch had. More than once, especially at night, I had stared at her hands—as she laid them on my mother, sick with *la grippe,* or on me, when I suffered from one of my fevers—and seen them radiate with an interior golden light, as if the very air around them trembled with subtle, glittering brilliance, with shining gold dust.

I was not surprised to see it; I thought everyone saw such things, that all grandmothers had a healing, golden touch.

But on that morning, I felt at last my Noni's touch withdraw, and heard her sigh; I opened my eyes to see her, still sitting, with a very grave expression.

"You fainted yesterday," she said, "at the burning in the square, and fell from the wagon. You hit your head; sometimes you slept, and at times, you raved about many different things.

"Do you remember what you dreamed?"

"I didn't dream it, Noni. I *saw* it. It was real."

She nodded, and, glancing about us to be sure we were alone, replied in a low voice, "It is a special way of seeing. Some call it the Sight. It is a gift from *la bona Dea* that very few possess. My mother had it, and her mother before her. You have it, too. Have you seen other things this way?"

"Yes," I murmured. Her mention of the Holy Mother made me remember the joyful, laughing Power that had inhabited the Madonna's statue in my vision. "Sometimes I See a golden light when you put your hands on someone sick."

She smiled. "The Touch is my gift."

"Last night, I Saw people burned—not in the square, but in my . . . dream."

Her smile fled. "Why were they burned, child?"

"I don't know. Bad people killed them. . . ." Without knowing I was going to, I suddenly added: "They are very bad, Noni; they are going to make more fire come, until it isn't safe anywhere."

A moment of silence followed; she looked away and sighed with great sadness. At last she said, "Sibilla, people fear what they do not understand. Very few are blessed with the Sight or the Touch, and so others are afraid of us because we are different."

"Like the Jews," I realized aloud. I had seen Jews before, the merchants and moneylenders in their funny horned hats, with yellow felt badges upon their breasts. I had heard from other children that they stole Christian babies, nailed them to crosses, and drank the blood; that unless they drank Christian blood, they would revert to their natural appearance—devils, with hooves and horns. But the stories made no sense to me; the Jews had babies, just as we did, and seemed to care for their children no less, and I had never once seen one with either hooves or horns. Besides, when I confided the story once to Maman, she had hushed me; and Noni had laughed aloud at its ridiculousness.

"Yes," Noni answered. "Like the Jews. Or the lepers. You are too young to remember, but when sickness came to the province of Languedoc many years ago, they blamed the lepers for poisoning the wells. So they burned many of them, but still were not satisfied; and then they said the lepers had conspired with the Jews, and many Jews were then attacked and killed."

I sat up and wrapped my arms around my knees. "Maybe the people I Saw were Jews. Or had the Sight."

"It is possible," Noni agreed sadly. "I do not want to frighten you, child, but it is perilous to speak of *la bona Dea*'s gifts to those who do not understand them. Your mother does not understand, poor soul, and so she is afraid; to speak of such things even to her—and certainly to anyone else, especially a priest—would put us both in great danger."

Tears rose in my throat. "Then I don't want the Sight, Noni. I don't want to bring danger to you." I grabbed her and buried my face in her shoulder.

She held me and stroked my hair. "Ah, Sibilla *mia,* I am sorry to tell you such hard things. But you have no choice: *la bona Dea* has chosen you, graced you with a special gift that can help many people. You must use it. If you trust the Goddess, no harm can come to you; but if you deny your gift, you will never find happiness."

I told her, then—as best I could in a child's words—of my vision of the Goddess, and she listened with an expression of growing pride. I did not tell her of the danger to myself, just as she, at that time, held back her knowledge of what the Goddess had shown her.

Then she leaned close to me and whispered: "I will tell you a secret. Before you were born, *la bona Dea* appeared to me in a dream and said that She had chosen you for a very special purpose in this world.

"We are of a race, you and I—the Race of those who serve *la bona Dea.* Some possess special gifts; others serve by protecting those with gifts. You—you have one of the most special gifts, and the most special destiny, of all." Then she sobered. "You must tell no one of your vision, or they will call you mad, or worse, a heretic, and kill you as those poor folk yesterday were killed.

"But remember: the Goddess has shown you these things for a reason. You must never forget them, but keep them in your heart, and wait for Her to guide you. . . ."

SUMMER

1348

IX

So, throughout my childhood, I remembered and waited. But the Sight did not come upon me again for many years—indeed, until the most terrible year mankind has ever seen since its creation.

Of the Black Death, they said it was the end of the world; I knew better. The world can withstand sickness of the body, but it remains to be seen whether it will survive the sickness that eats at the souls of our persecutors.

When the plague struck, it had no name. Indeed, what appellation could properly convey the horror of it? We called it merely the pestilence—*la peste*. Word of it traveled to us from the south and east—first from Marseilles, where it arrived in January on ships that had crossed the Mediterranean. It followed the coast to the Gulf of Lyons, where it came ashore at the port of Narbonne in February. In March, when we heard of its westward movement away from us to Montpelier, all in Toulouse breathed a sigh of relief, thinking we were spared.

That same month, Death sailed up the Rhône to Avignon, seat of the papacy, and it was whispered that God had at last seen fit to punish Pope Clement for his decadent excesses.

In April, our neighbor Carcassonne was struck.

I do not think we sincerely believed the terrifying stories we were told: of a disease that blackened men's tongues and caused lumps the size of apples to appear beneath the skin; of silent ships run aground, sailors dead at the oars; of convents in Marseilles and Carcassonne where not a soul escaped; of entire villages perishing without a survivor. We enjoyed recounting such ghastly tales, but never took them to heart: they were merely gruesome entertainment, like ghost stories. Such disasters might befall strangers, but never us. Never us.

Arrogant in our health, we took no action to protect ourselves, nor did we try to flee the coming scourge. God had smiled on us: the fields were sown and we had all joined in the dance around the Maypole. Now the world bloomed with the lush promise of summer, and we were smug in the knowledge that we would be fed while those in Narbonne and Carcassonne would starve, for they had not enough survivors to plant crops.

I was almost a woman then, in my thirteenth summer, and for the past several years Noni had tutored me in the ways of magic and charms. My lessons were conducted in great secrecy, when she and I were alone—which was rare, because my mother seemed to suspect what was transpiring between us. For that reason, Maman often took me with her to mass at our village church, and by that summer I was betrothed to the upstanding Christian and farmer Germain, a thirty-year-old widower whose wife had left him only with daughters—one of them older than I. I was unhappy with the arrangement; not out of dislike for Germain, who was pleasant enough toward me, but because I did not want to leave Noni and my magical studies. Nor did I care to give up my easy life in order to care for six daughters. But as I was already a thoroughly trained and respected midwife in my own right, my earnings and power to barter made me quite a marital catch.

So that summer, my thoughts were focused on the specter of marriage, not on that of the plague—until, that is, Noni fell ill with fever. We were terrified: had the pestilence come at last to Toulouse?

For two days, my mother and I nursed her with willow bark tea and cool compresses. I was beside myself with grief, certain that she would die; and the morning after Noni was stricken, I found an ominous sign: one of the village cats dead and stiff by our hearth, with the last rat he had killed still trapped between his paws.

But our dread eased when at last Noni's delirium passed. On the third day, she was able to sit and eat a bit, and at one point, clasped my hand and said comfortingly: "*La bona Dea* has shown me: it is not my time." We were overwhelmed with relief. This was not the scourge from Marseilles and Narbonne; or if it was, the stories we had been told were gross exaggerations.

It was on the fourth day of Noni's illness, when she was just well enough to stand, that a visitor knocked at our door. It was a kitchen maid, scarcely older than I, fair and plump in a stained white apron, with her dark skirt and sleeves dusty with flour; either she worked in the *seigneur*'s manor or she had come all the way from within the walled city. She looked and sounded as if she had run the entire way; several strands of pale brown hair had slipped from under the white cloth bound round her head.

"The midwife!" she gasped at my mother, who had responded to the loud knocking by hurrying to the door, the top half of which was open to let in the fresh morning air. "Are you the midwife? You must come at once! My mistress is having difficulty, and I cannot find the doctor!"

My mother glanced back at Noni, who sat on the bed, and me sitting on the stool beside her; the young woman craned her neck and looked uncertainly at us. I saw a flash of terror in her eye.

"It is only the ague," my mother said firmly. "And she is better now. She is the midwife; and so is my daughter, who will go with you."

The kitchen maid eyed me critically; at the reluctance in her expression, Noni called feebly: "My granddaughter is as skilled as I: for six years, I have trained her."

"And I will accompany her as assistant," my mother added. It was something she occasionally did for me and Noni, and she said it then to help assuage the woman's fears.

As she did, Noni leaned against me and whispered softly in my ear, "Take care you say and do nothing to arouse your mother's suspicions." For she knew that I often used the Sight to assist in birthings.

I nodded, aware of Maman's sudden sharp glance at us, as though she knew exactly what Noni had said.

"Let us go then!" the maid cried, wringing her plump, soft hands. I gathered up Noni's bundle of herbs and tools, and hurried out the door with my mother.

Beyond, harnessed to a sleek, well-tended horse, a sturdy cart waited; in it sat five weeping children. We did not ask whose these were, though clearly they were not the kitchen maid's: the girls wore brocade dresses trimmed with fur, the boys tunics of embroidered silk.

"Children," I asked gently whilst Maman and I held out our arms to comfort them, "why do you weep? It is for your mother? Do not worry; we will care well for her, and soon you will have a new sister or brother."

But they shrank from us, huddling closer together, and would not speak. In silence, we rode past the village square and the fields, past the manor and the great walls all the way inside the city.

A trip inside the city proper and back was a day's journey for us the few times a year we walked to market. The moment we rolled inside the gates, the world came alive with people of all manner and description. In the country, we saw only villeins like ourselves, but here there were poor cottars in rags and nobles on horseback dressed in bright silks and feathered caps, and merchants of varying wealth. We journeyed through the center of town, past the businesses: the smithy, the mill, the bakery, the cobblery, the tavern, and the inn. At last we turned onto the

Rue de l'Orfèvrerie—the goldsmiths' street. Here again stood a number of buildings all the same: four-story post-and-beam houses, much the same as those on the other streets, all leaning against each other with age; some painted blue, others bright red, some white-washed.

The bottom floors were all shops, with displays that jutted out into the busy street while their wary owners watched for thieves. Overhead hung colorfully painted signs: a candlestick for the silversmith, three gilded pills for the apothecary, a white arm with red stripes for the barber, a rearing unicorn for the goldsmith.

We stopped in front of the goldsmith's shop. The cook climbed from the cart, tethered the horse to a post, and, leaving the children to sit sniffling, helped us down and into the house. The shop itself was closed and shuttered tight; this struck me as odd, but I was too distracted by a sense of urgency to be alarmed.

The maid led us through a doorway and up narrow stairs into the dining area, where a dark hearth and oiled yellow parchment windows created a sense of gloom; even so, the room seemed sparkling clean to me, for the hearth had a chimney, leaving the walls unsmudged by soot. A good thing, too, for they were covered with beautiful tapestries, including one of the goldsmith's emblem, the unicorn, its white mane gleaming here and there with threads of pure gold. The inhabitants apparently shared the house with no other family—indeed, the house was so silent it seemed no one lived there at all.

At the other end of the dining area—with its large, disassembled trestle table atop which rested a pair of ornate silver candelabra—another staircase led to the third level. Here the young cook paused and pointed upward.

"The lady is upstairs in her chamber."

I turned toward her. "We need linens and water. Where can we find them?"

"I will fetch them," the cook said with sudden eagerness, and disappeared into the doorway that opened onto a large kitchen.

I can still hear the wood-against-wood clatter of my mother's and my peasant sabots against the steep stairs. I remember the puzzlement in Maman's voice as she asked: "But where are the other servants?"

Uneasiness descended upon me as I realized that it was mid-morning now, time for the servants to have dinner nearly prepared—but the hearth was unlit, and no sounds, no smells emanated from the kitchen. If those five wailing children belonged to the goldsmith and his wife, surely they were hungry by now for their dinner. Why did they still sit outside?

Despite my misgivings, I continued, with my mother beside me, propelled by a sense of purpose.

At the top of the stairs, the door to the master and mistress's bedchamber lay open, but the shutters were bolted, shrouding the room in darkness; it took my eyes a moment to adjust to the even dimmer light. Against the exterior wall stood two huge wardrobes and a chest, above which hung a large looking glass: inside, I glimpsed my own solemn, olive-skinned reflection, and that of my mother's, her beautiful, frightened face as pale as the white wimple and veil upon her rolled red-blond braids. The chest was opened, and had clearly been pilfered; it was empty save for a broken strand of pearls draped over the side. More pearls lay scattered on the floor beside it. In a corner of the room stood a wooden birthing chair, normally a welcome sight, but I was disturbed to see it empty.

An elaborately carved four-poster bed with brocade hangings stood with its head pushed against the center of the interior wall. From it emanated the sounds of suffering—not the candid, outright cries of a woman travailing in childbirth, but the weak, barely audible moans of the dying.

We are too late, I thought. *She has delivered and is near bleeding to death.* I started toward the woman—but was suddenly compelled to hold myself back. Something in the air, perhaps, for there was a faint but distinct putrid scent, one that I had never smelled before that terrible time; one I have not smelled since.

Whatever it was, Maman sensed it too; at the very second I paused, her hand caught mine to hold me back. I remember that instant with terrible clarity: for a long moment we two stood on the threshold in the thrall of death, doomed whether we took a step forward or back.

Then, pushing back the fear, I left Maman in the doorway and strode across the room to throw open the shutters. A shaft of light penetrated the gloom and illumined the woman lying on the bed.

By the time I was thirteen, I had witnessed all manner of distress: the screams of labor and the sight of blood moved me not a whit. I had heard women curse their husbands with words to make the Devil blush, and seen both mother and babe fade from life into death. All such I could withstand stoutly; but the sight of the woman on the bed sickened my heart.

She lay still—too still—save when the pangs of labor gripped her, jerking her high, swollen belly upward; when they passed, she fell back, limp as a puppet. A tangled heap of blankets had been kicked to the foot of the bed, revealing a soaking wet stain in the center. The woman's waters had broken in the bed, an occurrence most pregnant women avoided at all costs. Odder still, none of the servants had taken care to prevent the water from soaking into the linen-covered mattress beneath.

But the tableau grew stranger as we looked: the woman was still naked—which meant that her servants had never dressed her that morning—and her bare spread legs were covered from thigh to foot with black, mottled bruises; even her toenails were blackened. At first I felt a surge of anger: no doubt her husband had severely beaten her, though she was this close to delivering. Then I moved to the bed and saw her face, and nearly sank to my knees for fear. Her eyes were opened wide, but unseeing, covered with the dull film one sees in the dying. Perhaps she had once been a beautiful woman, but now her countenance was hideous, marred by the same violet-black mottling. Her mouth hung open, no longer able to contain the dark, swollen tongue that protruded from between blood-caked teeth.

My mother finally joined me at the side of the bed and raised a hand to her nose and mouth at the smell. For an instant I thought she would faint and I moved to catch her, but she steadied herself and lowered her hand long enough to call firmly to the woman, "Madame . . ."

"Maman," I interrupted her gently. "Maman, she is too near death to hear you."

Another groan, as the strong contractions forced air from the woman's lungs and caused her back to arch. The baby's bloody crown barely appeared; above it, on the mottled purple-black skin of the woman's abdomen, large suppurating boils oozed yellow-green pus.

It was my practice to place a hand upon the mother's stomach and utilize the Sight to determine the baby's location and health—but this time, fear so overwhelmed me that I could sense nothing at all.

To add to my dismay, behind me, my mother bleated in surprise; I followed her wide-eyed gaze to the floor, where a body—judging from the size, a man's—lay enclosed in a shroud. He had been there only a matter of hours, for he was still stiff.

"Marie Sybille," my mother said, in as commanding a tone as I had ever heard her use, "the pestilence has come to Toulouse. Bid the cook take you home at once and do not stop to talk to anyone."

"I cannot leave them." I pointed my chin at mother and child.

"I will stay," Maman countered instantly, and with defiant courage, walked to stand beside me at the bed.

That is the moment I try to remember, when my anger at my mother threatens to poison me: despite her fears, she loved me so much that she was willing to die in my stead.

"If you will stay, then find the cook," I said, "and learn what has happened to the rags and water." Normally, Maman would have boxed my ears for giving orders and ignoring hers, but in this case, I was the trained midwife and she was not. She compressed her lips into a thin line, then went at once from the room.

Hers were the only footsteps I heard, even on the level below; I knew that we would never see the kitchen maid, the children, or the cart again.

By the time Maman returned with the water and linens, the woman on the bed was writhing furiously. At first I thought with relief that the baby was coming—but after a time, her movements became unnatural and alarming. She stiffened, then jerked violently as if she were trying to throw herself from the bed, much as a captured fish tries to fling itself from land to water. Maman held her arms, trying to keep her from falling or hurting herself; as she did, the woman growled, then clenched her jaw and bit down so fiercely on her swollen black tongue, I feared she would cleave it in half. A thin, dark liquid squirted forth and dribbled down her chin.

Then her movements ceased abruptly, and her body fell limp against the mattress; her dull, clouded eyes stared beyond the ceiling at some horrific vision.

Meantime, I had fetched the small, white-handled knife from my bundle. Normally, I used it to cut the baby's cord, but this time, I knew that no amount of pulling would free the child from the womb; the widest part of the head had not yet passed. Maman's face went altogether gray, and sweat broke out above her lips, but she remained steady as I began to cut.

Blood gushed from the incision in the woman's swollen stomach. I had smelled blood and birth before, and I knew the foul, fecal odor of a person's insides. But I had never smelled anything so vile as when I cut the goldsmith's dead wife open.

I cut carefully, slowly, using the fingers of one hand to lift the plague-blackened skin with its layer of bloody yellow fat away from the child within. We saw his little buttocks first, glistening with dark blood and the pale yellow cheesy coating, and then his tiny back. Grimacing at the soft, slippery feel of blood and womb, I maneuvered my hands beneath its little stomach while Maman held the flaps of skin back. I had to pull away from the birth passageway in order to free the baby's head, which took uncommon effort; and then I pulled straight up. The child came free with a loud sucking sound and nearly slipped from my grasp. I smiled in exhilaration despite the grisly surroundings (the arrival of a child can dispel even the darkest grief), and handed the boy to Maman, who took him with one of the cloths and began to wipe him off.

Our sense of joy soon faded, for the boy did not stir, did not attempt to draw a solitary breath, despite our repeated thumps. Indeed, he felt limp as a smothered kitten in my hands.

My mother wrapped the poor thing in kitchen cloths and laid him between his dead mother's breasts; then I covered the dead woman's bloody corpse with blankets and retrieved my bundle. Together we walked downstairs.

Not a living soul remained in the house. The cook had indeed fled and taken the cart with her; I felt deep anger at her for deserting her mistress and the unborn child, and also for bringing us into a pestilence-ridden house. Yet I understood that she was probably a kind woman whose fear had driven her to evil. She had at least seen that the master's children were cared for, and that midwives would tend to the newborn; perhaps she hoped that the wisewoman's herbs could save her dying mistress.

Maman and I walked to the apothecary's next door, where she told the wife at the door that the pestilence had come to the neighbors, and asked her to summon a priest (for to the best of our knowledge, the woman and child had died unshriven, without the last rites that would permit them into Heaven). For our pains, we had the door slammed in our faces.

We would have walked the entire way home, but the Goddess intervened. My mother encountered one of the servants from the *seigneur*'s manor, who recognized us as Pierre de Cavasculle's wife and child, and let us ride in the back of his cart with supplies purchased for the manor. We walked the few miles from the castle to our village. By the time we arrived home, the sun had just set, and Papa was finishing the small supper prepared him by Noni, who seemed almost entirely recuperated.

Maman told them both the terrible story of the birth and the pestilence: the blackened skin, the oozing boils. My father listened grimly and said that one of the villeins who had worked on the *seigneur*'s demesne reported that the *seigneur,* who had recently entertained visiting prelates from Avignon, was himself ill. Everyone feared the pestilence had come to the manor, which meant it would soon be in the village.

Noni said nothing at all. But after we had finished our supper and gone to bed, she lit the oil lamp and sat up to sew four small cloth bags, which she stuffed with a combination of herbs, then drew shut with long strings that she tied so they could be worn as necklaces. From my place beside Maman, I feigned sleep and watched drowsily from beneath lowered lashes as Noni completed the charms.

Once she had reassured herself from my mother's wheezing, regular breath and my father's reverberating snores that they were asleep, she walked over to the open window and held the bags of herbs in her outstretched hands, as if offering them to the moon. She was silent a time, and as she stood holding out the charms, I saw her hands begin to glow with the golden healing light, growing brighter and brighter with each passing second.

Then she began to murmur a benediction in her native tongue. I knew only a few words of Italian then, so I cannot repeat precisely what she said, but there was one phrase I knew well: *la bona Dea. Diana, la bona Dea . . .*

She uttered the name as a lover gives a caress, and on her lips it became the most beautiful sound I had ever heard. As she spoke, the night clouds seemed to shift, allowing the moonlight to stream through the window onto the little bags; at the slow chant *Diana . . . Diana,* the golden glow in Noni's hands passed into the bags and merged with the silver gleam of the moon until each charm emitted its own radiant, golden-white aura. I drew in a breath at the sheer loveliness of the light. I think Noni must have heard me, for she smiled knowingly up at the moon. Then she roused me and my father and mother long enough to hang the charms round our necks. *Medicine,* she told them, *to keep away the pestilence,* but I knew it was much more. Even Maman accepted the necklace gladly; apparently the horrible sights we had seen that day were enough to silence all her suspicions.

In the darkness, I could see the charm glimmer golden between my girlish breasts. I settled to sleep that night feeling protected, secure in the warm glow of Noni's and Diana's love.

In a few days' time, my father was called to the manor to work the *seigneur*'s demesne, for the men who usually tended the lord's private fields had fallen ill. Papa grumbled at this, for his own crops needed attention, but he owed the *seigneur* several days' labor, and there was nothing that could be done. And so he abandoned his own fields and went to the manor with the intendant, who had come to fetch him.

On that same day, a visitor called at our door. Maman had gone to fetch water, and I was sweeping out the hearth while Noni prepared recently gathered herbs for drying in anticipation of the outbreak of pestilence. I set down the besom at once and hurried to the door, the top half of which was open.

There stood a stout middle-aged man, finely dressed in an embroidered short shift of red silk with long bell sleeves, yellow leggings, red velvet slippers, and yellow-plumed cap. Yet his face matched the elegance of his finery not all all; it was broad, with coarse, thick nose and lips, and tiny deep-set eyes. Behind him, tethered to the blooming lilac tree, a handsome black horse stood panting.

The man's forehead was furrowed with worry, and he shifted his weight from velvet slipper to velvet slipper in agitation. "The wisewoman!" he almost shouted—not in condescension, but in honest desperation. "Is this the home of the wisewoman?"

"Yes, *monseigneur*," I said, collecting myself enough to manage a small curtsey, and I slid the bolt on the door, thinking to open it and welcome him inside.

Immediately a hand gripped my shoulder with remarkable strength: Noni stood at my side. "No," she murmured, for my ears alone. "I will speak to him outside. Remain here."

I obeyed while Noni stepped outside. "I am the one you seek," she said in a tone that conveyed both graciousness and suspicion. "How may I help you, *monseigneur?*"

The man's face contorted; he lifted huge pale hands to his eyes and began to weep. I realized with a sudden chill why he had come, and why Noni would not receive him into our house. As I watched, I fancied I saw, even in the daylight, a soft golden glow emanating from Noni's heart, where the charm hung hidden beneath her clothing.

The man seemed unable to speak, and at last Noni asked softly, "It is the pestilence from Marseilles, is it not? Do they have the blackened skin and the boils?"

He nodded, and managed a few words punctuated by sobs and groans. He was a prosperous attorney whose wife and three children were all ill, and his servants sick or fled.

"Why did you not call a doctor?" Noni asked. Toulouse had six doctors; one whose exclusive task was to care for the *grand seigneur* and his family, and five whose services were available to the wealthy. For this lawyer to seek the services of a village midwife showed an uncommon degree of desperation.

"Those doctors who have not fled or fallen ill themselves are busy with the sick. Please, I am rich. I will pay anything. *Anything . . .*"

My grandmother considered this a moment, though her determination never wavered. "I will give you medicines to take with you. But I will not go with you into the city."

"Yes, yes!" the man agreed. "Only hurry! I fear they will all be dead before I return."

"Wait here," Noni commanded. She returned to the house and gathered up herbs for him as I watched, silent and somber, by the door. She gave him her fever tea and a yellow sulfurous-smelling powder for poultices. She put these in small cloth bags, went back out to the man, and explained how he should use them.

He listened with anxious eagerness, then said, "But *madame,* have you no charms as well, no magic I can use to save my family?"

Noni drew back as if scandalized and laid a hand to her heart, where the charm hung hidden. "*Seigneur,* I am a good Christian. The only magic I know is the medicine of herbs, which God in His graciousness has revealed to us."

The man began to weep again. "And I am a good Christian, but God in His graciousness has seen fit to strike my family with pestilence. Please, *madame,* my wife and children are dying! Have pity on us!" Again, he buried his face in his large hands.

Noni sighed, a little disconcerted at the thought of such a wealthy man addressing her as *madame,* and went back inside. With her back to the man, she made a little bundle of several herbs, tied it with string, laid her hands on it, and prayed a few words quietly under her breath. The bundle glowed ever so slightly, but with none of the radiance of the charms she had made for our family. She took it back out to the man and handed it to him.

"Wear this on your person at all times," she instructed. "Touch it often, and as you do, think of your wife and children as whole."

"May God and the Holy Virgin Mother bless you!" the man said, and in return handed her a gold coin. Both Noni and I stared at it, transfixed. We had never been paid in gold in our lives.

Noni thrust the coin back at him. "I cannot take this. You owe me nothing for the charm, only for the herbs. This is thrice a doctor's wages. . . ."

But the man hoisted himself back upon his fine horse and galloped away.

At that very moment, my mother appeared at the threshold with the water pail balanced upon her shoulder. She frowned quizzically at the disappearing rider, then at Noni, who stood admiring the gold coin between her thumb and forefinger.

"More pestilence in the city, and now the doctors are dying," my grandmother explained as my mother passed into the house. Noni followed, and I leaned toward her to carefully examine the coin. We later learned it was a genuine livre d'or, a beautiful shining thing. Noni placed it in her mouth and bit down hard; when it came away with the faint imprint of her teeth, she smiled. We were rich.

But our joy, purchased by others' grief, was at once interrupted. Behind us came a soft thud, the clatter of wood, the slosh and slap of water. We turned to see Maman sitting spread-legged on the earth-and-straw floor, her kirtle soaked, the bucket overturned between her knees.

She raised a hand to her face, and looking up at us both with a dazed expression, said, "I spilled the water."

"Are you injured, Catherine?" Noni asked as she and I each took an arm and helped Maman up. The flesh beneath my mother's damp sleeve felt uncommon warm.

"I spilled the water," she repeated, glancing from my face to Noni's with faint desperation, as if there were something important she wished to tell us, but could not find the words to convey.

"It's all right," I said as we helped her to the bed. "I'll take the bucket and fetch more."

"Is it cold today?" my mother asked with a sudden violent shudder. As we stripped the wet clothing from her, the feeble glow from the charm between her breasts flickered suddenly like a flame, then died.

Maman lay in the bed the rest of the day with chills and high fever. "Am I dying?" she asked weakly during the fleeting moments when she came to herself. "Is it the pestilence?"

No, we reassured her. Her skin did not blacken, and there were no signs of the vile-smelling boils. It was merely the ague Noni had been stricken with earlier, and she would recover soon.

We told my father the same when, weary and discouraged, he returned well after sunset. He was nonetheless very concerned about her, and tried to feed her soup himself, but the fever troubled her stomach and she could not eat.

Papa was only temporarily cheered by the display of the magnificent livre d'or; and after supper, he told us somberly of the trouble at the manor. "The pestilence is among us villeins now," he said sadly, his gray eyes focused downward on the barley stew Noni had cooked. "The seneschal, they say, is no more than a day away from death. His responsibility now falls to the intendant, an incompetent fool who knows nothing about managing fields or laborers. I saw a man myself, a laborer hired from another village, who fainted in the fields: he had a great red lump on his neck."

Noni's eyes narrowed at once. She stood at his shoulder; she never ate until her son had had his fill, and she waited with ladle in hand to refill his plate. As for myself, I sat across from Papa and listened with growing dread. I wanted to tell him not to go back to the manor, not to work the *seigneur*'s demesne anymore, and I could see from the fear in Noni's eyes that she wished to say the same. But for a villein to refuse to work the *seigneur*'s fields when ordered was a crime punishable by hanging; and so both of us held our tongues.

Still, Noni found enough courage to say: "Pietro, there is clean, sweet straw by the hearth. Sleep there tonight." And when Papa glanced up at her, his eyes alight with sudden panic, she added, with just the right amount of irritation to make him believe her: "No, not because I think Catherine has the pestilence from Marseilles. But if you lie with her and rise with the ague, it will weaken your strength, and make you more susceptible to the sickness at the manor."

My father refused, saying he would not leave Catherine to sleep alone, and perhaps the warmth of his body would soothe her. I slept by the hearth, on the straw beside Noni, who rose on occasion to nurse Maman. She would sit for an hour, the return to doze beside me while I took her place.

In the hours before dawn, I was summoned from the depths of sleep by shrill, feeble cries. I pushed myself up to see my mother flailing in the bed, unwittingly striking Papa in the face while my father struggled to keep her from rolling onto the floor. Noni, at the bedside, tried to help.

As I watched in horror, my mother in her delirium pulled the charm hanging round her neck with such force that the string broke, at which point she hurled the little bag to the ground.

Noni rescued it, but the expression on her face as she did so, gazing at her daughter-in-law, was hard—almost as if she were furious at Maman for what she had done, but I told myself I was surely mistaken. My father, his own face lined with grief, took the charm from his own neck and slipped it over my restless mother's head. Then he came and sat heavily upon the straw beside me, and I buried my face in his thick dark beard while we wept.

On the second day of my mother's illness, the smith's wife came from the city. Noni received her outside, gave her herbs, and sent her on her way, just as she had done with the lawyer. Then the people from our village began to come, one by one. Noni gave them all herbs until she had barely enough for our own use. At last, she closed the door, leaving the top half open barely enough to permit the smoke from the hearth to escape, and called to the desperate seekers who knocked, telling them where to find their own herbs and how to use them.

In between callers, while Noni napped by the hearth, I bathed Maman to bring down her fever. Her neck was slightly swollen, but I thought little of it, for such is common with fever. But when I loosed the ties on her shift and drew the cloth beneath her arm, I saw the swelling there: a hard lump the size of an egg, and red. The surrounding skin was speckled purplish-black, the color of old blood.

I woke Noni and told her Maman had the pestilence. We made a poultice and put it on the boil under the arm, and then we discovered two more swellings on Maman's groin, surrounded by the same darkening beneath the skin. I could think of nothing but the poor pregnant woman who had died.

In the late afternoon, my father returned from the manor. I was startled to see him for two reasons: one, because he never came home from his own fields until dark, and two, because he had returned on foot, and it was customary for the intendant to offer the villeins who worked the demesne a ride home in a cart.

I looked up from my mother's side at the thud of the door thrown open. On the threshold stood my father; he lingered there uncertainly a moment, his worn peasant's cap in his hands. I will never forget the sight of him: a handsome man, broad of chest and shoulder, coarse of blue-black beard, as dark as my mother was fair.

At the sound of his return, Noni hurried to tend to supper, which had not yet been put on the hearth to cook because of our visitors and the early hour.

"Papa!" I exclaimed. "Why are you home so soon?" I rose and went round the bed toward him.

He did not reply, but hesitated in the doorway, twisting his cap in his large, bloody-knuckled hands. I knew at once something was wrong: his eyes were those of a dazed, frightened boy. Noni sensed it too, and glanced over her shoulder at him from where she crouched by the hearth.

Yet despite Papa's confusion, he glanced first at my mother, then at me, and closed his eyes briefly in pain. "Catherine," he whispered, and I knew he somehow understood that the pestilence had come to our house. I felt an urge to comfort him as if he were the child and I the parent.

At last he slipped off his sabots and stepped inside (in his distraction failing to close the door behind him) so that the hearth light revealed dark stains upon his tow cloth smock. Upon inspection of them, I cried in alarm, "Papa!"

For they were deep red-brown, the color of dried blood.

He glanced down at them, as if faintly surprised to see them there, then said heavily: "No one else came to work the demesne, save one other villein, Jacques LaCampagne, who vomited blood and fell dead beside me as we worked. I tried to find help, but all had disappeared, save the priest, who came to shrive the *seigneur*'s mother."

"She is dead?" I asked in horror.

An odd expression crossed my father's face, as though he struggled to heed the words of some invisible soul. "I am very tired," he said suddenly. He went to the bed and lay down beside his wife, and did not rise again.

Despite the many years between what was and what is, the memory of my parents' suffering has not dimmed with time; the pain remains fresh.

My father fell at once into a deep delirium, and though I gave my glowing charm to him, as he had given his own to Maman, he never returned to sanity again. Although he too was afflicted by fever, his illness took a different course. The plague boils never appeared under his arm or on his groin; instead, the sickness struck his lungs so that he coughed up a vile bloody sputum. Within two days he was dead.

By that time, my mother had turned into a pitiful creature, her pale skin marred by black mottling and the angry, evil swellings that wept pus and blood. Such was the disease that it made those afflicted stink as the dead while they still lived.

The hour my father died, my mother cried out his name, then lapsed into silence. Noni and I were certain that she would soon follow her husband.

I was sore distraught. Ere my father had died, I had gone to the village in search of the priest to shrive them. Though it was midday, the village seemed eerily deserted; not a single villein toiled in the fields, not a single woman drew water from the well, though animals there were aplenty. Cows trampled unchecked through rows of tender young crops, eating what they willed, and a stray herd of goats, the females bleating pitifully for someone to milk them, approached me as they wandered untended.

The priest was in neither the church nor the rectory. As I crossed the churchyard, I came upon the gravedigger, shoveling another fresh plot. I inquired after the priest.

"Dead or dying," said the gravedigger, "or shriving the dead somewhere. It is only a matter of time before I bury him, too." His face and clothing were black with many days' grime and sweat. Unfazed by the tears streaming down my face, he spoke in a tone uninflected, that of one deeply fatigued and numbed by the sight of too much death. Beside him were more than a dozen new mounds and three fresh-dug graves while he toiled on the fourth; he gestured at the three. "But these will be filled before the morrow. If you have dead, bring them here yourselves, for there is no one left to help you. And best to bring them soon, while there is still room." He paused, tilted his head oddly, then added: "'Tis the end of the world, you know. The priest read to us from the Bible— the last Book, called Revelation."

He recited from memory:

When he broke the fourth seal, I heard the voice of the fourth animal shout, "Come."

Immediately another horse appeared, deathly pale, and its rider was called Plague, and Hades followed at his heels.

Heartsick, I returned home by dusk and told Noni that we would have to carry Papa's body to the graveyard without aid. And so, when my father's eyes opened in death we could only bless his body ourselves, and bathe him, and sew him up in his white shroud. We sat with him in vigil all the night, grieving and praying and checking on Maman to see if she still breathed.

In the morning, to our astonishment, Maman's fever had broken, but she still slept deeply, without stirring. So it fell to us to arrange for Papa's burial at once, as the weather was warm. Nearby lived Marie and Georges, the wealthiest of our neighbors, for they owned a donkey and wagon. I went to their house and, finding the wagon, and the animal tethered without, called within. The top half of the door was open, but all in the house were dreadfully silent. I took the donkey and wagon home without tarrying, for I suspected the owners would never again have need of them.

When I arrived, Noni and I set to the sad task of lifting poor Papa's body. The dead are far heavier than they ever were in life, and as I lifted my father beneath his arms, and Noni lifted his legs, I knew it would be impossible for us to lift the body high enough to place it in the cart.

At that dreadful moment, a knock came at our open door. Papa's lolling head blocked my view of our visitor, and Noni had her back to the threshold.

"Leave!" my grandmother cried angrily through her tears, stopping in our slow journey toward the door. "There is pestilence in this house—cannot you see that my son has died?—and I have no more herbs to give!"

A deep and beautiful voice replied: "I have come not to take, but to help."

A curious light came into Noni's eyes; gently, gently, she lowered her son's shrouded legs to the floor and turned. I too laid Papa tenderly down, and followed her gaze beyond the threshold.

Without stood a tall, weathered man with a white stripe running the length of his long, iron-gray beard. His large, heavy-lidded eyes and aquiline nose would have identified him as a Jew even had he not been marked by the yellow felt badge and horned hat. For a Jew to venture outside the city walls was unusual; for safety's sake they generally remained inside their designated quarter of the city, delivered their own babies, and tended their own sick.

I thought of the tales I had heard from others about Jews; but there was no trace of monstrosity in this man's appearance. His eyes were aged and liquid, the whites yellowed, the irises so dark the pupils were scarcely detectable; they were at once the most powerful and the gentlest eyes I had ever seen.

I knew then that he was a member of the Race.

Noni was clearly impressed by him, too, for she replied softly: "Why have you come, then, sir? It is not safe here: the pestilence has stricken us."

"It is nowhere safe," the elderly Jew replied, "and God has left me little enough time as it is." And without another word, he entered our house and gestured for me to step aside, then lifted Papa beneath his arms. How odd it seems now, from a distance of years: but at the time it seemed the most natural thing in all the world, to hurry to Noni's side and help her lift Papa's legs. I took the left one and she the right, and with the stranger's help we got the body into Georges's cart easily.

"*Monseigneur,*" I addressed him—a title of honor rarely bestowed upon Jews, "thank you for your help."

In reply, he drew out a small folded square of black silk from under his black cloak and held it out to me; I hesitated.

"We want for no money," Noni said quickly. "Your help has already been immeasurable; besides, I have received enough gold today because of the suffering of the sick."

He glanced at her, his expression warming with a faint, apologetic smile. "It is not a coin." He proffered it again, and this time, sensing the warmth that emanated from it, I took it and reverently opened the silk to peer at it.

It was indeed gold: a livre-sized disk of the thin beaten metal, attached to a thick golden chain. Etched onto its surface were circles, stars, strange letters. Though I could not read at the time, I knew these were in a tongue far more mysterious than my native French.

The disc glowed with a radiance far hotter, far whiter than any I had ever seen, the radiance of a star, and I knew: this Jew knew the Goddess; this Jew knew a magic greater and more powerful than any Noni had taught me. This was beyond healing charms or spells to protect oneself from an enemy or to make the crops grow.

"Keep it always," he said. "In times of danger—and such are now— wear it on your person. Great evil is about."

I looked up to thank him again, but before I could utter a word, he added, "Carcassonne is a place of safety."

Noni stared at him as if he were mad. "Sir, they are all dead and dying in Carcassonne!"

"Even so," he interrupted, and without a word of farewell, was gone—so quickly and quietly that Noni and I were astonished and confused by his sudden disappearance. When we gazed about the cottage, we saw no sign of him.

Noni lifted it from my hand, placed it over my head, and tucked it beneath my kirtle, despite my protests that *she* should instead wear the charm. "The Goddess sent him," she said of the mysterious man. "And the charm was meant for you, and you alone; for my sake, wear it always."

I yielded, for I knew her words were true. As the disc of gold slipped against my skin, I felt an intense warmth and tingling that made me start.

At last we climbed onto the cart and headed for the churchyard. On the road leading to the village square, we saw a woman's fallen body.

"Do not look," my grandmother ordered sharply, but I had already seen enough to sicken me: two dogs gnawed at the woman's rotting flesh, and one of them had nearly succeeded in detaching an arm. He held the elbow in his jaws and tugged, stretching the remaining shred of meat that held arm to shoulder.

"Holy Mother, save us," Noni whispered, and silently I seconded her prayer.

As we approached the square in front of the churchyard, I perceived the first signs of life in the empty village: I smelled, then saw, the black plume of smoke. Perhaps they were cremating bodies, I thought—then I heard shouting, followed by agonized screams that were distinguishable neither man from beast, male from female.

In the center of the square, a small bonfire burned; inside staggered the flaming outline of a man. I did not recognize him at first, for his cap was gone, and his clothes and hair and beard were ablaze, and his face black with soot. Struggling to escape, he stumbled to the fire's edge and fell forward on his knees, only to be jabbed back by a large villein wielding a pitchfork. With him stood three others—two men, one of whom brandished a dagger, and a woman, all of them jeering at their torched victim.

Noni gave a shout of outrage and reined in the mule, who sensed our horror and snorted, quivering.

The woman glanced over at us. Her skirt and apron were smeared with black blood coughed up by the dying, and her tousled hair spilled from beneath her headcloth. Her eyes were wild and fever-bright.

"He was sent by the Devil to poison the well!" she shouted to us. With the Goddess's eyes, I Saw a dark shadow over her breast, and knew the pestilence had already claimed her as its own. "The Jew came from the city into the village to bring the pestilence! He has murdered my husband and children! All dead! All dead!"

The man with the dagger joined in: "The Jew poisoned the well, and returned to finish the rest of us off! The Jew brought the pestilence from the walled city!"

Of a sudden, my gaze met that of the tormented soul dying in the flames—those dark, beautiful, agony-filled eyes—and I recognized the man who had come to our house. I stood bolt upright in the wagon and shrieked, startling the mule.

At that instant, he could apparently bear the pain no more, for he leapt forward and intentionally impaled himself through the heart on the outthrust pitchfork. The villein held him there as if roasting a morsel of meat, and watched with satisfaction until the weight of the body caused it to fall.

"By the one holy God," Noni called, her voice trembling, "I would curse you all to the thirteenth generation for your wickedness, but there is no need. Your families are perished, and you will all be dead by the morrow."

I fell into a half-swoon. In that state I rode with Noni past the fire into the graveyard. Of what happened afterward, I remember little save the sight of the open graves the gravedigger had been shoveling only the day before; these had been filled with decaying bodies, one on top of another, and left uncovered. Near them was a larger shallow pit, in which the dead gravedigger sat upright beside his shovel, which was thrust into the soil with the handle sticking straight up. Across his lap lay unshrouded dead, hastily thrown on top of him; he seemed a ghastly version of Mary grieving over the dead Christ.

How we disposed of my father's body, in all honesty I do not remember; the hideousness of the memory has caused me to forget it. I suspect we dragged him from the wagon and laid him atop the other bodies. Such was horrible, but what more could we or the other villagers do? We were too weak ourselves to cover the dead with soil, and to tarry near the stinking pits was to court the pestilence.

We must have returned home; but I do not recall that either, for my surroundings trembled and fell away. I entered deep into a fevered world that was part Sight, part dream, part delirium, a world comprised of pestilence and fire. And in the flames, I saw the face of the old Jew and the faces of each of my family—poor Papa, Maman, even Noni. Again I saw the shadows of the people trapped within the flames and heard their screams; again, I fought on their behalf until I was exhausted. And when I could fight no more I lay down, surrendering to the flames, and cried out: "What evil is this?"

And the Goddess said: "Fear."

I was hurled back into this world with a start, and opened my eyes to the interior of our little house and saw I was lying on my parents' bed. Day was breaking, and feeble sunlight streamed in through the open shutters. The fire in the hearth was almost extinguished, and beside it on the straw lay Noni.

Her apron was stained with blood, and she had removed her widow's wimple and unloosed the dark coils of hair that covered either ear so that the fat braids hung to her waist. Her face looked pinched and gray; she lay so still that for a terrible moment, I thought she had died of pestilence while I slept. I sat up and let go a wail, for I realized I was alone in the bed: Maman, too, must have died, and none of our family was left.

At once, Noni leapt to her feet and hurried over to the bed; I sobbed unashamedly with relief.

"Noni! I thought you were dead."

My beloved grandmother burst into tears—as did my mother, who sat near the fire looking wan and frail with a bowl of soup in her hands. When Noni could speak again, she explained that for three days I had lain raving, near death from pestilence. She could not speak frankly in front of my mother, but I knew what she thought: that when I had surrendered my own charm to my dying father, I had made myself vulnerable. I knew then that the Jew's charm had saved me.

Later that night, when I woke and found the straw mattress beneath me soaked with blood, I was terrified that the plague had come again; but Noni only smiled.

"Your monthly bloods have come," she whispered. "Soon you will enter the fellowship of the Goddess."

X

In the wake of the plague, life became an odd mixture of plenty and poverty. Both the miller and his wife had died, leaving no one to grind flour from the wheat stored in Old Jacques's barn. So many villeins, my poor papa included, had perished that the survivors helped themselves freely from abandoned fields and the *grand seigneur*'s orchards and vineyards, since there was no one left to guard them.

What we did not take rotted where it fell—as did most of the souls who died without surviving families to bury them. Such was the fate of our poor neighbors Georges and Thérèse, and all of their sons: despite the stink that wafted from their cottage, especially as the weather grew warmer, fear of the plague kept us from entering.

Nevertheless, we inherited part of their wealth: their donkey and cart, a sextet of pigs and several chickens, and all of the vegetables that grew in Thérèse's *potager*. Despite the lack of bread, we lived off all manner of vegetables, meats, and milk—for goats, sheep, and cattle wandered about in search of dead owners, and could be had by anyone.

At last I experienced the pleasure of a night's sleep on a full stomach. Even Maman began to fatten.

Yet grief pervaded our little village, alongside the stench of death. Germain, my intended, died, not of pestilence, but of the sicknesses that followed—in his case, one that turned the bowels to blood. I was filled with sadness (for he was a decent man) and great guilt over my sense of relief. For a brief while, I assumed the widow's black veil and kirtle, turning me into such a strikingly similar version of my grandmother that even Maman confused us from a distance.

Not just I, but everyone dressed in mourning; and every place we went—the market square, the riverbank, the fields—seemed empty, haunted by ghosts. Maman took me to mass every day, and lit a candle for Papa. She brought me because of loneliness for my father, in part— but also because she sensed I was being lured from the proper Christian path by Noni; and she was quite right.

For though I faithfully attended daily mass, my prayers were all directed to the Holy Mother, with the plea that I would soon come to know what I should do to fulfill my destiny. Noni had begun to teach me in earnest the knowledge of the *pagani,* the countryfolk, which she also referred to as the Race.

I soon came to realize that I had already observed much of Noni's magic; how she filled bags with herbs and charged them magically with a simple prayer. But as soon as I was sufficiently well, she took me with her into the fields to scavenge for food; being still too weak, Maman did not accompany us, and so my grandmother was free to speak openly of the old ways.

Most of the herbs I already knew, for they served a medicinal purpose; but Noni spoke to me now of their magical use. Here was lavender, used in healing spells; here, rosemary, used for protection and the restoration of memory; here was eyebright, used to aid the Sight.

But there were two herbs she showed me that had strictly magical purposes; these were dangerous and so used sparingly, and only by the trained—and when the time came, she would show me their use: henbane, which gave one the ability of flight; and—

And here, she whispered reverently, as we two crouched at the foot of an ancient oak, admiring a homely, gnarled fungus, *is the key to Beginning.*

Beginning, she always called it, though in later years I would hear it referred to as *initiation.*

One day, as we two were on our knees digging in the *potager* just outside the house, and Maman was inside resting, Noni lifted her face to the mid-morning sky, bright blue and cloudless. I followed her gaze and saw it, low on the horizon: the lunar ghost, a perfect circle of translucent ivory.

"A fine, fat moon," Noni said admiringly. "Tonight we meet; prepare yourself." And without another word, she went back to digging.

I was speechless with anticipation, else I would have deluged her with questions. Instead, I finished my work in silence and apparent calm, while my heart and mind flitted between joy and fear.

In the late afternoon, Noni prepared us a fine chicken and a stew of vegetables. I brought Maman's plate to Noni to fill and watched, startled, as Noni, her face like stone, ladled out a large portion of stew, then sprinkled a powder onto it and gave it a stir with Maman's spoon. Since our backs were to Maman, I gave my grandmother a sharp, questioning glance; Noni only shrugged and added a chicken leg to the plate.

With a thrill of anticipation and guilt, I took my mother her dinner, which she ate with better appetite than was her wont, and Noni and I settled down to our own lighter, untainted portions.

Within the hour, before dusk, Maman was snoring in the bed while my grandmother and I sat silently before the still-glowing hearth. We remained thus an hour, each in our own reverie and, certainly, each full of prayers for the events soon to come. I for one asked that the Jew's sacrifice—his life for mine—had not been in vain; that I would come to know precisely what I was, as Diana's servant, to do.

At last, night fell profoundly, though the moonlight streamed so brightly through the open shutters that it seemed as day. Hand in hand, we rose and proceeded out of our little cottage.

The grass and wildflowers were soft and cool beneath our bare feet as we headed away from the village, away from Toulouse, dark and towering against the moon-bright sky. I was not surprised to discover our destination was the great old olive grove. I had seen the wooden statue of Mary many times at the spring festivals, when it was garlanded with flowers; I myself had stood on the hallowed earth there before the image of the Virgin and made my floral offering alongside the other children. I had sensed even then that I stood on ground consecrated to the Great Mother, and Noni had later said that the wooden statue replaced an ancient Roman one of stone—of Diana, crowned by the crescent moon.

So it was that we made our way into the grove, beneath branches of gnarled silver and leaves of pale powdery green; my attention at once became focused on the clearing just beyond, whence emanated a feeble blue glow.

At last we arrived at the clearing, with its bright ceiling of moon and stars. There within a thin, wavering globe of blue were three: the statue of the Holy Mother, garlanded with rosemary, and two weeping people, a man and a woman, sitting inside a freshly drawn circle in the earth. As we approached, they looked up at us—or rather at my grandmother—their tear-streaked faces suddenly bright with joy.

"Ana Magdalena!" the woman cried; at the same time the young man exclaimed: "We thought you dead!"

"My children!" Noni cried, then, motioning for me to remain still, approached the circle and with her forefinger cut an opening in the blue glow; with her foot, she erased part of the arc scribed in the earth. I obeyed her gestures and quickly made my way inside the opening; she followed, then sealed the cut so that the blue globe once again contained us, and redrew the arc with her forefinger.

That done, she embraced the woman fiercely. "Ah, Mattheline! My Mattheline! Are we all that is left?"

"All," replied Mattheline, sobbing. She was a matron of perhaps twenty, or even three-and-twenty, for she had the type of childlike face that would never look old, and she looked thin as a starving bird. Her hair was dark gold, with streaks that were almost brown, and her eyes were of similar color. "My Guillaume is gone—and my little Marc, my little man!"

My grandmother held her at arm's length. "But the baby, your Clotilde—"

"Alive." The misery in her voice did not ease. "But she suffers so from colic, she will not eat food, and I have no milk. . . ."

"Ah, my poor ones!" Noni put her hand gently behind the woman's head, and pressed Mattheline's forehead to her lips. "We are together now, with the Goddess to help us—"

Mattheline pulled away, bitter. "Where was She when my son and husband died?"

"You sound like a Christian, Mattheline," the young man said reprovingly, his voice deep and calm despite his recent tears. He bent down and gave my grandmother an embrace signaling utter affection, utter respect, and at that moment, I understood that Noni had always been the leader of the group.

"Justin," she murmured. And as they both drew back, she asked quietly: "And whom have you lost, my son?"

By trade a blacksmith, Justin was tall and powerfully built, known for his slow, serene manner; but his long face shuddered with repressed tears as he replied: "My father. My mother. My sister Amelie, though the others are all well. And my"—here, he drew in a breath, struggling to maintain control—"my Bernice." And he hung his great head and sobbed unrestrainedly while my grandmother stroked his arm, and said tearfully:

"And my Pietro gone, too. And where are Lorette, and Claude, Mathilde, Georges and Marie, Gerard, Pascal, Jehan, and Jehanne-Marie?"

"Alas!" Mattheline cried. "We were thirteen, and now we are only three." Suddenly owl-eyed, she unleashed a torrent of fear-filled words at my grandmother. "The priest says it is all because of *witches,* who in secret worship the devil. They kiss his arse and lie with him. Father Jean says they use magic, as we do, but theirs is always evil, and they love nothing better than to put curses upon us simple folk. They wander at night through the forest—my heart is in terror that I might meet one. Also, they steal small children, and render their fat to make magical unguents; I cried when I kissed my little Clotilde good-bye tonight." At last she paused, took a gulp of air, and continued: "It sounds as if the Devil is a very powerful god—and if it is true that his magic is strong enough to bring the pestilence and almost destroy our little circle, then perhaps he is stronger than our Goddess—"

"Enough!" Ana Magdalena commanded, at the same time the younger woman uttered the final syllable. "Mattheline, this is what comes of listening to the priest: fear and mistrust. For thirty years I have come to the forest at night, and I have seen no evildoers. Nor will I listen to any suggestion that their Devil, a minor god among their four, is more powerful than She Who Is Mother of All Gods.

"No, this story of evil witches who brought the plague is the very same madness that flourished here twenty years ago, when the crops failed and famine came to all Languedoc. They are burning Jews again: many have already headed south, to the safety of Spain." She paused, and a heaviness came over her expression. "Now *we,* as a group, must take care never to be discovered working a spell or meeting here in the forest—or we will find ourselves accused as witches and burned. For whether there be witches or no, the priests and the villagers will be sure to find them."

"If there be no witches," Mattheline countered, with such simple heartbreak that my eyes stung with unshed tears, "and if the Goddess's magic is the most powerful of all, then why did it not save our loved ones from horrible deaths?"

"The Goddess brings life and joy; therefore, She must also bring death and suffering. Such is the cost of entering this world; how would we know one if we do not know the other?" Ana Magdalena asked softly, and clasped the younger woman's hand, gently drawing her back toward our little group. "But look: *we* are alive. Is that not cause for joy? And we are not three only, but four. Here is my granddaughter, Sybille."

The introduction seemed unnecessary: I had known these two people casually all my life. Though my family had never had need of a blacksmith, we had often passed by Justin and his father as they worked near the village square, or seen Justin looking, smitten, into his fiancée Bernice's eyes; and I had often seen Mattheline and her husband around the village, especially at market.

Still, I felt awkward as a stranger around them, for now I was seeing them in an altogether different aspect.

Mattheline gathered herself with red-eyed dignity, stepped forward, and gave me a feather-light kiss on both cheeks. "Welcome to the fellowship."

Justin did the same, though his kisses were distinctly shyer—yet stronger, and the brush of his beard against my face made me catch my breath. At the sound, he glanced directly into my eyes, and I at once noticed two things: that his eyes were green, and that I was utterly disconcerted by the sudden bloom of warmth that began deep within my belly and ended—most obviously, I am sure—upon my cheeks.

Now I will tell you something that will convince you I am insane, for what I Saw was quite impossible; but I Saw it nonetheless; and I tell you, Brother, that you would See such things too if you could only remember how to Look.

As I withdrew from Justin's embrace, I noticed beside Mattheline—slavishly hovering over her, and a good two heads taller—a great dark cat, taller than the tallest man I have ever seen. Standing on its plump hindquarters, it clasped its paws together like hands, and its face (a frightening one, with great thick fangs springing upward from its lower jaw, although its expression was gentle) was bent close to its mistress, as if fearful it might miss a whispered word or small change in her expression. From time to time it began to fade so that I could quite see through it, and once it almost disappeared altogether. In truth, I worried myself that I had gone quite mad, or that Noni had slipped some strange herb into my dinner—but the rest of the world seemed quite undistorted.

Until I looked over at Noni, hoping to whisper a comment about what I had seen; and there standing serenely beside my grandmother was a thin wraith of a young, handsome man, his head wrapped in the white turban of the Turk. The creature steepled his ghostly hands together and, smiling, bowed his head low in greeting to me; I gave a small nod that I hoped was not visible to the others.

As for Justin, he was attended closely by a sweet female spirit that looked like his beloved Bernice as a child.

I had Seen things before in dreamlike visions, quite apart from the waking world, and I had seen babes inside their laboring mothers' bellies. But I had never stood upon my two feet and seen creatures clearly not of this world, and it unsettled me. I reached for Noni's hand, and upon noticing my troubled gaze, she gave me a warning glance to hold my tongue. So I did, dissembling as best I could throughout the rest of the event, since neither Mattheline nor Justin took notice of our unearthly guests; and I believe even Noni saw but little.

At last, Noni let go my hand, and with a gesture indicated that we others were to take our places behind her in the circle. We did, I with an eye upon the others that I might imitate their movements.

Ana Magdalena faced due north—where, beyond the wooden goddess and the shadowy gray veil of olive leaves, the city of Toulouse slept, dark and impenetrable. In a deep guttural pitch she began to chant words in her native tongue (or so I assumed, for I understood not one of them), slowly at first, then a bit faster, her pitch gradually rising. . . .

I lifted my face to the sky, and saw the moon and stars throw forth their light to a point high above our little circle, and there the light grew strong, stronger, until it began to move. . . . *Deosil,* Noni had explained earlier; clockwise, the direction of invitation, of joining. Round and round it swirled, a vortex dropping lower, lower until it finally penetrated the feeble blue veil surrounding us, and enveloped Ana Magdalena.

How beautiful she became! Though I could not see her face, I watched her posture grow straighter, stronger, taller, as if the light inhabited her very bones and lifted her toward heaven. And when she flung up her arms to welcome its descent, her sleeves fell back, revealing flesh no longer brown with sun and mottled with age, but incandescent, limned by a glow as strong as the moon's. So strong that I squinted, and in the glare could no longer detect the gossamer form of the Turkish spirit.

Her head fell back, and her wimple fell away behind her, revealing loose blue-black hair, streaked with luminous silver, that hung well below her waist. She straightened and lowered her arms, then, pointing due north, cried out a command in a high-pitched tone.

Unable to contain my joy, I giggled aloud, for the air had become alive, vibrant, as if filled with the energy of a thousand buzzing bees, or the whirling of a mighty storm. On either side of me, Justin and Mattheline stood at rapt attention, unmindful of my jubilance.

Then Ana Magdalena—and something far greater than Ana Magdalena—turned to the east; and as she did so, her forefinger scribed at waist level a thick golden band of light. I still remember the sight of her face in profile; how beautiful, how ageless it had become.

Another turn, and then another, and we were once again facing north, completely enclosed by the shimmering ring of gold; about us, what had once been a feeble veil of blue was now a sturdy sapphire globe, flecked with golden sparks.

A globe I could see through: to my surprise, I Saw beings standing just outside the circle. At each of the four directions Noni had faced, giants towered almost to the sky, each radiating a different color: the mossy greens and browns of earth; the shimmering yellow of sunlight; the searing reds and oranges of flame, and the deep blue of the sea. Giants, I say here, but only two of them, the yellow and the mossy green ones, took on a vaguely human appearance; the others, red and blue, were more pure force, columns of prismatic living light that resembled sun or star or moon more than any person or creature.

Their aspect was as utterly heartless and matter-of-fact as a stone, or Death, yet I had no fear of them, for it was clear they stood as sentinels, guarding us, and were willing to serve us, should we command them.

Beyond them, outside the bright comfort of the circle, hovered a plethora of dark, shapeless beings eager to take on any form impressed on them; others eager to attach themselves like leeches to those lacking the will to cast them off.

My attention was soon drawn from them, for Noni turned toward us, a living representative of the Goddess whose statue stood behind us. Her face was radiant, her hands and arms spread slightly in the same inviting gesture I have seen on many statues of Mary. The brilliance emanating from her—from *within* her—pained my eyes, yet the sight was far too lovely for me to look away.

Even Justin and Mattheline stood awestruck beside me, though they had certainly seen the Goddess in my grandmother many times. And when Ana Magdalena asked: "What do my children require of me?" Mattheline bowed, and with genuine reverence said, "My child, my Clotilde, is sick; I would that she were well."

In reply, my grandmother stretched forth her hands in invitation to Mattheline on my right, Justin on my left; they in turn took hold of my hands.

Immediately I felt a spark, such as one feels in the winter sometimes when it is dry, and a surge from them into me, and through me, like the tingling of lightning before it touches the earth. The sensation increased as we began to walk slowly sidewise, making our little circle inside a circle begin to move deosil. Ana Magdalena led, gradually increasing the pace and chanting in a low voice words I again did not comprehend, save for one phrase:

Diana, Diana, la bona Dea . . .

The others joined in the chant and I followed as best I could, until Mattheline leaned her face next to mine and repeated the chant slowly, then explained: "We are imagining a great white cone with its point in the center of our circle; it will grow stronger and stronger until we send it to my Clotilde."

And indeed, that is what I Saw in our midst: a vortex of white light, spinning faster and faster as we danced faster and faster ourselves. The night was cool, but soon we were all dripping with sweat—not from the dancing, but from the incredible heat generated by the cone, and the pitch of our chant had risen so that I felt it could rise no more, and then continued still to ascend.

The heat and the current of power and the chant that vibrated in every part of my body had become near unbearable in an ecstatic way; by then, the cone had grown so wide and tall that it pierced the top of our blue globe and engulfed us; and so opaque that I could not see Noni across from me.

At this point, I heard my grandmother cry out.

"Now!"

Our dancing ceased with a collective gasp as we stumbled against each other. Noni, Justin, and Mattheline flung their arms straight up into the air (which of course made me raise mine); as they did so, the power traveled upward and outward from us. Open end up, the cone went sailing out up into the night sky, seeking Mattheline's baby.

Find her it did: I *Saw* it whirl through our little village, inside the slightly open upper door of a cottage, where upon the large straw bed a child of some months lay swaddled and sleeping fitfully. Pale and sickly she was, bald as a newborn, with yellow skin and sunken cheeks, and shadows beneath eyes too big for such a small face. The cone of light engulfed her, wide end swallowing her first, much as the whale had taken Jonah. Slowly, the light was absorbed into her person until she seemed to radiate from within and the sallow cast to her skin eased, replaced by a gentle pink, like the blush on a peach. As I watched, she gave a sweet, small sigh, and sank into a deep, renewing slumber.

The others did not See, but their eyes were bright, their faces flushed and exuberant. All of us were exhausted and sweating from the experience; I felt exhilarated, too, for I had experienced the Goddess's power in a new way.

That was not the only spell we did that night; Noni had brought herbs with her into the circle which we all charged with magical power, then ate, with the intent that the Goddess would help our village through the coming autumn and winter.

There were outright prayers, too, and requests that were addressed by Noni's chants; at last, Ana Magdalena went to the four quarters of the circle and began to dismiss our towering guardians, one by one. I felt disappointment, for never had I felt such freedom in the Sight, or the presence of the Goddess so constantly; I wanted the circle never to end.

At the precise moment when the shimmering yellow giant turned to depart, I caught a glimpse of a globe of white light just beyond, steady as a beacon, and it filled me with inexplicable joy, for I knew it awaited *me*.

But when the sapphire guardian of the west moved away, I caught sight of a column of the darkest black—

Nay, to use the words *dark* or *black* to describe what I saw is to revile them both. For without the sweet relief of darkness and the jeweled black of night, we should come to hate the brightness of day; but this was a void, neither dark nor light, but the desolate absence of all: all life, all hope.

And it, too, awaited me.

My knees began to tremble; somehow I managed to stay on my feet while Noni unmade the circle. And when she had dismissed each guardian, and erased with her foot the last bit of arc scribed in the earth (causing the blue globe and golden ring to vanish, along with all other-worldly creatures), I asked: "Is Circle always so short?"

Mattheline answered swiftly, before Noni could speak: "No. Oft-times it lasts almost to dawn; but you have not begun the Path and do not know its secrets. In time, perhaps a year—"

"Her beginning ceremony will be at the next moon," Noni said—no longer the Goddess but most definitely my grandmother—with a sharpness that dared dissent.

Mattheline's thin, colorless eyebrows flew upward. "A *month*? Why does the priestess's granddaughter wait a month when I myself waited eight, and Justin here nine?"

"Matthe," Justin reproved her, putting a hand on her shoulder. "She *is* the priestess; she has the right. . . ."

Mattheline calmed herself and said no more, but a small crease of disapproval remained upon her brow.

"You have always known my Sybille is doubly gifted with the Sight," Noni explained. "Her whole life has been one of training in the Path: I have brought her now only because she is ready. Next moon, she will begin."

No more was said that night until Noni and I had taken leave of the others, and we two walked home through the meadow. After a long silence, my grandmother said: "Justin is a fine lad. He is not so strong in the Sight as was his mother, but his people are of the Race."

"Mattheline's are not," I said, testing.

She drew in, then released, a sigh. "They were, in generations past; it has been bred out of them through poor marriages. Even so, she is drawn to the Path."

Another period of silence passed; I felt unsaid words hanging in the air between us, but bided my time until Noni at last said, "It is your destiny, child, to move beyond our little circle. The pestilence has eased its grip, but there are worse dangers coming. Your Sight is far stronger than mine; and within a moon, your magic will be, too. When that time comes—"

"But what magic is there in the village that is greater than what I have seen tonight?"

"The magic within you, Sybille. Your destiny lies elsewhere." She spoke so sweetly, with such deference, that I was taken aback; yet I knew she was filled with the utmost gravity, since she rarely called me by my French name when we were alone.

"But I don't understand. . . ."

"In time you will. Here." She drew out of the pocket of her black kirtle a small black cloth bag, tied to a string, and held it out to me.

"This will protect you from all harmful influence during this important time; for never have you been more vulnerable."

I took it and gratefully hung it round my neck—but Noni still held out her hand, now expectantly. "The gold charm—you still wear it, yes?"

Yes; but I felt a sudden overwhelming reluctance to part with it.

At my hesitation, Noni gestured, impatient. "My child, there can be no other influence upon you now save that of the Goddess. The Jew's talisman has no doubt protected you, and saved your life from the plague—but this charm of mine will protect not only your life in this world but in the one unseen, the one that now knows of your presence. I have need of that talisman now. Can you trust me?"

Without further protest, I slipped the gold talisman on its fine chain over my head, and dropped it into my grandmother's cupped hand.

"I will take especial care of it," she said, smiling, and it was not until some time afterward that I would truly understand what she had meant.

In the month before my Beginning, I had time to consider what Noni had said; but never before had the Goddess seemed so distant, or my thoughts so muddled and conflicting. *Your destiny lies elsewhere. . . .*

A foolish idea; what cause had I to leave my village? Never in my life would I abandon Noni and my mother. Never . . .

When such frightening thoughts visited me, I diverted them by trying to imagine my life as a blacksmith's wife. Only days after my first circle, Justin called upon Maman and convinced her that I should be affianced to him at once, given the shortage of eligible men. The deed was done; a date in September, the following month, was set, and he presented me with his departed mother's fine oak loom. The notion of marriage to Justin was not disagreeable, for he was fine-looking and young, with a kindly temperament and muscles upon his chest and shoulders that stirred within me decidedly unchildish thoughts. Maman was pleased because Justin and his surviving sisters were among the wealthiest in the village, so that she would be well looked after in her old age; she spoke of nothing else all day but the upcoming marriage. But a dark change had come over her since Papa's death, leaving her with no appetite, gaunt hollows in her cheeks, and eyes ever filled with suspicion.

I listened respectfully to all her advice in the evenings while we sat by the hearth-fire and worked upon my wedding quilt, Maman often weeping as she thought of the quilt she had made twenty years before, on her engagement to Papa. But my heart and my mind were focused more on the beginning to come, and the odd distance that was growing between me, the Goddess, and the Sight.

At last the day came—or rather, the night, a night where leaden clouds obscured the deeper black of sky, and spilled a warm and steady rain. As Noni and I fastened our cloaks while Maman snored, I found myself overtaken by nerves. My fingers trembled, and I felt not the excitement and anticipation I had expected, but true dread. I could not meet Noni's eyes, and she did not try to meet mine, and when we stepped out of the cottage into the rain, we spoke not a word. My grandmother moved with unusual speed and determination, and in the humid air I soon began to sweat beneath my cloak and kirtle as I kept pace.

We were headed toward the olive grove—or so I thought until Noni suddenly veered to her left, and the hills that lay east of the village. Into the forest of oak and evergreen we went, slipping from time to time on the slick carpet of dead leaves, up the slow incline where the boughs of ancient trees half protected us from the rain.

A figure leapt out at us from behind a tree: a tall man, masked and cloaked in black, in the night a mere silhouette, but there was no mistaking the flash of his sword.

'Twas a gendarme, I thought wildly; now we would be arrested and burnt as witches. I cried out and sank to my knees.

"Go no farther!" he commanded. With wild relief, I recognized the voice as Justin's—and yet not, just as my grandmother's voice as priestess had been hers, and yet the voice of something more. A smaller figure, also masked, came from behind him: Mattheline, I realized. These were only Justin and Mattheline performing an ancient ritual, but as she tied a blindfold round my head, and as I felt the razor-keen tip of the sword nick my kirtle and almost pierce the skin between my breasts, I felt a thrill of fear.

"Woe to you," Justin said, "if you reveal the names of any of your brothers and sisters to those not of the Goddess, or if ever you disavow Her. For then you shall be accursed with all Her wrath and fury, and ours, and we shall seek you out not just in this world, but all others; nor just in this life, but all to come. Do you understand?"

"I understand," I replied, in a voice so weak I hardly recognized it as my own.

"Do you then swear upon your life and magic that you will be faithful to the Goddess and the circle, and never, even upon threat of death, reveal the names of your brothers and sisters to anyone not of the Race?"

"Upon my life and magic, I swear."

"Then begin," he said, and the sharpness between my breasts withdrew.

I was forced to my feet, not at all gently or kindly, and shoved along further up the hills, wincing when I stepped upon a fallen cone. Upward we climbed, until I heard the others all gasping behind me; finally, the hill began to level off, and I was led over wet rocks inside what I presumed was a cave, for the rain ceased as suddenly as the ground beneath my feet grew dry.

I was pushed into a sitting position against a cool stone wall; above me, Noni's voice ordered: "Swallow."

A bolus was pressed to my lips; I accepted it, and began to chew, for it seemed too large to swallow easily. So vile-tasting and bitter was it that I gagged at once, and nearly spat it out when I felt a cup at my lips, and heard the command: "Swallow." I took a gulp from the cup and was relieved to taste plain peppermint tea. Even so, the bolus went down reluctantly, and for some moments I huddled against the cool stone in nauseated misery while Noni gave me further sips of the tea.

Finally the queasiness passed, and I moved to stand and take off the blindfold; but before I could do either, my three companions pressed me down to a prone position, pushing upon my limbs, my ribs, my shoulders. Already the beginnings of lassitude were coming over me, and without further struggle I let them push me down.

Down, down, down to the earth, down to the Goddess . . .

Outside, the drumming of rain; inside, the near-deafening sound of my own breath.

My sodden cloak was gently unfastened and removed while two pairs of small hands, feminine hands, lifted my skirts and began to rub my legs, slowly and steadily. Within a short time I realized an herb-scented unguent was being rubbed into my skin. The effect was almost immediate: my breathing grew heavy and slow, my attitude deeply passive and content; the gliding of worn fabric over the skin of my arms, my torso as my kirtle and undershift were pulled up and away was pure pleasure, and my nakedness no cause for alarm. . . .

Outside, there was thunder, beautiful, deep rolling thunder, and I lay entranced inside the cave, feeling the rumble within me as three pairs of hands moved slowly, sensually down my arms, down the length of my body, all humming a wordless chant in absurd harmony. The pitch grew higher, higher, until it became the foolish buzzing of bees, and I laughed aloud.

Abruptly, the touching slowed, and I could no longer differentiate the separate hands; I felt touched by one great caress, felt my body begin to contract and expand like a woman in childbirth—without pain, but with the same sense of struggle and desperation to give birth to something, to free myself. . . .

At once my body was consumed by a terrible cold fire; I sat up, rolled onto all fours, and vomited.

Immediately I felt better. I sat back and freed myself from my blindfold to discover that I was quite alone, and that the cave was bright as day—blinding, it seemed to my poor bedazzled eyes—because a fire had been built near its mouth, about as far from me as I could hurl a stone. It was a fair distance, but I could see it with impossible, indeed supernatural, clarity: a fire as bright as the sun and prismatic as a gem, bejeweled with tongues of sapphire, ruby, emerald, threaded with strands of copper, silver, gold. If there was night beyond, I saw it not, for the whole world, it seemed, was ablaze.

If I remember anything of the experience, it was the brilliance of the light.

I raised a hand to shield my eyes from the pain, yet such was its glory that I could not look away. The fire roiled, growing taller and wider with each breath I took; and as it grew, the colors within it deepened: gold, silver, and copper melted to ominous crimson, sapphire and emerald to black.

These were dark flames, devouring and merciless; I cringed, clutching vainly at the cold stone wall, watching blood-red tendrils reach for me; a single glowing spark shot high into the air and floated downward, a jet cinder by the time it landed on my leg and made me scream in fear and surprise.

Still I could not look away, for I knew that within the flames lay visions and destiny. At the same time that I recoiled, I drew closer to the fire, and peering carefully within its heart, I Saw:

In miniature, a thousand thousand men, and a thousand thousand women, born a thousand years past and a thousand years hence, and all the years in between; Moor and Jew, Christian, pagan and unbeliever, leper and whole, slave and serf and merchant, lord and lady; all of these trapped within the flames and crying out in pain. Many crying out to the Goddess, by all Her names; others not of the Race, crying out to their own gods, or to humanity itself, pleading for an end to such cruelty. All of them ablaze as if for perpetuity.

In desperation, I cried out the secret name of the Goddess.

And She answered with a sudden flood of warmth at my heart that was not at all painful, but pure comfort, pure life.

At once I was in the cave again—a fair distance from the fire, which no longer seemed as threatening or as bright. Yet I was not free to rise; for Justin lay atop me, his flesh pressed hard against mine, his lips moving over my cheek, my neck, his left hand cupping my breast. His right hand smoothly but firmly moved between my thighs, separating them; then he raised his upper body by balancing upon one arm. He, too, had left the boundaries of the real world to be with me; his eyes were the clouded gray-green of a storm-tossed sea, his pupils large and infinitely black.

How like a savage he looked that night, his hair tousled and wild, his naked body glistening with unguent and smeared with earth from the cave's floor; the muscles in his arms, his chest seemed far more beautiful to me than any artist's carving or sculpture. Awestruck, I raised my hand to them, and laughed softly when they quivered beneath my touch. I swept my fingertips over them, from shoulder to chest to abdomen. There I paused at the dark, soft nest of his pubic hair; from it, his male member emerged, fully erect and flushed with blood.

I touched it tentatively, filled with innocent curiosity and a sudden violent craving to be resoundingly pierced by it; beneath both, a small silent voice spoke.

Now is not the time. . . .

Before I could say aught, Justin took his hand from my breast and guided his male member between my legs, then arched his back and with a groan thrust himself inside me.

The sensation was one of fleeting pain mingled with intense pleasure; a second thrust, and I groaned, too, with desperate longing.

But not for Justin. Not for Justin . . . *Now is not the time.*

An impossible strength seized me; as easily as I might flick away a fly, I reluctantly pushed him off and sat up.

He fell back onto one hip, gasping, and in that one instant, I saw an eternity of emotion pass over his face: the lust, then genuine hurt, followed by grief at the realization that he would never find in me his beloved Bernice.

Lust overtook him again, and he reached for me; I pulled away and said, gently as I could: "No. You are not the One."

"But you must," said he, plaintive as a child. "It is the way to begin."

"Not for me." I stood, and found that strength had returned to my limbs and that all dizziness and discomfort had gone. As for poor Justin, he protested no more, but sank back upon the ground, his eyes staring blankly at the ceiling.

I ran lightly to the mouth of the cave, feeling no fear of the fire, only enjoyment of its warmth. Leaning one hand against the stone wall, I peered out.

The rain had stopped, and the veil of clouds had been drawn away to reveal stars so aglow their rays almost touched the earth; the moon was huge and opalescent, veined with shimmering blue and rose, so radiant I could see each trembling, shining drop of moisture that hung from every leaf in the forest.

The Goddess was with me once more.

I laughed softly, and as I did I espied a small white orb of light in the distance, traveling through the trees. It grew as it neared, and by the time it stood before me, it was taller and wider than I.

This was the light I had seen waiting for me outside the circle the previous moon; hoping I might now receive a vision of the Goddess, I knelt . . .

. . . but what emerged from the light was an old man, his iron beard and curls falling to his waist. The Jew who had saved me, stooped and dressed just as he had been in life, skullcap hidden beneath his horned hat, yellow felt badge pinned to his somber merchant's tunic. Such infinite love resided in his dark eyes, with their age-yellowed whites, that tears came to my own.

"Jacob," I greeted him—marveling that I should know his name, and at the same time realizing that I had always known it, just as I had always known and loved him as teacher and guide.

"My lady," he said, to my utter surprise; and, taking my hands in his, drew me up to my feet, then knelt and pressed his lips to my knuckles, as a knight might do when he swears allegiance to his queen.

"No," I said, aghast. "Jacob, you must not kneel to me." And as if following a command, he rose promptly, then turned and gestured behind him at the great white orb, which still remained.

My gaze followed his direction; and before my eyes, I saw another figure coalesce within the brilliance: yet another man, this one with hair the pink-gold of copper when it is finely polished, and delicate, handsome features. He was dressed in the velvets and silks of nobility, and at his hip he bore a great sword.

I knew him—and at the same time, knew him not, and so turned to Jacob to ask: "Who is he?"

"Edouard. One of many," Jacob said. "You will come to remember us again."

The figure inside the globe of light transformed to that of a cleric; then again to that of a third man, and a fourth—then it began to shift so rapidly that I became dizzied, until it became that of an ancient chieftain, upon whose head a crude golden crown rested.

"And him?" I asked.

"One of legend," Jacob replied. "His name meant Bear."

And then an elderly man, with trimmed white moustache and beard, dressed in the simple chain mail armor of a knight from the century past: over the armor at his breast he wore a loose tunic of pure white, emblazoned with a blood-colored cross. His face was long and severe, his eyebrows thick and still fiercely black; and I watched as beard and brows and hair were consumed by flame.

"Jacques," I whispered as the chevalier's fire-kissed face dissolved to that of my beloved Jew. "Jacob…" I glanced up at my spirit companion and held back tears. "Jacob, how many times must you be martyred for me?"

In reply, he merely smiled and nodded at the globe of white light, which still hovered before us.

And I looked into the light and saw the face of *him,* my Beloved, the One whom I have always loved and always will. A near unbearable yearning overtook me at the sight of him, a yearning I had not known, until that moment, I had always possessed. It was a physical ache, a sexual desire that consumed my body like the fire—as it does even now, when I speak of him—but even more a true longing of my soul. In hopes of fulfilling it I had permitted myself to be engaged to Guillaume, and then Justin, and twice been disappointed. For *his* sake, I had pushed away Justin, and been relieved when poor Guillaume died; for *his* sake, I would not stop seeking until I had found him again, in this life. For without him, I and my destiny would never be complete; without him, I and our Race would never survive the flames.

"There is a time and place for charms and chants," said Jacob. "And talismans." Upon the last word, he gave me a curiously pointed look before continuing. "But you must learn the highest form of magic if the Race is to continue.

"For in this generation, my lady, an especial evil awaits us; one so great that even a seer as gifted as you cannot know for certain the outcome—whether we will survive, whether any of us will be able to escape the flames. And if we die, then surely all men and all women are lost without our guiding influence, doomed to murder their neighbors and themselves until the world is empty."

"Then teach me this magic," I insisted, but he shook his head sadly.

"Would that I could this moment, and save the earth; but it remains for lord and lady to find and instruct one another. . . ."

As he spoke, I felt myself swooning with pleasure beyond imagining at the thought of coupling with my lord; for a time, I knew nothing else, and then I heard Jacob say: "Only then will their magic be the highest, the most powerful. It will need to be, to combat the enemies of the Race and humankind."

Jacob turned somberly back toward the shimmering globe—and to my sudden terror I saw that it was light no more, but dark. Nay, deeper than dark: it was the void of all voids, the negation of negation, the sum of all hopelessness—the horror I had sensed awaiting me outside my first Circle.

I looked within and saw the faces of different men: again, a nobleman armed with a sword, a cleric and others, all different men from those I had seen in the light—Enemies, and yet somehow strangely similar.

"These men are also of the Race," I said, aghast.

"Yes," Jacob answered, his voice and manner deeply calm, even reflective—while I managed only with the greatest difficulty to keep my trembling knees from collapsing beneath me. He turned toward me and gave me a look of pure compassion.

"But why?" I asked, and he replied swiftly: "They fear who they are. The tragedy, lady, is that most of them seek to do good. But even a force as powerful as love, when it is tainted by fear, can lead only to evil."

Once again, he gazed into the terrible void. His compassion gave me a measure of strength: I looked back into it as well, and at the progression of faces there, and thought that I had never seen anything so piteous.

And then the void—

Forgive me, Brother Michel, my voice catches; I cannot speak. I beg a moment to—

No, I am well. I will not weep.

I will not weep.

Then the void emptied, yet remained swirling before me, ominous, waiting. An even deeper dread betook me, as beside me Jacob said:

"Here is our greatest Enemy of all."

And within the void formed the body of a man . . . gradually, indistinctly, as though shrouded inside a slow-dispersing veil of mist. The features were last of all to appear, and as they did, such a hideous sense of horror descended upon me that I cried out: "No! No! I cannot look! I cannot—!" I sank to my knees and covered my eyes.

Jacob crouched next to me and whispered into my ear: "You must, lady. You must, else we all are lost. . . ."

Yet I could not bear it; I had seen enough horrors for one night. I kept my palms firmly pressed against my eyes and cowered there upon the wet earth and leaves. I know not how long I remained there, kneeling and shivering, but when at last I uncovered my eyes, Jacob and the void were both gone.

The sky had changed, too, from the deep of night to the less intense darkness of the hour before dawn, and the stars had begun to fade. No longer did they seem impossibly radiant—though still they were brighter than ever I had seen them—nor did the forest seem light as day.

With a start, I realized that the night had passed, and soon Maman would be rising: I ran back to the cave to find Justin gone and the fire dead. Fortunately, my shift, kirtle, and cloak were there, carefully folded, and the cloak dried; I dressed quickly, and ran down the hillside to our cottage.

Maman was in bed snoring, and Noni, too, as if she had never been to the forest the night before. I undressed and slipped in beside them, trying to slow the rapidity of my breath.

I could not sleep in that hour before Noni rose; even though Jacob had disappeared, it was as though he now resided in my mind, and all the questions that had troubled me since my very first vision now, one by one, were being answered. I remembered how he had stood outside the door of our cottage that last day of his life, and said: *Carcassonne is a place of safety.*

Sir, my grandmother had cried, *they are all dead and dying in Carcassonne!*

But I suddenly knew, in the gray twilight before dawn, that he had spoken not of safety from the plague, but from that greater Evil that now faced us—the flames set by our Enemies to destroy us.

The sooner I hastened to Carcassonne, the sooner my destiny would be fulfilled.

My destiny: Noni had been right. It did not lie here, in our village's little circle, but elsewhere—aided by the men I had seen within the brilliant orb of light. Most of all, it did not lie with Justin, but with the One whose face I could never forget. I was compelled to go and find him; for only then would we save the Race and defeat the Greatest Evil.

I could not wait to tell Noni all that had happened to me: at the same time, I felt sorrowful. How could I tell her that I would leave her alone with Maman for the rest of her days, would deny her the right to deliver her great-grandchildren into the world?

When Noni finally rose, we said not a word to each other, but maintained a casual silence as we set about our morning chores. Maman would soon waken, after all, and it would be foolish to risk speaking of the night before—especially when there was so much to be said. We had long ago announced our plan to harvest the last of the summer berries that morning—on the *seigneur*'s property, which produced too much fruit for his decimated household, and now was open to the villeins—knowing that Maman, still grieving, would as always remain home. That way, Noni and I were sure to have time alone to discuss all that had happened the night of my Beginning.

As it was, Maman awoke in an agitated state, saying that she felt oddly unwell. As Noni and I passed her, baskets in hand, on our way out to the fields, she gripped my forearm with unusual strength, pleading:

"Stay with me, Marie Sybille. I am falling ill to something serious, I know it; I will need your help, and besides, your very presence comforts me."

I hesitated, and looked askance at Noni. As a dutiful daughter, it would be unheard of for me to refuse my mother; but I hoped that perhaps my grandmother might say something to reassure Maman that we would be home quickly.

Noni hesitated but an instant; then, to my surprise, she said, quietly but most firmly: "Stay with your mother, Sybille. She clearly needs you."

What could I say? I could not disobey both mother and grandmother. Reluctantly I set down my basket, and my grandmother walked through the door alone. As for Maman, I put her to bed and started dosing her with pain-relieving tea, just in case, though I saw no sign of fever—only a strange, disturbing wildness in her eyes. Grief, I decided, had finally taken its toll upon her nerves, despite the calming, sleep-inducing potion she had been given the night before. I gave her more calming herbs, then sat upon the bed with her and worked upon my wedding quilt, telling her all the amusing goings-on in the village in the hope of easing her anxiety.

But she only grew more restless with each passing hour, glancing out of the unshuttered window. I looked up often to follow her gaze, and saw only the dirt road leading up toward Toulouse, and the great city lying to the north; and closer to the east, the *seigneur*'s castle and vineyards. And each time I would rise to do some menial chore, she would again grasp my arm, begging for me to stay beside her.

So I did, though by mid-morning, she was so agitated she could barely sit still. "What is it, Maman?" I asked again and again, but she would only mutter: "We will see, we will see," and continued to stare out of the window.

At last she leapt from her bed with astounding alacrity and motioned for me to join her. Leaning one elbow upon the sill, she pointed to a spot far in the distance.

"Marie Sybille. Your eyes are better than mine; tell me what you see."

I did as requested. In the distance a cart drawn by two black horses rumbled toward our village, and behind it rose a small plume of dust. Nearer and nearer it came, until at last the two men sitting on top of it became clearly visible.

"Who are they?" Maman gasped, breathless. I took note of the swords at their hips, their identical caps and tunics.

"Gendarmes," I said, wondering what matter could be of such grave import that it would bring city police all the way to our little village. I noticed then that in the back of the cart sat a third man, dressed in black. "Gendarmes, and a cleric."

Beside me, Maman began to tremble so violently that her legs gave way beneath her; I caught her just before she fell. As I half carried her to the bed, she clutched my shoulders with painful intensity, and, eyes wide with madness, cried out:

"You are my daughter, Marie Sybille—my only child! You know that I love you more than my own life!"

"I know, Maman; I know. Now hush," I soothed, smoothing the blanket back over her spindly legs, settling her back against the pillow—but she would not be comforted. I glanced back out of the window, though Maman clutched my shoulders, my arms—and noticed that cart and horses had turned toward the east.

"Look, Maman," I said cheerily. "You have nothing to be afraid of—they are taking the road to the *seigneur*'s castle. They are not coming here."

But my words failed to calm her. "I love you, Marie Sybille; you must understand how much I love you!"

"I do, Maman; and *I* love *you*," I replied, fearing that perhaps she was in the first stages of brain fever, for her shivering and agitation continued. Yet her forehead and cheeks remained cool; so I crawled back up onto the bed and sat sewing beside her, vainly trying to reassure her and distract her from her mysterious ailment. She calmed but slightly and at last fell silent, sitting rigidly against the pillow, her eyes wild and fixed upon the world outside the window, her hands gripping her blanket so tightly that each knuckle turned the skin above it to ivory.

After a time, she gave a small cry, and I looked up from my sewing to see her staring out of the window again—at the gendarmes and the cart, now retreating from the *seigneur*'s castle.

I rose and went to the window. "It is all right, Maman; can you see? They are heading back to the city; they are not coming here. . . ." But even as I spoke, a sense of dread overwhelmed me. For in the back of the cart was not one person, but two.

Certainly I could see neither detail nor feature, so far away were these two—only a general impression that one was a cleric, and the other, also dressed in black, was a woman. But all of us have an ability to recognize those dear to our hearts, even from very great distances.

Ere I could turn to my mother in horror, she stood beside me, grasped my wrist with uncanny strength, and pulled me round to face her.

"It is only because I love you, Marie Sybille, that I do this," she said. "Look what I have found. Look at what that woman has done to me!"

So stricken was I in that moment that she was able to drag me over to the bed. With one hand she produced from beneath the mattress an object wrapped in tattered black silk. This she threw upon the mattress, and opened the silk to reveal the contents therein:

A doll, sewn from undyed fabric scraps and filled with leaves and soil. It was clearly female, embroidered to give the impression of hair and features—all in black, since I had been weaving and sewing with the lighter thread and would have noticed were any of it missing. Bound to its breast with black string was Jacob's gold talisman, and over its eyes, a small strip of black fabric had been tied like a blindfold.

Black: the color of protection, when worn voluntarily.

Black: the color of binding, of containing, when not.

"A curse," Maman hissed. "She put a curse upon me, just as she put a curse on your poor father—murdered him, do you understand? But she cannot kill me; I am a Christian woman, faithful to God, and He has saved me, that I might save you. Father André says it is so. She has always wanted to corrupt you, sweet Marie, and lead you to the Devil. Always; but I will not let her. I am surprised she has not simply strangled me while I slept. . . ."

I heard my mother's words, but could find none of my own: my Noni, my own dear Noni, would use such a thing as magic to control me. . . . Impossible. Yet here was the truth before my eyes: and as my mother watched, I unwound the golden talisman that linked me to Jacob and those who had for lifetimes served me.

Then I pulled the blindfold free: immediately I Saw, and cried out in pain and anguished love at the knowledge of what my grandmother was about to do for me. For the Race.

I clasped the talisman tightly in my hand and, without a word of farewell, left my mother forever.

. . .

I ran. Ran down the dirt road toward the grand city of Toulouse as fast as I possibly could, until both lungs and legs were burning; even then, I continued at full speed, my mind full of terrible images. Of my beloved Noni, being tortured by her captors; of my Noni, crying out in pain with no one to help her.

Of my Noni, writhing in flames, just as those poor victims had that day so many years again in Toulouse's public square.

Of my Noni, who meant to sacrifice herself for me.

A voice, sinister and low, whispered in my mind, as if an invisible being had just spoken in my ear:

That shall be her fate, you know, if you do not rush to save her. They will burn her; just as, someday, they will burn you, too, if you do not hurry to the jail at once, the jail in the belly of Saint-Sernin. . . .

The very idea sent a bolt of fear through me, and I hurried my pace until I was gasping: yet in the midst of all my agitation, the memory came to me, distinct and slow, of Noni saying: *Trust in the Goddess. . . .*

And so I prayed as I ran. *Holy Mother of God, let your peace descend upon me. Guide me, and empower me to help my grandmother in whatever way I can. Show me the magic I need to protect her from all harm. . . .*

I began to calm, and slowly became aware of the sinister voice's source; this was the darkness I had seen so long ago in my childhood vision, and again in Circle, and a third time at my initiation—the darkness that sought to consume the light.

Stop, Jacob's voice commanded, and I did as bidden, coming so quickly to a halt that I coughed in the dust raised. And as I opened my heart further to the Goddess, instinct told me to turn about in my tracks—not completely, though, which led due south back to the village, but south and east, to Carcassonne . . . and safety. This led me entirely off the path, and into the wood, where I wended my way around trees and bushes—for hours and hours, until night fell, and the darkness forced me to stop.

Even so, grief would not permit me to sleep for a time. When at last I slumbered, I fell into a dream. . . .

In the city, I knelt inside a great cathedral—one I recognized from childhood visits as the massive basilica of Saint-Sernin, its great western doors open to the rays of the afternoon sun. Beside me in the main sanctuary were more people than I had ever seen: nuns and monks, of course, but also folk of every description, peasants and merchants and lesser nobility, all praying and weeping.

On the altar, candles for the dead, hundreds of them; in the aisles, penitents lying facedown, arms spread and legs together to form a Roman cross as they murmured Our Fathers and Hail Marys, all beneath a concave bas-relief of Christ in his majesty. Some beat themselves with nail-spiked strips of leather, kneeling with bloodied backs as they prayed.

Even in my desperation, I felt a trickle of awe at the sight of the sanctuary, vast enough to house five thousand souls, tall enough to touch the sun; and somewhere beneath the beauty and serenity, my grandmother suffered. Heaven above, Hell below.

I moved to a spot far from the altar, and there knelt upon the cool stone and prayed my earlier prayer once more: *Holy Mother of God, let Your peace descend upon me. Guide me, and help me to help my grandmother. . . .*

Over and over again I repeated the prayer, until at last some measure of calm betook me; and with a sense of love and relief, I allowed myself to be led, step by step, to my destination.

Five cavernous naves there were. I watched as my feet made their way to the third; there, I spied a small transept that led to stairs. These wound downward to a dark corridor, which terminated at a locked wooden door thrice my height, and twice as wide; with a dreamer's confidence, I passed confidently through the very wood, as if I were a phantom.

Just inside stood a tall, muscular youth perhaps two years my senior, with a downy boy's moustache the color of sweet cinnamon and hair to match. In his right hand, he bore a short sword most threateningly.

Without a word, I walked past him, over the threshold into a dark stone corridor.

At its termination, behind bars of iron, sat my Noni.

Smiling she was, so sweetly and with such genuine gladness at the sight of me that I wept tears of joy, even though I sensed that they had already somehow hurt her, and she was in physical pain; but that is the manner of dreams sometimes, that we do not always see everything clearly.

"Sibilla," she said, and reached up through the bars. I reached down, clasped her hand, and sat; and it was as though the bars between us melted away, so that there was nothing between us, nothing at all—neither distance nor walls, nor even age or the bodies in which we were, for this lifetime, clothed.

My tears grew bitter with salt and sorrow. "Why, Noni, why? Why did you hide my Sight from me?"

Still smiling, she replied, "Child, why do you ask me questions to which you already know the answers?"

'Twas true: had I known of the danger, I would have insisted on going with Noni to the *seigneur*'s orchards, in an effort to protect her; I would not have permitted her to climb into that cart, to enter that jail alone. And so I persisted:

"Must you be here? I can come to you, bring Justin and Mattheline, and we will find a way to free you, we will find a way. . . ."

"Look into your heart," she said, and for a moment she appeared infinitely young; I saw her as she must have been as a young woman, with her hair glossy and dark, her lips full and crimson, her entire being beautiful. And I wept bitter tears.

"Ah," said Noni, "you see, you cannot deny the Goddess either. She has told you what must happen."

"But I cannot bear to let them harm you. Surely," I whispered, "surely there must be another way."

"Indeed there is, and you know as well as I where the path of safety leads. To the eventual deaths of us all, my child. To the extinction of the Race, which will lead in time to the destruction of all men. How should we live, knowing that a few years of our happiness was purchased at such a price?" And she put a hand, warm and firm, against my damp cheek—I tell you, that touch was no dream, for I felt it, as surely as I feel the pain from the torturer's beating now. "I am happy with my choice. Indeed, I made it the day you were born, when the Goddess showed me my destiny, and yours. Yours is the harder, Sibilla; for you must now learn to become more than human." She paused and withdrew her hand. "And you must then find *him*—for only you can save him from the Evil that threatens; only you can show him how to truly begin as the two of you were meant. Once joined, God and Goddess are the greatest power of all, and no Evil can defeat them.

"Now hasten on your path," she continued, "and beware returning home, for your poor mother is now thoroughly in the Enemy's hands and a true danger to you; all your magic cannot save her. A blessing upon you, child, and all the Goddess's gifts; in you they will increase a thousandfold."

"I cannot leave you suffering so!" I insisted, but it mattered not; *she* had already left *me,* and I woke to find myself sitting in darkness, my lap filled with dead autumn leaves.

For three days, I made my way through the forests, judging my direction by the sun and the pull of my heart. They say the patriarch Jacob wrestled with God in the form of an angel; well, those days I wrestled with the Goddess after a fashion, praying fervently with each step I took, like a supplicant who grasps his benefactor's leg and will not let go until his request is granted. Of Noni, I sensed nothing—her magic, I supposed, to spare me further grief.

Until the afternoon of the third day. Fatigued, I had fallen asleep beneath a copse of oaks only to waken with a pounding heart as the Sight came full upon me.

I stood in the great square in the shadow of the Basilica Saint-Sernin. In that square, a berm had been built, and upon that berm had been erected stakes; and to those stakes, prisoners in chains were being led.

I let go a gasp, but was so stricken that no sound, no tears, came.

There were several prisoners being led out, I am sure; to their spirits I apologize for my lack of compassion and attention, for on that terrible day, I saw only one being dragged by her heavy iron shackles to her final destination:

Noni.

My precious Noni, all life and beauty stripped from her. Gone was the sturdy matron I had known; in her place was a feeble crone. Her long shining hair, ebony streaked with a few strands of silver, had been sheared away, leaving a ragged cap that had gone almost entirely white since I had seen her. Her cheeks were deeply sunken, for they had broken most of her teeth, and her eyes were swollen shut so that she was quite blind. How I recognized her, I do not know, for even her body had been horribly altered: legs bowed, arms hanging useless.

All the prisoners were shackled to each other at ankles and wrists, and the guards urged them to keep moving; once, Noni, being the weakest, stumbled and fell. The guard lifted her to her feet, then bludgeoned her across the back, which almost caused her to fall again.

When at last she was unchained from another prisoner and ordered to kneel at the stake, she sank down with a profound sigh of acceptance—as if the worst of her suffering was now past, and what remained a mere formality. Two executioners had already been moving among the other prisoners; now one came to Noni. With a key, he loosened one of her ankle shackles, and situated her so that the stake was between her shins before relocking the shackle. He did the same with the chains at her wrists, loosening them, drawing her arms behind her (so that she grimaced in agony) and again refastening the shackles.

This made escape impossible—even for someone strong—but this was not enough, for there was still the chance that she could faint or surrender, sag forward into the flames, and die very quickly. To prevent this, the executioner bound her torso several times with rope, to hold the

spine straight and ensure that death would come well after the agony of
the fire.

Once he had finished, the second executioner arrived and encircled
my kneeling grandmother first with kindling, then logs to make certain
of a hot, fast-burning blaze.

As he did so, Noni began to chant:

> *Diana e la bona Dea*
> *Diana e la bona Dea*

The words were slurred, indistinct, but I strained until at last I
understood. She continued to repeat it proudly—a magical chant, perhaps, and indeed a declaration, one she had never before felt free to
utter in public, or even in her own home.

The crowd finally understood, too, and began to boo; someone
hurled a rock, which grazed Noni's cheek. She smiled, revealing
bloodied gums, and sang weakly on:

> *Diana is the good Goddess, the Holy Mother*
> *All hail, Diana, la bona Dea!*
> *She Who has always been*
> *The Mother of God*

A second stone was hurled, then a third; both missed. The gendarmes waved swords threateningly at the perpetrators; the people settled at once, though some continued to jeer at Noni's intolerable
blasphemy.

Ana Magdalena, however, seemed not to hear them. Still chanting,
she lifted her face toward heaven; gruesome as her battered visage
seemed, it was nonetheless radiant.

Then she turned her face toward one of the clerics who sat watching
on a nearby platform. I tried to make out his features, but his figure was
cloaked and hidden in shadow.

Ana Magdalena sang to him:

> *Diana e la bona Dea,*
> *Diana e la bona Dea*
> *Domenico, you who broke the glass so long*
>   *ago in the cathedral*
> *You the treacherous breeze at the baby's*
>   *birth*
> *You the crow on that cold summer morn*
> *You think your hate has finally won*
> *Do you not see? It has only allowed Love*
>   *to win again, to become*
> *Stronger than before.*
> *This is Our victory, not yours.*
> *Turn your heart to the Holy Mother*
>   *once more and find peace . . .*

What can I say about death?

We have been told of saints and heroes who, pierced by arrows, inverted on crosses, plucked clean of their eyes, do not cry out, but greet their ends blissfully, their faces agleam with rapture. I tell you now that these are but tales, that there is in a painful death neither dignity nor mercy, gallantry nor beauty; we mortals go screeching like swine.

So it was my Noni went too—at first. For once the kindling caught in earnest, the flames licked the prisoners' feet. Most began screaming at once, but not until the kindling grew hot and the logs began to catch did Noni surrender her chanting and let go anguished shrieks.

Like Jacob, I seized the Goddess, and held Her fast, praying with every muscle, every bone, every shred of flesh in my being: *Take her pain. Take her pain, and give it to me.*

There was no magic to it: no charm, no spell, no chant, only pure will. Will coupled with love, and perhaps these are the greatest magic of all, for at once I was consumed by an agony beyond any I had ever known, and I pitched forward, screaming, to the earth, both glad for my swift answer and driven to madness by the pain.

We have all through ignorance or accident touched red-hot cauldrons; such is the pain that the afflicted arm or hand or finger, unable to bear it, at once pulls away. Afterward, the suffering is so acute that children learn at once never to repeat the error. How, then, shall I describe the sensation of immersion in fire? The body writhes perpetually, unable to escape from a pain that cannot be endured, a pain that blots out all thoughts, all emotions, all memory, until there is only the pain and no self, no world at all. . . .

My voice joined those of the others in an unceasing chorus of misery, as undergarments turned to ash and sailed into the air as glowing cinders, revealing the heat-reddened skin beneath. The fire consumed cloth up to the shoulders, then leapt past neck and chin to the scalp, where it erupted in a Pentecostal blaze. All hair vanished in that spectacular instant, leaving behind pink scalps that rapidly reddened, then paled with blisters, then blackened, only to slough away to redness again. . . .

But in the midst of my unbearable labor, I realized that my grandmother's voice was not among those screaming, and I squinted at her with streaming eyes.

Noni had become a living flame: not a charred, pathetic spectacle like the other prisoners, but a living embodiment of the Divine, a woman young, beautiful, strong, glowing incandescent, hair and flames together streaming about her shoulders, forming a golden halo. I realized I looked upon no saint, but the very Goddess in the flesh—the Goddess smiling, triumphant, and the tears of agony on my face turned to those of joy.

She spoke, in a voice that was also the loveliest music I have ever heard, to the Enemy who sat watching:

You think you have won, Domenico. But here is the magic: the victory is ours. . . .

How long my physical torment continued, I cannot say, for the time came when I was too weak even to writhe, to scream, to whisper, and I had become quite blind; the agony had become a deep ache in the center of my being as the internal organs began to cook.

But the moment came at last when my grandmother died—for at first the pain lifted abruptly; and then I felt her spirit pass. Indeed, I experienced a strange surge of electric warmth as though she had entered me.

She, and Something greater . . .

I must confess that at the time, I understood what had happened intellectually not at all; but my heart and intuition had understood entirely that Noni's sacrifice for me—and, in some way, my sacrifice for her—had been a necessary exchange, else I would have fought her death with my entire being. But that day I Saw clearly that the manner of her end was a great honor, a destiny she had been truly glad to fulfill; that she had died without pain, and triumphant.

The sensation brought with it acceptance, and peace, and as the last of the sun's rays colored the clouds coral, I felt comforted by the presence of the Goddess and Noni's joyful spirit.

But I am human, too; and as night fell, the sense of Noni and Diana eased, and grief came in their stead. Restless, I rose and began to run. I ran until the forest changed to mountain and back, until I could no longer move, but collapsed gasping upon stones and leaves and rich-smelling earth.

Destiny is sometimes bitter.

Above me, black-on-black clouds roiled and thundered, echoing mightily off the mountains. When at last the summer storm broke, I broke too, and with the rain, wept.

PART III

Michel

CARCASSONNE

October 1357

X I

After vespers Michel returned to Father Charles's room to find the priest Thomas waiting outside the door.

"Good news," Thomas said, though his hushed, glum tone signified anything but. Torchlight glittered off his high brow, to which stuck strands of pale hair, darkened a shade by perspiration. "I have just returned from the bishop. He has given provisional approval to your ordination, which shall be deemed to have occurred today; a letter stating such is being forwarded to the archbishop at Toulouse. It is all but done; and of course"—here his tone turned prideful—"Chrétien will give the final approval because I ask it."

Michel sighed, but there was no relief in it. Thomas would never have agreed to help had he known of Michel's intent concerning Sybille—*Mother Marie Françoise,* he corrected himself swiftly.

With his head, Thomas motioned at the door and said sadly, "I'm sorry to see he fares no better than my poor scribe; though, thank God, no others have fallen ill." He paused as they both looked inward at Charles, who lay still ashen and motionless against the pillows. "It is hard to see them suffer so; we must pray, Brother. We must pray sincerely." And he rested a hand briefly, awkwardly, on Michel's shoulder.

"At least he is no worse than last night," Michel said, though Charles certainly looked no better. It was impossible to guess whether he was gathering strength or dying, for he remained still as stone and just as gray; only the faint rise and fall of his ribs distinguished him from a corpse.

After a pause, Thomas turned to him. "The abbess. Did it go well with her today?"

Michel lowered his gaze. In truth, it had gone far from well; he had been intrigued and engrossed in her story—especially the tale of her initiation. It was only after leaving her cell that he realized that, by the Church's standards, it had been a boldly Satanic rite, and that she had confessed outright that her destiny was to work sexual magic with her "lord."

Yet he had been—and was—honestly moved by her recounting of her grandmother's death; he knew all too well the suffering the old woman, heretic or no, must have undergone, and it was clear that Sybille—that is, the abbess—had truly loved her and still felt great grief.

Abruptly, the jailer arrived to tell him eventide had fallen and Father Thomas had long ago left. Michel had quickly summarized to the abbess the essence of her heresy, and urged her to repent and accept Christ; she had answered him with silence.

Silence, and that magnetic gaze.

Then she had insisted that the next day, she would speak of her "Beloved"; Michel had again refused, pointing out that the investigation was of her, not anyone else—and that there was time only for her story.

Again, she had fallen silent, and would say no more.

Even now, he felt the same odd mixture of fascination and irritation, remembering how she had innocently referred to the "old knight" in her vision. A peasant she may have been born, but in Toulouse, where surely everyone knew of the Knights Templar. *Jacques,* she had called him; and surely she had heard of the martyred head of the order, Jacques de Molay.

What she was suggesting—that this order still existed, and that she had contact with it—was the purest heresy; for the Templars had practiced the most depraved and abominable sort of magic. Or so King Philip the Fair had proclaimed a century before, and on that account the order had been disbanded and de Molay (and any others who had failed to flee the country in time) executed at the stake.

And for her to weave into her story the ancient chieftain with the golden crown . . . Bear. *Artos.* Arthur . . . There had been a band of knights in that legend, too.

Madness at best, blasphemy at the least. Yet he could not help finding the story intriguing. . . .

With abrupt dismay, he censured that train of thought. At least her story displayed a woman of noble character and good heart—not to mention a determination that had led her from life as a serf to that of a powerful abbess. She reminded him much of the misguided Saul, a well-meaning soul who spent the first portion of his life persecuting Christians with great zeal.

Who was to say she could not be converted and become as Saint Paul—a great force for good within the Church?

"I cannot say how it went," he told Thomas, choosing his words carefully. "What the abbess tells me is not so much a confession as a tale of wild invention; but she has admitted she is not a Christian." He did not mention that he intended to use that admission to prove she was not *relapsa.*

Father Thomas gave the monk's arm a reassuring thump. "Continue your good work, Michel; if she feels she can trust you, she will eventually reveal enough to ensure her conviction. I knew I was right to have faith in you." He paused. "Rigaud also told me that Cardinal Chrétien is on his way here."

"Really?" Michel feigned curiosity at this unusual development. Technically, as head of the inquisition, Chrétien could seize control of any proceeding, and he had been the presiding cardinal at Mother Marie's arrest; but custom dictated that the matter should be dealt with by the local bishop—Rigaud.

Thomas gave a somber nod. "He will arrive the day after tomorrow. He is . . . most concerned to hear that Father Charles is ill, and eager to see that Mother Marie Françoise's case is handled properly. However, due to the growing unrest, Rigaud has ordered that the executions be carried out beforehand."

"Executions . . ." Michel echoed, stunned. "Thomas, surely you don't condone Rigaud's desire to ignore proper inquisitional procedure and execute a prisoner before guilt can be properly established."

Thomas's features grew taut with disgust. "You are a greater fool than I thought. How could you have been raised by Chrétien and still remain so utterly naive as to the political workings of the Church?" He paused. "The fact exists that the pope himself was threatened, and *that*—"

"That has yet to be proven," Michel countered, but before he could complete the sentence, Thomas said loudly, drowning out the monk's last words: "You *will* do as ordered, and find her guilty. Or your ordination will be revoked. Which shall it be?"

A long and hostile silence ensued, at the end of which Michel cast his gaze downward in feigned humility. "I will endeavor to work as swiftly as possible."

When night had fallen in earnest, Brother André came, and at his insistence, Michel was obliged to stay in the guest room adjoining Father Charles's, with accommodations far more comfortable than the monks' cells. The previous nights' lack of sleep and the stress of the day had removed all resistance to comfort; when Michel fell upon the soft feather mattress and cool, slow-sinking pillow, he fell soundly asleep.

And as he slept, he dreamed . . .

·   ·   ·

His cheek leaned against a firm shoulder covered in musty-smelling wool, and his face was turned toward a tanned and corded neck, one he clasped with small hands, a child's hands. He drew in an oddly familiar smell of sweat, sun-warmed hair, and horses. Strong arms bore him aloft as down a spacious corridor of stone they passed, the walls lined with gilded tapestries.

A servant with a sword at his hip preceded them; abruptly, the servant stopped at a tall, arching wooden doorway bound with black iron, and lifted a heavy wooden bolt. As the door swung open, he entered first, then gestured for the man holding the child to follow him inside.

Inside, a lady-in-waiting knelt, her silk-wimpled head bowed so low her face was eclipsed. The room was furnished with great chairs and a massive table, several silver candelabra, cushions of scarlet velvet, and more tapestries.

Two open archways led to other rooms, but the men were not interested in those; instead, the man holding the child tightened his grip and stood back while the servant drew his sword, then cautiously unbolted a smaller door that might have led to a closet. Only then did he venture a tentative step inside, and wave for the others to enter behind him.

The chamber was surprisingly larger than those preceding it, its walls whitewashed, wainscoted, and painted with delicate pale roses; one entire wall was hung with skeins of thick thread in scarlet, turmeric, indigo, and forest green. In a corner stood a large loom, on which was displayed a tapestry in progress: women plucking bright oranges from a tree. The smell here, other than a faint vegetal odor from the dyes, was marvelous: the stone floor was scattered with lavender, pennyroyal, rosemary, and the petals that had fallen from bowls of pink and white roses.

In the midst of it all, a woman sat, her head turned from them, at a spinning wheel. At the sound of their entry, she reacted not one whit—not until the man said: "Lady Beatrice. I have brought our son."

She turned toward them, her expression frighteningly slack—but at the sight of the child, it grew incandescent with joy. She was a beautiful woman, with features fine and even as a Roman statue, and skin just as pale and smooth. Her golden hair was braided and coiled at the ears, and her eyes were an amazing deep blue-green. She wore a shift of creamy wool beneath a kirtle of lavender silk.

Without a word, she rose from the loom, knelt, and held her arms wide; the boy impulsively pushed against his father's chest, wanting to run to her, but to his frustration, his father held on to him, and the servant stepped between the woman and her child.

"You know the rule, Luc," his father said. "You must stand next to me at all times. Understand?"

"I promise, Papa," the boy replied in a piping little voice; with ease, his father set him down, but rested one large hand upon his shoulder, as if ready to pull him back.

Maman tilted her head, sinuously, sinisterly, and beheld her husband with narrowed eyes lit by something predatory, wild; to the child Luc they seemed to glow like a cat's eyes at night.

At the same time, Papa spoke with forced cheer. "Luc, why don't you sing the song your uncle Edouard taught you this week?"

Slowly, the Lady Beatrice lowered her arms, with such unhappiness on her lovely features that the boy wanted to weep. At once Luc sang the requested song, a sad one of the Crusades, of a poor pilgrim entering a hostile land, perhaps never again to be seen:

> *Chanterai por mon coraige*
> *Que je vuil reconforter*
> *Ne quier morir n'afoler*
> *Quant de la terre sauvage*
> *Ne voi mais nul retorner*

As he sang in his fine high voice, he watched her expression grow more melancholy, then agitated; at last, to his horror, she began to cry, then sprang past the servant toward him.

At once Papa scooped the boy up out of the woman's reach. "That's enough. Your mother needs to rest." And he hurried out the door while the manservant held Maman at bay. Once the servant made good his escape, the door was bolted over her, but Luc could hear her moaning his name: "Luc, my Luc . . ." Never another word did she utter, but as his father bore him through the lady-in-waiting's chamber and out into the corridor, her voice rose to a feral howl.

"*Luc . . .*"

And Luc wept because he could not understand why life could not be sweeter and simpler, why his mother lived apart from them, why he could not run to her when she smiled at him and opened her arms. Wept, burrowing his face into his father's neck as he was carried out onto the covered pentice (its fireplace lit, warming the passageway) that connected the lady's chamber to the lord's. His misery was compounded by the realization that his father was brooding over something more than his tormented wife. Trouble hung in the air like smoke, and the child, being more sensitive than any adult, read eyes and face, hands and bodies, heard every word unsaid.

Though no one spoke to Luc of it, he knew the adults were anticipating a coming event: his father wore his best mantle, fastened with a gold and ruby brooch over a tunic of saffron silk. Luc, too, sported his finest clothing: a tunic and leggings that were already too short and a gentleman's velvet slippers with curling toes that were slightly too large.

A long journey through bitter rooms, then outside stairs. After a time, the child Luc found himself sitting in a vast high-ceilinged hall, at a long table set upon a platform that overlooked two dozen other tables filled with diners—lords and ladies, a hundred knights all dressed in clean white surcoats embroidered with a hawk and roses. At the head of the grand table sat his father, auburn-haired, with fierce eyebrows of such dark red it was almost black; Luc sat three chairs away, to his father's right.

He was small within his wooden chair, just able to reach the thick slice of bread that served as plate, and the cool silver goblet filled with hippocras, the castle's best spiced wine; he took a sip and smiled. A familiar sense of joy stirred within him at the smell of the food as it began to arrive: stewed eels and fish, roast mutton, hares grilled with vinegar and onions, peas with saffron, and a porray of leeks with ham, cream, and bread crumbs. Beside him, Nana cut up the meat with her knife and placed it on Luc's bread. Over the music of the harpers, she whispered: "Remember, now, to take small bites, and chew with your mouth closed—and please, this time remember to use your spoon for the peas and the porray."

At the sound of her voice, both familiar and strange, he glanced up: here was a matron, her iron hair braided and coiled beneath a wimple with a long, gossamer white veil tied tightly beneath her jaw to lift a double chin. Her mantle was a striking brocade of dark purple against lilac: *To hell with black,* Nana liked to say. *All my youth I wore widow's dress; now, I'm simply an old woman and will do as I please.* Her manner could sometimes seem hard, but her heart was soft as her plump, full-bosomed body; and Luc, who shared her bed and spent more time with her than with either parent, was grateful to be the object of her greatest affection.

"Nana," he mumbled happily at the sight of his grandmother. As he spoke, another voice at the table drowned him out.

"We have to set an example," the archbishop said. His eyes were blue with bloodshot whites, his face full and round. "We must remind the people in Languedoc that the Church no longer tolerates any form of heresy. And I think they want to be reminded. With all the sickness and poor crops lately, they need a reason, someone to blame. Who's to say it isn't God punishing us?

"Now, heresy is like a weed; it spreads swiftly, with its roots hidden. It was thought de Montfort killed all the Cathars, and that King Philip the Fair did the same for all the Templars. But in truth, they lurk among us. . . ."

From behind Luc, a familiar voice asked lightly, almost teasingly: "The Templars? I thought they were all dead or gone to Scotland."

"Uncle Edouard!" Luc cried, and before Nana could grab hold of his tunic, he whirled about in his chair, almost overturning it, and let himself be hoisted into his uncle's arms.

"Ugh! Edouard Luc! I do believe this is the last year I shall be able to lift you," Sir Edouard said. Were Luc's mother a man, she would appear as her twin Edouard did: with the same amazing malachite eyes and fine features, but with a squarer jaw, thicker eyebrows, and golden hair kissed with red, the color of beaten copper when it is new. Edouard placed his nephew back in the dining chair, then turned to his brother-in-law, who had risen.

"Seigneur de la Rose," Edouard said, and bowed formally, then, as Luc's father reached smiling for him, added: "Paul. How fare you, Brother?"

"Well," Paul replied as the two embraced with deep affection; then Edouard drew back for an instant and searched his brother-in-law's eyes for an answer—one clearly negative, for Paul's gaze was evasive, defensive. A dark glimmer of disappointment passed swiftly over Edouard's face. He sat himself at once, and said, "My apologies, Your Holiness. Pray continue. . . ."

So the archbishop did: "It was the Templars, you see, who brought the Devil's own magic from Arabia, when ostensibly they were to protect pilgrims and fight the Saracens in the Holy Land. Yes, some of them were noble, in the beginning, and sacrificed themselves to regain the Temple in Jerusalem for Christendom. But the truth of it is . . ." And here the old man leaned forward, his voice dropping to a near-whisper. "Some of them discovered beneath the Temple magical documents, writ by Solomon himself; and with them, a source of inestimable power. And what they learned, they shared with the Jews and the witches. It is part of the worldwide conspiracy of evil."

"But the witches," Nana said politely. "I didn't know they learned magic from the Templars. I thought theirs came from the old pagan ways before the Romans."

"Some of it does," the archbishop allowed. "But women, as the witches mostly are, are fickle, and just as they will be fickle, flitting from pagan god to god, and spell to spell, so they will happily steal magic from any available source. It all comes from one, though: Lucifer, and so he is their god, regardless of the name by which they invoke him. And though the Templars much preferred their Satanic orgies with men alone, the Templars and the witches had—and still have—the opportunity for . . . how shall I put this delicately? Interaction."

Luc's father kept his eyes upon his plate and ate during the archbishop's statement; at its end, he looked up, his gaze direct and intense, and said pleasantly, with neither conviction nor disapproval: "Indeed."

Nana smiled up over at the archbishop and said nothing, but Luc felt her tense beside him and realized that she—and his father—disliked the man intensely. Why were they all pretending to agree with the archbishop, when they disagreed so strongly?

Abruptly, the archbishop was processing through the great hall past genuflecting diners, with Paul de la Rose at his side. Nana and Edouard followed at a respectful distance, with Luc between them, the child's right hand grasping his grandmother's, his left his uncle's.

From Edouard's hand, Luc sensed warmth, strength, and a tinge of sorrow—which meant he had been to visit his twin Beatrice before coming to dinner. Edouard's love for his sister was fierce, as was his love for her only child; and Luc, knowing this, returned that love with equal fervor.

Despite any sadness, Edouard's touch was always the same: filled with joy. Not a wild, wavering euphoria, but the determined, steady happiness, even in the face of tragedy, of a man who knew what he believed—and who believed in something wondrous and beautiful.

Today, even that joy was dampened by some unspoken horror—the same unspoken dread that emanated from Nana's soft hand. They were putting on a flawless performance for the archbishop and the assembled diners, these adults, but they could not fool a child.

Suddenly, they were outside: Luc, sitting on a gilded saddle in front of his father, astride Paul's fine black stallion. A fair distance in front of them, aides settled the archbishop in a magnificent four-wheeled *chariot*, its wood covered by white and gilded leather into which symbols of Christianity and the archbishop's family crest had been elaborately tooled. A matching tapestry of white brocade embroidered with gold thread served as canopy while the old man settled his frail bones against cushions of scarlet velvet.

Swift images:

A noisy public square, the buzz of a thousand voices. His father's whisper in his ear:

"Remember always what you are about to see and hear; and let it remind you, in all circumstances, to guard your tongue."

Ascending a wooden platform, where four men waited: two vicars, a monk, a priest named Pierre Gui. Beneath them, in the cleared center of the square, wooden posts protruding from the ground.

The sky, bright and blue and as piercing as his father's gaze. Luc shivering as he clutched his father's hand and watched the flames, flames the color of blood, flames that transformed living human beings to charred, blackened stumps.

Luc had turned his face away, but his father firmly guided the boy's chin back without a word.

So he had watched: and when everyone had finally died, and the gendarmes had broken the charred bodies into pieces with pokers so that they would burn more quickly, he had returned with his father and uncle to a small supper at the castle. He was able to eat but little, and that he vomited.

Dizzy and weak, he curled up in a favorite spot: a window seat in the solar that offered a strategic view of the castle grounds, and the land beyond its walls. The sun had heated the small room between the lord's and lady's quarters; and as Luc drowsed there, he heard his father and Uncle Edouard arguing:

You said nothing, then, to the boy.

He is my son, Edouard, not yours—or your precious Templars'.

His uncle's voice, dropping low but still audible: *For God's sake, Paul, what if the servants hear? Besides, names are irrelevant: I've told you, I'm no more a Templar than a Cathar or a Moor or a Christian—maybe I'm all four, or none at all. The truth is the truth, regardless of what label you put on it. And the truth is your son—*

My son, *remember.*

A sigh. *Yes, your son, Paul. Yours, and Beatrice's. And he cannot escape his—*

Papa's voice, rising with anger: *Would you have him go mad, as his poor mother did? Or be roasted like a suckling pig, as those poor fools were today?*

Edouard, calmly. *Without your help, Brother, and mine, he might well go mad; and without counsel, he may well use his talents unwisely, in the presence of the wrong people.* Quickly now, and louder, as Paul made a noise as if to interrupt: *Oh, yes, he is talented—as heavily as his poor mother is, however much you may hate the fact.*

Paul: *How can you say such a thing? He has shown not an inkling—*

You have not seen it because you do not wish to see it. A long pause, then Edouard added: *Paul. Let me have the boy. Let me train him. It isn't safe here, not with Beatrice as she is. She serves as our adversary's ears and eyes, and the longer the boy is here, the graver the danger that the Enemy might find a way for her to—*

From his father, a sudden hoarse sob. *How can I let him go, seeing what his mother has become? Tell me, what has she done to deserve such torment? I ask myself, is it a punishment from God? Simply madness? Or—*

I cannot say the why, Edouard countered. *But I can say the who.*

Abrupt silence.

One of us, Edouard said; and though Luc did not understand the significance of the words, his skin prickled.

One of the Race? No. No, impossible. How could one so gifted become so corrupt?

It has happened, Paul.

No, no; it is my fault, I tell you. We pushed her, you and I. She has always been sensitive. Perhaps it is no attack at all. Too sensitive—you, her own twin, know that better than anyone else. I have done what you have asked, always, what you and she said was my destiny—and look at what it did to her! All the visions, the magic, finally drove her to madness.

Edouard, soothing: *Those with the greatest gifts are at the greatest risk. I should have sensed something, should have realized her own fear would overwhelm her. I should have forbidden the two of you to work outside my presence—or at the very least, should have coordinated the day and hour when distance separated us. We all made mistakes: you, Bea, and most of all, myself. But Bea comes naturally by her talent, and while on rare occasions, those heavily gifted fall into insanity, I know now how we could have prevented it. The boy can be carefully trained so it will not happen to him. It is his destiny, Paul, just as it was Bea's destiny to bear him for the good of the Race. It would be a tragedy if we did not now—*

A loud clatter of metal striking stone; perhaps a goblet of hippocras being hurled against a wall. Luc flinched as, on the other side of the wall, his father shouted: *Destiny be damned! There can be no greater tragedy than this!*

Silence a time, and then Paul's voice again, suddenly quiet and sorrowful: *She is a jewel, Edouard, a precious gem, the love of my life. How can you speak to me of destiny when she sits nearby, trapped behind walls and bolts to keep her from harming herself or her son, suffering God knows what manner of mental torment? What care I for the Race when my Beatrice is lost to me?*

Give me the boy, Edouard said firmly. *Even if my sister is beyond saving, we can still help the child.*

Paul, hoarse: *No. Do not presume to ask, Edouard. I have lost my wife. Luc is all that is left to me.*

And ignoring who and what he is will not change things, Brother. Fate will find him, whether he is prepared for it or not. Edouard paused, then spoke again, his tone ever calm, reasoning. *Give me the boy.*

No.

Give me the boy.

Give me the boy. . . .

Luc lapsed into delirium; perhaps he cried out, for he remembered his father's worried face above him, then Edouard's, then Nana's. He tossed, agonized, in the bed he usually shared with Nana.

And tormented—not so much by the unbearable memory of the suffering he had witnessed, but by the terror that he was doomed to become as his mother.

That, and the recollection of a glimpse of another child, as he had stood upon the platform, looking down at the living flames: A dark-haired peasant girl, hair in a fat braid, dirty bare feet balancing on a cart's edge as she screamed . . . then fell backward and lay still, as if struck dead. A small commotion had ensued as her family scrambled to reach her, then lifted her back into the cart; they had left the public burnings at once—with difficulty, given the size of the crowd.

Why Luc should have noticed this at all remained a mystery, for the one small cart was one of many in a crowd of a thousand peasants and merchants, and he and his father, the *grand seigneur,* were separated from the commoners by the execution berm and the flames.

Yet, in the aching waves that swept over him, Luc relived the moment again and again, as if he had been next to her and not seen it from afar: her black eyes, wide and anguished, her parted lips, her tanned arms flailing in an effort to keep her balance. . . .

Then the scream, the plunge backward, the fall. And, as the crowd parted, her silent form . . .

On his sickbed, Luc thrashed about, haunted by the peasant girl. He found himself desperate to save her, to find her, to know whether she still lived. Of all the curious, cold onlookers in the crowd, he knew that she had felt, as he had, the suffering of those in the flames; she had understood, as he had, the full horror of what occurred there.

And he had thought, *Of everyone here, she is most like me. And if she is dead, then I shall die, too. . . .*

He asked the faces hovering over his bed—Papa, Edouard, Nana—if any of them had seen the little girl who had screamed and fallen from the cart. None of them had, and each of them had smiled patronizingly at his real distress, then tried to distract him from it; he was too young to label their condescension for what it was, but it infuriated him nonetheless. For he had thought that if he could perhaps learn her name he might find her, might content himself that she had recovered and was well.

And in the night, the monk Michel half woke briefly, his mind still tangled in the dream, his heart welling with a satisfaction so deep it brought tears:

Sybille. Her name is Sybille. . . .

Almost at once, he fell into another dream:

A year later, perhaps two, the child Luc woke in a vast bed, one so tall that when he placed his legs over the edge, his feet dangled a precarious distance from the floor. He half slid, half leapt down to the cold stone, and walked outside his nursery onto the covered pentice, cold now with the onset of winter, even though the fire was lit. Calm, yet driven, he felt as though someone had taken hold of his heart and tenderly but surely guided him by it—from his bed, onto the pentice, down the corridor past the sleeping sentinel at the entrance to his father's chambers.

Surprisingly, the door was ajar—just enough for a child to enter, as if someone had conspired to allow Luc passage.

Inside, his father Paul lay alone upon the great feather bed, covered by bearskins and blankets of fine wool; a dying fire colored the scene a faint orange. In a bedside chair, the loyal manservant Philippe sat in attendance; in another, Nana—both snoring with the abandon of old age.

Luc moved stealthily to the bed and, on tiptoe, craned his neck to see his father. The *grand seigneur*'s face was frighteningly pale and drawn; droplets of sweat glistened upon his brow, in the gold-red stubble on his cheeks; it was a stern face, the forehead furrowed deep in a scowl even in unconsciousness.

Then Luc's father stirred and let go a moan—low, weak, anguished. He was in pain, terrible pain; despite the physician's efforts, the gaping wound in his leg had become sore infected, and was expected to kill him.

Pierced clean through by a lance, his thigh was, at a jousting tournament to honor the king. Most skilled and experienced of all the knights there, Paul had been chosen the king's favorite—yet he had fought without heart. . . . *Almost,* the servants had whispered, *as if he had wanted to die.*

Pity, compassion, and adoration all surged through Luc so strongly he felt for an instant he scarce could stand, and before he realized his intent, he had crawled up onto the bed and pulled back the blankets to reveal his father's wounded thigh, shrouded in damp dressings and hard swollen to twice its normal size. What skin the bandages did not cover was a taut, shiny violet.

The sight was horrific, not to mention the smell—of acrid mustard, rotting meat, bitter sweat—but Luc felt no fear, only an instinct that provoked him to lay his small hands upon the hot, damp poultice.

At once, he felt an odd sensation—of heat, of the buzzing of a thousand bees—surge through his body and pass through his hands into his father's injury. His palms grew increasingly warmer, and the vibrations stronger, bringing with them a sense of bliss so profound that he became immersed in it and lost all sense of time. Indeed, the boy remained there until the leg beneath his hands moved; startled, Luc glanced up to see his father gazing at him, eyes widened with astonishment.

"Luc," he whispered, and pushed himself up slowly on his elbows. "Luc, my God . . ."

The boy followed his father's gaze to the bandaged leg—swollen no more, the flesh yielding to the touch and now a healthy hue.

The child clapped his hands and let go a laugh of delight; yet shyness kept him from throwing his arms around the *grand seigneur*'s neck. At once, the old servant Philippe snorted loudly and twitched in his chair, near waking; Luc's father lifted a finger to his lips, then signaled for his son to quietly crawl forward and embrace him.

So the boy did, clasping the man's neck and pressing his soft child's cheek against his father's weathered, stubbled one. To Luc's joy, his father wrapped his arms tightly about him.

"My son, forgive me," Paul said; the elder's cheek grew suddenly damp with tears. "I have wronged you by trying to forget the truth, out of sorrow over your mother. I had hoped ignorance would protect you from your heritage—but I can see it will overtake you with or without my help. Better it be with, my boy. Better it be with. . . ."

In the darkness, the monk Michel pushed himself upright, hands sinking deep into the soft mattress. The onslaught of images—from another man's mind, another man's dreams—left him dazed and violated.

"*So,*" he whispered. "She thinks to bewitch me. . . ."

The next morning, he headed earlier than his wont to the prison. As the jailer escorted him back to the abbess's cell, the door opened from the inside, and Father Thomas emerged, the hem of his satin aubergine robe rustling against the earthen floor.

"Brother—or should I say Father?—Michel," Thomas said smoothly, and smiled . . . but something threatening lurked behind that smile.

"What brings you here so early, Father?" Michel asked, managing to keep his features stern, though the sight of Thomas provoked anxiety. Had he gone to interrogate the abbess himself, discovered her heresy, and that there was already enough evidence to deem her guilty—which would also show that Michel was slowing the proceedings to protect her?

The smile vanished. His expression opaque, Thomas tilted his head and regarded Michel intently. "I was curious to see how the abbess was doing. She will not speak to me, of course, but it does seem that you have chosen not to make further use of the torturers." His tone was soft and even, but Michel sensed the ever-so-faint danger in it.

Before Thomas could ask the obvious question, Michel stated firmly,

"There was no need, Father. As I told you last night, she spoke quite freely; I shall soon have all the evidence I require."

"Mind that you do," the young priest said in the same unsettlingly quiet voice, "for to our thinking, you now stand in Father Charles's stead. No doubt you were present with him during his audience with Bishop Rigaud; no doubt you understand we intend to deal with any . . . missteps in the abbess's interrogation. We will tolerate no delays, no misguided ideas of mercy."

Without any change in expression, Michel gave a slow nod. "Censure is a most reasonable penalty for a miscarriage of justice."

He had not finished uttering the last word when Thomas countered swiftly: "We do not speak of such mild things as censure or defrocking, Brother . . . or even the far more serious punishment of excommunication. Perhaps Bishop Rigaud did not make the Church's feeling clear: those in sympathy with Mother Marie Françoise are, like her, in league with the Devil; and like her, they shall suffer the same penalty."

Again, Michel reacted outwardly not a whit; but in his mind's eye, he saw a mallet arcing through the air to come down, ringing, upon a stake driven into Carcassonne's rich soil. "I understand."

"Good," Thomas said. "And I hope that you are take this most seriously . . . as seriously as you take your own life."

He took his leave then with that same bright and shallow smile, and headed down the corridor toward the communal cell. Michel watched him go.

Inside her cell, the abbess sat upon the wooden bench. Her face, while still swollen, was less puffy, and the bruises had darkened; her once hidden eye was now mostly visible, as dark and shining as the other.

The instant the jailer closed the door behind them, Michel said bitterly: "Tell me why I should not convict you now, Mother. I have heard your testimony, in which you freely confess to engaging in witchcraft. I have given you a chance to repent and receive God's forgiveness, which you refused. Why should I listen to you any further?"

"You should not," she answered softly.

"In addition, you have tried your best to bewitch me. You have sent me the dreams of another man, a heretic influenced by the Devil." He paused, realizing finally what she had just said, and sat in confused silence. He felt as though both his mind and his heart had been riven. As a Christian, he knew intellectually that her tale of magic was heresy, and her candid talk of sexual matters unchaste. But he could not deny the strong emotions, both sacred and profane, that drew him to her. Despite her confessed evildoing, he still regarded her as a holy woman, a true healer sent from God; at the same time, he continued to be filled with a profound lust such as he had never felt—one mixed with a love pure and holy.

"I did indeed send you those dreams," the abbess said. "They tell the story of my Beloved, Luc de la Rose. He was no heretic, but a hero. He healed rather than destroyed, and in the end, sacrificed himself for love. Any suffering I undergo is nought compared to his; and I will see his story told. If you will not hear it by day, then you shall dream it by night." She paused. "You gave me no recourse." Then her tone softened again. "My hearing is quite good. I know what Father Thomas said to you in the doorway. It seems he has threatened your life, no?" And when Michel did not reply, she continued: "My poor brother, your destiny is linked to mine. There is no way around it. Here, let me refuse to repent: again and again and again. Now, you have given me several chances as the law allows, and you need feel no guilt at condemning me. My fate was determined before I was brought to this prison; but yours lies in your own hands. Go, and tell Father Thomas you have obtained a conviction."

Michel considered her words; it seemed logical to condemn her. She was a confessed witch, she had refused to repent, and by following the law's letter, he could save his own life. And yet . . . Yet he could not deny that, despite her story, her every action showed her to be the saint he had expected her to be. Even now, she was concerned for his welfare, seemingly fearless concerning her own fate. Heretic or no, there was much that was *good* in her; and even if there were not, she deserved, as did all God's children, the opportunity to come to know Him before her death.

And he still could not rid himself of the hope that, once she was converted, Rigaud might be swayed to mercy.

He drew in a breath and said, matter-of-factly, "Mother, we haven't time for such debate. Pray, continue with your story—and quickly."

Her lips were quite too swollen to smile; but her eyes conveyed the gesture as she began to speak. . . .

PART IV

Sybille

CARCASSONNE

Fall 1348

XII

I slept where I fell, exposed to the rain and the animals, and woke wet and shivering to a humid dawn. Skirts damp and heavy about my legs, I began again to walk. My destination was near; indeed, I sensed I should find it that very day.

I wandered through forest and meadow, deserted fields and an empty ghost of a village. There, outside a small hostel I found hanging from a tree an odd sight: the white habit of a nun, rustling gently in the breeze. No doubt it had been left there months before by those who had nursed its wearer, now perished along with all the others, for it was stiff, as though it had endured much sun, wind, and rain.

But it had also escaped the storm I had encountered the night before; and so I quickly shed my damp clothes and replaced them with the habit, veil and all, glad not only to be dry once more, but also to be disguised.

My increased confidence led me to walk where the ground was more even, and cleared: eventually, I made my way onto a path leading toward inhabited villages and a city—from the look of its famous wooden ramparts, Carcassonne.

Despite my sorrow and fatigue, I smiled faintly at the sight. *Carcassonne, a place of safety.* I would be able to find food there—for I was ravenous—and shelter. My gaze focused on the city, I quickened my pace and moved ahead—almost colliding with a great dark figure who stood in my path. I glanced up and saw a stocky monk in a black robe, its hood lined with white: a Dominican.

An inquisitor. There was something amiss about his appearance, something I could not immediately identify; despite my awareness that the Goddess was with me, I could not stifle a sudden thrill of fear. Had he been sent by the Enemy to find me?

"Good afternoon, Sister," said he with a smile. "Tell me, what has led you to be traveling alone in this part of the wood?"

I thought, *If I run, that will only give him cause for alarm. He is merely a monk; he has not come from Toulouse, and he does not know me.* So I replied evenly, "Good Brother, I might ask you the same."

"Ah," he said, and his fat ruddy cheeks rose further, almost eclipsing his eyes, "but I am not alone."

The proof of that immediately apprehended me: strong hands seized my wrists, forcing me backward against the body of another unseen man, at least as tall and strong.

I kicked and yelled out for aid. For an instant, I succeeded in half turning to find my captor likewise wearing the Dominican habit.

They had caught up to me at last, I decided; the Evil had sent them, and I was lost—but I would never surrender. I sank my teeth into a hard, muscled forearm until the man behind me groaned and let go of my left hand.

The first Dominican caught it and held it firmly.

"No purse," the other reported, to which his partner growled.

At once I heard the thunder of hoofbeats and the creaking of wheels, and a woman's voice crying: "Off! Off, you brigands! You dogs!—though by no means *canis Domini*. I have found the poor monks from whom you stole those clothes, and they stand ready to accuse you! Off, I say!"

The crack of a whip; and again. And again.

Something hard—a stone?—struck my head, and suddenly I was falling backward, backward, with no arms to catch me; only the cool soil, the hard stones, which knocked the wind from my lungs. The monks disappeared from my sight.

In their place, parenthesized along its periphery by the boughs of tall trees, was the sky. It was bright and blue, and a dry, insistent breeze dismissed the earlier clouds left from the storm.

At once, another face eclipsed the blue: a woman's, long and square and pale, encircled by a white wimple, crowned by a white veil. *Mother,* someone murmured behind her, and I knew that it was the Goddess. She was dressed exactly like me, and when our eyes met, hers were filled with such compassion that, grieving and dazed as I was, I began to cry.

"God has brought us both here," she said, and, wiping away my tears, smiled.

Her name was Mother Geraldine. In time, I would come to know it in entirety as Mother Geraldine Françoise, but that day I knew only what the other nuns called her. She helped me up into a large wagon with a canvas roof to shelter us from the sun. I have clear memories of that ride; of the donkeys' wheezing brays, of the constant rumbling and jostling in the cart that pained my head and my back, still aching from my fall. I remember the kindnesses of the women, how they offered me bread and a cup from which to drink, and let me rest my head upon their soft laps. Most of the time, they whispered prayers:

Hail Mary, full of grace; blessed art thou among women. . . .

The ride continued until dusk, when we stopped to make camp. Night followed quickly. I slept fitfully, and recall that Mother Geraldine spent a good deal of it watching over me in the wagon. The nuns had built a large fire, whose wavering light painted my benefactress's skin and white habit an ominous pale orange.

. . .

The next morning, the nuns traveled in silence; I vaguely recall that we arrived at a vast stone building that stank of death, and that I was helped to a bed, where I fell into a profound sleep.

At last I came to myself, fully awake—to the sight of a white-wimpled, black-veiled sister standing over me, her lips and nose obscured by a kerchief tied round her face. At the sight of me, the corners of her eyes crinkled and she clapped her hands, saying with muffled glee: "God and Saint Francis be praised! How do you feel, Sister?"

"Better," I croaked, wondering if the kerchief were a lingering apparition from the delirium, when I noticed that the peculiar, unpleasant odor—a faint undertone of what I had smelled in the goldsmith's wife's bedchamber—remained, and was apparently quite real.

I had no time to inquire after it—my nurse had left the room quickly, and returned, enthusiastic, with a bowl of soup.

She was a young, pleasant woman, and surprisingly talkative for one who had taken the habit. As I slowly ate, I learned from her my circumstances: that we were in a nunnery in Carcassonne, that her name was Sister Marie Magdeleine, that, yes, there had been some dead in the chamber next door, but they had been removed and that the other sisters were scrubbing the place down now, and the smell would soon be gone.

They had feared I might die from the blow inflicted by the robbers, as I slept overlong and could not be roused. Mother Geraldine, the most pious and compassionate of women, had spent last night praying at my bedside.

Weak though I was, I was lucid enough to start suddenly, and press my hands to my scalp, expecting to feel the long coiled braids that would expose me as a fraud. To my relief, I felt only the fine linen of the wimple covering my head; my veil had been neatly folded and rested in the corner.

If Sister Magdeleine had noticed my hair beneath the linen, she showed no sign of it, for she asked politely: "And how is it that you came to be alone in the wood, Sister?"

It is of course unheard of for a woman, especially a nun, to travel alone. My mind raced to find an explanation, but encountered none; after several seconds of staring at her, I said, "I do not know."

"You do not remember?" A crease appeared between Sister Marie Magdeleine's eyebrows. "Ah, poor thing! Who knows what those brigands did to you—or your other sisters! Was it the blow to the head? Or perhaps—" This last thought struck her as too horrible even to voice.

"I do not remember," I echoed her swiftly, immediately grateful that she had just provided me with an explanation to cover my many failings.

But it could not explain my hair. Thus it was, when she left me at vespers to pray, I slipped off the wimple, took the small knife that rested beside the plate of leeches next to my cot, and in the flickering candlelight cut off the hair that had grown untouched since my birth. I fed it to the flame, watching it singe and curl upward into nothingness, recoiling at the horrid smell and thinking of Noni.

The next day, I was stronger, well enough to get up and make use of the chamber pot in the corner—though not of a mind to attend prayers in the chapel with the other nuns, for such would reveal my ignorance and atrocious Latin. My caretaker, Magdeleine, did not spend the day beside me, but came only to bring and remove my meals.

It was during one of her absences that the abbess's head appeared in the doorway. Smiling, she asked: "May I come in?"

"Of course," I said, moving to rise—for she was clearly of noble birth, and I nothing but a peasant girl. But she gestured insistently for me to sit, and so I did, propped against the pillows. She took a most informal seat at the foot of my cot.

Of Sister Magdeleine, I had intuited that she was a sincere girl, one who meant no harm to anyone; the Sight had told me as much just sitting next to her. But the abbess—

Of the abbess's heart, I could sense nothing, See nothing, as surely as if an invisible wall had been erected about her—this despite the great affection and trust I had felt for her the night she had rescued me. Perhaps I had been discovered, I told myself; perhaps she or one of the other sisters had seen the gold talisman round my neck when they attended to my shoulder. Perhaps one of them had seen my long hair before I managed to cut it.

Apparently unaware of my discomfort, the abbess said kindly: "My name is Mother Geraldine Françoise. And yours . . . ?"

"Marie," I said automatically, then amended: "Sister Marie . . . Françoise." I dared not give the name Sybille; Marie was ubiquitous enough to be safe, and in my dread, I repeated the second half of the abbess's name, quite by mistake.

But her eyes widened with delight. "Sister Marie Françoise! At last, we are formally introduced!" And with impulsive affection, she seized my hands—my rough, callused hands, and hers so smooth, the nails short and clean—and gave me a kiss upon each cheek. "Forgive me, dear Sister," she continued, "for not coming to you earlier to introduce myself and explain who we are, but as you were weak, I thought it best not to come to you directly after removing the dead—"

"The dead," I interrupted, remembering the terrible smells the first night I had spent here. "Yes, Sister Marie Magdeleine told me someone had died in the next room."

"In more than one room, I dare say. More than sixty Franciscan sisters, all taken to Heaven by the pestilence," said she, matter-of-factly, and at my expression, explained: "There was no one to bury them, and so, with the dispensation of the bishop, we are doing so ourselves—with the help of some very kind Benedictine monks, the few of them God left. I am so sorry for the smell; but soon, our first task will be done, and we can set to the second task of repopulating the convent.

"Which is why I have come to you today." She paused, and tilted her head downward so that I could barely see the eyes beneath her lids. Her smile faded. "Sister Marie Magdeleine said that you had difficulties with your memory yesterday. Has it returned to you?"

"I am sorry, no . . ."

"But you remember your name. Is there anything else you recall? The cloister from which you came, perhaps? The sisters traveling with you?"

"I . . . No. I am sorry."

"Clearly you have come a long way; you wear the habit of a Franciscan, that is true, but there are few of us left these days. I think the nearest cloister now is in Narbonne, but news travels so slowly after the pestilence; I do not even know if any of the sisters there survived." And she lifted her head, showing me her long face and steady, penetrating eyes; the intensity of her gaze was disconcerting.

"Narbonne?" I hesitated. If I were going to survive, I had to be forceful in maintaining the lie Sister Marie Magdeleine had offered me. "Mother, I do not wish to be difficult, but I simply cannot remember."

"Ah," she said, her tone too guarded for me to interpret. "Well, I will write to the sisters there and ask them whether they know of a Sister Marie Françoise . . . although it is a common enough name in this order. It is the least I can do to help you find your rightful place." She rose to leave—but after she had turned her back to me, she paused a time, then turned again to face me. I kept my expression carefully neutral.

"Sister . . ." Her tone and manner were hesitant. "I do not mean to be presumptuous, but when I saw a Franciscan nun, and a professed apostolate at that, I could not help but believe that God had intended for our paths to cross. All I have here are postulants and novices, none professed; I need an experienced sister to help organize and teach the others.

"Will you help me until we can find your home? For one so young, barely at the age of consent, and already professed—clearly, God has moved powerfully in your life. Will you stay with us?"

It was my turn to hesitate. Unlettered as I was, I knew next to nothing of nuns, except that they could read, for I had (on those few times when Maman had dragged us all to pray at Saint-Sernin when we had other business in Toulouse) seen the veiled sisters in the sanctuary, following along in their little books while another sister read. At that moment, I could not have told a Cistercian sister from a Dominican, or a poor Clare from a Fontevrist. Yet I had no choice other than to rely on this woman's good graces for the time being; the Goddess had led me here for a purpose, and here I would remain so long as it was safe.

"Mother Geraldine," I said, with some honesty, "I am afraid. I know not who I am; I can barely remember my Latin; I fear I might not even be able to read, or remember all my prayers. You have been so kind to me . . . I cannot refuse to repay such charity. But how can I be of use to you when I cannot even recall the experience you desire?"

"Do not fear," she said gently, and with her fingers lightly touched my cheek in reassurance. "Time will return your memory to you; and even if it does not, I can be of assistance to you. We can begin your lessons as soon as this afternoon, and have you lettered within a month. I remain convinced that you were sent here to help me, not the reverse."

I smiled, for the moment somewhat relieved. For I knew that if I remained here a time, learned to read and write and effect the manners of a well-born lady, the inquisitors would never recognize me as the peasant girl I had been.

If I could manage to keep the nuns fooled as to my identity. This mother superior seemed a highly intelligent woman. There might have been genuine compassion in her large eyes—but there was also shrewdness, a shrewdness I was convinced would someday look right through my disguise and see the liar there.

Within another day, I had recovered sufficiently to begin my life as a nun. It was more different than ever I could have imagined: I had always heard that it was a life of terrible privation, of fasting and flagellation, and cruel penances, of never-ending work.

And perhaps it was—for a noblewoman, but to the daughter of a villein, it was a life approaching luxury. I had my own straw mattress, my own cell, and enjoyed the unthinkable convenience of an inside *garderobe* located on the very floor where we sisters were housed. You are well-born, Brother: you cannot imagine how glorious it is to be freed from relieving oneself outside in the midst of winter.

The daily ritual was likewise comfortable. Five times a day we met in the sanctuary to chant in Latin, and to pray, and to hear a reading from the Gospels; once a day, a priest from town came to celebrate the Eucharist.

The remaining hours were given to personal prayer, the morning and evening meals, work, and study. *Work*, they called it, though to me it seemed more recreation, compared to the work of the fields or midwifery: we tended the sick in that part of the great cloister turned into a hospital, with the help of a few lay sisters who, having been widowed by the plague, depended on the monastery for food and shelter. Since the population of poor in Carcassonne had already been decimated, there were few left to care for, even when Mother Geraldine opened one wing of the convent to those lepers who had survived the wrath of angry, plague-stricken mobs. Thus, each nun was required to spend only a few hours each day tending to the sick; and every sister worked the same number of hours.

Of all things new to which I adjusted, the equality among sisters was the most difficult: I often found myself beginning to curtsey to the high-born nuns upon greeting them, and it took some time for me to learn not to defer to them. This was the legacy of the good Saint Francis, who, though born the son of a wealthy merchant, treated all men—no matter how poor—as his betters.

And each afternoon I spent two hours, sometimes more, in secret with Mother Geraldine, learning my letters—in French, then in Latin. A miraculous thing, the written word: I had approached the first lesson in terror, for, being peasant and female, I thought myself perhaps too stupid a creature to learn. To my amazement, I took to the alphabet and its sounds quickly, and within little more than a week was able to sound out short words. The abbess attributed the swiftness of my learning to the stirring of my dormant memory, and I did nothing to disillusion her.

After the grief and terror I had experienced, the convent provided a pleasant haven. The regular rituals provided an outlet through which I could commune with the Goddess; and to an extent, they soothed my grief, for they were beautiful, and it is through the experience of beauty that we remember what was best and beautiful about the life of our lost loved one. If you had seen me at prayer, my expression calm, even serene, you would have thought that I was as good a Christian as the others.

But when, at the prescribed time, I knelt alone in my solitary cell, it was only in case I was seen by one of the others. And when, as a good nun, I murmured the rosary, my prayer was not only to the Mother of Jesus, but to the Mother of All.

Every day I prayed, and every day asked the same questions:

What is my destiny here?
When shall I find my Beloved?

Here, I knew, I would find the answers. My grandmother was dead, but she had planted a seed. In the safe and nourishing soil of the convent, it began to grow.

So I remained at the nunnery, living with the other sisters in the spirit of obedience, poverty, and chastity, as Saint Francis had bidden. Only so much time can be spent upon one's knees without reflection; only so often can one gaze upon the faces of one's sisters, rapt in prayer, without being similarly moved. I began to find peace at the convent. True, I never believed myself to have been born such a craven, wicked creature that a man should have to shed his blood for me; certainly, I could not worship any god that demanded such blood in order to spare the world an eternity of torment, or who judged such torment to be appropriate punishment for sexual peccadillos or failure to attend mass regularly.

But I began to suspect that God could be another name for the experience I knew as Goddess; I could see it upon Mother Geraldine's radiant face, could hear it in her exuberant voice when, at vespers, she spoke of the beauty of Brother Sun's rays streaming through the windows of the chapel, of how Saint Francis was right that the glory of Nature far transcended the beauty of any creation of man. All of earth is a magnificent cathedral, she said, and we the lucky souls who worship therein.

I could not disagree with such a statement; and I retired that night to my little cot knowing that the Goddess encircled me, protected me, dwelt within me.

But once I fell asleep, I dreamt of Jacob, his beard and long iron curls aflame, his right arm stretched out in supplication, saying: *The flames grow closer each day, my lady.*

The flames grow closer each day.

In the second year of my stay, I went to work as usual one mid-morning in the lazaret, accompanied by Sister Habondia. Habondia was a frail bird of a woman, with few teeth, bright, darting eyes, and a face furrowed with deep, drooping lines; I cannot honestly recall seeing her smile. She was a widow whose lips curled at the very mention of her children; she had been forced by them years before into the nunnery, and given her sour temperament it was not difficult to see why. I pitied her charges, for she attended them in surly silence, without sympathy, and on days when her mood was especially dark, I often heard her patients cry out at how roughly she bathed them or dressed their sores.

Ah, yes, I can see your discomfort at the mere mention of lepers; after so many years nursing them, I can no longer fear them as I once did. I, too, was terrified the first time Mother Geraldine bade me take care of them. Our makeshift hospital had a ward for lepers too sick to be cared for by their own, who lived in the hills outside the city and its villages.

But every nun I spoke with had little fear of contracting leprosy; many had nursed lepers for years and none had ever fallen prey to it. The secret, it seemed, was a basin of water, regularly refreshed, in which each sister washed her hands upon leaving the lazaret, and the special prayer to Saint Francis that was uttered over the water as it was drawn from the well. Francis, after all, had been a special friend to lepers; upon returning home from war before God called him to a life of poverty, he had encountered a leper upon the road. The poor afflicted creature had hidden his face beneath the dark cloak he was required to wear, and rung his bell to warn the saint away—but Francis, overwhelmed with compassion, had leapt down from his horse, embraced the suffering man, and left him happily dazed and with a sizable purse.

Certainly I was horrified the first time I entered the great chamber that comprised the lazaret. I had been raised to fear the afflicted: they had come only rarely to the outskirts of our village, when hunger drove them. I remember huddled forms draped in ragged gray cloaks, deformed feet and hands bound in rags, shadowed, marred faces lurking beneath hoods, bells and clappers sounding—and my mother pulling me along by the arm as we hurried toward the safety of the cottage, while my father tossed them spoiled fruit from a distance. I remember, too, the look on Maman's face when we went down to the river to wash laundry, and discovered upon a rock the gray-white, bloodless top half of a finger.

The first leper that I bathed was a well-born young woman who said that she had once been beautiful. She wept for shame as she removed the gray cloak that marked her as unclean, and I wept for pity: her face was scarcely recognizable as human, the bridge of the nose having caved in, and an egg-shaped mound of swollen, shiny white flesh erupting from the corner of her lip and extending upward to partially obscure her eye. She had come because she had lost the feeling in one foot—and with it, three of her toes—and could no longer walk; and, like most of the others, lived in terror of being discovered by the cityfolk and burned in retribution for the plague. Despite our ministrations, she died soon after, the gaping wounds left by the loss of her other toes having turned gangrenous.

How silent was that chamber, and muted the suffering: true, many of the afflicted suffered deformities of mouth or jaw that left them unable to speak, but the others had been silenced by shame. Most had been officially "buried"—that is, proclaimed dead, and had attended their own funeral rite at a church empty of all save the priest, who stood quite a distance away.

So it was with one of the men I tended that morning: an old peasant named Jacques, with a quick wit and an impossibly jovial spirit, given his circumstances. The disease had eaten away both his feet to the ankles, but he used his hand-carved crutches to move haltingly about and take himself to the *garderobe* (for he insisted he would rather die than piss himself in bed). This was remarkable because he had only his thumbs and no fingers, and a countenance so deformed any other person would not have made the journey for fear of being seen; the bridge of his nose had collapsed so deeply that he had had to cut away the rotting flesh and cartilage in order to expose the holes right in the skull, and so breathe. One of his eyelids had been eaten away, leaving the eyeball to dry out, then ulcerate in its socket.

All in all, Jacques's appearance was unquestionably grotesque, but he had been at the lazaret for five years, and I had grown so accustomed to him and the other hospital inmates that I saw beyond the disfigurement and could imagine the man he had been. Indeed, we had become fond of each other—on my part, because I half imagined that he was my father grown old, whom I was being allowed to nurse; and I believe he had a daughter, whom he could no longer see because of his disease. In that way, we comforted one another.

Every morning, he met me with "Good day, my dear Sister Marie! And how does God treat you?" and I would of course reply, "Well," and inquire as to his own well-being, to which he would answer: "Never better! To live such a life of comfort and leisure, and tended by such beautiful women—ah, it is a far more marvelous life than ever I dreamt of when I toiled in the fields! Never did I suspect that in my old age, I would be able to shit inside, just like a *grand seigneur.*" And he would smile with his misshapen lips to reveal gray, toothless gums, and I would smile in return as he proffered his sores to be cleaned.

Surely his wounds were as terrible as those of any of the others; indeed, his body had been most ravaged of all by the disease. But some-how he outlived all the others; somehow he managed to escape the curse of gangrene and certain death.

So, back to that particular morning with Sister Habondia. Our first task upon entering the hospital was to empty and clean the chamber pots at the pump in the nearby *garderobe.* Having accomplished that, we re-turned to the lazaret to clean those unfortunate few who were too crip-pled or too sick with infection to make their way to the chamber pots.

As I returned, I waited for Jacques's usual greeting; but that morn-ing he was ominously silent. Thus I went straight to my friend's side— and discovered, to our mutual embarrassment, that he had for the first time soiled himself. Had it been anyone else, I would not have felt the slightest discomfort; but this was Jacques, who prided himself on taking the chamber pot to others. I was worried that his disease had suddenly worsened; but he averted his eyes, apparently ashamed, and said not a word, even after I had brought a change of clothing for him.

This cast a pall over the morning. I tended my other charges less cheerfully than was my wont, while Sister Habondia did so with her ha-bitual, unpleasant muttering.

Perhaps an hour later, after I had begun to dress a grievously angry sore on the leg of an old lepress, I heard a noise—soft, like the muffled clearing of a throat, yet it also possessed an edge of keenest desperation.

Many in the ward groaned and coughed continuously; normally, I would not even have noticed such a faint noise. But something caused me to pause, wet rag in hand, basin on the floor at my knees, and turn my head.

Behind me, Habondia likewise knelt on the stone floor, tending to a leper's wounds. Just beyond her, Jacques lay on his straw mattress, hands clutching his throat.

At once I Saw—Saw with a compassion that beheld only Jacques and not me, not my own fears, not my own potential loss. Only Jacques, and the brave, loving soul he had remained under circumstances that had broken many a lesser man; only Jacques, and the strength and kindnesses he had shown not only his fellow lepers, but also his caretakers.

And I Saw, with utter clarity, his leprous tongue—which had come detached and now lay lodged in his throat.

"Sister!" I cried across the chamber to Habondia. Startled, she dropped her rag into the basin, splashing water, a darker stain upon her dark habit. "Tend to Jacques! His tongue!"

Still kneeling, she glanced over her shoulder and frowned down at Jacques, whose mouth now gaped silently.

"Hurry!" I cried, at the same time flinging down my own rag and struggling to my feet. "He has swallowed it! He is choking!"

So slowly did Habondia move, and so quickly did I that we both arrived at Jacques's bedside at the same instant, though she had been beside him and I at the other end of the chamber.

Upon closer inspection of the patient, Habondia threw up her hands in dismay, finally understanding what was happening; but, led by the Sight, I knew there could be no delay.

With one hand, I pried Jacques's mouth open as far as it could possibly go—then, with swift certainty, knowing what I would discover, I slipped the fingers of my other hand past his slick, ridged gums. The smell of his breath was exceeding foul, but I thought only of getting my fingers tightly around his swollen, fleshy tongue. Only the very tip remained, as he had swallowed the root.

Once I won purchase, I pulled—then pulled hard, harder, until with a great sucking sound, the member came free.

Completely free. For an instant, I studied the object—gray and glistening as a slug—that had come away in my hand. Beside me, Sister Habondia covered her mouth and stared with a look of such dismay and disgust that I was surprised when she did not vomit or faint.

At the same time, poor Jacques drew in a great, hoarse gasp of air through both his gaping mouth and the slits that served as his nostrils.

A peculiar thing then occurred.

A sense of—how shall I explain it?—rightness came over me, a sense of peace where there was love and nothing else. A gentle warmth descended, spreading from my head downward, as if I were standing beneath the rays of the sun. For a timeless moment, I dissolved into it, quite mindless of myself. It was the same feeling of the Goddess's presence I had experienced after Noni's death.

And when I heard a small gasp beside me, I turned to observe Sister Habondia's gaze, and followed it to the object in my open palm: a tongue, no longer pale gray, swollen and misshapen, but perfectly formed, healthy and pink. And about my hands, visible even in the daylight, shimmered a radiant golden glow.

Noni's hands; hands blessed with the Touch. I had no doubt that her glorious death had purchased this moment, for I sensed her standing beside me.

There were no thoughts, no surprise, no fear, no turmoil; only the doing of the one action that felt right—to slip the tongue back into Jacques's still-open mouth, to feel the intense but pleasant heat in my fingers, to let them rest gently upon the root of the tongue for a moment, then just as gently withdraw. . . .

At once, time began to move swiftly again; I became aware of myself, of what I had just done, and was startled beyond speech.

Kneeling, I stared down at Jacques, who lay upon his mattress. Abruptly, he sat up, his one good eye wide with wonder, his face (though still marred and pitiful to look upon) radiant with joy. He reached forward, grasped my hand (the one that had held his leprous member), and began to kiss it repeatedly.

At last he looked up at me with disturbing adoration, and proclaimed: "You have healed me! You have saved my life, and restored my speech!'" And he turned his face about the entire chamber so that all the lepers could hear him speak—more clearly than he ever had been able since his arrival:

"Hear, everyone! This good nun is a saint, a miracle worker sent from God! Last night, my tongue came loose in my mouth—and I, discouraged that I should no longer be able to voice my thoughts, and finding that the tongue was so swollen I could not spit it out, determined to let it remain. I hoped to swallow it, choke, and die swiftly.

"But this angel"—and here he gestured dramatically at me—"not only recognized from a distance my plight, she dislodged my great tongue after I had swallowed it—*and* she has made it perfect again, and through a miracle put it back in its place so that once again I may speak.

"God be praised for sending us a true saint—Sister Marie Françoise!"

Along my spine, I felt heat—no longer pleasant, but electric, the cold burn one feels from touching an icicle to the skin. At once my communion with the Goddess was severed.

For from beside me came a soft sound—a sound I should not have heard in the cacophony of cheers and questions that followed, but one that nonetheless caused the hairs on the back of my neck to lift.

"Magic," Sister Habondia breathed. "Witchcraft . . ."

How can I describe the peculiar mix of emotion I felt? Certainly, I was joyful to see my friend Jacques restored to the power of speech, and deeply grateful for Noni's sacrifice, which had made the act possible; at the same time, I was not prepared to admit the miracle I had just performed. Indeed, Sister Habondia's reaction evoked in me a desire to deny what had just transpired.

The lepers, however, felt quite differently; those who could rise limped toward me as fast as their infirmities allowed, and clutched at my apron with their partially fingered hands, begging pitifully for me to have mercy upon them, to grace them with a touch.

But by then, self-consciousness had overtaken me, blotting out the Presence entirely, for the first time since Noni's death. Sister Habondia and I could only beseech them to return to their beds, that we might continue our work.

This they did only with the greatest reluctance, and there was not one who, when I came to tend to him, did not plead for me to touch his wounds and make him whole; many clutched my hand and pressed it, palm down, against their open sores. So desperate were they to be healed, and so helpless I to oblige, that by the time Sister Marie Magdeleine came to take my place, I was quite near weeping.

Sister Habondia had neither uttered another word to me nor met my gaze since the event with Jacques; indeed, when we left, she took care to walk several paces behind me. Her mistrust made me consider flight, for I knew she would gossip and poison the mind of every inmate against me; in no time at all, I would be turned over to the bishop, then the inquisitors.

With that in mind, I hurried to join the others in chanting the Opus Dei in chapel. If I fled at that moment, everyone in the convent would be alerted, so that I might soon be overtaken; but if I left after sundown and vespers, no one would be aware of my disappearance until matins the next morning, giving me hours of darkness.

So I put on my best face and sang the hours along with my sisters, in my agitation making several mistakes; and the entire time, I was aware of Habondia's gaze upon me, though she glanced away each time I met it.

After chapel, each nun was required to fulfill a specific task—in my case, setting out bowls—before the evening meal, and at last, the time came for us to sit together at the long trestle table and bow our heads as Mother Geraldine gave thanks for the food.

The rules forbade the sisters from speaking casually in chapel, or during the communal refection that followed; Habondia would have only a small period of time in which to make her accusation before the nuns retired to the cells for solitary prayer. It would be impossible for any authorities to be alerted until the next day.

Yet when I raised my face to the assembly, I noticed a strange phenomenon: the women, who tended to sit every day in the same place at table, had rearranged themselves. More than half sat with their bodies and smiling faces slightly but surely inclined toward me, at the left side of the table; the rest, huddled and tight-lipped, sat inclined toward Sister Habondia on the right.

Only Mother Geraldine sat in her usual place in the center. After thanksgiving, she rose and began to serve us, one by one, from the cauldron overhanging the great hearth. While the abbess was so engaged, Sister Habondia glanced over at me and pointed two fingers at me in the gesture against the evil eye.

Geraldine saw: and though the rule forbade speaking during meals except in the direst emergencies, the abbess looked sharply over at Habondia and said, "You are excused, Sister. I will speak to you later. Go now to your cell and pray to God about what you have just done." Then, her expression stern but otherwise unreadable, she turned to me and added: "You also are excused, Sister Marie Françoise. Come with me." Without a further word, she proffered her ladle to the astounded Marie Magdeleine.

I followed the abbess, my knees unsteady with fear. Yet after many months at the convent, I trusted Mother Geraldine, for she had always treated me well.

In silence we left the refectory, passing through the kitchen and out into the corridor. To my surprise, the abbess led me directly to the empty sanctuary; and there, in the late afternoon shadows and the glow of candles that burned perpetually for the souls in purgatory, she paused to regard the altar, then crossed herself and knelt upon the cool stone.

I did the same; how could I not? But as I knelt, my heart grew cold, for her expression remained unfathomable, her manner grave, her eyes averted from mine: I expected any moment to feel a hand upon my shoulder, to gaze up and find a Dominican in his black robes and white-lined hood, a carrion-eating crow.

None ever came; and after a time, the abbess rose, again crossed herself, then—once I had done the same—gestured again for me to follow.

This I did. Soon we were in the lazaret, where Mother Geraldine went directly to Jacques's cot and brightly said, "Dear Jacques! My good friend!" And, as if it were the most natural thing to do, she knelt before him, clasped his fingerless hand, and kissed it.

"Sweet Mother," said he, still rejoicing at the clarity of his articulation. "And my sweet Sister Marie, whom you should by now know is a true saint, sent us by God! She has performed a true miracle, and restored my tongue to me. I was dying, Mother—"

Her face remained oddly composed as she interrupted him. "Dear friend, might I inspect the evidence? I can hear the improvement, indeed, but if our sister is to be hailed as a saint, another eyewitness will be needed."

He agreed gladly. The windows of the lazaret faced west, and through them came the rays of the setting sun. Mother Geraldine handed Jacques his canes, and permitted him the dignity of limping unaided over to an unshuttered window. I cannot forget the tableau: Jacques, crouched over his short crutches, the taller nun bending down to peer into his throat; both of them dark silhouettes limned with crimson light.

And then they returned to me, so at last I could better see the abbess; how shall I describe her? Her lips were pressed firm together; the breast of her habit moved visibly up and down with quickened breath. She was moved, and deeply so, holding back emotion and words—but in my anxiety, I could not tell whether her demeanor boded ill or good for me.

"Thank you, my friend," she told the leper. Once he was settled comfortably again on his cot, we took our leave, with Jacques calling out behind us: "God be praised! God be praised, and may He eternally bless Sister Marie Françoise!"

The abbess led me swiftly and silently to her cell, the smallest and sparest of all the rooms, without even a cot. Though it was custom for the nuns to leave their doors open, she shut the door behind us, and at last faced me, her gaze direct.

"So, it is true, then," she said—or rather, asked, for she clearly desired my confirmation. "As Sister Habondia said: somehow you knew that Jacques was choking, and when you removed his tongue, it became whole in your hand; and you restored it to him."

How could I deny it? She had seen the proof with her own eyes, and had the word of two people that I was the culprit. True, she was fond of me, and if it had been simply my word against Habondia's, perhaps I might have lied; but I could not accuse Jacques of telling a falsehood.

And so I cast my gaze downward and said, "It is true. But it was God who accomplished it, not I."

"Habondia says it is witchcraft," she responded softly, and I felt a chill. I said nothing, but remained with my head bowed until at last Geraldine added: "There are many people like her; and in these dangerous times, it is best to be cautious."

Hope dawning, I raised my face slowly to look up at her. She continued:

"Perhaps you remember when we first met, how I told you that I felt God intended for our paths to cross. Did you think it accident to find a nun's habit, and a Franciscan one at that, hanging so conveniently in the wood? 'Twas I who put it there."

As I absorbed this in astounded silence, she added: "You see, I Dream: I had Dreamed of finding you, attacked by the brigands, Dreamed of today's event. It is my destiny to serve you, Sister, just as it is your destiny to go on to achieve much greater things."

I sank to my knees as she spoke, my white habit rustling about me. "I cannot—I must not—" My voice dropped to a whisper as I pressed my palms to my eyes. "I am a fraud, a lie. . . . Mother, I am not a nun. I am not even a proper Christian."

Gracefully, she knelt beside me and caught my hand; she was much taller than I, a fact I found oddly comforting in that moment, as if she were truly the consoling mother and I the child. "God is greater than His Church," she said. "Greater than the doctrines of man, greater than any of us can know. So it is by whatever name we call Him—or Her, as

Goddess: Diana, Artemis, Hecate, Isis, Saint Mary . . ." She fell silent for a moment, then at last added, "When we first found you, I saw the Solomon's Seal around your neck."

I blinked at her, stunned.

"The gold talisman with the star and the Hebrew letters upon it. You still wear it, yes?"

Speechless, I nodded. How was it that this Christian woman knew the name of the magical medallion when I, its wearer, had no idea?

"Good. It protects you. It helped to bring you here."

"I do not even know what it means," I admitted. "And I have never done such a thing as happened with Jacques today. I do not know why suddenly—"

"I do," she said. "It is the legacy left you by your grandmother; the result of your supreme initiation, accomplished by her sacrificial death.

"For you are meant, my dear Sybille, to become more than human; and your grandmother has magnificently accomplished her role in that task. Great power shall come to you; and it is our purpose to guide you in its use. . . ."

XIII

By the next morning, all at the nunnery had heard of the healing of Jacques—if not from his own mottled gray lips, with joy and praise, then from Habondia's, with fear and venom. The lines of loyalty drawn at the dining table became even more apparent at the next meal: six of the sisters became ardent supporters of Habondia and her suspicions. The group moved together, tight as a school of minnows, whispering with veiled heads together, casting furtive glances back at me, praying audibly for protection and cursing the devil whenever I passed.

Like Sister Habondia, I too was surrounded by my own disciples. It was too late to deny my involvement in healing the leper, but I took care to point out to all that God, not I, had actually performed the miracle. Most understood this, but sought out my presence as if believing that, having once been visited by God, I still possessed some of His radiance, in which they wished to bask. Some, however, canonized me in their hearts. Chief among them was Sister Marie Magdeleine, so smitten by religious fervor that she tried to play Saint John the Divine to my Jesus—walking so close beside me that our habits brushed against each other, holding my hand, pressing it to her lips, her eyes rapturous as she begged: "Talk to us, sweet Sister, of God. What does He say to you this day?"

"I am no saint," I insisted. "God speaks to me as He does to you—through liturgy and scripture."

That night I lay sleepless. I had come to care for many of my sisters, especially my protectress, Geraldine, who had not spoken to me since her amazing revelation that she was to become my teacher. But I lived in terror that she, as well as I, would soon be discovered for what we were. . . .

On the day following, as I attended my duties in the lazaret with Sister Habondia, Sister Marie Magdeleine appeared in the doorway, breathless and flushed as if she had been running. Ignoring Habondia's narrow-eyed scrutiny, she called to me: "Mother Geraldine has summoned you to her office. You are to come at once!"

Once we were outside in the corridor, Magdeleine caught my hand. "I am to take your place in the lazaret," she whispered. "But I had to tell you. . . . Sister"—and here she jerked her head to indicate Habondia—"had Father Roland tell the bishop about the miracle." She squeezed my hand excitedly.

I stared at her, aghast. "You mean the father *and* the bishop both know?"

"More than that." She broke into a broad grin. "The bishop is *here*."

Here? I mouthed the word, too dizzied to utter it aloud.

"To see *you*. Isn't it wonderful? I must go now; but afterward, you must tell me everything." And she interlaced her hands at her waist, and let the full sleeves fall to cover them; with the faint rustle of wool over stone, she glided swiftly back toward the lazaret.

Numb, I took several long strides in the opposite direction—until my legs gave way beneath me, and I sank to my knees, hand pressed against the wall. My breath grew short: this was the very thing I had feared; but at least no one was implicating Geraldine. If they tortured me, would I be strong enough not to utter her name or the names of any other sisters?

Goddess, help me, I prayed silently as my head bowed beneath the weight of my fear. And such was the intensity, the desperation, and the will behind those three words that I knew they were heard.

There I remained for several breaths until I gathered my wild thoughts. Any attempt to run would seal my guilt; besides, the bishop's *chariot,* horses, and attendants were no doubt waiting outside.

I had no choice but to face my questioners. Then at least I could feign innocence and ascribe responsibility for the healing incident to the Christian God.

That decided, I let go a deep, steadying sigh . . . and lifted my face to find Mother Geraldine and the bishop standing a slight distance in front of me.

The bishop was a regal man, an old man, a gaunt-cheeked man with deep shadows beneath world-weary, heavy-lidded eyes; he was stooped and painfully spare, as if his very flesh were consumed by the responsibilities he bore. On that day, he wore the informal black robes of a priest with a bishop's skullcap.

"Sister Marie Françoise," Mother Geraldine said, her manner strangely formal, distant. "You know the bishop."

I did. He had visited us several times over the past years in his official capacity, to inspect the convent's finances and to celebrate with us the anniversary of our arrival in Carcassonne.

"Sister," he said, in a voice reedy with age, and took a stop forward to proffer his ring. I sank to my knees before him to kiss the band of cold metal and precious stone. When I had completed the ritual, he took my hand and helped me to my feet. "Come," he said, and we made our way to Mother Geraldine's small office; he gestured for us women to enter first, then closed the wooden door and stood with his back to it, and one hand upon the iron bar.

For a time, he did not speak, but scrutinized me with unsettling intensity. His eyes were intelligent, piercing; his gaze might have been admiring—or it might have been that of a raven studying a carcass upon which it intended to dine.

"Tell me your story of how the leper came to be healed." His tone was soft, even encouraging. I took heart and, keeping my eyes respectfully downcast, told him very simply what had happened: that Jacques had choked, that I had realized this and pulled out his tongue, which was then miraculously healed. I insisted that God, not I, was responsible, and that I had no idea how it had occurred. I was a humble nun, not even a very good one at that; God had not seen fit to use me again since that time.

To all this, the old man listened in silence. The more I spoke, the more I felt he was listening not at all to my words, but rather observing *me*.

This unnerved me far more than any accusation could have done. In the midst of my story, I broke off in the telling, having forgotten the next words to say. For a moment, I stood dazed, unable to speak; but through the Goddess's grace I recovered myself, and stammered through to the end.

Still, he maintained silence—for so long that at last I dared glance up.

He was scowling with disapproval. "Sister Habondia says it was witchcraft, that your hands were surrounded by a strange glow, brighter than day. How do you answer this charge?"

I looked down again immediately. "Your Holiness, it was not witchcraft, nor anything I accomplished. God healed Jacques, not I."

"You have the right to hear from your accuser," he said, and in a loud, stern voice, commanded: "Sister!"

At the same time, he unlatched the door to admit a nun, her head so deeply bowed that her face was altogether obscured by wimple and veil; but I had no doubt as to her identity.

"Holiness," she said, her voice frail, wavering—indeed, quite pitiful; she knelt, kissed his ring, then—almost losing her balance midway— let herself be helped up.

"Sister Habondia, tell us what you saw the morning that the leper Jacques was healed."

Inspiration and righteousness so illumined Habondia's features and smoothed away lines writ by anger, that one could see she had in youth been pretty. In a voice filled with passion and conviction, she said, "Your Holiness, I was caring for one of the lepers when, across the room, I heard a terrible sound—the sound of Sister Marie Françoise shouting."

Calmly, the bishop prompted, "And what were her words?"

"Terrible curses, Holiness; curses against God, and Jesus . . . And a prayer to the Devil."

I gasped in amazement, a sound which provoked attention from no one.

"I know this is difficult for you, Sister Habondia, but . . . what were her *precise* words? We need to know if this is to proceed to trial."

"Oh, *Holiness,*" she said, stricken by such a thought, and pressed her palm to her bosom in dismay. But she obeyed, her face reddening, as she uttered: "I believe she said 'Damn God' and 'Damn Jesus'"—and here she crossed herself—"and then, 'Devil, give me power . . .' Or no, it was '*Lucifer,* give me power.'" Finished, she crossed herself again and lowered her countenance again until her features disappeared.

"And then?" the bishop prompted.

"Oh. Then she pulled out the leper's tongue and stuck it back in. And her hands," Habondia added, speech swiftening, "there was a very odd yellow glow about her hands, each of them. It stayed for some time."

"But these are lies, pure lies!" I insisted.

"Mind your impudence, girl—you shall address me properly!" The bishop whirled to face me, brow furrowed in anger. "So now you say you did *not* heal the leper, when you have already admitted it?"

"No—Holiness. I am saying that I have never cursed God, and certainly did not pray to—"

To my further amazement and despair, Mother Geraldine swiftly interjected: "*Monseigneur,* she is not even a nun or a Christian; she has confessed as much to me. She is a peasant fled from Toulouse because her grandmother was convicted of witchcraft there and executed." She pointed, her arm a straight, unbroken line of accusation from shoulder to fingertip. "Ask her, Your Holiness, what she wears about her neck!"

I could only stare at her, aghast, while the bishop insisted, "Well, then, let us see."

What would resistance win me? I struggled for some seconds to withdraw my arm from its sleeve into the body of my habit, where I found the skin-warmed disc of metal. I pushed it upward, through the top of my collar and the wimple wound about my neck, and for the first time since leaving Carcassonne, revealed the talisman to another. There it hung, bright and incriminating, upon my breast.

A period of solemn silence ensued.

"This is magic," said the bishop, "magic most sinister. Sister Habondia, you are to come with me into the city; Mother Geraldine, escort Sister Marie Françoise to her cell, and see that she remains there through the night. I shall return on the morrow with formal charges, and will see that the accused is escorted to prison myself."

As ordered, the abbess led me back to my cell; such was my astonishment and bitter pain at her betrayal that I could not speak as we walked, could not bear even to look upon her. The wound she had dealt me was deep; but even deeper at that moment was my confusion. She was one of the Race, without doubt: she had spoken lovingly of my grandmother's sacrifice; she had known of my impending arrival and left the nun's habit for me to find in the forest. How, then, could she so cruelly betray me to the bishop?

It was beyond my understanding at that time. So in silence we walked—Geraldine offering no explanations for her cruel disloyalty— and when at last we arrived at my little cell, I entered without protest and at once knelt and sat back upon my heels. And the abbess said, without shame or gloating but with pure ease, as if nought terrible had passed between us, "Remain here. I will go and summon a sister to stay outside your door tonight."

Her willingness to leave me alone only added to my confusion. Did she so trust me not to escape? (Of course I would not; not until I was sure enough time had passed for the bishop's *chariot* to have left.) Did she think a single sister sufficient enough to hold me back? For I was small, but strong, stronger than many of the sisters with greater height, and I also wielded magic.

Or was this an attempt to provoke me to escape—which would quickly seal my guilt and my fate?

Mother Geraldine left; and in the hour that passed before the large and gentle Sister Barbara appeared to keep vigil outside my door, I found myself torn. For I remembered all too well the anguish of the flames I had both seen and suffered on Noni's behalf, and I knew I could not bear to face them again; my entire body trembled without respite at the memory.

And I recalled Noni crying out to her tormentor, the one who had sent her to her death: *Domenico*. . . .

'Tis the Enemy, I told myself, shivering. *I have fallen into the hands of the Enemy, the hands of those who would destroy the Race.* I had to escape at any cost. . . .

Yet all the while, my heart whispered that it was not yet time, not yet time to leave this place, that here I belonged.

Thus I sat for hours on the cold stone, as daylight waned and night fell, at which hour Habondia appeared with two lit oil lamps. One she handed to Sister Barbara; the other she kept. For once, she cast no baleful stares in my direction; indeed, she altogether avoided my gaze and, task accomplished, turned immediately to leave.

Through the night I remained quite still, save for the waves of trembling that shook me when fear overwhelmed me. I remained also of two minds: one set on escape the instant Barbara took to sleep; and one set on staying precisely as I was, for I felt such was the Goddess's will.

But the time came when my body refused all further contemplation of fire and death, even though Sister Barbara remained adamantly awake even into the latest hours of night. Soon would come the time for lauds, when the community awakened in the darkness for prayers, only to return once more to sleep; in desperation, I determined to cast upon my unwitting sister a spell.

An odd sense of power came to me, and I knew at once that, just as I had been capable of restoring Jacques's speech to him, so could I strike down Sister Barbara if I chose. I Saw clearly how to silence her tongue, that she could not cry out, clearly how to paralyze her limbs that she could not give chase.

For an instant I actually considered this—then felt an unspeakable revulsion at the thought. Even so, my terror would not permit me to remain; thus I evoked a globe to contain her body. And within that globe, sparkling jewels fell gently as snow, a soothing snow that brought slumber. 'Twas so easy, accomplishing that spell, and I wondered that I had ever bothered with making charms and potions and drawing circles in the earth.

Within a moment, she was snoring serenely, head fallen forward, chin resting comfortably upon her breast, folded arms hidden beneath long sleeves—all the while maintaining the straight and graceful pose of the nun at prayer.

Ignoring the stiffness in my legs, I rose silently to my feet. In my mind's eye, I had already slipped past Sister Barbara, down the corridor, out of the rarely used door between the *garderobe* and the lazaret, into the night and the wood and the mountains. . . .

But in the realm physical I did not move; *could* not move, for my heart and will would not let me, as I knew the Goddess's mind. My destiny lay here; here, in this cell, at this convent, in the hands of Mother Geraldine and the bishop.

Disgusted at my misuse of magic, I sat down again and promptly dissolved the globe that enveloped Sister Barbara. She woke with a small start, blinked to clear her gaze, and looked about herself; and, once satisfied that I was still in my cell, took the ring of beads at her belt and began softly to pray the rosary.

Calm settled over me; not the weary and hopeless surrender that overtakes the doomed, but the true peace I had found after Noni's death, in the presence of the Goddess. There I dwelt until morning came.

And after the bells for prime had rung, and the sunlight came full through the window, Sister Barbara looked upward as if prodded by some invisible touch. She rose, and in a voice composed and serene, said: "Sister, come."

She led me to Mother Geraldine's office, and after a timid knock, unlatched the door. It opened onto the abbess, Habondia, and the bishop, severe and regal. A flutter of fear passed through me as the door shut firmly behind me, but I quelled it by remembering Noni and the Goddess.

Mother Geraldine spoke first. "You have performed well, my child, enough for the first lesson: that fear dispels the Goddess; and magic worked in fear brings great evil. The time will come, though, when you must be fear's master—for any hint of it in your heart will destroy you. We have much to accomplish before you are ready to embrace your destiny."

As I stood, thunderstruck, the bishop came forward, and genuflecting upon one knee, kissed my hand. "My lady."

He withdrew, and Habondia followed in his stead. "My lady," she said most fervently, "forgive me for being the one chosen to bring you pain."

Geraldine, clearly leader of the group, took her turn bowing, and after she had added her solemn kiss to the others', said, "My lady, you will always be safe here with us; for we are sworn to protect you."

"What *are* you?" I asked, amazed. "Are you witch or Christian?"

At this, Geraldine graced me with the broadest of smiles. "Perhaps none, my lady. Perhaps both. Women we may be—excepting our brave bishop here—but we are no less Knights Templar."

And with a swift motion, she brought from beneath habit and wimple a necklace on which hung a bright and shining disc, inscribed with Hebrew script and stars: a golden Solomon's Seal.

"The most important thing you must learn now," Geraldine said after the bishop and Habondia had both left and we stood alone in her office, "is who you are.

"Perhaps you know to an extent; perhaps your grandmother told you the tale as she learned it from her own teacher. Perhaps not. But surely as a child, then as a young woman, you went to mass, and heard the priest tell the story of God made man.

"Let me tell you another story, one just as old—perhaps older—of a child who became a woman. She lived by a lake called Galilee, in a land where lions roamed.

"Her name—Magdalene—meant Watchtower; and those who knew her as a child thought she was named for the town whence she came. But those who loved her as a woman knew it was because she Saw far, far further than the rest.

"And she knew he who was God made flesh, for she, the Goddess, was his equal. Together, they were Mother and Father of the Race. They shared a single destiny: to aid mankind, to teach compassion, to guide those who shared their blood and talents to do likewise.

"But soon danger faced them both: for there were those jealous of their power and their influence on the people. Evil raised its head and proclaimed what they had found sacred to be profane; and it sought to destroy them both.

"My lot it is to warn you of this Evil, which has stolen the highest magic and even now perverts it to a wicked end in order to keep you both from finding your joint destiny; and to teach you to discover and perfect the powers that you now possess.

"Generation after generation, the pattern is repeated: the two must find each other and unite with one purpose, and defeat the evil that works against them. Over the past generations, your Enemy has grown stronger, because some of those possessing holy blood and holy powers have been swayed to evil; now the danger facing you is grave indeed. For now it is more than your own deaths that you and your lord must face; it is the eradication of all our kind, so that those who dwell on the earth will be left without help, without hope, trapped in a present and future filled with war and hatred."

"So you are all here Templars?" I asked, still amazed.

She smiled. "We are, my lady. True, we women do not bear swords and lances; our battles are fought in a different realm. Nor, being female, could we ever have belonged to the Order of the Knights of the Temple of Solomon—but the men who with us served Lord and Lady had formed an inner order of the Templars, and were persecuted for their beliefs: thus, we came to refer to ourselves as such, for we served with them. Their task was to protect and train the Lord; ours, the Lady. And when the order was officially destroyed and the men executed or fled northward—save for a very few whose association was never discovered—we women remained, for who would ever suspect us as belonging to part of that inner order?

"But for the thousand years before that time, we simply referred to ourselves as disciples.

"A few of us here have blood in which the talents are strong—the Sight, the Touch, the Dreaming, and many more—but most of the others, less magically gifted, believe and wish to serve in whatever capacity they are able. Sister Habondia is such a one; she lends her physical and mental abilities—and, as you may have noticed, her peculiar talent for pretense."

"But I am no different from you," I countered. "You know the Goddess better than I; you are more powerful than I. You knew that I was coming, and I was not even sure whether you had betrayed me."

Most somberly, she said, "Untrue, my lady; I possess not a whit of your power—or rather, the Goddess's power. Do you still not understand what occurred with your grandmother's death? Your supreme initiation?"

Tears burned behind my eyes at the memory, but I remained composed. "I know . . . that I felt the presence of the Goddess more strongly than ever. I know that I received the power of the Touch."

"You received far more than that." Geraldine paused; ever so slightly, she inclined her head, so that her black winter veil draped upon the straight, strong line of one cheek and fell gracefully at her abrupt, square jaw. Her eyes remained focused on me; yet at the same time, they looked beyond my physical form to behold something deep and magnificent. Her expression softened, and I was reminded suddenly of the wooden statue of Mary in the olive grove. "It has only been done once since the Race began: you, my dear Sister Marie, whether you believe it in your heart or not, though you have yet to discover it within yourself, have become the incarnate Goddess."

XIV

Over the next few years, there were many things Mother Geraldine explained to me; one was that the two means of initiation—that is, obtaining magical power for good or ill—were death and love, the latter being interpreted by practitioners of common magic as the procreative act. True, she admitted, the physical act alone did accomplish some degree of initiation; but the attainment of the greatest power lay in an act of compassion that transcended self, and in that sense sexual congress between lord and lady had indeed achieved great levels of power in generations past. (Forgive me for speaking so frankly, Brother; I did not mean to make you blush.)

What Noni had done for me was to combine selfless love and a willing surrender to death; thus, my initiation was doubly powerful. So it was, Geraldine said, that I could then find and more powerfully initiate my Beloved.

First, however, both I and the lord had to be especially trained and prepared, since in this generation the danger was particularly great; until then, I was exceptionally vulnerable to the Enemy's attack.

This began in Circle with the other sisters of the Race ... a Circle very much like the one I attended with Noni. There came the invocation of the Light, Geraldine drawing it down into herself with what sounded like the very same words Noni had used—Hebrew, Geraldine explained later, not Italian as I had believed; for in the days that the Templars were forced to flee for their lives, many witches sheltered them, and each taught the other what they knew of magic. There were the towering beings of different colors—the archangels Raphael, Michael, Gabriel, Uriel—and the stars and circle.

All this was accomplished deep within the cellar, in a legacy left by the many times Carcassonne had seen invaders: a small hiding place with a cold earth floor hid behind earthen walls. Surrounded by rough-hewn, mildewed stone, without a window to ease the blackness, we bore no tools, no magical items of any sort, only an oil lamp and our hearts; nor did Geraldine even bother to scribe a physical circle in the earth. But the presence of the unseen was unutterably vivid; in the dark, I feel, we See best.

There, in the little chamber, under the abbess's and my sisters' protection—and that of many unseen others scattered in many towns and lands, who attended in spirit rather than body—I took my first steps in learning to focus the Sight.

"Think on your Enemy," Geraldine murmured in that first Circle, once we all were safely ensconced inside a globe of shimmering blue-gold. She came and linked one hand with mine; my other was caught by Marie Magdeleine, and hers was caught by Sister Barbara's, and Barbara's by Sister Drusilla's, and Drusilla's by Sister Lucinde's. ... Six of us there were that night, and all six of them I bless, for without them, the Enemy would surely have detected me. As it was, with the good nuns' help, I was to him invisible, unknown, completely safe.

"Think on your Enemy in your heart," Geraldine continued, "and slowly his image will appear. ..."

I drew a breath, unsettled by the very thought. Surely these women were deluded, and I, too, to dare think of me as Goddess, as a worthy vehicle of Her power. I was all too human: weak, anxious, afraid. . . .

Beside me, Magdeleine squeezed my hand, and I turned to see her profile in the lamplight, the gently concave slope of brow, the relaxed curve of closed eyelid, a sweep of lashes set upon a golden arc of cheek: a portrait of serenity. I felt that same peace descend on me, felt the flutter of my own eyelashes against my skin, felt my fear dissolve.

And I heard Noni, crying out:

Domenico . . .

You the treacherous breeze at the baby's birth . . .

At once, I fell into a vision:

The silhouette of a man tall and heavy-set. He stands before an altar, a cube of onyx. Upon its polished surface rest two candles, one white and one black; a white dove in a small wooden cage; a circle of salt; and a golden censer. From the last, smoke spirals, and behind its thick, myrrh-scented veil, frescoes of pagan gods cavort in the wavering shadows. Here, a pearl-skinned Venus couples with Mars, golden waves of her hair washing over them both; there, the mortal Leda lies in the shadow cast by the great wings of a divine swan.

Directly above the man's head, the cupola glitters with inlaid gold stars and astrological signs; before him, a magical circle—with symbols for fire, water, earth, and air set in glittering mosaic—ornaments the white marble floor.

A golden sconce as tall as the man and half as thick adorns each quarter: the eastern one, directly behind the altar, is elaborately fashioned in the shape of an eagle, the southern in that of a lion. West and north are represented by the face of a man and a bull. Atop each ornate holder, a taper flickers, adding to the glow cast by the candles on the altar.

A woman adorned with the sun, the magician whispers, *standing on the moon, crowned with twelve stars. In the agony of childbirth, she cries out. . . .*

He steps forward to the altar and opens the small wooden cage. The dove inside shrinks back slightly when he puts his hand inside, and jerkily cants its head to regard him with one pink and entirely expressionless eye. When his hand closes over its back, it tries to stand and ruffs its feathers, sending down and dander into the smoky haze; but the instant the magician draws it forth and gently smooths its feathers, it settles, unresisting, into the cup of his palm.

Such a small life it is: nothing more than a soft, weightless spot of warmth and a swift-beating heart there in his hand. He strokes it absently, his mind utterly focused on what that small life will purchase, until the bird so relaxes it begins to groom itself, reaching for a feather on its snowy breast and preening it.

Abruptly, the magician seizes its narrow neck between thumb and middle finger, and wrenches it to one side until he feels and hears the delicate, tubular bones snap; simultaneously, the dove defecates in his cradling hand.

Without reaction, he transfers the limp bird to his other hand and lets the green and white syrup roll from his palm onto the marble flooring, then quickly wipes his hand on his robe before placing the bird inside the small circle of salt poured on the gleaming black altar.

There he takes the ceremonial dagger from his belt; its blade flashes once, twice in the candlelight as he quickly severs the dove's head from its neck. Hot blood spurts forth onto the dagger and his fingers, staining white feathers crimson-pink, collecting in a small pool against the salt barrier.

Immediately the magician steps back and in his mind's eye creates a protective circle about himself, one that excludes dove and altar. Once the barriers are firmly in place, he thunders the name of a demon—one who has served him well before, but at present performs no task—and commands it in all the holy names to show itself within the circle of salt.

Those less experienced, less gifted, might miss the subtler signs: the odd physical sensation rather like that of cool satin being drawn slowly across the skin, the sudden flaring of the candles on the altar, the abrupt death twitch of the dove. The censer begins to billow smoke. It streams over the dead bird, then swirls slowly upward in a column—hovering, gathering, until at last the magician sees the face forming in the smoke. And a monstrous one it is: that of a wolf with long, deadly tusks, a darting tongue like a serpent's, and great, sharp teeth. . . .

It wants badly to frighten him, to make him run away out of fear, to trick him into leaving his protective circle. For then it could master him, rather than the reverse—and fear is the easiest means for it to obtain what it wants. Therefore, the magician permits himself to feel not a whit of fear; indeed, if he feels like reacting in the slightest, it would be to laugh at the spirit's blatant attempt at bravado, to remind it that it was entirely in his power.

Thus, when the demon is fully formed within the smoke, the magician again speaks its name, and commands: "You will destroy the one I seek, the one who shall See more clearly than I. And in this manner shall it be done. . . ."

From his robe, he withdraws a long taper, the end of which he touches to the tip of the western quarter candle; and, without stepping forth from his circle within a circle, he holds the flaming tip to the wooden cage upon the altar.

It catches fire at once, and in the space of two breaths is consumed; the glowing structure collapses on the dove in its salt circle, and the smell of scorched feathers follows as the small corpse ignites.

And at once I Saw the magician no more, but the small cottage in which I was born; and within, my mother squatting on tares of fresh-cut wheat, her belly swollen with me. So young she was; younger than I am now.

She was screaming—screaming with the pangs of labor, screaming in fear and fury at Noni, who knelt beside her. And Maman reached out and, with a wild strength, a strength she had never before or after possessed, slapped my grandmother to the floor.

Noni fell onto her side, and with her shoulder, struck the small lamp resting nearby on the straw-scattered floor. I watched the fire ride the spilled oil, pouring across the straw, across my grandmother's dark skirts, toward the stack of tares where my mother strained to give birth to me; and I thought of the little cage reduced to glowing cinders upon the smoldering body of the dove.

Death, I realize; *the deaths of others are his source of power.* No wonder, when Noni died, that he thought he had won; and how bitter he must have been when that power came, not to him, but to me.

No wonder, then, that he pursued me and my Beloved. Not so much out of a desire for revenge on Ana Magdalena, but out of a hunger for our great power.

"Enough," Geraldine commanded, and in Circle I came to myself.

"This is your Enemy as he was in the past," the abbess said. "You will look on him thus until you are strong enough to face him in the present."

So I faced him again, in other Circles on other nights. I saw the magician work in a dozen incidents I have not told for want of time; incidents in which, had it not been for Noni's intervention, I might have died. I saw him work when Maman seized Papa's charm from his neck, before he died of plague, and when poor Maman discovered my bound Solomon's Seal and betrayed Noni to the gendarmes.

In Circle—and in my solitary cell, but always under the protection of my female knights—I learned to meditate, not upon the cross or other sacred objects as the cloistered are taught, but upon the Goddess Herself, until I reached a state of profound calm.

In that state, I practiced directing Her healing power at will; and although it may sound easily achieved, it was a slow, difficult process. And while in the lazaret we had many willing to receive my fledgling Touch, to my great disappointment, Jacques (along with several others) refused to be healed any further. "Some lepers must remain, lest the people talk and become too suspicious," he said. "And if there must be lepers, then let me be one of them. I shall serve you no less, my lady, so long as God and Goddess give me life."

But many others I learned to heal: always minor things, the curing of an open sore there, the restoration of a bit of flesh here; though nothing as dramatic as I had done before with Jacques, nothing more ambitious. Those stricken by the plague either grew well in their own good time or worsened and died, despite my touch. When I bemoaned my failures to Geraldine, she simply said, "You must forget yourself; forget the human body you inhabit, and remember only the Goddess."

Indeed, there were longer and longer periods when I *could* remember and achieve that meditative state of calm, that grace, that sense of the Living Presence. At those times, I began slowly to contemplate my fears: for only when I conquered them could I be strong enough to protect myself and others, thus freeing my sisters to do the same.

Only when you are strong enough, Geraldine told me, *will you be allowed to meet your lord in the flesh; only then will you be able to initiate him, when your heart is right.*

So it was the Enemy Domenico I learned to think upon first, until—having learned to focus my Sight, and overcome my terror—I could See him and feel naught but the Goddess's compassion. Thus strengthened, I dealt with all manner of fear—including my special aversion to fire and the pain inflicted by it, which I so keenly remembered. I speak of it quickly now, but all told, the process took years; it was years before I could evoke such things in meditation and remain at peace, in the Presence. I could allow no darkness to remain in my soul, for it could be turned against me.

And when I had learned to look upon my present Enemy—even at last finding the strength to See his face with equanimity—Geraldine spoke to me alone, one night after circle when all the others had left the dank little cave and we remained behind, sitting on our heels, shins pressed to the cold ground, a candle dispelling the dark between us.

"It is not enough," she said, the taper's flame casting a wavering cone of light that illumined her breast, chin, and lips, but left eyes and brow in shadow, "that you have Seen our Enemy in past and present. You must look upon the Enemy who will come in the future. This is the last and greatest fear you shall have to conquer."

I hesitated; I opened my mouth to protest, to say (for what reason, I know not) *I cannot;* but before I could speak, she countered: "Understand, it is for the same reason that you are limited as a healer. You forget at such times who you are: you remember only the woman, Marie Sybille, and forget you are also Goddess. Your limitations are Hers."

By then I had grown accustomed to dwelling most of my hours in the Goddess's Presence; perhaps I had even come to be a bit prideful about it, for when the abbess spoke, I was humbled by the horror that welled up within me. I knew she spoke about the greatest Evil to come—the one I had not been able to bring myself to look upon when Jacob, in my earliest initiation, had urged me to. It was the purest hopelessness, the purest void, which I had seen waiting for me outside my first and last circle with Noni as priestess, and I thought: *How shall I look upon it with peace when I cannot even bear to hear it mentioned?*

But I knew that all my training was directed to that very goal: and that, once it had been achieved, I would at last be ready to encounter my Beloved. So I began, most tentatively, to make attempts in Circle and meditation; and, being tentative, I failed, again and again.

However, my attention was soon diverted by a different threat.

We had been at war with England for as long as I could remember—indeed, longer—though I had never experienced it firsthand: the sporadic skirmishes had thus far occurred north of us. Through the bishop and Father Roland, who administered our daily Eucharist, we heard that the Black Prince, Edward, had invaded Bordeaux. He and his army did more than simply kill the inhabitants: he laid waste to the city and all its outlying villages, slaughtering pigs and cattle, destroying crops, trees, vineyards, and wine vats, setting fields and buildings on fire. "The land," Father Roland had told us one day before mass, "is blackened and pitted, and the poor survivors are now forced to starve; they do not even have bread, because Edward burned down the mills and granaries. All because they remained loyal to the French king."

When my sisters heard that Edward's army was marching south and east—toward Toulouse, and then Carcassonne—it caused them great concern. True, the fact that we lived in a religious community should have protected us, as it certainly would have done a hundred years ago. But in these modern times, respect for nuns and monks had so dwindled that we were as likely to be murdered and violated as anyone during war.

Our worry increased daily with Father Roland's visits. "They have the Armagnac" became "They have arrived in Guienne," then "They are headed for Toulouse." Mysteriously, Toulouse was spared; and Father Roland decided to celebrate with a special mass of thanksgiving, reasoning that if Edward would not bother with the ripe, succulent plum that was Toulouse, he certainly would not trouble the grape that was Carcassonne.

Besides, our city was a citadel, a fortress, with not one but two city walls: an inner, wooden rampart built by the Visigoths almost a millennium ago, and an outer one of stone a mere century old. True, our cloister sat just outside the city walls—but the reputation of those walls certainly should have been enough to discourage the English from coming here.

Or so most of the city's inhabitants thought, with the results that no preparations whatsoever were made, no precautions taken.

Marie Magdeleine spoke often of it to me, and perhaps even hinted that she should like to know what future, if any, I foresaw, concerning the invasion; I cannot say, for I was too distracted to pay her heed. After five years of training under Mother Geraldine, I was consumed not only by my failure to bear looking upon the face of my future Enemy, but by my increasing conviction that my Beloved was in special danger of attack. How could I help him if I could not yet See him safely? This talk about war and the looming English meant little to me, and I directed no energy, no thought, to their possible arrival.

. . .

One day near the end of the mass, during the beautiful strains of the Nunc Dimittis, we in the choir were startled into abrupt silence by the painfully loud slam of the chapel door; indeed, so hard had the door struck the stone that the heavy wood split down the middle.

From the doorway, one of the lay brothers, the shepherd Andrus, propelled himself forward into the center of the sanctuary and sank to his knees—not out of reverence, but agitation. As Father Roland, the choir, and the other nuns beheld him in astonishment, he shouted:

"The English! They are here! God help us! They are here!"

A ripple of murmurs spread through the assembly, whereupon Mother Geraldine stepped forth from the choirbox, to motion for silence—then turned, and gave the choirmaster a nod.

Once again, the singers began the Nunc Dimittis, their voices tauter, higher than before:

Lord, lettest now thy servant depart in peace. . . .

This time, the liturgy was completed; and when Father Roland had given his hasty blessing, he ran full tilt from the chapel in his vestments while we nuns moved out in our customary orderly fashion behind the abbess.

They moved steadily down out of the hills, the English, more than five thousand men, all told: lancers, foot soldiers, the much-dreaded archers with their bows the height of a man. Dark locusts spilling out in irregular swarms, they had been on the march for months and no longer bothered with the precise lines of formal battle; nor did they need to. There were no herald trumpets, no bright banners flying, nor should there have been.

This was not warfare, but knavery.

Like all the other towns they had taken, Carcassonne was not ready for their attack. A small army consisting of the *grand seigneur*'s men and commoners had been mustered, but these were no more than two hundred; we stood out in the fields north of the cloister and watched aghast as these few gathered against the approaching enemy.

The day bore an exceptional chill; the night before, we had lain straw on the crops to protect them from frost, and that morning in the drafty chapel, my fingernails had taken on a decided shade of blue.

Now I stood outside, having forgotten my cloak, and the cold I felt was not that of the body. My thoughts and talents had been focused elsewhere; I had given the approaching war only passing consideration, but at that moment, I Saw glimpses of what it was to bring us. I slipped my hands beneath my long sleeves and rubbed my upper arms to try to warm myself.

Despite her training, Marie Magdeleine's eyes had filled with tears; she clutched Mother Geraldine's arms and said in a low voice, her words emerging as white mist: "Mother, we must flee or they will kill us all, just as they killed the poor souls in Bordeaux."

The abbess looked over at Magdeleine and, seeing the tears, Geraldine's face softened. "Go if you must go; stay if you must stay. As for me, I must stay." In a louder voice, she said to all the other sisters, "Those who wish to leave, take the cart and the horses and gather up as much food and wine as you can."

Not a soul stirred; the shallowest arc of a smile graced the abbess's lips, then disappeared. "What do you See?" she asked me.

I thought of the sheep and cattle grazing in the fields before us, of the straw-scattered leeks and peas, of the trees still heavy with apples, pears, and nuts, and Saw that all of it would be gone in a matter of hours. I Heard the thud of English feet upon the cloister stairs. "They are coming here, to the convent."

"What else?" Geraldine asked, contained and brusque as a haggling merchant.

I was taken aback, for at that moment I could See nothing else. With a sense of humility, I realized that it is one thing to overcome one's fears in meditation; it is quite another to overcome them in reality. When I did not respond, Geraldine continued: "Barbara, Magdeleine, go to the garden and gather up what you can of vegetables and apples, then hurry to the cellar. The rest of you, follow me." And, catching up her skirts, she broke into a full run.

We followed. We went first to the lazaret and took those lepers who were well enough down with us to the cellar; likewise, those in the regular hospital who could walk were also escorted down; and three nuns hurried to the kitchen to fetch whatever food and drink they could carry.

Numbed, I worked beside Geraldine in the lazaret—where old Jacques instructed other cripples to hold on to his back while he carried them down the stairs. We sisters carried those who were too feeble to move, interlacing our fingers to make temporary chairs. Our destination was the hidden magical chamber, into which we crowded food, lepers, plague survivors, and sisters, then swung the earthen wall closed.

I trusted Geraldine utterly and never questioned her commands, for she knew the Goddess's will as well as I, if not better. But when darkness closed over us with the rumble and scrape of stone against stone (for we dared not bring a source of light, lest it shine through a crack or crevice and reveal us), I thought: *Now we are trapped.*

Blind we were, but not entirely deaf. Through crevices placed in the chamber wall for ventilation, we were able to hear the shouts of the encroaching English, the screams of the fleeing French, the rumble of hoofbeats.

At last we heard what might have been dozens of footsteps above, and a bit later the clank of metal on the stairs. Finally, a singular pair of heavy boots scuffled down into the cellar, accompanied by the sound of heavy breathing.

The voice of a man, rasping and crude, barbarously unable to properly utter a single French vowel, as he called out: "Very well, ladies! If you are hiding somewhere here, you will not escape us. If you call out to me now, I promise none of you will be harmed. . . ."

We said not a word, but huddled together in the darkness, so close that my shoulders and knees were pressed tightly against Magdeleine's on my right and Geraldine's on my left; in front of me, Jacques sat, the base of his twisted spine pressed against my feet; I could feel their breath warm upon my face.

"Sisters," the Englishman called out in his tortured French. "If you are here, we will find you. Save yourselves and call out to me now. . . . We will reward you kindly for surrendering." He was a large man, surely, for we could easily hear his footfall as he moved about the great cellar.

Suddenly dozens of footsteps rang out on the cellar stairs; strange, deep voices cried out questions in a foreign tongue, and our Englishman replied. After a pause, we could hear more men entering the cellar.

A few of the sisters, not of the Race, moaned softly with terror.

For hours, we remained in our cramped condition, while soldiers came and went; we could hear above us more soldiers on the stairs, in the cells, outside on the grounds. At last the cellar became filled with the sounds of an army settling in for the night: men dragging in mattresses and supplies; I imagined I smelled roasted chickens and sacramental wine. They talked and laughed well into the night; and, when I finally believed they never would, fell silent and at last began to snore.

La bona Dea, I prayed, with the words my grandmother had loved so dear. *Good Goddess, I am in your hands; show me what to do.*

For I sensed that the survival of our community rested on me at that moment, and the starkness of that realization—that I *had* to evoke the Sight now or forfeit our lives—made me turn my cheek toward Geraldine and say, in a voice softer than a whisper:

"Circle."

She understood at once, caught my hand, and squeezed it; on my other side Magdeleine, who had impossibly overheard, did the same. A sound something less than a sigh passed through the room, and with deliberation and caution, those who were of the Race moved to the circle's perimeter and joined hands, while those who were not moved to the center, where they would be safe.

Those of us who could silently evoked a protective circle. As I surrendered myself and my fears, a potent peace—indeed, a sense of joy—at last descended upon me. In the space of a breath, I Saw clearly:

The English, finding in the convent shelter and ease, using it to shelter a portion of their legion; and, once they were gone, setting fire to the place. I smelled the smoke of three days hence: I heard the screams of the helpless lepers, of my sisters; I felt the heat of the flames, felt the stone walls surrounding us grow red-hot.

And I Saw the city of Carcassonne, its turrets, its watchtowers nestled behind ramparts of wood, and behind those ramparts, walls of stone. And the people said, *They shall never get in; we are well fortified. These stones have held a thousand years. . . .*

Fire sailing through the air, riding the tip of an English arrow, a deadly thing, hurled with the incomparable force of the longbow. Wooden ramparts set ablaze; wooden gates buckling against the battering ram.

In the city, death, death, and more death, followed by flames.

Including the distressing image of a sharp sword being raised; and Magdeleine and Geraldine standing beneath it, both crying out, both with hands raised to shield themselves from the blow.

All this did I See; yet I mastered my fear. For I Saw, also, what I was meant to do—and in that same breath, I felt again heat—not of fire, but of power, in the Solomon's Seal round my neck, in my very heart.

I knew logically that it was not safe to venture from our place, that the mere sound of the stone wall scraping against the ground would rouse the soldiers at once. I knew, too, that there would be watchmen surrounding the convent, and we, without weapons, were no match for them.

But I was past logic at that point: the joy that transcended all reason, all fear and doubt had overtaken me, and I was filled with a compassion that saw both tired warrior and terrified civilian, killer and victim, and utterly loved them both.

At once the Goddess gave the solution for sparing both, and I laughed softly.

"Do you feel it?" I whispered to Geraldine, and in the darkness sensed her smiling nod.

A warmth had descended upon us, a tingling ebullience; around our group of some three dozen souls, the blackness began to glitter with tiny golden sparks, like a star-scattered night. With my mind, I directed it to envelop our assembly, as the delicate shell surrounds an egg; and when it was safely in place, I said in a normal tone of voice:

"In this state, we cannot be seen or heard; and now we shall open the door and depart. Dear lepers, remain here. Sisters, come with me. Let us all pray to the Goddess, and we will all be safe."

Together, Mother Geraldine and I found the proper crevices in the unfinished stone, and pulled with all our weight: with a rumble, the door—shaped, I imagine, like the rough boulder that blocked the entrance to Christ's tomb—slid open.

Whether we were enveloped in a sphere or whether the entire world was aglitter with golden dust, I could not say; the effect was the same from my vantage.

Geraldine and I stepped out first, with Magdeleine just behind us; and the three of us froze immediately. For, lying on the ground no more than a thumb's length from the pushed-back stone—and from our very feet—was the freckled, balding head of a well-fed English soldier, his greasy auburn curls hopping with lice. Beside him rested his helmet; not the gently pointed domes with visors such as our knights wear (which recall the central blade of the fleur-de-lis), but a cap like an inverted bowl, with a broad, flat brim, tarnished to a dull brown.

Magdeleine looked at me swiftly, her eyes wide and aghast; for an instant, the shimmering gold surrounding us flickered. "Do not be afraid," I urged, squeezing her hand. "See? We have opened the door, but he is still sleeping."

At that very moment, the soldier released a snort as loud as any pig's, then blew out a gust of air that set lips and wiry red moustache flapping.

With my free hand, I clutched my side, laughing silently; Geraldine, Magdeleine, and some of the other sisters, too, bent over, shaking with hilarity, faces flushed. At last we recovered ourselves, and, smiling, moved forward, undaunted by the realization that so many men were sleeping so closely together that we had to lift our skirts high and pick our way around them.

At the cellar's far opening were two seated sentries, playing dice and arguing with one another in low voices; to them our approaching group were unseen ghosts. Inside the cellar proper lay perhaps forty men, wrapped tightly in the wool blankets that we made for our patients and the poor, for it was colder here than above. Twenty of these were the common English; but then we passed through a different group.

At once I became aware of unrest in our protective circle—in Magdeleine, who had just stepped beyond its invisible, protective boundaries with a surge of rage that would not be contained.

"French!" she cried, pointing at their helmets, their swords, their banners. "Look at them: traitors, every one!"

"Hush," Geraldine said, reaching for her, but it was too late: Magdeleine became quite visible. And at that instant, the abbess willed herself visible as well. (I, firmly rooted in the Presence, kept myself and my charges within the glittering veil.)

The soldier nearest us stirred; and then another. "Well," said the first, a thin, long-limbed man with an equally thin blond beard, and an accent that marked him as a noble and a Norman, "what have we here? Two ladies have decided to reveal themselves." His voice was ragged, weary, in the way of a man who has been forced to exceed his physical limits far too long, in the way of a man who has seen and committed too much cruelty. "Now, where there are two ladies . . . there are un-doubtedly three or four, or even more. Pray tell, where would the others be hiding? Do not be coy; I command here, it is I who decides your fate."

By the time he finished speaking, he had unwrapped himself from at least three blankets, and taken up a finely wrought sword with a handle of engraved gilt. The men surrounding him had done likewise: all bore well-crafted swords and were dressed in undergarments of fine wool—and all wore the same mocking half-smile as their commander. These were no common foot soldiers, but the trained elite, knights.

And all northern French.

Fury eclipsed any fear in Magdeleine's heart; she took a bold step toward the blond Norman and chided: "Here you are—Frenchmen—murdering your own people! No true chevaliers would do such a thing!"

"Take my hand," I told her, knowing the soldiers could not hear or see me. Yet even as I said it, I knew she would not; and even as I knew she would not, I felt no fear. Instead, I watched the drama from a place of repose and peaceful distance—while at the same time, my compassion was utterly engaged.

The Norman stepped up to her at once. He had held his sword loose in his right hand; now his grip tightened, and the muscles in his arm grew taut. With a blindingly swift movement, he bent his elbow, bringing his forearm up and back across his chest, right fist pausing briefly at left shoulder.

"No," Mother Geraldine said; not with outrage or terror, but with gentle, firm insistence.

As the sisters and patients watched in horror, she stepped between Magdeleine and her attacker. The Norman struck out with the sword as if issuing a backhanded slap.

Silence fell, so profound that one could hear the rip of fabric as the blade sliced through Geraldine's wool habit—as easily as it pierced the flesh above her breast. When she lost her balance and staggered toward him, he drove the blade in deep.

He stepped back then, and let her fall—forward, onto the weapon up to the very hilt, so that the greater length of the blade protruded directly out of her back, just beneath her right shoulder.

"Anyone else?" the Norman asked brightly.

Magdeleine fell sobbing, and pressed Geraldine's limp upraised palm to her lips. Beside me, within the veil of invisibility, the others wept silently.

But the commander would have none of it; he sheathed his sword, then seized Magdeleine's elbow and wrenched her to her feet. She struggled, but he managed to pull off her veil and wimple, revealing cropped pale curls.

"You are lucky you are beautiful," he said. "For that, you will be permitted to live another day or so and provide me companionship . . . *if* you tell me honestly where the other women are. Refuse to do either, and you will die, like your homely sister here." And he nodded dismissively at Geraldine's body.

In my life, I have experienced the slowing of time: this was just such a moment. Surely I felt compassion and grief at the sight of Geraldine fallen; but I also felt an odd sense of the *rightness* of things. This was as the Goddess willed it. Thus with a growing sense of joy, I called out to the Norman, with an authority far beyond my own:

"Let her go."

There was no anger in my words; no grief, no hatred, only justice.

An odd thing happened: the Norman of course drew his sword, one hand clutching Magdeleine, and turned toward me . . . but rather than lash out, he paused, his gaze unfocused, his expression quizzical.

"Let her go," I repeated, only to see him tilt his head, further mystified. His men had stopped their satyric leering to look in my direction, equally perplexed.

I laughed aloud as the realization struck me: I was still invisible to them. I closed my eyes, in my imagination dissolving the protective veil, and stepped forward as if emerging from an occluded doorway. I did not need to continue to hide the others; I knew they would be safe.

The commander's eyes widened, and his skin grew paler than his scraggly beard; thoughtlessly, he let go his grip on Magdeleine, who stared gape-mouthed at me and sank reverently to her knees.

"Holy Mother of God," the Norman sighed, and did the same. One by one, nuns and soldiers crossed themselves and knelt.

I cared not what they thought they saw: I knew only what was to be done. Containing my grief, I knelt by Geraldine, gently turned her on her side, and with some effort, withdrew the sword. She groaned as it came free, for she was still alive; alive, but from her grievous wound blood spilled, soaking the ground, dark against her darker habit, against my sleeves. Soon she would bleed to death.

I sat on the cold earth and gathered her into my arms.

She had been destined to be my teacher; she had not been meant to die. I knew I was poised on a precipice: I could react with bitterness. I could renounce the Goddess and curse my destiny. I could run from what must be.

But I would not.

I closed my eyes and pressed my hand hard against her wound; my skirts were already heavy with her blood. She was limp and gasping in my arms, dying.

I smiled at the illogic of it all. I dissolved.

Union. Radiance. Bliss.

A murmur moved through the crowd, like the fluttering of birds' wings.

I opened my eyes to find myself staring into Geraldine's brown ones: no longer dull and distant, but bright and alive—and looking *down* at me, for she was sitting.

My hand was still pressed to her wound; slowly, gently, she pulled it away to reveal black wool—untorn, unstained.

She rose, radiant, and gave her hand to lift me, suddenly startled, to my feet.

"You have just witnessed a true miracle of God," she told the kneeling assembly, and the Norman commander began to weep.

X V

Only later did I learn why both soldiers and sisters had knelt: not just because I had appeared to them out of thin air (which I had), but because I had appeared to them as the Virgin Mother, in her guise as Queen of Heaven, with blue veil and golden crown. Only after Geraldine had raised me to my feet did I appear as myself again.

The others regarded us in silence for a time; then, slowly, both nuns and soldiers rose. Geraldine's skin was truly aglow, like parchment held before a flame.

"I have seen the face of the Mother of God," she whispered into my ear. "She is here, with us."

The Norman approached us, his pale eyes troubled, his manner timid, penitent, his palms pressed together as if in prayer. "Sister," he said, "tell me what I must do. I am not a good Christian; I have not gone to mass in months, nor even made a proper confession in a year. But I cannot deny what I have just witnessed."

"Pray to the Holy Mother," I told him with an authority that surprised me. Had it been myself alone speaking, I most certainly would have added that he was to leave us unharmed and become an ardent supporter of good King Jean. "Listen carefully to what She tells your heart, and pay no heed to any man who contradicts Her."

"But what penance shall I do?" he persisted.

"Ask Her," I said.

The English and Normans were at first horrified, then angered, to discover that we had both lepers and plague survivors hidden with us. So we had meant to infect them, had we? But Sister Geraldine gestured at all of us sisters and said, "See our faces? Are they mottled with buboes? Do we show signs of leprosy? Yet we have nursed some of these patients for years. God and Saint Francis—and the Holy Mother—protect us, and will protect you, if you but believe."

"I will hear no ill talk about the sisters," the commander reprimanded his men, and ordered for us and our patients to be allowed to return to our usual quarters and given blankets, food, and wine. Miracle notwithstanding, we were apparently not entirely trusted, for sentries with lanterns filled the corridors; one stood watch just outside my cell.

The moment I was full of food and wine and comfortably warm, I fell asleep at once, for the events of the day had left me sorely weary. But after a time, even through the veil of sleep, I felt movement beside me, heard a faint rustle, sensed a presence. I opened my eyes and saw dark silhouettes kneeling about me, faces black and invisible, forms lit from behind by the sentry's lamp.

English soldiers: behind those nearest me were at least twenty others. The moment I opened my eyes, they crossed themselves as if I had just uttered a prayer.

I pushed myself up to sit; it took all my years of training in the mastery of mind and emotions to repress a grin and instead scowl peevishly at them. "Go away," I said. "The Holy Mother is sleeping."

These soldiers apparently spoke no French, for at my little joke they looked in confusion at each other.

"Go away," I said, making the same sweeping motion I might to shoo a goat. "Go back to England." And as my perplexed worshipers rose and began to leave, I called after them: "And tell your friends that you have seen the Holy Mother, and She is French."

The English housed us in secret kindness the next day—it could never be told, they insisted, or they would all surely be killed by their comrades. But on the day after—that terrible third day I had Seen in my vision—they herded us into wagons before dawn and carried us out to the forests west of the city; they would, the Norman said, be marching south and east. From there, we climbed up into the hills (leaving the lepers down in the forest, since they were likelier to be left alone—indeed, avoided—by any stragglers).

Finally we found a cavern that served as an excellent vantage point; and there, we watched the destruction.

Since the miracle, our captors had been courteous, even respectful: but the commander warned us that they would have to do certain unpleasant things in order not to be killed as traitors.

In the hours after sunset, we watched as the city—a great, oval collection of buildings, both wooden and stone—was slowly consumed by fire. From a distance, it seemed as though a flint sparked here, a taper flared there, a lamp over there—until at last the entire town no longer seemed a collection of separate candles burning on the altar of earth, but one great conflagration, yellow-orange against the smoke-laden sky, the clouds leaden against the deeper dark of night. The inner stone walls did not burn, but what remained of the outer wooden ramparts glowed red-hot, a circlet of ruby about the blazing jewel that was Carcassonne.

And then the fires erupted outside the city, devouring fields, trees, flowers, anything living, anything green. We watched as the thatched-roof houses of villagers were consumed in a brilliant burst of carmine; we watched, too, as tongues of flame snaked out of the windows of our beloved convent. The structure was of stone, and much of it might well survive to be rebuilt: but all the shutters, the wainscoting, the altar and altar vestments, the statues of Mary, Jesus, Saint Francis, the medicines and bandages and lovingly tended gardens of herbs—all these would be destroyed.

The east wind blew smoke and ash toward us, stinging our eyes and throats, prompting tears to course down our cheeks.

I wept not at the destruction of physical things, nor even at the deaths of the innocent—for all things were transient, even life, and suffering; and all that was destroyed would be transformed and reborn.

I wept because at last, in the flames that engulfed Carcassonne, I saw my Beloved. A shadow he was at first; but then I Saw him more clearly: a young man, sincere and tormented, as I was, by the distance between us.

My tears were those of pure human yearning—and disappointment at myself, for not yet conquering the fear that kept us apart.

All this I Saw in the raging fire, until I felt a touch, gentle and loving, upon my arm; a touch meant to soothe my heart, to ease any pain.

I stopped my tears, turned and saw Geraldine. She smiled gently, comfortingly.

But I found it not within myself to smile back. For the time was not right; our hearts were not yet right, and there was naught for us to do but wait.

The days after the English marched south were difficult ones. Those who had survived the siege wandered about the city streets and the fields just outside the ruined walls, but everywhere one looked, the earth was burnt black; all that remained of centuries-old orchards and vineyards were charred stumps. Even the water had been befouled: the English had dumped the corpses of victims into rivers, streams, and wells.

The convent well, however, had not been despoiled. We had sweet water and a modicum of food; the Normans had buried for us stores of flour, fruit, and vegetables in an untouched field behind the convent so that we would not starve. For the first few days after the burning of the city, we were alone, and believed ourselves the only survivors. Only scarred earth and rubble remained of the village that had housed the peasants who tilled our fields and the shepherds who watched our flocks.

Our abbey lay in only partial ruin: the dormitory had been set fire, destroying any cloth or wood within, but though the rooms were filled with debris and ash, the stone building remained solidly intact. During those hours of relative peace, we cleaned the blackened debris from the great chamber used as the hospital, which was of all rooms in best repair. There all of us, nun and leper and layperson alike, slept and lived, and those who were able worked to repair our home.

But those who had successfully fled the English returned to Carcassonne to find their homes reduced to ash; those who had remained and miraculously survived both invaders and fires wandered outside the city walls in search of sustenance. It did not take either group long to discover us, and the food left us by the Norman commander. Soon the convent, which had for so many years remained but a third occupied, was overrun. In addition to the starving and thirsty, there were many injured by fire and sword, many ill from tainted water. We had more sick than we could care for, and not enough food to feed them all; many I healed with the Goddess's power, and sent on their way. Even so, we nuns gave up our own portions, with the result that we went hungry; and still there was not enough. We prayed for help.

It arrived in the form of the bishop. Unannounced, unattended, wearing the garb of a poor village priest, he arrived one cold morning at the reins of a cart pulled by two donkeys. To our delight, the cart was filled with treasures from Toulouse: cheese, wine, apples, a bevy of chickens and a rooster, all bound at the feet, flour and olive oil, and a ram and two ewes tied alongside the cart.

We all rejoiced at this gift; and then the bishop summoned Mother Geraldine and me to a private conference. Again, we went inside Geraldine's office and closed the heavy door.

The bishop lowered the hood of his worn black cloak to reveal lips and brow drawn taut, eyes fierce and falcon-sharp. "My presence here is not official," he began grimly, his words rising heavenward as steam in the cold air. "But I must tell you that word has reached the Church concerning the miracle of Jacques the leper, and the vote was almost evenly split in terms of whether the initiator of that startling event was God or the Devil; mine broke the tie. It is thus now the official position that the healing was a miracle of God—but no special consideration is to be given to Sister Marie Françoise. Being a woman and of common blood, she was merely the crude vehicle of God's grace—so says the archbishop."

Geraldine and I considered this calmly for a time, then the abbess said: "You should know, Your Holiness, that Norman and English soldiers invaded our cloister, and their commander mortally wounded me. Sister Marie healed me in full sight of all of them, so it is no great surprise. Word will spread quickly now among the commonfolk. This is all as it was meant to be."

He listened to her carefully and nodded with great respect; and then she added: "I have taught her all that I know, Bernard, and she has learned well. She needs my instruction no longer. With your blessing, I shall surrender my position as abbess. Sister Marie Françoise shall take the position in my stead. This is as it must be; I have Dreamed it."

Within a week I was officially proclaimed abbess, and our little flock became known as the Sisters of Saint Francis of the Queen of Heaven. As life slowly improved in Carcassonne, our abbey grew, and so did my reputation as a miracle worker. A stream of sick and lame, blind and disfigured came for my Touch; some I cured, when the Goddess bade it. Rich believers inflicted upon us gifts of gold, horses, vineyards, and property. (I know not how I would have managed without the assistance of the novice Sister Ursula Marie, a merchant's daughter skilled at counting coin and keeping records.) So many lay brothers and sisters volunteered to help us nurse and tend crops and animals that we nuns were able to spend more time in study and prayer.

As for me, my heart's impatience overwhelmed my judgment. I

spent less time meditating on how I should overcome my fear—and instead considered when I should begin to seek my Beloved. After a year, knowing that the time was growing short, I used the magic Geraldine had taught me to Dream of him.

How handsome he was—with features classic and strong, as if they had been sculpted by an artist of ancient Rome—how courageous, and how good. At the sight of him it took all my effort not to weep with joy.

He stood at a crossroads and faced two men, both of whom I had seen the night of my initiation. One was the shadow-veiled magician, with his great thick hand raised to block, to stop. One was a knight, with complexion and hair like my Beloved's; and his hand was outstretched to assist, to guide. *Edouard,* I called to him; for I knew he served my Beloved as Mother Geraldine had served me.

Help him, my lady, Edouard said, gesturing at his charge. *I am merely a teacher; I have not your power to aid him. See, he falters on the Path. . . .*

I turned to the one I loved; I called his name, and he turned to me with a look of such devotion, such determination, I scarce could speak. Yet for his sake, I gathered myself, found my voice, and said:

Fate is a spider's web. At birth, we stand at its center, facing out at a hundred radiating paths. Our truest destiny lies at the end of one, and only one. We may not initially choose the right course, or others might intervene to distract us—but it is always possible to stop and instead travel one of the crosswise strands to the true Path. Indeed, it is possible to walk a hundred paths not our own—and then, at the end of our life, cross over from strand to strand to silken strand and ultimately arrive at our best destiny.

Did he hear me? I could not say; I came to myself with a sense of foreboding. Something was sore amiss: the Enemy had spent years setting a trap, which my Beloved was finally about to spring.

At once I directed my Sight toward the source of the coming danger:

The Enemy in his glorious, incense-veiled chamber, beneath the gaze of the gods. In one hand he cups a healthy young rat, with snowy fur and a thin, long tail of naked pink. Motionless, it breathes deeply, languorously, the black pupils in its tiny eyes large against thin circles of rosy iris, as if it has been charmed by a serpent.

Indeed, with the swiftness of a viper, Domenico strikes. He seizes the rat's tail between thumb and forefinger and holds it aloft above the onyx altar and the waiting circle of salt. Its torpor fled, the male rat struggles valiantly, curling its head and chest upward, trying to scramble up its lower body, reaching for its legs, its tail, the hand that grasps it. Reaching for purchase that cannot be found, small pink feet working furiously, tiny translucent claws swiping at air.

The magician draws a freshly sharpened razor. The instant the little animal uncurls and stretches backward, searching for a means of escape behind it, he slices firmly across its breast, his lip twitching ever so slightly as he meets the resistance of delicate bones.

Blood spills down into the salt circle. The hanging rat spasms violently, causing the wound to open further. The wound is deep, very deep: the ribs have been pierced, and I can see its still-beating heart.

I can See its beating heart.

And as I watch, the tiny red organ throbs slowly, slower, slower until it gives a final shudder and grows still. . . .

I sat, fully alert, my own heart pounding painfully, and gasped, hand to my breast: "Luc . . ."

These were the days when the Black Prince marched his vandals and brigands south and east (just as the Norman had said) to Narbonne and the sea, then back north to Bordeaux, with all the gold, jewels, tapestries, and other riches stolen from the once wealthy French. In the following months, there followed skirmish after skirmish to the north, and the Black Prince's father, Edward III, landed at Calais with an invading force, only to be forced back to England by good King Jean's loyal army.

That was before Jean rashly imprisoned Charles de Navarre, a member of the Norman nobility whom he accused of conspiring with

Edward, and seized Navarre's estates. The outraged Normans once again sought the help of the English king. Rash though Jean's action might have been, he was shrewd enough to foresee its consequence; in spring of the following year, 1356, he issued the *arrière-ban*, the call for all loyal Frenchmen to take up arms.

The king's foresight proved correct: in midsummer, a second army of Englishmen, led by the Duke of Lancaster, landed at Cherbourg in the far north, and headed for Brittany at the same time that the Black Prince and eight thousand soldiers left Bordeaux on another raid, this time headed north.

Good King Jean, meanwhile, had amassed an army twice that size; and at summer's end, accompanied by his four sons, he led his men in pursuit of Edward.

This news I learned in various ways—from travelers, townspeople, and from the Sight.

As I sat gasping after my terrible vision of the magician, I realized the Goddess had spoken to me most clearly: the war to come threatened not only the fate of France, but the very continuation of the Race. My Beloved's life, his future, was endangered.

Beside me upon the hospital floor, Geraldine slumbered peacefully, her lips parted, her head pillowed upon a stone. Dawn was still hours away, but the moon was bright, and I rose at once to crouch beside the former abbess.

Flanking us, the other sisters were snoring.

I should have woken her, my teacher; the exact danger that threatened my Beloved was unclear, my Sight unfocused. But my heart cried out like cathedral bells on the eve of war: catastrophe is coming, doom, the death of the Race. I could not stay and let Luc face that alone.

I was not ready for this, I knew; I had not faced my greatest fear. I went into battle like Achilles.

I stole silently away from the sleeping women. I took a small amount of food and water, a blanket; I mounted a strong horse.

To those unSighted, unmagical, this must have surely seemed like madness. I was an unarmed woman approaching two armies in full darkness on the eve of war. How should I keep from being mistaken for an enemy or a spy? How should I keep from being killed? At the very least, how should I keep the horse from stumbling in the darkness and becoming lame?

At the moment, there was no time left for such trivial worries.

I was late.

I may have already been too late. And I was not magically ready. . . .

X V I

For two days I rode upon my brave and tireless steed; leery of English soldiers, I avoided Aquitaine and the Garonne River, instead staying east alongside the mountains. From there I headed north, just past the city of Limoges; and on the third day, I reached the city of Poitiers in the hour before dawn.

From the city gates down toward the meadow and the army, I rode. The distance was not far, but it seemed that with each stride my mount took, the blackness of night eased more and more to gray; at the same time, a heavy mist began to form, shrouding the countryside, condensing in cool, fine droplets on my habit, my face. The moments before dawn have always seemed to me the quietest, when all nature is still; but then, as I retreated from the walled city of Poitiers, the air itself seemed to tremble. The two armies had made no secret of their existence: although the fog muted a great deal of the noise, I could hear on either side of me the sounds of warhorses snorting and stamping in innocent anticipation, the voices of men eager for glory and too arrogant to believe they faced their own deaths, the clang of armor and weapons being readied.

There was the smell of men, too, for they had been encamped there three days while papal legates argued vainly for a truce; it grew viler as I neared the latrines, and there was also the strong but less offensive odor of manure.

Twenty-five thousand men had amassed for the purpose of killing each other, on a field smaller than the one on which my father grew wheat. But that day the war was between me and the magician; and only one of us would emerge victorious.

I was not alone; he watched. I knew he watched.

And he knew, just as I did, that my protection was incomplete. My fear for my Beloved had compromised me, distracted me, indeed, so overwhelmed me that at times I forgot the Goddess and could think only of him.

I followed the noise and the smells, and made my way through an apple orchard; in the thickening mist, the trees were distorted wraiths, black boughs reaching out as I hurried past.

Beyond the trees lay an open meadow; and beyond that, hidden in the drifting, earthbound clouds, were ghostly silhouettes: the profiles of men on horseback. A dozen men in single file, I thought at first, until I drew close enough to see that it was but a trick of the fog. For the line of men stretched to my right and left farther than my physical eye could see, and behind each rider was a row of his peers that stretched to infinity.

They were facing to my left, where their enemy lay in wait.

I kept my Beloved's face foremost in my mind as I drew a breath and rode further into the open meadow, toward the soldiers. I knew what I must try to do this day; but the Enemy was close, very close. My Sight was clouded, sporadic; only my heart was sure.

The first ray of light streaked through the fog, dappling the gray with small, fleeting rainbows; as I neared the mounted soldiers from their flank, colors began to come alive. Black turned to scarlet, gray to blue, white to pale yellow: such were the bright banners flying. Here sat nobles dressed in costly armor, their helmets grandly plumed, their surcoats and banners bearing family crests. There were gilt lions and bronze hawks, white lilies set against backgrounds of blue, red and green dragons, yellow castles, golden crosses, brown stags and bears. The nobles sat upon the finest horses I had ever seen, also outfitted with armor on head and chest and draped in surcoats to match their riders'. I had not seen such assembled finery since I was a girl in Toulouse, watching the jousting tournaments; indeed, I never saw such finery even then.

The one nearest me, on the outermost position, glimpsed me on his periphery and turned his head toward me, one mesh-gloved hand reining in his anxious horse. He was old; his visorless helmet could not entirely contain his bushy white brows. "Eh! A woman! What are you doing here, Sister? Don't you know the fighting is about to begin? Go hide in the city!"

He was utterly, irreproachably French, down to the last detail of his clothing and armor; so were the others who took notice and directed scowls at me. Horses stamped, impatient. "A nun? Is she mad? Tell her to go!"

"Soon it will be too late," the old warrior insisted. "Do you hear? That is our spearhead charging."

As he spoke, trumpets sounded: dawn had come at last, with the thunder of hoofbeats and the war cries of men. The mounts whinnied their protests. "God be with them," the old knight prayed, eyes sweeping shut for an instant; then, as the assembly began to move— slowly, a step at a time—he glanced back down at me. "Now, you— go!"

I went. Not in the direction he wished me to, toward the city, but further toward the army's center, snaking around the slow-moving horses and infuriating the riders, some of whom took halfhearted swipes at me with their lances. "A *woman*," I heard them say to each other in wonderment and annoyance as I passed. I was looking for a standard with the image of three roses and a hawk; I was looking for an uncle, for a father and his son.

I knew these three rode somewhere ahead of us, and I spurred my tired horse on—in vain, for now that the knights were in slow motion, and many thousands of men in front of us proceeding in earnest, speed was impossible. With increasing difficulty, I struggled toward the heart of the battalion; and once there, saw a perplexing sight: twenty men dressed exactly alike, with black armor beneath a white surcoat embroidered with black fleurs-de-lis, and in the midst of them, a man bearing the scarlet Oriflamme, the fork-tongued banner of the kings of France—of King Jean, who was dressed like the others in order to confuse the enemy in case of an attempt at capture or assassination.

I urged my mount forward in the slow-moving current of warhorses; I tried to listen, but heard nothing of the battle. I looked into the distance; the battalion in front of me was on foot—even though they too wore knights' armor—but I could not see beyond them to those on the battlefield. Even so, something caught my eye above it: a great flock of dark birds, so large they obscured the sky. They arced upward, then swooped suddenly down: arrows, propelled with such force by the English longbow that they were well capable of piercing French armor.

At once I heard hoofbeats, clashing swords and battle-axes, war cries—and added to that cacophony, the death-shrieks of horses and men.

The Sight bade me let my valiant steed go: I dismounted and set him free, and he trotted happily toward the now distant meadow. As for me, I ran past skittish horses into the next division of soldiers. The men on foot there were all nobles too, every one in armor and fine surcoats, with banners and attendants. I ignored them, even though they shouted indignantly as I passed: *Mad whore! Come back tonight, when the war is won!* I ran until I could go no farther—not because of fatigue or loss of courage, but because the tide of soldiers on which I was swept was met by a current of men marching out of the mist *toward* them.

The battlefield, I thought at first. *These are the English.*

But no: these were the French, perhaps two, three hundred of them. They ran toward us, some bleeding, others splattered with blood, others with arrows caught in their armor. *"Retreat!"* they shrieked, visors up, each face a rictus of horror. *"We are dead men—they are killing us all! We are all that remain!"*

The cry went out before us—and behind us as well—weakly at first, and then more strongly: *"Retreat! Retreat!"* The soldiers near me stopped and watched their comrades in the first battalion go running past. For a moment, they hesitated in confusion, being filled with anticipation of war. But the fear on their fellows' faces was compelling. Moments before the official word was given, they turned and went running back toward the walled city, taking up the cry.

But I could not retreat; my battle had not yet begun.

It was near impossible to stand against the wave of fleeing flesh. But there was one soldier in front of me, his face still turned, like mine, toward the fight. He was large and strong, his legs like tree trunks, his arms mighty boughs; I pressed behind him and let him shield me from the tide. And when he looked to see who had hidden behind him, revealing his broad, corpulent face, he smiled, and said: "Behold, a woman is braver than them all. Pray for me when I am dead, Sister."

We stood fast until the swell of those retreating passed, then slowly made our way forward, my protector hampered by his heavy armor and battle-ax, but holding his shield high. It caught three arrows as I ducked behind him; each time, the loud *thunk* of the arrow striking the shield and the following reverberation of wood and metal caused me to jump, though I felt no conscious fear.

The sun had begun to burn away the mist. I peered around my knight's broad flank and saw, on our immediate horizon, what remained of our soldiers: a few clusters of Frenchmen—every one of the nobility—and a few German mercenaries were still on their feet, but the retreating first battalion had told the truth. Everywhere, dark, dirt-smeared Englishmen removed their weapons from French corpses. My knight saw this, too, raised his battle-ax, and began to charge....

Yet before he could react, he stumbled and fell forward onto an obstacle sprawled at our feet: a handsome young noble lying on his back in full armor, his eyes wide, lips slightly parted in surprise.

Nearby, the noble's squealing horse labored with its forelegs to rise and could not: its unarmored rump had been deeply pierced by an arrow, rendering its hind legs useless; its fine surcoat, embroidered with gold and blue thread, was soaked in blood. Inconsolable, it bared its teeth and reared its wild-eyed visage toward the sky.

"Here now, here now," said our knight softly to the downed young rider; the former managed to catch himself before he was entirely down—and by pushing with one arm against the horse and the other against me, he managed to rise again, but only with much groaning and creaking of armor. "Let us set you aright, *seigneur,*" he told the noble, and with amazing strength reached down and began to lift the fallen man.

But the handsome young man's expression did not change: his eyes stared into the far distance, and his body remained limp as the knight struggled to lift it. Indeed, his head lolled backward, and it was then that we noticed how it canted at an odd angle.

"Hell and damn," said the older knight as he gently laid the younger man to the ground. "Hell and damn. His neck." Then with a swift, startling move, he swung his ax under and upward to connect with the keening steed's throat. Blood gushed forth like a spring, and the poor animal sank down immediately, its suffering ended at last.

It was then that I saw more clearly what lay around us and just ahead of us: a field of fallen bodies. Horses dead and dying, a few wandering without their riders; knights fallen, some crushed beneath their mounts, some hacked down by sword and battle-ax. And everywhere, sprouting from bodies animal and human, armor-clad or no, the shaft of English arrows: so long, that were one to have been driven all the way into my skull, leaving only the feathered tip showing at my crown, it would have extended below my knees.

The sunlight seemed suddenly too bright, my human vision too clear. The way before us was suddenly so covered in blood and flesh that we could scarce make forward progress.

An arrow whistled between us, so close and shrill that my ear was momentarily deafened; the knight reacted by raising his shield between us.

Immediately, from on top of a dead horse, a dark figure leapt at us: I recoiled, gasping, and watched the enemy attack my protector. The former was an English commoner with a tarnished bowl of a helmet on his head and a badly dented breastplate; he swung a bloody iron battle-ax with both arms, muscles standing out in cords.

Inferior weapons and, some would say, an inferior man. But his eyes were wild as he roared, and my Frenchman was undone.

His fine shield took the worst of the first blow and he tried, my knight, to counter with his own finely polished ax; but the momentum of the blow forced him down on one knee. He tried to swing again, but there was no room for him to launch a proper blow, and the next strike from his attacker made him fall back onto the ground. The armor was too heavy for him to rise unaided.

There was a time and place for miracles, and it was not I who controlled them. As desperately as I wished to intervene, it was the Frenchman's time.

As the killing blow came, I knelt beside him, closed my eyes, and began to pray—aloud, so that he would hear it as he took his final breath.

Warm blood spattered my face, as fine and gentle as the morning mist. And when I opened my eyes, I gazed up at the English soldier, who had again raised his weapon to strike.

I kept my palms pressed together, my visage composed. I Saw the force within, behind, beyond the ignorant soldier. "Go ahead if you wish," I told him calmly. "Go ahead; I am not afraid. But first, you must know that the Holy Mother loves you."

A curious, indeed bewildered, expression crossed the Englishman's dirt-smudged face; slowly he lowered the ax—then, as if suddenly lashed by a whip, he ran on.

I rose, the knees of my black winter habit heavy with damp earth and blood, and made my way over and around bodies—thousands and thousands of the dead, as far as I could see in either direction, too much death for any one heart to contain. Naught could I do but harden mine: for at my right, one man stood screaming with his arm severed, and I was forced to clutch him for balance lest I slip on the gleaming entrails of another who lay groaning. And these were but two in an impossibly vast tableau of the most grievous suffering any can imagine: I could not but think that only the untested have ever uttered the word *glory* in relation to war.

Around me English archers had emerged from their hiding places behind hedges and hastily built palisades to pull arrows from the dead, standing upon the corpses and using their feet to aid in leverage; and the English foot soldiers, the same commoners who had marched into Carcassonne and burned most of the city to the ground, ran after those who had retreated, or fought the small pockets of living French who remained. They paid me no heed, as if I had been incidental, a harmless dog who had wandered accidentally into the midst of war.

Behind me, trumpets blared again. The soldiers were on foot, not mounted: I heard them march. In the far distance near the city, hundreds of warhorses grazed on the grassy slopes.

At both sounds, the archers looked up, then ran back to their palisades for shelter, and the English foot soldiers took up a war cry and ran faster toward more approaching French.

It was the last battalion, led by King Jean, and foreboding overtook me: I had seen not one peasant, not a single member of the bourgeoisie. Our dead were all noblemen, the finest of France, more knights than ever I knew existed in the realm. The king—too brave to join the others' retreat—had seen the folly of riding horses with unprotected rumps in a war against the longbow, and had ordered his men to shorten their lances and cut off the long, pointed toes of their *poulaines,* designed not for marching but to hold their feet in the stirrup. Their steeds now grazed serenely in the distance, indifferent to the fate of their riders.

Again I was surrounded by chaos: by a stream of bodies moving in opposite directions, clashing with the sound of metal. I staggered forward in the melee, for my sense of urgency had become overwhelming: I had to find *him,* and soon.

I could progress forward only very slowly, ducking swiftly to avoid swinging weapons aimed at others, sometimes crawling on my hands and knees on the torn and bleeding ground. I was covered in blood: my habit, my once white wimple, my veil, even my face. I stopped licking my lips because they tasted so strongly of iron. I crawled over stones and fallen weapons, over motionless golden spurs, until my own blood flowed with the others' to nourish the ground. My palms, my knees, the cloth that covered me, were tatters.

Of a sudden, I heard hoofbeats very near and thought that perhaps it was Black Edward's final assault on our king. But no, there was only one horse; and the instant I realized that, I also realized that the sound had stopped, and the very hooves I had just heard were now standing directly beside me.

My lady.

I heard it first silently in my head, and looked up. The horse wore a scarlet plume and a white surcoat over its armor to match that of its rider: black armor, like the king's, and the surcoat embroidered with a peregrine perched above a descending triangle of three crimson roses.

The knight opened his visor. "My lady."

I rose and studied his face. I knew it well: I had first seen it the night of my Beginning. The features were fine and well-balanced, the nose aquiline and unmistakably noble. Beneath the brow of his helmet, his eyes were the color of a pale sea, his beard red kissed with sungold. He, too, looked ragged and blood-spattered, and had broken off the shaft of a single arrow that had pierced the shoulder of his armor but left no wound.

"My lady," he repeated; I extended my hand, and he kissed it. In the midst of an ocean of fighting, we were alone and untouched.

"Edouard," I said. "Thank God. You must take me to Luc at once."

Immediately he pulled me up onto the horse. Ducking behind his shield, we rode away from the front, with those who were retreating.

"Wait!" I cried. "Wait—I can feel him; he is back there, behind us. We must turn around at once."

"You are foolish to have come, lady!" he bellowed over his shoulder. "It is a trap—do you not see? Luc, too, was lured here by the Enemy; my own Sight told me as much. Now he has disappeared in battle, and I do not know what has become of him. We dare not lose you, too!"

"No!" I screamed in pure fury, half rising behind him. "It is *you* who do not understand! 'Tis a trap, to be sure, but he will die, Edouard! He will *die* unless I find him! The trap must be entered—but we shall find a way to escape."

But Edouard's mount did not slow, nor did its rider turn. Desperate, I half slid down the horse's sweat-and-blood-soaked surcoat, then flung myself down, landing on palms and knees on the tortured earth.

I recovered and ran. Ran and did not see the chaos surrounding me; ran and did not think of danger, or war, or the Enemy. I thought only of my Beloved, and my Sight—veiled by emotion, unsure—was nonetheless strong enough to lead me toward him.

After a time—an eternity, a heartbeat—I stood upon the ground where fighting first commenced, where the flower of French nobility, the *grand seigneurs,* the noblest-born chevaliers, were first struck down. The field terminated a short distance further on, giving way to marshy ground, then to a mature vineyard, then to hedges and slopes perfect for hiding archers. English foot soldiers were still slogging toward us through the marsh, sinking ankle deep; no wonder they were so filthy.

Beside me an anonymous knight lay in profile, his armor forever bound to him by more than a dozen arrows that pierced his breast-plate, his unprotected arms, his legs, even the visor designed to protect his hidden face. He still clutched the reins of his downed horse. The poor creature also lay dead on its side, its flank and rump pierced by a full quiver of arrows. Their surcoats were scarlet, with patches of white.

Torn by the fact that I could not help all I saw, I almost moved past the pitiful sight—and then I stopped and let go a hoarse, rasping sob. The surcoats were not scarlet, but bloodied; and the crimson stains had rendered the roses near invisible beneath the dark falcon. There was a dreadful sense of finality emanating from the tableau; this was a death I could not prevent, a man whom I could not help.

This was the *grand seigneur* of Toulouse, Paul de la Rose.

Metal whistled through the air not a hand's breadth from my right ear—so loud that I cried out, cupping my palm to my head, and stumbled upon an English corpse. I recovered and whirled about to face the weapon.

The English battle-ax was dark: congealing blood over black iron, and the soldier who swung it back over his shoulder, this time to split my skull, was blond and impassive, a mercenary, protected by a battered helmet and scarred leather shield.

I dropped to my knees.

A screech of metal against metal: sword clashed with ax to send up a constellation of blue-gold sparks that glinted dazzingly in the sun: eternal splendor, white-hot brilliance.

The body that wielded the sword stood with its back to me: a French knight, whose stained surcoat bore the image of the hawk above the trio of roses.

Edouard, I thought. But his legs were longer, his shoulders broader.

At the very instant the name came to me, I knew I was mistaken; and I knew on whom I looked. At the sight of him in the flesh, I let go a small cry.

With a slight hesitation in the movements of his arms, his back, he swung his sword to counter the ax, and the two weapons collided with such force that blue-gold sparks leapt into the air. He swiveled his head

over his shoulder, swiftly trying to catch a backward glimpse of me, to
see if another soldier threatened—

—but the very act slowed him, permitting his enemy to wield an
unanswered blow. The English soldier drew the heavy ax back over his
right shoulder, then, putting the entire heft of his body into it, began to
straighten his arms.

At the same instant, Edouard appeared behind him on horseback
and thrust downward with his lance. From the Englishman's belly the
weapon's point emerged, the iron dulled by violet-brown blood.

The man fell forward, but his weight only added to the heavy ax's
momentum as it arced implacably down on my young paladin. I could
not see the actual act; but I heard the screech of the blade cleaving metal,
then the lower-pitched, muted thunk of it biting into flesh and bone.

My Beloved dropped his sword and teetered backward, arms flailing
for balance that could not be found; with a clatter of armor, he fell
faceup upon the damp ground. Upon his breast lay the Englishman.

Edouard leapt from his horse and pulled the English corpse away.

Sunk deep into my Beloved's chest, almost to the handle, was the ax.

Bending at knees and waist, Edouard pulled mightily upon the
wooden handle. The blade came free, not without a great deal of suction
and a torrent of blood. Weeping silently during the entire action, he
loosened and removed the cloven breastplate, its edges dangerously
sharp, then moved quickly to one side and knelt, watching.

It was not a time for self-indulgence: it was the moment for which I
had come. I swallowed all my grief, and pulled the heavy helmet away
to reveal my Beloved's face. His eyes were wide, directed heavenward; I
put my face between them and the sunbright sky. For an instant, they
did not perceive me; the veil of death was slowly being drawn over
them—and then, with the final release of breath, they focused and
looked directly at me.

My own eyes filled with tears, not from sorrow, but at the exquisite
rendering of love and recognition upon the human face before me.

He had seen me and known me.

That alone was sufficient to quell my every fear, my every doubt. Still on my knees, I pressed my hands against his wound. Too hard, for the gouge was deep and wide; it opened, and for an instant both my hands slipped inside his chest, past shattered breastbone and sharp ribs.

I was touching his heart.

His still-beating heart.

The image of the magician and the rat rose unbidden; and as I held my Beloved's heart in my hands, it spasmed—once, twice, then a third time, slowly . . . and then it stopped.

He was dead, my Beloved.

Luc de la Rose was dead.

For an instant, no more, the grace of the Goddess remained with me— then the Enemy, ascendant, struck. A torrent of mounted English soldiers, the last charge, came sweeping down upon us: I was knocked down, away, shrieking as my legs were crushed beneath a dozen hooves, but it was not the pain that made me cry out. I was separated from my Beloved, from his body—I lifted blood-slicked hands to the war-hidden sky, but I could not See what had become of him.

I shrieked, and was trampled again; then cold metal hands seized me, lifted me, slung me over a horse, and carried me away.

PART V

Michel

CARCASSONNE

1357

XVII

And Michel watched as Sybille, her eyes and thoughts focused on a different place, a different time, emerged slowly from that dreadful moment in the past. Her gaze had been directed beyond him; but now it receded until she beheld him and her present surroundings. After staring at him for an anguished instant, she lowered her face to her hands and let go a soft, bitter cry.

With dismay, Michel leaned forward and murmured: "Hush, Mother, do not weep. Do not weep. . . ."

But her despair was profound; without thinking, he put a hand upon her forearm to comfort her—and quickly withdrew it, startled by the electricity in that touch.

At that she looked up, dark eyes glittering with tears but ashine with the same charge he had felt.

If only she were a Christian, he thought, she would certainly be the saintliest person he had ever known, and the most loving. How kind she had been to the lepers, how greatly she had loved her grandmother and her abbess. In her beliefs—sadly heretical—she was devout, and in her actions, compassionate and brave. To go into the midst of battle alone and unarmed—

An amazing woman, Michel thought—then recoiled internally at the realization: This was not a prisoner he could simply surrender with sadness to the civil authorities for execution, a prisoner whose fiery death he could watch with grief and pity, whose damnation he would mourn. Her words, her strength, her very presence had moved him, and he had lost his heart.

However long he lived, he would divide his mortal existence into the time before and the time after he had met this woman.

God forgive me. God, forgive me for my lust; do not let it interfere with a proper interrogation. Let me humbly complete the task You have sent me to do.

"Luc died then, did he not? Were your efforts in vain?" Michel asked gently. "Is that why you cry, Mother?"

She shook her head, and with noticeable effort, regained her composure. "I cannot speak of it even now. I am tired; I must rest."

And she lowered herself gingerly into a reclining position on the wooden board.

"Mother," Michel said with honest alarm, "you *must* find the strength to continue. Bishop Rigaud will require something far different from this testimony if you are to be found innocent. Turn your heart to Christ; confess to your crime, and perhaps we will be able to free you from this jail."

"They want my blood," she said, her voice hollow with exhaustion, weary beyond all emotion, neither repentant nor fearful. "And they will have it, regardless of what I say."

Michel let go a small, plosive sigh of indignation. "How can you know such a thing, Mother?"

"Ah, but I do, poor brother." She looked upon him with infinite pity. "Just as you know more than your mental prison allows. The dreams of Luc are vivid, are they not?"

Her unexpected question stung him. With his heart, he believed in her story, and that the dreams were indeed the memories of the dead Luc; with his rational mind, he believed in Christ and the Church, and knew that what she spoke was the vilest heresy, and that he was on the verge of losing his mortal soul.

He lowered his face and shook his head at the perplexity of it.

"I . . . The dreams of Luc, they trouble me. They fill my waking thoughts," he said at last, then stopped himself at once; he had not intended to make the admission.

"You know why you are sensitive to them, Brother."

It was a statement, but he looked at her askance.

"You are one of us," she said. "One of the Race."

His lips parted as his jaw dropped slightly, and he stared her intently before at last finding his voice. "I will not hear such a thing!"

"It is why the dreams come so easily to you; why you feel drawn to me, why a part of you believes my story. These things have happened not because of any spell or by coincidence, but because of who you are. Bewitched you are, Brother, but not by me. The struggle is not for *my* soul . . . but for yours."

Before she could finish, Michel had stiffly replaced quill, inkhorn, and parchment into his bag. "I—if you will not continue your statement further, I must leave to go pray. Father Charles—and Bishop Rigaud— were right. You are an exceedingly dangerous woman."

And as he turned to call for the jailer, he glimpsed for the merest fraction of time her face. There, in the dark eyes and the parted swollen lips, he saw the purest mix of such love and sorrow that it seized his heart; but he steadied himself and moved on.

Father Charles appeared no better. Brother André clearly had nothing new to report, but merely rose from his bedside seat, nodded at Michel, then hurried off to refection.

Michel, however, had no appetite—for food or for prayer. Instead, he sat in the backless wooden chair vacated by André and studied his mentor's face. Father Charles's pallor had taken on a yellowish cast, and his cheeks and tightly shut eyes seemed to have sunken even further; the lips were drawn tautly over the teeth and cracked to the point of bleeding, despite the wet rag Brother André had left behind for moistening them. Charles seemed capable of expiring at any time.

"Bless me, Father, for I have sinned," Michel whispered to the unconscious priest. "I have fallen in love with the witch Sybille. I listen to her stories of heresy and magic, and hear only good in them. I hear her speak of her Goddess and feel inspired. I am being led like a dumb beast to the slaughter; I have failed, and she has succeeded."

In the flickering light from the hearth fire, Michel leaned back. Head against the wall, he stared up at the shadows writhing across the ceiling.

Mere phantoms they were, and nothing more; black falsehoods projected from a simple, concrete reality. Was that all that the abbess's story was—or was she telling the truth? Were his feelings for her merely the result of a powerful spell?

He squeezed his eyes shut and pressed his hands to his ears with a force intended to blot out all thought, all memory, all internal sights and voices. Harder and harder he pressed, fingers trembling, and in an effort to drown out the sounds, he whispered, "Hail Mary, full of grace; the Lord is with thee. Blessed art thou . . ."

Over and over he repeated the prayer until a deep peace descended upon him. Despite his shut eyelids, a vision coalesced before him: the Holy Mother, robed in dazzling white, veiled in sky blue. She reached forth with her hands and blessed him.

This was Holiness Unquestionable. Michel took his rosary in hand and fell upon his knees.

TOULOUSE

September 1356

XVIII

In a flurry, the images of another man's life descended upon him:

Of Papa, healed—and, reluctant to give up his only child, retracting his promise to train his son in the use of his powers.

Of six-year-old Luc, still living at his father's home, running against a backdrop of brilliant-colored skeins and tapestries, crushing underfoot the herbs and flowers strewn on his mother's chamber floor: pennyroyal, mint, rosemary, lavender, and rose, all mingling to make a heady perfume.

Slipping free from his father's grasp, past the guard, heading straight into his mother's waiting arms—then gasping as, with a single motion, she caught his neck and tried to wrench it, as if breaking the tender neck of a bird.

So soft her hands, so cool, so surprisingly strong.

He had tried to scream and found himself unable to draw a breath. Surprise left him incapable of struggle: instead, he had stared up at his mother's face—her beauty marred, her features contorted, fearsome as a gargoyle's, but Luc had looked beyond the wildness in her eyes, at the love and anguished apology there.

By that time, Papa was already upon her, gentle and swift—but her strength was supernatural, and Papa and the guard were forced to wrest her to the ground and lie upon her while she howled, limbs flailing in a futile effort to reach her child.

Within two days, Luc's things were packed and he was sent to Uncle Edouard's estate.

It was grand, though not so large as Papa's; but the atmosphere there was happier and somehow safer; Luc felt free to flourish. It was the happiest time in his life, certainly, for Edouard's joyfulness never fluctuated, and the knights in his small *mesnie* were the same.

There Luc received his training as a squire. He excelled at all: dancing, which he was forced to practice with the knights' sons (which generally left them in giggles over who took the role of lady, and with how much affectation); falconry, which gave him a thrill each time the handsome bird with its thick, strong talons lit upon his glove, flapping its great wings and tilting its head to regard him with a singular and piercing eye; swordsmanship, for which his talent was acute; and horsemanship.

He learned the arts of chivalry and war easily—though not quite so easily as he mastered his other training: the secret training that he had sworn upon his life never to reveal.

It began in his thirteenth year, well after sunset, when night had rendered the world monochrome. Edouard had come to Luc's chamber, and whispered to the boy, awake in his bed in the moonless black: "Come. It is the time."

Without a word of challenge, the boy had risen. Edouard had given him commoner's clothes and a dark cloak to wear, and led him down a narrow, secret passageway leading from his uncle's chamber outside, to the stables. There they had taken mounts, and ridden half an hour over starry-skied meadows to the nearest town.

Edouard led his nephew not to any structure befitting two knights of noble birth, but to rows of tiny narrow houses—shacks, really, built of wood and thatch instead of stone, all clustered on an impossibly narrow street, and all dark, it being well past the time of cover fires for the common folk.

Commoners, Luc realized, *and poor ones at that.* But this place lacked the hopelessness and filth of other ghettos he had seen; the edifices were clean and well maintained, the neighborhood free of the stench that permeated other city streets.

The houses appeared identical; but Edouard rode confidently up into the center of the cramped ghetto and to one structure in particular, then dismounted and rapped upon the door.

As no light shone from any window, Luc expected all the inhabitants to be asleep, but the door opened almost immediately. Within, the hovel was dark, and their host illumined by the single dying flame of a candle stump. In the dimness, he appeared a hulking shadow, a great shaggy beast that dwarfed Edouard. He spoke not a word, but gestured urgently: *come in, come in.*

Edouard in turn signaled to Luc, who dismounted with a sense of both intrigue and dread. Their host led them through an outer room, where a faint aroma of supper lingered: a stew made with unfamiliar, pleasant spices, and yeasty ale rather than hippocras. Overlying this came faint wafts of a fragrance Luc had never smelled outside the great cathedral: frankincense.

There he heard the breath of sleeping children, caught the gleam of a woman's suspicious gaze in the feeble candleglow; when they passed into an inner sanctum, their host shut the door behind them.

This room was dark as the first—unlit, with shutters drawn—but the moment the door closed, Edouard reached into the folds of his cloak and handed over a gift: several long tapers and a flask of oil.

In a deep, melodious voice, their guide said, "My thanks, Edouard. These will ease our task." He put all but one aside; this he touched to the dying flame in his hand. The shadows that hid his countenance began to dissolve, and when he used the flask to fill a large oil lamp, then lit it, Luc saw him at last as he was: a broad-shouldered bear of a man with uncommon hair, hair that streamed down his back in stripes of ivory, iron, and ebony, as thick and tightly curled as a winter coat on a ewe. Hair that streamed from his face—in a beard so long it was tied round his belt lest he trip over it—in tight, regular kinks, as a maiden's tresses hang when recently unbraided. Hair that protruded a full finger's length from his brow, shading his eyes most dramatically; between these, a prominent nose emerged downward.

And when Luc noticed the small black cap on the crown of the stranger's head, and saw pinned to his dark tunic the yellow felt circle that marked him as a Jew, he was mystified. Jews were the worst of all heretics according to the Church (not that he gave the institution much credence), and to be found consorting with them was cause for questioning by inquisitors. Why would his uncle have brought him to such a dangerous place?

Edouard, however, took the weathered hand of the old Jew, lifted it to his lips, and kissed it with remarkable reverence. "*Rebbe. Rebbe,* I bring to you my nephew, Luc."

The old man waved the respectful gesture away as unimportant, then bent down to peer at Luc. "At last; at last. Luc, hello. I am Jacob."

For a year he studied under Jacob's aegis; and during that time, Edouard forbade all contact with his parents, even at Eastertide. "You cannot see them," Edouard had told him mournfully, "especially your mother."

"Why?" Luc had demanded again and again; and the answer, always unsatisfactory, came:

"Because your mother is tied to the Evil that threatens you, your Beloved-to-be, and the Race. For you to be with her, to expose yourself to her, is to expose yourself directly to your Enemy."

"But Jacob can protect me," Luc had argued. "Both you and Jacob, and nothing will happen to me. . . ."

And Edouard had sighed. "Luc, you must understand. . . . Your Enemy is exceedingly powerful; and Jacob and I fear too much for your sake to rely on our lesser abilities to protect you. Look at your poor mother—at the good I was able to do for her." And he lowered his head in shame, so stricken and sorrowful that Luc had put a hand on his shoulder in an effort to comfort him. At last Edouard gathered himself, and added:

"In time, Luc—after you have received your initiation—you will be a powerful magician. More powerful than all your enemies. Then, perhaps, the time will come when our Beatrice, your mother, can be restored to us. But until then—beware, for your Enemy wants nothing more than to keep you from that moment."

In order to avoid further upsetting his uncle, Luc had said nothing more; but he swore to himself that, the very moment he became magically strong enough, he would wrest his mother from the Enemy's grip and restore her to herself.

So Luc began his true studies. The first lessons were simple: to learn to sit straight as a pillar, to breathe slowly and steadily, to empty his mind of all. He progressed swiftly and learned to create a circle of protection, scribing an imaginary line of blue flame and golden stars that in his mind became as real as the flickering lamp that lit Jacob's chamber.

"The circle is a place of protection," Jacob said one day after Luc had begun the lesson in the typical way, by casting a circle with his forefinger, carefully drawing the stars and each cardinal point and whispering (in such a deep way that it caused the inside of his chest to vibrate) the Hebrew names of God and the archangels. "But it is more importantly a safe place to awaken within yourself the power of God."

From the folds of his robe he withdrew a small, polished piece of glass and held it carefully between thumb and forefinger; then he moved his hand until the glass caught the lamplight at a precise angle.

Luc drew in a breath. For the bare wooden wall was suddenly painted with a rainbow of color, from red to yellow to blue to deepest violet.

"God is light," Jacob said softly. "He shines with eternal white brilliance; yet such is His glory that it cannot be contained in any one place. It spills over, separating into manifestation after manifestation, just as the light from the candle separates into all the different colors. So there is within each man the different virtues and power of God, each evoked by different colors and sounds. This is ancient knowledge, but it has been lost for a long time. You will keep it secret, of course, passing it down only to your heir; for when the knowledge is needed again by our people, an angel will reveal it to another."

Thus Luc learned to meditate in a circle on what Jacob called the spheres of power: Kether, meaning the Crown, the ineffable white light that hovered just above his head. From it he drew the power down: to red Geburah (Severity) and blue Gedulah (Mercy) at his shoulders, then to the sphere of gold at his heart, Tifareth, the place of perfect balance. There came the violet of the astral, Yesod, at his sex, the place where all magic was accomplished. Last came Malkuth, the world of reality at his feet, divided into the four quarters of black earth, citrine, clay, and wheat.

From Edouard Luc learned the art of sigils and talismans—with the stern warning that they were to be used only for that good directed by the God within him. He made a talisman that healed old Philippe from pleurisy, and one that rendered him, Luc, invisible to the knights of the *mesnie*. Then, with deep respect and joy, he made a Solomon's Seal out of the purest gold for his beloved teacher for protection.

"When shall I be initiated?" he asked Jacob seven months into his tutelage.

The *rebbe,* half his face in shadow, half illumined by Uncle Edouard's candle, regarded Luc mildly.

"True union cannot occur in the presence of fear." He paused at Luc's puzzled expression, then added, "I cannot initiate you for a very practical reason: It is a woman you seek."

Luc drew in a breath. "The girl," he whispered to himself, "the one who fell from the cart, the one with the dark braid and the dark eyes . . ." He realized with a sense not of surprise but of rightness that he loved her, had always loved her.

"Yes," Jacob murmured beside him. "The girl. You are a proficient magician. But there are other gifts you lack, including that of the Sight, which you will need in order to fight your enemies. And she alone can give them to you. Of all the Race, only you two shall have many gifts and be the most powerful." He paused as his eyes focused on a spot far beyond Luc. "It was predicted more than a thousand years ago by a group of mystics in the Holy Land. Two messiahs would appear: one kingly, one priestly, and united they would save their people. For such blasphemy, the mystics were chased into the desert, where they hid for centuries. You, Luc, are the king, and you are bound to find your priestess. So it must be each generation."

Luc listened with only cursory attention, for at the thought of seeing the girl again a thrill passed through him. "*Rebbe,* when can I—when shall we two . . . meet?"

Jacob shook his head wistfully. "That I cannot say. But I can tell you this . . ." And he turned to point at the painting Luc had made of the different-colored spheres of power, organized in rows, which hung near them. "Here, at the top, is Kether—the white light, the brilliant Divine, the Crown. And here at the bottom is Malkuth, the Queen who rules the Kingdom of Earth. Do you see? Here is the path the groom must take to reach his bride; he must pass through many obstacles before he reaches the bliss, the power of Divine Union."

All of a sudden, Luc's very heart began to ache; and for the first time he understood the restlessness that had driven him, the sense of emptiness he had felt even in the company of loved ones. "How can I wait?" he whispered, near tears. "How long must I be apart from her?"

And Jacob, a tender look of pity upon his craggy face, said, "You must look into your heart and purge the greatest fear hidden there, the one fear your Enemy can use against you, the one that will sap your strength and make your magic powerless. Only then is it safe for you and your Beloved to be united."

"Tell me what to do and I shall do it," Luc answered stoutly.

"It is not for me to name your fear; you must discover it for yourself. I can only help as I am bidden; I can bring her no closer to you. Let the knowledge of what awaits you serve as balm for your soul." With his great hands—gloved in tattered wool, with each icy fingertip exposed—resting upon the boy's shoulders, he began to chant in a voice so strong and sonorous that the very atoms of air in the room seemed to vibrate.

Jacob's cold, bony hands grew suddenly warm, and through them streamed a power like a bolt of lightning—dazzling to mindlessness. It seemed to Luc that he had lived a blind, shadowy existence, and only now could he truly see . . . see the Light—nay, *become* it, in all its glory and beauty. Within it were no limits: no life, no death, no time, no Luc, no Edouard, no Jacob, no Papa, no Maman, no Church, no magic, no Torah. Only a vast, all-encompassing Joy that knew no Sorrow.

And a Voice spoke. *"Jacob, you shall take our talisman to the country-side, where our Beloved dwells. Death dwells there, too, but a greater life follows, and the greatest reward."*

The words were uttered with Luc's own tongue, but so great was his bliss that he heeded them not at all. He remained in that wordless state for an hour or perhaps a day, a year, a lifetime, a single heartbeat—he knew not. But when at last Luc returned to his normal mind, he found Jacob had knelt facedown upon the floor. And when the *rebbe* at last lifted his head to gaze upon his pupil, Luc saw the radiance of God reflected on his countenance.

Luc crawled off the stool at once and helped his aged, groaning master to his feet. "Never to me! *Rebbe,* you must never kneel to me."

"To what is within you I kneel," Jacob answered, smiling. "You have learned the mechanics of magic well, my lord. Your lady is learning to dwell in this, the Presence. She is your heart, Luc; and when the time comes for her to initiate you, you will dwell in the Presence together."

Determined to overcome all fear, in order to become strong that he might meet his Beloved, Luc practiced his rituals daily. And in secret he began to experiment by holding his finger to a flame. Only for an instant at first, then longer, until at last he could gaze unblinking at the flame with his palm pressed to it, watching for moments as the flame licked his skin. And each time he drew his hand away healthy and unblistered.

Likewise, he stole a spindle from one of the chambermaids and steadied his concentration until the sharp point, though it pierced his skin, elicited neither blood nor pain. In time, even his hunting dagger drew no blood and left no wound.

The following summer, the plague had arrived; word came from home that Nana had died, and Papa had fallen grievously ill, but had recovered. Amazingly, no sickness came to Edouard's estate—none of his servants, nor the knights in the castle *mesnie*. But the city was hard besieged, and beg though Luc might, Edouard forbade his nephew to continue the visits to Jacob.

In the month after the worst of the outbreak had past, Edouard had gone to Luc in his chamber and said gently, "Dear nephew, I have the most difficult news: They have burned the ghetto down."

The boy refused to believe it until he had ridden to the very site where Jacob's house had stood and knelt weeping in the ashes. Even then he told himself: *He has escaped. He is alive somewhere and will return. . . .*

But in his heart he knew that his beloved *rebbe* was dead.

In the years that followed, Luc became an accomplished squire, then a knight; he fought in skirmishes against the Black Prince and gained renown as a warrior. He also dreamt often of the girl, though he could never clearly picture any face save that of the five-year-old with the black braid. He knew, though, that Edouard regularly practiced the Sight in Circle, and one night when they dined in Edouard's private quarters, he begged, "What have you seen of her? Where is she, and what is she doing?"

"You are not strong enough, Luc."

"But I am," he insisted. "Sight or no, my magic is as strong as yours."

Edouard had regarded him sternly. "Swear to me that you will never again see your mother, and I will tell you."

Luc drew in a hitching breath. "You would tell me now to abandon Maman, when she has given her sanity for mine?"

"I would," Edouard said grimly. "You are linked to her on the astral plane. In your presence, she knows your heart and your mind; and because she is linked also to your Enemy, he knows, too. If you go to your lady now, yet do not cut yourself off from your mother physically, mentally, emotionally—you put her in jeopardy as well."

"I cannot abandon my mother," Luc whispered, embarassed by the sudden constriction of his throat caused by imminent tears.

"And there is something else, of far more importance," Edouard continued. "You must seek out your greatest fear and conquer it. When those two things are accomplished, the Enemy cannot harm you."

Luc rose eagerly from his stool. "But I *have* conquered my fear, Uncle. I am not afraid of pain, not afraid even of dying. Look!" And he stepped over to the hearth and thrust his right arm directly into the flames. After an instant, Luc pulled his arm from the fire; and though his sleeve was blackened and partially burned away to the elbow, the skin beneath it was unblemished.

"Do you see, Uncle?" He held up the uninjured arm like a trophy then seized from his belt his dagger, which he thrust into his left palm. The shining blade completely pierced the hand, yet when Luc pulled it out it left no blood, no wound. "Do you see? I have begged God to help me do whatever I must. Let the Enemy cast me to the flames; I will not burn. Let him try to slay me with a sword; I will not be cut. How then shall I be defeated?"

"Through your own mind," Edouard said quietly. "Fear can make you vulnerable again." And as Luc began to protest, Edouard continued, "It is true, Nephew, you are far more powerful a magician than I. But the danger is more than physical; the fear you must yet conquer is not that of your own death." He placed a hand upon Luc's shoulder.

"Sit. I can see the time has come." And he disappeared without reply into his inner chamber. When he returned, he bore in his hands a tiny flask containing a dark liquid. Luc watched as his uncle, with reverence and gravity, poured two drops, no more, into the lad's wine.

"Drink," Edouard said.

Luc drank. The taste was nauseatingly bitter; but after several moments, he forgot the unpleasantness and instead grew fascinated by the hearthstones, which seemed to be drooping like flowers wilting in the summer heat. He opened his mouth to relay this and found himself without words; suddenly he laughed until he howled and fell halfway from the chair.

Edouard caught him and helped him to his feet; Luc, unsteady, let his uncle bear the brunt of his weight into the inner chamber, where he fell most gratefully onto Edouard's great bed.

"I . . . am . . . sorry . . ." he stammered, giggling.

"Laugh all you wish, Luc. I have sent the servants away. If you need help, simply call for me." And Edouard shut the door to the bed-chamber behind him.

Luc burst into a fresh paroxysm of laughter, for though he heard Edouard's words, they made little sense to him. All of it made no sense: that he, a normal young man so far-removed from sainthood should be chosen to lead the Race, to be a Teacher, indeed to be the Voice of God. He was no holy messiah; surely Edouard, so wise and good, was more suited to the task, or the dead and blessed Jacob.

His mirth turned at once to sorrow. Edouard had been right: his pride had led him to believe he was ready to find his Beloved and fight the Enemy. He had been so caught up in the study of magic that he had not Spoken with the Voice for years and had almost forgotten what it was like to dwell in the Presence.

"You will remember soon enough," a voice said. "The time will come again for the Voice to Speak."

Luc sat up swiftly, all lassitude fled and his limbs responsive, to find beneath his hands not the rich brocade on Edouard's bed, but dry, crackling leaves and cold ground. In front of him a campfire burned, and on its other side Jacob crouched over the flames, rubbing his bony palms together to warm them. Around them stood a great, dark forest.

"*Jacob,*" Luc whispered as tears flowed hot against his cheeks. "You're *alive.*"

"Even better," the *rebbe* replied, showing yellowed ivory teeth.

"I . . . I want to please God," Luc said, "and want to find *her,* but something keeps me from her, from initiation. I have studied magic that I might be of service; I have worked to become immune to pain. I know not else what to do . . ."

Jacob nodded. "You have learned tricks, as any common sorcerer might do. Talisman and ritual, these are but outer props meant to lead us to the most difficult, the most powerful magic: that of the heart. You must leave behind your most deeply held fears and learn to trust."

At once Luc was no longer in the forest but was a babe swaddled and suckling at his mother's breast. Enrapt, he looked up at her: beautiful Beatrice with gold-fringed malachite eyes full of love, her skin warm as the sun, pale as the moon. She sang to him in a voice womanly and low.

Then, with a howl, she hurled him to the floor, her face abruptly monstrous, and he screamed with terror. Her hands were upon his neck, and he was near losing consciousness while Papa and the guard struggled to free him.

His mother's face was stretched in a hideous shriek, and, as Luc watched, she began to grow younger, a mere child, dark haired, dark eyed, bare feet balanced precariously on the edge of a wagon.

You merely looked at her, and she fell.

"No!" Luc cried out, fist pounding the dead leaves, the shimmering brocade on his uncle's bed. "No! Jacob! Help me!"

At once Edouard was beside him, helping him sit and drink sips of pleasant-tasting tea. "It is over," his uncle said soothingly. "Here, this will help you rest."

Luc calmed and at last slept. When he woke, he began work on a talisman of silver, inscribing it with his mother's astrological signs. This he did in secret; and in secret, too, he bade his own squire to make the journey to Toulouse and deliver the talisman in person to the Lady de la Rose.

Ere the squire returned, Prince Edward's forces were joined by another group of invaders in Brittany, and the French king issued the call to arms. Uncle Edouard and his knights began to prepare for the journey to battle. The plan was to meet Paul de la Rose at his estate, and proceed thence northward to join with King Jean's forces and intercept the enemy.

In the hours before dawn on the morning they were to depart, Luc (too anxious to sleep) prepared: sharpening sword and dagger, repairing his shield and armor. In truth, he dreaded war; for though he had little fear that he would himself be killed—he was, after all, skilled at protecting himself magically—he could not bear the cruel horrors it inflicted upon others.

But a part of him was eager, for years had passed since he had last seen his parents, and he tried to picture them as they appeared now. Surely, his father would have some gray in his hair.

As he tried to imagine them, a sharp rap came at his door. "Come in," Luc said, and Uncle Edouard entered.

"Luc," he said in a low voice, "I have Seen great danger awaiting you upon the battlefield; I beg of you, do not come."

In recent years, Edouard's copper hair had begun to silver quickly at brow and temples, and lines of worry had deepened about his pale eyes. Now his forehead was furrowed with concern.

Luc lowered the dagger in his hand, as well as the stone he had been using to sharpen it.

"I speak of your life," Edouard continued. "Perhaps even worse—"

"I have been on battlefields before, Uncle, and not once been injured," Luc countered respectfully.

"I know, Luc. I also know that if you decide to come, there is nothing I can do to hold you back." After a pause Edouard added, "But for *her* sake, I beg you not to come. For if you come to battle, you will not only bring harm to yourself, but terrible suffering to her." He drew a breath, then released his frustration in a torrent. "Blood and hell, Luc, I wish I could make you See. Why does the Voice that dwells within you not warn you? The Enemy will try to use your fear against you."

At that, Luc lowered his head, ashamed; Edouard obviously realized that his nephew had tried to face his private terror and fled from it, a coward.

"I am sorry," his uncle said immediately. "I say these things not to cause you pain, but out of concern for you. Will you stay, Luc? Will you meditate on the Presence and remain safe, for the sake of the Race?"

"I will," Luc replied, but his eyes remained downcast.

"God bless you," Edouard said.

"And you." But the lad kept his gaze on the floor and listened rather than watched as his uncle turned and walked deliberately from the room, opening and closing the door behind him.

Luc sat upon the edge of his bed with a troubled sigh. He loved his uncle well and knew that Edouard would never have come to warn him without good reason.

As he sat upon his bed ruminating and listening to the sounds of the household waking, and the knights entering the great dining hall for breakfast, he fell into a strange state, half awake, half asleep:

And he saw his Beloved call to him from the battlefield, mired in mud and surrounded by grapevines. *Luc, Luc de la Rose, help me!* She was kneeling upon blood-soaked earth while thousands of soldiers wielded ax and sword and shield. A merciless torrent of arrows fell around her. *Luc, Luc! Save me!*

In the murky darkness, her flesh alone was pale and bright, ashine like a beacon; even as she called to him, her face was composed, transcendent.

As he watched, a great shadowy figure ran toward her and hefted a great ax above its head, then brought it down to strike, to cleave that shining face in twain. Her expression did not change; she merely lifted a white hand gracefully, in a gesture of forgiveness.

In the midst of the vision, Luc stood, dagger clutched in his fist.

Sybille's face and form changed into those of his mother, her features beautiful and pale after a different manner, her posture straight and graceful—and her eyes . . . her eyes so lucid, so sure. She was slender still, her hair still burnished gold, and she stood, fine hands emerging from long, elegantly draped sleeves, and pressed together just above her heart.

Luc, she said in a tone impassioned, *you must join the other soldiers at once. Your Beloved needs you. . . . Protect her before it is too late. . . .*

When Luc came to himself, it was mid-morning—indeed, many hours past dawn—and to his alarm the house was silent; he flung open his chamber shutters to discover that the great yard, where all the *chariots* and carts had been assembled, now lay empty. Impossible, that he had slept so long, had failed to hear the rumble of the wheels and the hoofbeats of the horses as they commenced the journey to war.

Luc rose. From the stables he rode upon his white stallion, Lune, to the northeast, where home lay. The ride took no more than a few hours; but by then it was past midday, and Luc, glad to see the outline of the great castle, with the gaping teeth of the watchtower turrets dark against the sky, was nonetheless disappointed to find the courtyard empty of soldiers and carts. Papa and Edouard had already gone.

Luc rode up to the castle's main door and there tied his horse, and went silently up a side pentice to his mother's chambers.

He was no fool; even trusting in his talisman and the vision, he stripped himself of sword and dagger and put them in the chamber outside hers. There would be no weapons in her room, and Luc was more than strong enough to protect himself against her physically.

True, it had been years since he had seen her—but he still remembered where the key to her chamber was kept, and Papa had never moved it. With dread and yearning, he put it into the rusting lock and pushed open the heavy wooden door.

A lone figure stood gazing out of the barred but unshuttered window onto the vineyards below: a slender woman clad in emerald wool with an apron of gossamer silk the color of seafoam, and a wimple of the same hue, on top of which rested a gold circlet. Her braids were coiled, and when she turned round to face Luc, arms folded in front of her, she gazed on him with great, expressive eyes of deep blue-green.

He gasped aloud, having forgotten her profound beauty.

"Luc," she said, in the very tone she had used in his dream. "Luc, thank God, my darling, my son . . ." She held out her arms, floor-length sleeves of gossamer spreading like angel's wings.

In the beat of a heart he made his decision: to go to her, to risk that blissful moment he had only dreamed of.

So he went; and in that moment found that bliss, of his mother's arms wrapped around him, of her voice, tearful with love, whispering in his ear: "Oh, my son, my son, how I have made you and your father suffer all these years. . . ." She drew back suddenly and held him at arm's length to admire him. "Look at how tall you have grown!"

And how small you have become, Luc thought as she continued: "How like your father you look. How am I well? It is a miracle," said she, and laughed, a sound so beautiful that Luc laughed with her, his laughter punctuated by sobs. "Luc, my darling, was it you?" She seized him again, so impetuously that Luc was at first startled—then laughed again.

She squeezed him with admirable strength, then let go again, arms still loosely about his waist; her expression and voice grew suddenly somber. "But you heard my warning. You came, even though Edouard feared for you."

He nodded. "I came."

"'Twas I who sent you the vision. Your Beloved is in danger. Edouard has sensed this, but his Sight is not so great as mine; and perhaps he worries that you will somehow endanger yourself trying to protect her." She paused, and reached up to brush a stray lock of hair from Luc's forehead; her touch was warm and delicate, so maternal that Luc struggled to restrain fresh tears. "It was so strange. . . . The misery was terrible, unspeakable"—this she said without any self-pity or regret—"and I remember that Paul came to me before he left with Edouard. He told me where he was going, what he was doing . . . he told me, too, that you were staying behind, safe at Edouard's estate. He meant, I know, to comfort me.

"I was still in the Enemy's grip. I had Seen the danger to Sybille, yet I could not tell him, could not utter a sound; and with my last ounce of strength, I fought to keep from harming him myself. I tried even to weep—but the Enemy forced all my tears inside. And so your father left, without my being able to warn him or Edouard."

Her expression grew suddenly radiant, beatific. "And then—oh, my son, I soared swift from Hell to the Divine in an instant; for the moment I watched from yon window as my husband and my brother and hundreds of their knights and squires departed, the madness left me at last, and I was myself again, and able to send you a warning. The Goddess has intervened." The corners of her lips curved upward toward dimples, and her eyes grew knowing. "It is your destiny to go, my son.

"And you must go now—quickly, before it is too late." And she told him which direction she had Seen the men take; then, as tightly as she had earlier embraced him, so did she now push him firmly toward the door.

He rode hard. By the time the sun was low in the sky, he dismounted and led Lune to a fast-moving stream to drink, and there drank himself, sitting on his haunches, cupping his hands to draw the shining water.

"Thank you," he whispered humbly, then raised his hands to his lips, and drank.

In the distance behind him, voices, the slow drum of hooves against earth, the creak of great wheels: an army of hundreds. Luc rose at once and mounted Lune, then drew his sword: he had stayed well to the east of the lands now dominated by Edward the Black's men, and from the cadence of the voices, he supposed them French. But the danger existed of encountering English raiders, and some of Edward's soldiers were French traitors.

Thus he approached with caution, staying behind the cover of trees until he could clearly see the army, which had just begun to encamp. And when he saw the banner—the falcon with the roses—he smiled and rode out, shouting a greeting.

Inquiring as he went, Luc made his way to the center of an army of half a thousand men—more than three hundred from the de la Rose *mesnie,* two hundred from the Trencavel, with its watchtower banner—past knights with their squires, attendants, and standard bearers, and their plain wooden *chariots* for carrying armor, the grand attire of war, bedding, food (including bleating sheep tied to the wagons), cooks, and servants. It was like making one's way through a small city—one replete with the smells of roasting mutton, which made Luc ravenous—and by the time he reached the red-and-white-striped canopy of the *grand seigneur*'s encampment, the sun had set in earnest.

There, in the yellow glow of a stone-encircled fire, the elder de la Rose sat outside his tent upon a carpet of sheepskin; the lower half of his body was covered by furs. Distracted as he was by a serious conversation with his second-in-command over a map, he did not see his son tie his horse with the others, then approach from the shadows.

For a moment, Luc paused; he had not seen his father in seven years, and in that time, Paul had aged astoundingly. His dark auburn hair was now mostly silver, though his eyebrows were still dark and thick—indeed, wild; inaction had thickened him at waist and chest and face, leaving folds of flesh, and sorrow and sleeplessness had engraved dark circles beneath his eyes. Even his moments were slow, those of one numbed by grief. His heart, Luc decided, had been broken again, by something equally as tragic as his wife's madness; and with a surge of heartrending pain, Luc realized that Paul had lost not just wife, but son.

That thought, combined with his father's pitiful appearance, inspired in the younger knight a sharp intake of breath that caught in his throat.

And at that small sound, the *grand seigneur* raised his lined visage from the map and gazed out at the darkness; lips parted, eyes wide, he wore a look of dawning recognition, of hope that dared not hope, lest it be dashed.

"Luc," he whispered, rising to his feet, mindless of the furs that fell forward into the fire, and of his second, who scrambled to rescue them.

The two men moved toward each other, arms wide. Beside the crackling fire, each held the other so tightly neither could breathe, but tears flowed unchecked.

And as Luc clutched his father, a figure emerged from the shadows behind Paul: Edouard, his features half in darkness, half in light, and upon them a look of defeat more profound than his nephew had ever seen.

The second-in-command and all servants were dismissed. Edouard stood nearby, arms folded, gazing into the fire while Luc sat beside his father with a plate of mutton and explained how he had dreamt of his mother, then ridden to the estate and found her sane.

"Sane," Paul whispered. "Luc, do not toy with me. Do you mean—"

"I mean what I have said, Father. She is well; she is herself; she is concerned about you." Luc looked down quickly, struggling to keep the deep emotion he felt from showing on his face. "She rejoiced to see me again."

He glanced up in time to see the spark catch hold in Paul's eye; it spread outward, softening his features, suffusing them with radiance.

If there was one moment Luc had awaited with a yearning equal to that of his meeting his Beloved, it was this: to know his mother was restored, to see all sorrow banished from his father's eyes.

"Beatrice," Paul said to the darkness before him; his lips trembled with a growing smile. "Is it possible? My Beatrice is returned to me. . . ."

"Paul," Edouard warned, kneeling before his brother-in-law with a swift, solitary movement, catching the *seigneur*'s arms above the elbow so that Paul had no choice but to regard him directly. "I have no wish to steal your joy. But I believe this is the Enemy's trick."

Paul recoiled from the notion with utter loathing. "A *trick* . . . With what purpose? To break an old man's heart?"

"To harm your son."

"Uncle, let me explain," Luc countered swiftly. "I did not come here out of rebellion against you. I had made a talisman for Maman to free her—and it has worked! If only you could see her, you would believe. She was worried that harm would come to my *Beloved*. She—Sybille— is coming here, Uncle. And she will be endangered—without my inter- vention, she will die. Why would the Enemy warn me of such a thing?"

Edouard whirled on him with contained heat. "To send you into harm's way."

Luc rose. "If he meant me harm, why did he not attack while I was alone with Maman?"

"And I told you, I foresaw danger to you on the battlefield. Say, then, that you have come only to bring this news to your father, that you have not come to fight."

"I will not leave his side, Uncle. Not until I see him and my Beloved safely home."

"Edouard." Paul's voice, eyes, and expression had suddenly dulled at his brother-in-law's words, as if someone had extinguished an internal flame. "Is this true?"

Edouard nodded, his gaze still severe, still fastened on his nephew.

Paul turned to face Luc. "Then you must not come with us. Your uncle's Sight is sure, my son; I have never known it to fail. What good is it to me to hear such joyous news, to have the honor to fight by your side, if I know you are endangered? Perhaps"—and here he patted Luc's shoulder comfortingly—"perhaps it is true that your mother is with us once more. Who can say? But we must also listen to Edouard."

"I must do as my heart tells me," Luc persisted.

At this insolence, Paul's eyebrow quirked up, and a familiar stoniness that had made the child Luc tremble crept over his features; but this eased quickly to an expression of uncertainty, as he glanced askance at Edouard.

Luc's uncle sighed. "There is nothing we can do, short of killing him—and that would prove difficult enough. He has learned Jacob's lessons too well." He drew in a deep breath and moved closer to Luc, and with a heartfelt humility his nephew had never seen in him before, said: "But perhaps *I* have been a poor teacher. Perhaps I have not emphasized enough to you, Luc, the importance of remaining safe until you have conquered your fear."

"But that is the point," Luc said, smiling. "My greatest fear was that Maman would never be restored to us . . . but now she has."

"Oh, Luc," Edouard said, and with a sigh he sank down until he crouched upon his heels, arms wrapped about his knees. "There is more for you to face—trust me. You have brought yourself to danger."

"Your uncle is most wise. Listen to him, and for my sake, stay," Paul begged his son, to which Luc replied:

"For my Beloved's sake, I must go."

Within a day, the slow-moving caravan that was the de la Rose and Trencavel armies merged with those of King Jean himself; the great and growing beast (fed by the arrival of other noble houses' *mesnies*) continued its journey northward, for scouts brought back word that the Black Prince had crossed the Loire River and arrived near the town of Poitiers to join forces with the English army led by the Duke of Lancaster in Brittany.

During that time, Luc rode beside his father, who had obtained a suitable set of armor for his son from the *mesnie*—while Edouard most conspicuously and uncharacteristically remained with his own knights, not even joining his nephew and brother-in-law for meals. The gesture stung Luc, not so much on his own account—for he told himself that when they returned from the war, Edouard would behold Beatrice sane and well with his own eyes, and be sorry he had shunned his kinsmen— but because it clearly pained his father, even though Paul never mentioned it, and feigned cheerfulness during his long conversations with his son as they traveled together.

On the third day, just as the army paused for mid-morning dinner, word came: the English prince had crossed back over the Loire, headed for the city of Poitiers. Black Edward's contingent looked less than half the size of King Jean's, and his men were battle-weary after months of raiding the countryside. A French victory was assured.

On to Poitiers! the heady shout spread throughout the massive encampment until the ground beneath Luc's feet trembled with it, until his very teeth and skull vibrated with the mighty sound, and he himself took up the cry: "On to Poitiers!"

For it was there, he knew in his heart, that he would at last meet his Beloved.

For two days after the armies' arrival at Poitiers, the French and English rulers, spurred by papal legates, made halfhearted attempts to negotiate a settlement: but in the end, neither would yield. The fate of all France was at stake.

The third day was Sunday, and neither side would violate its sanctity by shedding blood.

Just before dawn of the fourth day, Luc sat in full armor with Lune, in an equine helmet adorned with curling scarlet feathers, quivering beneath him. Beside him sat Paul de la Rose, his surcoat the color of untouched snow.

On either side of them sat no one; and before them stood meadow and mist—and the unseen English. They were the first of the spearhead to attack, and behind them stood four standard bearers, and behind *them,* eight knights from the de la Rose *mesnie.* Paul had volunteered to lead the attack, and Luc would have no place other than beside him. They did not speak—partly from the tension, partly from the fact that the helmets dulled noise so that normal conversation was impossible to hear.

Behind Luc, the shrill blast of trumpets: the signal for the charge. Beside him, the great old warrior Paul de la Rose roared and hefted his long sword with his right hand; with his left, he clutched his shield and the reins, signaling his gleaming jet stallion onward.

In reply, the two hundred knights in the spearhead roared, too, a deafening sound; Luc's heart began to pound as wildly as the horse's hooves when the charge into the swirling fog, wet upon his face, began. The cacophony began to coalesce into an intelligible phrase:

For God and for France!

And two arms' length away, Paul de la Rose, still hoisting his sword, shouted:

"For the Lady Beatrice!"

"For the Lady Beatrice!" Luc cried, and also hefted his sword just as figures came running toward him out of the fog: a dark tide that flowed between him and his father and forced the two of them apart. The rest of the knights in the spearhead surged forward around them, quickly engulfing the fewer English foot soldiers.

Luc grimaced as he brought the bright, sharp blade of his sword downward on the neck and shoulders of a commoner in dirty clothing, with a dirty face; how unfair it seemed! The enemy had clearly presumed that the French would wage war in the usual fashion, bringing their commoners in on foot, and sacrificing them first before the nobler, mounted warriors were brought in. . . .

He said a prayer for the Englishman as the soldier cried out and sank to his knees in pain, while around him, his fellow knights were crying out joyfully: *Victory! Victory is already ours!*

And in the midst of exuberance, madness descended like locusts. From the sky the arrows came, so deadly swift, so dark and devouring that Frenchmen delivering up the cry of *"Victory!"* smiled while uttering the word's first syllable, and were dead the next.

All about his periphery, Luc could see the blood, could hear the screams and the death rattles of knights and their animals, and the song of shuddering wooden shafts fresh in their targets: yet he could permit himself to feel no fear. Though he could not see his father, he kept within his mind the image of Paul protected, and felt satisfied the older man was safe. Luc was likewise protected: arrows hissed dangerously past his helmet, his body, his horse's unarmored rump—only to pierce the ground or some unfortunate behind him.

In the course of less than an hour, as Luc continued to fight, unable to penetrate past the line of English commoners that streamed forward, he became aware of the mortality that surrounded him, courtesy of the longbow: so many French bodies, men and animals included, lay on the savaged field that even the English stumbled as they tried to advance.

Around him, the frenzied cry in French arose: "Retreat! Retreat! They are killing us all!" And he sensed, rather than saw, the movement of a hundred men, a thousand, fleeing behind him, back toward the walled city: but he remained, determined to stay until king or father ordered him to go. Surely they could not permit defeat: the Black Prince had not half as many men.

For hours Luc fought, until well past midday, by which time the sun had burned away all trace of mist and heated his armor so that the clothes beneath were drenched in sweat. Lune was staggering—from thirst, and from the ground, now piled with so many corpses that the horse could make its way only by stepping on them. For the animal's sake, Luc dismounted and set it free; it trotted at once back toward the city and the meadow where other riderless horses grazed.

He continued on foot: difficult though it was to maintain balance, it was no easier for the English, who with their far inferior hand-to-hand weapons and armor were clearly relying on their longbows to keep their advantage.

Almost immediately, Luc became engaged again in combat, as a tall, pale foot soldier with dirty clothes staggered toward him, rusting ax raised above his dented helmet. Instinctively—for in battle there is no time for reflection—Luc raised his sword and blocked the blow, wincing at the spray of sparks. . . .

. . . And behind him there came a cry: soft and low—too much so to be heard above the clash of metal, the shouts of victory and the shrieks of dying, yet he heard it nonetheless. A distinctly feminine sound, one oddly familiar, and at it he turned his head and looked.

If she dies, I shall die too. . . .

No dream or enchantment could be as clear as the experience of seeing her again in the flesh: a child with long braids no more, but a veiled and kneeling woman, with a heart-shaped face that was to him the essence of beauty, the face of the Goddess Herself, the countenance he had waited for years to see.

In a happy instant of sacrifice—so short he had not time even to speak—he knew her. Knew her, realized the danger to himself, and gladly weakened his golden circle of protection to place one around her, that she might continue.

There came the ax's bite—a sensation primal, savagely unbearable, cleaving both body and mind so naught existed but pain; then a sudden cold that extinguished the suffering—indeed, all physical feeling. He floated free and blissful, staring up at the brilliant blue sky. A flock of dark birds soared overhead—or was it his own vision failing? Or worse, a covey of English arrows?

At once, it was all blotted out by her serene madonna's face, smiling, beatific, and he thought with wild happiness: *I have seen her; I can die now.*

Darkness.

Then a warmth, emanating from the core of his heart—her touch upon him, alive and electric, *moving* from inside his chest to his very bones, then outward to his flesh. . . .

He woke to find himself alive and without pain, without even the ache in his arms and shoulders that came from hours of wielding a heavy sword. His thoughts, his vision were exceptionally clear: the woman Sybille had not been a dream.

Indeed, as he sat up to find his helmet and cloven breastplate removed and lying beside the bloodied ax, he caught the briefest glimpse of her—a small, dark, black-veiled figure—in the distance, separated from him by a fresh surge of English soldiers. She was riding away, held in front of Uncle Edouard on his horse; and though Luc was relieved to see her safely escaping the battle, he cried out after her:

"Sybille! Sybille!"

Luc's words were swallowed up by war cries and the clash of arms, as more Frenchmen arrived to counter the enemy—but he had not come this far only to be parted from her again. He looked about, desperate to find a mount, remembering that he had set Lune free. He rolled onto his side and with great effort pushed himself to his knees. Beside him lay the arrow-ridden flank of a dead horse; he clutched the corpse and slowly, gracelessly, pulled himself to his feet, hampered by his remaining armor.

Edouard's steed had already disappeared into the moving mass of metal and horseflesh and Luc had no hope of following, of seeing which way they had gone through natural means. He had always depended upon Edouard's Sight to guide him when such means were not enough.

Yet in his mind, faint but unmistakable, he heard his Beloved's voice whisper:

I shall see you again in Carcassonne....

Even as her silent words formed in his mind, a sinister sensation stole over him.

He had swooned, indeed, *died;* Edouard had been right. His, Luc's, magic had not been strong enough to protect himself, which meant it could not have been sufficient to protect his father....

Luc did his best to run—staggering from the weight of his remaining armor, the uneven footing of a ground hidden beneath layers of corpses, the onrush of colliding warriors. He possessed not the Sight, only a soldier's instinct and a son's heart; these were enough to guide him, after several moments, to the marshy land that separated the English entrenchment from the battlefield. Beyond, behind ancient grapevines, behind thickets and the sheltering side of a hill, the hastily constructed wood-and-earth palisades protecting the longbow men were visible.

Nearby, half sunk into the ravaged marshland, Paul de la Rose, *grand seigneur* of Toulouse, lay in profile, shield raised to protect, sword lifted to strike—perhaps having been thrown from his great black stallion, or perhaps having decided to engage the enemy on foot. No other bodies lay near his, for he alone had penetrated so far into English territory that it had been his undoing.

So close had he come to the archers' palisades that a full quiver of arrows emerged from his breastplate—having pierced so deeply through metal and flesh that the sharp tips emerged from the back of his tattered surcoat.

With a cry, Luc dropped to his knees and gently removed his father's helmet. The elder de la Rose's hair was damp, his face still agleam with sweat; and in his open eyes, framed by scowling black brows, was no fear, no hate, only singular determination.

For the Lady Beatrice....

With impossible strength, Luc tore the arrows one by one from his father's body, slicing his palms, embedding deep splinters in them, until at last he was able to lift the heavy breastplate. Beneath, his father's chest—in a great oval from breastbone to navel—was naught but a deep pool of congealed blood.

Sobbing, he drew in a breath and struggled to summon the bright warmth that had overtaken him years ago—when, as a child, he had crawled into his father's bed and laid his hands upon Paul de la Rose's hard-swollen thigh.

And he sank his hands deep into the thick, sticky blood welled upon his father's chest, and bowed his head, waiting; waiting for the warmth, the peace, the tremulous vibration. It never came. He had healed Paul once, and over the years only grown stronger in his talent; why now had God, Goddess, the Divine power of Kether, forsaken him?

Turning his face to the sky, Luc screamed with fury: not at the English or himself, for his failure to protect his father, but at the cruelty of fate, which had decreed that the lovers Beatrice and Paul, so many years separated, should now never meet again in the flesh.

He wrested the great sword from his father's tightly clenched fist. Swinging it wildly, without shield or helmet or breastplate as defense, he thrashed howling into the midst of the battle.

How much blood he spilled, how long he fought, he could not have said, for grief steals the present and leaves only the past. But before the sun set, most of the last battalion, comprised of the highest nobility, had been slaughtered or captured; and the overwhelmed King Jean, in a poignant gesture, surrendered his glove to the enemy.

And Luc—amazingly untouched, though his heart ached with doubled grief—lowered Paul de la Rose's sword, and walked back to his father's side, where he lay himself down.

He spent the night beside his father's corpse, playing dead himself when the English came near in search of survivors; by dawn, the field was abandoned by all but the dead and the hungry ravens. The English had taken the de la Rose gilded carts and fine stallions, but Luc managed to find a sturdy mare and an uncovered, rickety cart. He pushed his father's heavy body onto the cart with great difficulty and a goodly number of torn muscles; only the desperation of grief made it possible.

While he had yearned desperately to leave the battlefield and follow after Sybille, he knew not where she had gone, and his grief overshadowed all but the sense of love and duty he bore toward his parents. How could he deny either the right of having Paul de la Rose buried on family soil?

The ride home was a blur of the fiercest pain, unbearable in its agony, as he thought of the task ahead; of periods of utter emotional numbness; of a cold, physical heaviness that settled over him and made the slightest movement enormously difficult.

But nothing was more difficult than the moment when, having arrived home and turned Paul's body over to the servants, Luc stepped across the threshold of his mother's chamber, and she turned to look at him.

Her great blue-green eyes were blurred by a veil of tears that spilled continuously down onto her pale, shining cheeks, and before Luc could say a word, she gave him a tremulous smile and said, her voice husky: "I know he died with honor, and with my name upon his lips. I know, too, how you protected him unto your own death. Let your heart be free of any shame, my son, for you have acted bravely and true.

"It is my duty and privilege to tend to your father's body. Stay with me, Luc; let us ease one another's sorrow."

"Mother," he murmured, and, weeping, enfolded her tightly, bending down so that they stood, wet cheek pressed to wet cheek. "Mother, I have come to return Papa's body. But I cannot remain here. I must—"

"Find *her*." She held him fast, with surprising but gentle strength, and cupped his other cheek with her palm. "I understand. But where has she gone, my son? Do you know where she is?"

"In Carcassonne," he answered promptly, remembering the unspoken message Sybille had sent him.

"Carcassonne," Beatrice whispered, as if this news was a revelation. "Ah, but she has not returned there; her way has been impeded. She is lost and finds herself in danger, and now needs your help. . . ."

Ere any reply could come to his lips, his mother's chamber dissolved around them—indeed, he could see neither his own body nor hers—into a forest dense with ancient trees whose heavy-laden boughs near blotted out the sun. Cooler it was, and darker, redolent of evergreen and colored with the first brilliant flames of autumn; from time to time, the distant cry of a raven pierced the silence.

He thought at once of the tales Nana had told him long ago, of enchanted forests where wizards lived inside trees, where lost children wandered for centuries and never aged, where fairies crouched beneath toadstools for shelter; this seemed such a mystical place.

Through the tangle of branch and vine, a forlorn and solitary figure, body cloaked, shadowed face hooded in black, struggled to make its way over a dappled carpet of dried leaves and needles, releasing with each step the fragrance of pine. Its build was short and slender, its movements feminine, graceful, strong.

"Sybille," he whispered, as much to her as to himself. "Mother, where is she?"

He tried to detach himself from Beatrice's embrace—and found himself gripped fast. For the first time, a thread of fear, delicate as that spun by a spider, wound itself about his heart.

With all his physical strength, he pushed against her, his face reddening, his forehead growing beaded with sweat, until the muscles in his arms shook and ultimately failed. And still his mother held him, pinned so that he scarce could move.

"Lost," Beatrice replied, her voice woeful. As she continued, it grew distorted, low as a man's. "She is lost, even as your mother is lost, in a world of madness."

"No," Luc whispered harshly, but even as he said it, panic welled up in him. It was true, he was afraid—had always been deeply, secretly afraid throughout his life—that when he and his Beloved finally came together, he would cause her to go mad . . . just as he had his adored mother.

In an instant, he saw Uncle Edouard's wisdom: that in learning to distance himself emotionally from Beatrice, he would attain the stability necessary to distance himself from his secret fear about Sybille. *Love is not attachment,* Edouard had once said. *Real love is compassion, which never leads to grief; but attachment, which springs from our craving for security, is a trap.*

And now he, Luc, was caught in just such a trap, flailing in the toils of terror, and the Enemy had cast the net.

"Oh yes, my darling," Beatrice whispered, in a low parody of a feminine voice. "Such is the curse you bring to the women who love you. Would you like to see her, as she is now—see what you have done to her?"

The cloaked figure turned toward them, and in a different, deep voice—one Luc knew with certainty, but agonizingly could not place—taunted: "Do you not know me, Luc? For I know you, your mother, and your uncle, and the woman who plagues your dreams very well. . . . *I* am your true Beloved, for I alone wish to see you achieve your finest, your holiest, destiny."

"Let Sybille and my mother go," Luc demanded. "Let them go—only a coward would choose to attack in such roundabout fashion. It is me you have always wanted; well, then, show yourself, and let us have it out alone."

Even as he said the words, he realized the acute danger he faced: at the same time, he knew he dared not flee it, for the sake of the two women he loved.

I can at least save them, if not myself.

He would risk death, if it meant saving Sybille.

"Yes, save her, Luc," the Enemy chided, using Beatrice's lips, "and I will show you the face of a foe even greater, the face your fair Sybille could not bring herself to look upon."

Slowly, deliberately, the cloaked figure lowered its hood, revealing that of a broad-faced man wearing a cardinal's red skullcap; as Luc stared, the cardinal's countenance began to change—to waver, shimmer like water beneath a skipping stone—to that of another.

Ere the transformation was complete, Luc cried out in horror as mind and will were stripped from him, even as his mother's hands were strong around his throat. . . .

XIX

In the middle of the night, Michel came to himself: he could not honestly say that he woke, for he had not been asleep, but quite consciously aware that he looked upon that which had been Luc de la Rose's life. And though his faith in God had become no less devout over the past two days, neither had his honesty—and in truth, he felt less like a man bewitched than one capable of Dreaming.

Thus when the vision ended, he felt a desperate yearning to rescue Sybille. Nevertheless, he prayed to the Virgin: *Holy Mary, if Sybille's and Luc's stories be blasphemy, restrain me; else give me a sign that I should go to her.*

Once more, a great peace descended upon him, and a tingling warmth upon his scalp, as if the Holy Mother had lain her hands there in blessing.

Despite the darkness, he refilled the near-empty oil lamp and carried the flame with him.

His heart full, he hurried outside the still monastery into the chilly city streets, and from thence to the jail.

It took no small bribery to gain entrance, for the sentry assumed the scribe had come at that late hour to take physical advantage of his prisoner. Michel agreed, without an instant's regret, to deliver a gold livre by the next day, or have his misdeed reported to the jailer.

Once inside the abbess's cell, he discovered she had not been sleeping; to the contrary, she had been sitting up, as though she had been awaiting his arrival. At the sight of her—frail, beaten, weary—he felt a surge of love and admiration so strong that the urge to kneel before her, to kiss her hand nearly overpowered him. She was worth any price: excommunication, the stake, damnation.

But Michel wished not to startle her with declarations of his feelings. Thus he sat and said, "You *did* heal him on the battlefield. Were you so aware? You healed him at Poitiers; he returned home to his mother, whom the Enemy used to kill him. So now I know, from both what you have told me *and* what I have dreamed, exactly how he died. Yet I do not understand why knowing his sad end was so important that you sent me the dreams."

"You do not yet know the whole of it," she answered. "And that you *must* know, as he knew it."

"I fail to see what more can be known. But I *do* know that I must help you," Michel countered. "You know why I am here, Mother; we have no time left us but this night. Rigaud is the Enemy; he will stop at nothing to see you dead. I have paid the sentry to leave. Can you walk? Here, take my cloak, and raise the hood—"

She waved the proffered garment away and said in a tone of pure misery, "I must not."

"No, you *must,*" Michel urged. "We are speaking of your *life,* of the continuation of the Race!"

Sadly, she shook her head. "It is my destiny to remain here, to tell the rest of my story ere I go to the stake."

"Mother, no . . ." Near weeping, he knelt before her. "Please, let me help you . . ."

She laid a swollen hand upon his head and managed a small smile. "You *can* help me. Listen to my tale's end, for it is my destiny to tell it, and yours to hear it, before our fates are decided. That is my greatest hope for survival: that one of the Race hear the complete truth—and remember. Will you do this for me?"

"If there is no other way," he said.

PART VI

Sybille

AVIGNON

October 1357

X X

It was Edouard who miraculously recovered his horse, and pulled me thereupon, my legs crushed, revealing bone and blood. This I know only from what he told me—for the pain was overwhelmingly great, and I had fallen so far from the Goddess's Presence into agitated mortality that I could do naught but scream out Luc's name. Cheek pressed against the horse's sweat-soaked surcoat, I remember struggling to push myself away, to return to my Beloved; but Edouard held me fast.

The clash of metal: again and again and again, so near my ears that my teeth sang. This seemed to continue for hours, while I, in dreamy agony, struggled to See Luc, at least to sense his presence, to know that the resurrection I attempted was successful.

Nothing. Nothing. I knew not whether he lived or was dead.

At last I fainted from the pain (amusing, is it not, that I cannot heal myself?). When I woke again, I was in a hostel far from Poitiers, upon a bed, with Edouard and Geraldine sitting at either side.

I smiled up at Geraldine, truly glad to see her again. But her normally sweet expression was pulled taut, and in her eyes were such rage, such grief, such profound disappointment in me that my smile faded, and I emitted a low cry of panic.

For as I directed my Sight back to my Beloved, as I struggled to sense where and how he was, I sensed . . .

Nothing. *Almost* nothing. Before I saw him clear as a bright, flickering flame—but at that moment, I sensed only the last wisps of smoke from the extinguished wick. *'Tis the ghost of his spirit,* I thought, and began bitterly to weep.

"Yes, weep," said Geraldine, and in her voice was no pity. "Weep, because Luc's spirit is entrapped by the Enemy, and only you now can free him. Weep, and swear upon the Goddess that you will never again directly confront the Enemy until you have faced the greatest fear. Only then can you free your Beloved from an eternity of misery."

I thought of that eater of fearful souls: thought of all those, perished in the flames, he had consumed, and so increased his power. And I ceased my tears, and swore.

I would never permit the Enemy to possess either my Beloved's spirit or his magic.

Thus I returned to the convent, and was nursed by Geraldine and Marie Magdeleine for many months. Grief and defeat often threatened to overwhelm me, as well as guilt for listening to my heart instead of the Goddess. My foolishness, my hubris, had cost my Beloved everything; but I put such self-indulgence aside. There was but one thing to be done: to find his spirit, to free it from the Enemy's shackles.

During that time, I worked carefully under Geraldine's tutelage in order to restore my Sight; but try though I might, I could See naught of Luc—only sense the ghostliest wisp of his presence like the smoke from an extinguished fire—and naught of the Enemy.

For months, I could not walk without aid. But I traveled much, sending my Sight throughout the world: *Luc de la Rose . . . Where have you gone? Friends, Templars—have any of you Seen Luc de la Rose, in this life or the next?*

None had. Even Edouard—who had taken refuge at our convent in the guise of a lay monk—could sense no trace of the nephew to whom he was so deeply tied.

"He is dead," he wept. "Perhaps I should have stayed with him— perhaps . . ." But then reason returned to him, and he remembered that, had he not rescued me, I most certainly would have died.

Time passed. Many magical methods I tried, in the convent's belly, in Circle surrounded by my sisters and Edouard: all failed. It seemed my Beloved's soul had been entirely consumed.

During the same time, I worked in Circle to confront the future Enemy, that void of all voids that I had seen during my first Circle with Noni, and again, at my initiation with Jacob: and each time, as the image began to form, I cried out in terror and would See no further.

Still, I knew it awaited me outside the safety of Circle.

For such cowardice, I give no excuse.

Then—after more than a year of searching, of hoping, of dwelling with failure—I sat resting in the afternoon sun after working for a time in the convent garden. The air was sweet that day, with an underlying autumnal coolness, but in the sun it was warm, and I closed my eyes and lifted my face to the sky.

After the physical exertion—I had recovered sufficiently to walk and work almost normally—and in the relaxing heat of the sun, a sense of deep calm overcame me; a calm that, during the months of my desperate search for Luc, had eluded me.

There, in the garden, which smelled of cool, rich earth, adorned with the vines of peas and the spreading green fans of leeks, it was given me to know that my Beloved's soul teetered between good and evil. Now was the time of his crisis; now was the time that he required his helpmeet most, or his very essence would truly be consumed by the Enemy.

Yet my Sight was hobbled: I was powerless to find him, to help.

With full humility, remembering my mistake, I prayed to the Goddess:

I surrender. I surrender grief and fear and hope; I surrender heart and mind to You. I surrender even the search for my Beloved, until such time as You wish to reveal him to me; and I surrender my terror of the Enemy to come. Whatever destiny I believed was mine, I empty into Your hands.

And I bowed my head in submission, away from the sun; but its warmth stayed on my cheeks. Indeed, the warmth spread throughout me, as though the Goddess encircled me in her arms, and I was filled with such deep compassion that in my heart dwelt room for no other emotion.

And in such a state of bliss, of utter surrender and acceptance, I returned to that moment at my first initiation, when Jacob stood beside me as we watched a dark, swirling globe, filled with the faces of those of the Race who had rejected their heritage. Lurking within was the horror I had sensed awaiting me outside that first Circle with Noni: the void of all voids, the negation of negation, the sum of all hopelessness.

And I heard again Jacob's deep, beautiful voice: *They fear who they are. The tragedy, lady, is that most of them seek to do good. But even a force as powerful as love, when it is tainted by fear, can only lead to evil.*

Ah, how I understood those words now, for my anxious love had brought my Luc only harm.

He was with me, Jacob, at that very moment as I sat in the garden, as surely as he had been with me so long ago, on that night of my initiation; and I felt his love and support as together, we gazed back into that ominous, swirling void. . . .

Which emptied abruptly.

Dread threatened to settle upon me, as it had each time past at this confrontation. But this time, I kept my heart settled firmly in the Goddess's compassion; this time, I rested in Her strength, in Jacob's, in my own, and gazed steadily into the void as an image began to coalesce.

For it was naught but that of a man, his face obscured by the hood of his loose robe. As I watched, he raised his hands, wide sleeves falling back to reveal well-muscled but pale arms, and slowly lowered his hood.

Darkness covered his features; yet as he pulled his hood back, the shadow rose slowly, like a veil—revealing first a square chin, firm lips, strong cheeks, pale eyes. A handsome man, whose forthright expression revealed no guile, this Enemy to come; but his bearing, his eyes spoke of sublimated power. Soon, too soon, he would become more powerful than any of the Race, including myself; soon he would replace my old Enemy and put an end to our kind. For he was one of the Race, possessed of his own awesome powers; and when the older Enemy died, the younger would consume all his accumulated power from all the stolen souls; and add to it his own natural abilities.

Thus he would become the most fearsome Enemy ever known throughout the generations the Race had been in existence.

This was the danger I had seen so many years ago, as a young girl: for he would send the all-consuming fires to extinguish us all. My destiny had always been to stop him at any cost; my destiny, to confront him directly. He was not a threat. Not yet, not yet; but soon . . .

At the Sight of him, I permitted myself no fear, no guilt, no trepidation. Only compassion, calm, and a renewed sense of destiny.

Of a sudden, a mist lifted from my vision and I Saw clearly, for the first time in a year, him whom I so desperately sought: a young man on a precipice, his soul sublimated to this new Enemy, and soon, soon to be altogether consumed—unless I went in rescue.

I felt inexpressible horror; and at the same time, relief, elation, radiant love.

"He is alive," I whispered, but only the Goddess heard.

He is alive, alive and in Avignon—the Lord of the Race, my Beloved, my Luc de la Rose.

. . .

Alive and in Avignon, lair of the Enemy old and new, where our joint destiny awaited. He was held, a prisoner in their grasp, his powers stripped from him, his mind held fast.

Whereas I had gone to Poitiers out of a sense of fear for my Beloved, I went to Avignon at the Goddess's bidding.

Was my heart any less engaged? Any less tormented by the thought of my Beloved, soon to be corrupted by the Enemy? Ah, no. But I was obliged to act only out of compassion, not from selfish or fearful love.

The current Enemy was ascendant, as he possessed the Lord of the Race; but because I had faced my last fear, our powers were evenly matched. At times I would able to sense him clearly; at others, not. But I knew I was bound to take great care myself to remain in the Goddess's presence, else he would be able to sense *me*.

By night and by day I rode alone, empowering my horse with supernatural strength and vision. To my Templars I said naught: but those sensitive to the whispers of the Goddess and the pull of fate followed after, in the event they might prove of service.

Of the outcome, I saw nothing. As I said, the contest between myself and the Enemy was evenly matched, and therefore unpredictable—as were the choices of my Beloved. The danger to Luc and to me was great, but I left it in the Goddess's hands, and rode swiftly to the holiest city in France.

What shall I say about the city proper? Heaven and Hell, it is. Never have I ridden through streets narrower, filthier; nor seen more whores, brigands, beggars, and charlatans gathered in one place. (They say in Avignon there are so many reliquaries containing a lock of the Magdalen's hair, it must have been long enough to encircle the world; and so many fingers belonging to Saint John the Divine that he was obviously a monster, graced by God with a dozen arms.)

Likewise have I never beheld such beauty, such grandeur, such wealth. More ermine resides in Avignon, they say, than in the rest of the world combined; and I can vouch for it now. On my arrival, I let myself be led by the Goddess into the great square in front of the papal palace, and watched the glorious display of finery: the nobles in their canary, peacock, and purple silks and brocades, the papal gendarmes in uniforms blue as the broad Rhône, the cardinals in wide-brimmed carmine hats and snowy furs.

Across from me stood the Palais des Papes, the Palace of the Popes, that magnificent cacophony in stone, built upon a cliff that dropped precipitously to the shores of the Rhône. Tall as a great cathedral, it was much broader in span—in fact the size of a king's estate, grand enough to house several hundred, its massive walls enclosing dozens of spires and turrets. And those walls faced a great city square.

As I neared the papal palace, my steed atremble as if he sensed the Evil residing there, I saw a platform.

A platform for inquisitors, and before it an execution berm. Immediately I remembered the scaffolding I had seen so long ago in my native Toulouse, when I was but a child of almost five in braids, in a cart with my Noni, Papa, and Maman, and our neighbors Georges and Thérèse. That city square had been far cleaner, with fewer people and far less grandeur.

For in Avignon, lines of papal gendarmes in smartly matching caps, tunics, and iron swords formed a continuous ring about both platform and berm. The platform itself was permanent—no hastily erected scaffold of timber here, but a structure of carefully painted and gilded wood adorned with scrollwork, gargoyles, and the likenesses of saints. A striped red-and-yellow awning had been rolled out to protect those who sat there—on tufted stools covered in crimson brocade—from encroaching dark clouds that spoke of a coming storm.

This was the side of Avignon presented to the public: decadent beauty.

Yet with it came the overwhelming stench of sewage, viler than anything I had ever smelled, as if beneath the glittering layer of finery and color, the city itself was rotting like a gloriously attired corpse in summer.

And upon the gilded platform, sitting in comfort upon the tufted stools, were three men. *Two crows,* as my Noni would have said—Dominicans in black robes, their hoods thrown back to reveal the white lining—*and one peacock,* a great cardinal in a gown of dazzlingly red silk, trimmed with white ermine at necks, cuffs, and hem. Given the gravity of his mission, he had forgone the broad-brimmed hat in favor of a simple skullcap.

Two crows and a peacock. Of them, the peacock was the Enemy, and the handsome younger crow the Enemy-to-be.

And I, like the child Sybille standing tiptoe on the cart, gazed at last on my Beloved.

A single prisoner, prodded by a guard, moved on the execution berm. He was a young man, near skeletal from months of imprisonment and starvation, hobbled by shackles and chains on his ankles, stooped by the same upon his wrists. Though his body was painfully weak, his spirit was strong, for though each halting step, no greater than the span of a hand, was plainly agony, his bearing revealed pride.

Had he ever been handsome? So much of God's wrath had been unleashed upon his features, it was impossible to tell. The bridge of his nose was half crushed between his eyes, whence it veered to the left at an alarming angle; the skin there was hot, shiny purple. His nostrils and upper lip were caked with black blood.

The sight of him released in me unutterable pity; but I dwelled in the Goddess. I maintained compassion for both inquisitor and victim, and I waited; waited for direction. I would not endanger my Beloved this time.

The prisoner was led to the stake awaiting him, and fastened there; the faggots were heaped about his knees, to the level of his hips.

And then the peacock cardinal called out to him an irregular question: "Have you any last thing to say?"

"Yes," the prisoner cried out. "What you worship as God is in truth a Devil—a demon who controls your world through fear, and blinded your eyes to the true God—"

"Gendarmes!" the Enemy-to-be cries out, and in response the guard escorting the prisoner struck him harshly with the blunt handle of his sword.

The prisoner was caught at the edge of his left temple, and the handle slipped into the orbit, half dislodging his eye. As he screamed in raw, feral pain—helpless to cup the damaged eye, hanging forward by green and blue threads onto the skin just above his cheeks—the crowd of genteel nobles, wealthy merchants, and pious clergy roared its approval.

The grief and outrage I felt at this threatened my calm; but I held fast to the Goddess's compassion, even to the Goddess's joy, and Saw my Path. I dismounted, whispering a magical command to my steed, and through the crowd I ran—faster and more easily than was possible: more than human through a wall of impassable flesh and wooden *chariots*. Indeed, I stopped not even at the line of gendarmes encircling the berm, but easily passed through, though there was no opening. They did not notice me until I reached the prisoner's side, until I had stooped down and cupped his crushed and bloodied eye, warm as pudding, in my hand, until I had replaced it in its socket and shared with his soul the wildly joyful communion of the Divine.

Smiling, I drew my hand away; and he laughed, all fear and rage dismissed, filled now only with singular delight.

"I have been rescued by an angel," he said happily, his sweet, tortured features radiant with joy as we gazed upon each other for that infinite moment. "A true angel sent from the true God."

The previously conversational, indeed noisy, crowd, fell silent for a time; the gendarme who delivered the blow stood nearby and watched the exchange, too stunned to react. At last some crossed themselves and whispered prayers; some shouted, "It is a miracle! He is innocent!" and "She *is* an angel!"

Others remained silent, faces taut with uncertainty, even fear. They looked to the men upon the platform for direction.

The largest, the eldest—the peacock, my scarlet Enemy—stood looking down at me and his prisoner with teeth-gnashing fury. "Hear me," he cried in a booming voice to the crowd. "He is a heretic of the worst sort—you have heard him call our Beloved Lord the Devil with your own ears. And she who has healed him is merely his magical consort—a witch, come to deceive you into thinking him innocent."

"But, Eminence—" one of the Dominicans on the platform began.

"Silence!" His Eminence snapped. Then ordered: "Gendarmes! Arrest her and bring her to me! The rest of you, proceed with the burning at once."

As an executioner came forward with a torch and held the flames to the coals at the prisoner's feet, I was dragged away by the guards; for the moment, the Goddess did not grant me the power of escape. My heart protested wildly, yet I knew this was as She willed it, and I had to yield, else a worse evil would come. But first I struggled, first I cried out to my Beloved:

"Luc! Luc de la Rose, I swear I shall find a way to free you!"

I was then prodded to the back side of the platform, where my Enemy, the cardinal, had already descended to meet me. He was thick of bone and broad: a square head upon a square body, and tall; I had to tilt my face half skyward to see his. Beneath his red skullcap, his graying hair was thick and wavy; a pale round mole sat to one side of his short nose, and the bags beneath his eyes weighed down the lower lids, exposing the inner reds. An air of gloom surrounded him; his presence seemed to consume all joy, all air, all light. At one time, I might have been seized by fear at the sight of him; now I felt only compassion and pity. For his power was born of a self-hatred so great it extended to the rest of the world; self-hatred, and the accumulated misery of terrified souls.

It was that misery, directed at Luc's mother, Beatrice de la Rose, which drove her mad.

Had he been startled by my sudden appearance? I could not tell. But on his face was an expression of gloating, of evil pride that seemed to say: *So, you have seen what I have reduced your Beloved to. You have lost him forever; and now, you also are in my hands. . . . Who is now the more powerful?*

He expected me to weep with horror at what he had done to Luc, to be full of fear at what he would do to me. But there were no tears in my eyes.

Instead, I forced myself to hold on to a shred of the Presence, to smile at him. I even managed to love him; he saw it in my eyes, and it infuriated him. "At last, Your Eminence," I said. "We meet in the flesh."

"You will pay for it, Mother," he threatened. When his mouth opened to speak to me, I imagined it consuming my Beloved, limb by limb, eating his very essence, while I stood, temporarily powerless and smiling beside him. "You have just performed an act of witchcraft in the presence of hundreds of witnesses." He turned his back to me; leading the way, he bade the two gendarmes accompanying me to follow.

I followed, too, remembering the two crows remaining upon the platform, and the prisoner still kneeling at the stake, surrounded by firewood—touched now by flame.

My heart was breaking. There was so little time before Luc's soul was lost, and I could not bear to be separated from him once I had seen him again. But the Goddess spoke: *In order to save him, you* must *leave him now.*

This was the only way. It was not given me to see the outcome: I had to walk through this torturous trial step by step, yielding to none of the pain, only the joy.

I had never realized how hard my destiny would truly be.

His Eminence the cardinal led us through a side doorway into the Palace of the Popes.

The palace is the strongest and most beautiful house in the world, they say, and it is true. I walked down long corridors, through chamber after chamber, and everywhere I looked—floor, walls, ceiling—I saw a masterpiece, whether rendered in tile beneath my slippers, or in paint and gold leaf above my head. The previous pope, Clement, had been much scolded for his lavish spending during his life, and even more so after; surely he had paid the painter Giovannetti alone a fortune for the years spent toiling here. Bible stories unfolded scene by scene upon the walls as I passed, while saints and angels glared down from above, and glittering mosaics of mounted knights pursued fantastical animals into gardens of stylized flowers.

All this was housed in chambers so spacious that, though we passed many people—officers of the Curia, priests, nobles, cardinals, and all their attendant aides and servants—never once did any of us brush against another person.

I walked through brilliance and beauty: but all I saw was the ugliness, the evil beneath it; all I sensed was the suffering of tortured souls.

My hosts escorted me silently to what seemed a private chamber, for the door was closed. The peacock knocked once, brusquely, then, with an air of infinite confidence, opened it.

He strode in swiftly; the gendarmes and I followed with equal alacrity, and the door was closed behind us.

This chamber's scale was smaller than that of the other rooms I had seen; but it was no less glorious, with murals of pastoral themes upon the walls, of archers shooting deer, and nude bathers.

There, upon cushions of velvet in a great and gilded throne beside a desk, sat Pope Innocent VI. I had seen a likeness of him before, but it resembled him not at all. The Goddess Herself told me whom I faced.

I could not understand why my Enemy had brought me here, instead of escorting me directly to a dungeon. Surely he—and the Goddess—had a purpose.

Five years upon the throne, at the age of seventy-five, Innocent's beard still contained a surprising amount of black. Instead of the glorious papal crown, he wore a close-fitting crimson velvet cap that covered his ears; but his robe was a heavy scarlet brocade embroidered with so much golden thread, it glittered with his slightest movement, weighing him down.

Clearly he had once been a robust man, with great shoulders and broad chest, but now his back was stooped, his chest and stomach caved so far inward that his ribs approached his hipbones. His skin was an unhealthy yellow, his lips pale, but he was still possessed of most of his teeth. His nose descended from still-dark brows in a sharp, straight line and ended in a V, like the tip of an arrow pointed downward.

"Holiness," my Enemy said, moving to him, then both genuflecting and kissing Innocent's ring so quickly that his knee did not bend, nor his lips touch more than air.

"Domenico," the old man said with annoyance. "You can see I am in the midst of . . ." Rather than finish his sentence, he lifted the oft-kissed, blue-veined hand from the armrest of his throne, and turned it palm up, three fingers slightly curled, index finger pointing at a young scribe, who read to him from a scroll.

"My apologies, Holiness," the Enemy said. "But I have a dangerous prisoner who must be dealt with swiftly—"

"Oho!" countered Innocent. "So you have brought the danger to *me*, in my private quarters? How thoughtful." Eyes clouded with age, he squinted at me, a corner of his mouth quirking at the notion that such a small woman presented such an immediate threat. "Who is this?"

"The abbess of the Franciscan cloister at Carcassonne, Mother Marie Françoise," my Enemy said. The gendarmes accompanying me did not react to this information at all, as if it were a perfectly natural thing for such a high-ranking cardinal to recognize a lowly nun from distant reaches.

"Ah." The pope's expression grew focused; his intellect had remained keen after all his many years. As the man Etienne Aubert, he had been a professor of law in Toulouse. "This is the abbess in Carcassonne who healed the leper, yes? Many people think she is a saint, Domenico. The opinion of the Toulouse diocese is that these are miracles of God. Is there reason to think otherwise?"

"Indeed," replied the Enemy. "She has healed again—but this time, an evildoer scheduled for execution, from another of the cults springing from the original Gnostic heresy. She would have kept him from a just death, had we not stopped her."

"But even Christ healed sinners—" Innocent began mildly, and then his mouth shut so abruptly, his teeth clacked, and his head jerked unnaturally toward the cardinal as if pulled by an unpolished puppeteer.

Again, the gendarmes gave no sign that this was an extraordinary event.

And the cardinal, his eyes upon me, shining with victory, his lips curved upward in gloating, said to the Holy Father: "You will dictate to this scribe now a writ dispensing with the normal number of witnesses required to bring charges and make an arrest; a writ that also dispenses with the traditional requirements necessary to sentence a heretic to execution. Mother Marie Françoise, that is the name of the criminal."

As he was told, so did poor Innocent do—and his scribe wrote, while the gendarmes waited, all of them behaving as if nothing unusual, nothing magical was occurring there.

My Enemy, still looking to me, bared his teeth, and at last I understood why he had exposed the pope to my possibly dangerous presence.

Cruel arrogance. He was proud of the control he had won over Innocent and his minions; he reveled in the fear I might feel at witnessing such control. He wanted no more than to see me suffer, to see me *know* that it was he who inflicted the suffering.

Perhaps he felt that my temporary compliance was due to his strength, not my devotion to the Goddess's will. Perhaps he gloated also because he felt he had won, that I was hobbled without my Beloved. That I was the Goddess without her consort, the lady without her lord—like my Enemy who had become, by his own choice, a lord separated from his lady, the lady Ana Magdalena. For he had been born in Italy to an Italian mother and French father as Domenico Chrétien.

Ah, but he did not understand the sacrifice Noni had made for me; he understood only fear, not love, and therefore was ignorant of my supreme initiation.

As he stood in arrogant triumph, he at last turned his face to watch the pope fulfill his bidding; and I found myself suddenly free within the Goddess, to move and do her will.

Again, my heart ached that she did not direct me to the side of my Beloved at once; but I yielded, trusting. While Innocent dictated, I faded from the visible world, and slipped unnoticed from the gendarmes, from my Enemy, from the papal chamber.

Invisible, divinely guided, I ran swiftly to a different part of the palace, where members of the Curia lived with their attendants and servants in magnificent apartments. From chamber to chamber I moved, then down a dim passageway, until I arrived at a magnificent private suite, with a vast anteroom warmed by a blaze in the arching hearth. Here were gilded chairs cushioned with shiny gold brocades, tiled floors covered by carpets of ermine, walls hung with the finest tapestries of biblical scenes, including a striking one of Eden before the Fall. A pair of great golden candelabra rested upon a dark table, inlaid with pale oak in the design of a six-pointed star. The ten tapers had all been lit— recently, judging by their height—in expectation of the owner's return.

I picked up a candelabrum, then moved to the tapestry of Eden and lifted up a corner of it to reveal a wall mural: a mournful Adam and Eve being cast from the garden, fig leaves covering their nakedness, Eve's fine pale hair cascading in waves over her white breasts. I pressed forcefully upon the image of the archangel, sword in hand, ready to prevent those evicted from paradise from returning; there came the scraping sound of stone against stone as the wall slid *inward,* opening onto darkness.

I entered.

Through the Sight I had already been to this place, and knew what awaited me here; yet upon entry, I let go a gasp.

The winters in Carcassonne and my native Toulouse are rarely fierce; but there are times when *le mistral,* the winter wind, blows so bitter, so cold, it steals my breath away. Such was the sensation upon entering that small windowless chamber, hid within the thick walls of the palace: a chill so profound, I scarce could breathe. Yet by no means was it physical. It was a cold that burned, the whispers of a thousand souls perished in fear and agony, the voice of my Noni calling out: *Domenico . . .*

Here in my Enemy's lair was the smell of smoke, both astral and physical.

I held the candelabrum high, casting a glow over the circular room. At each of the quarters—east, south, west, and north—stood a sconce as tall as a man and half as thick, each decorated with a different image: eagle, lion, man, bull; in the east rested an altar of gleaming onyx.

Upon that altar lay a gruesome sight: the charred carcass of a bird, surrounded by ash and scorched splinters, the remnants of a small cage. On the cold marble floor lay three white feathers, two of them speckled with fine drops of bright blood; I closed my eyes briefly at the image of the dove, thrashing its wings against the flaming wooden bars that held it prisoner.

You the treacherous breeze at the baby's birth . . .

Wrapped around the dove's blackened wings, around its neck, was a chain culminating in a golden talisman. The legend inscribed there was unreadable, for the metal had melted quite thoroughly and molded to the bird's breastbone, to its still, small heart.

I knew who the dove represented: the Enemy *did* know that I had Seen Luc before my coming here. He had been waiting for me, preparing a trap for me. At first I wavered and asked the Goddess: *Why did you bring me here? To desert me? To surrender me to the blaze?*

But I quickly begged forgiveness for such thoughts. Instead, I fixed my urgency on looking for a particular talisman.

Beginning at the east and proceeding deosil, clockwise, I lit the candles, touching a flame from the candelabrum to each wick in turn. The gloom lifted somewhat, revealing that I stood in a magical circle rendered in mosaic beneath my feet; on the curving walls and domed ceiling, images of frolicking gods flickered in the shadows.

When I had finished, I set the candelabrum down and again closed my eyes—not in pain this time, but in surrender to the Goddess, for I desperately needed her protection and aid in this place of Evil.

Help me, I prayed silently. *Help me to find what is hidden here. . . .*

And through the Goddess's eyes, I Saw, hidden beneath the scorched remnants of the poor dove, a piece of silver on which there was inscribed a sigil. It was wrapped in black silk, and wound about with cord.

This was the talisman I so yearned to find: for it controlled the heart and mind of Pope Innocent. I walked forward to the altar, and, in my state of calm, I displaced the limp, broken bird without emotion. I unwrapped the sigil, and with the Goddess's magic, reversed the charge and freed the pope from the Enemy's grip.

To the other souls there, I whispered a promise: *I shall return someday to free you as well.*

And then I paused, and centered upon the Goddess, and opened myself, my Sight, asking the question: *Where shall I find Luc's talisman?*

The answer came quickly: *The talisman is not here.*

It was not there.

Panic threatened, but I steadied myself, and prayed again: *What must I do here, that my Beloved might be saved?*

No answer.

Again: *What must I do here, that my Beloved might be saved?*

Nothing.

There was nothing I could do to save my Beloved then. Nothing; and as I let go a moan at the very thought, I lost my divine center, and realized at once that the Enemy had sensed me, that he knew where I had gone, that he was in pursuit.

All I could do now was to flee.

So, invisible, I ran: ran through the great palace, my very soul afire. In my mind's eye, I was the dove, beating my wings till they bled against the glorious gilded cage that surrounded me: it was as though the paintings of the saints stared down at me through a wall of flame. How many of them, I wondered, had been martyred so?

Saints and sacrifice, death and burning; I felt smothered by smoke, but I called out silently to my Templars, to my knights, whom I knew had followed me to this holy, heavenly, desecrated and infernal city.

Come! Come! To the execution berm! The Enemy pursues, and I know not what has become of our lord. . . .

Outside, the sky had opened. Late afternoon it was, but dark as night. The rain came down not in drops, but a single great sheet, and the wind blew it, stinging like the bite of an asp, into my face.

I did not waste my power protecting myself from the rain; I had no heart to. For the inquisitor's platform was empty, the chairs removed, the striped awning furled and tied back, though the violent wind had already torn it as it was pummeled against the palatial stone wall.

The square itself was empty.

And upon the berm, the stake to which the prisoner had been bound was charred and toppled. The logs there had been consumed. Any bones, any remnants of the body had been removed; I knelt there and wept, a hand upon the few remaining ashes while the wind and rain together swept them away.

My Beloved was gone. Again, I asked the Goddess: *Why? Why have You led me here, only to show me defeat? He belongs to the Enemy more than ever now. . . .*

The muted rumble of hooves against mud. My knights had come; they had brought a horse for me. I wiped my cheeks with my dirtied hand, smearing my face with tears, death, and ash in the instant before the rain washed them all away.

Yet at first I could not rise; I could not leave this place where last I saw my Beloved. I yearned to follow after the inquisitors, to find what remained of him.

Would that I were not human, and had no heart.

Luc's uncle, Edouard, dismounted his steed to pull me to my feet, to guide me onto my horse.

Home, toward Carcassonne, we rode. It was the greatest foolishness, I knew, the first place my Enemy would seek me. But this was my Path, shown me by the Goddess; it was like a lantern. I could see only so far into the dark future, and no farther.

At the taste of destiny in my mouth, sharp and metallic as blood, I spat.

For hours, we rode; through night and rain that never ended, over rough, slick stones, over hills, through valleys and meadows until I smelled the fragrance of crushed lavender, of rosemary, beneath me. We were nearly home.

At last, exhaustion and continual prayer calmed me sufficiently to See a bit further. In flight, there could be no victory; for the future held only more encounters between me and my Enemy, none of them providing my Beloved release from his horrific prison.

Surrender, the Goddess whispered. *It is the Race's only chance. Surrender.*

Only the slenderest hope of success remained; a thread so fine the smallest tug would cause it to snap. But because it was the only hope, I yielded. Against their protests, I sent my knights away.

Then to the Goddess, I surrendered.

To my Enemy, I surrendered.

I surrender.

That is my story. There is no more to tell.

PART VII

Luc

XXI

"If your story is true, then I am the Enemy-to-be," Michel said, with quiet sorrow. "And I am to blame for the suffering and death of Luc."

For he had been upon the inquisitors' platform that day in Avignon, seated between Cardinal Chrétien and Father Charles. He had been what Sybille had called "the younger crow," the future Enemy. It was he who had called out in anger to the gendarme to punish the prisoner's heretical statement, then been horrified in the extreme at the result. It was his first burning—the one that had caused him to stagger off to his cell and retch; and Chrétien had held his head and comforted him.

He had seen Sybille—that is, Mother Marie Françoise—not knowing who she was; like the crowd, he had been astonished to see her suddenly appear beside the prisoner, and even more astonished when she had restored the beaten man's displaced eye.

He had known at once in his heart that he had just witnessed a true miracle of God; he had known at once that she was a saint, for he had been filled with what she called "the Presence": the sweet, free, undeniable presence of the Divine. When he learned that she was the abbess of Carcassonne, famous for healing the lepers, he was doubly convinced that she had evoked in him a true mystical experience, and that Cardinal Chrétien and Father Charles were wrong to call the act witchcraft.

Thus he had been greatly disturbed when Chrétien had arrested her and taken her away at once.

And to watch, worrying about what had become of her, the death of the man she had just healed seemed to Michel monstrous. God had spoken: God had wanted to spare that man, but the two men Michel loved most made sure that the healing was wasted, that the man died in utter agony.

To realize now that the prisoner had been Luc . . .

He lowered his face, clutching forehead and temple with his fingertips, and let go a sob.

"You are the Enemy-to-be," Sybille confirmed softly, even kindly. "But you did not kill Luc de la Rose."

He looked up from his still-cupped fingers, angry at himself, at his moral weakness. "Perhaps not directly; that honor lies with Chrétien and Charles. But I was their accomplice, obliged to speak out against wrongdoing, and I did nothing to stop them—"

"Father Charles is naught but a misguided innocent. But you still do not understand," Sybille interrupted. Her lips parted as she beheld him, her gaze filled with sorrow, pity, love, hope. "Luc de la Rose is not dead."

"Not dead?" He sat straight, thunderstruck. "But I saw him die. They fanned the flames strongly, so the execution would be carried out quickly, before the storm."

"The prisoner that I healed was not Luc de la Rose." She paused and focused upon him intently before saying carefully, slowly: "Luc de la Rose *is* indeed alive. And he sits before me now."

For the longest moment Michel could make no sense at all of what she said; after a silence, she added: "*That* is why I surrendered to the

Enemy; because I Saw that his arrogance would lead him to send *you* as scribe, for it would torment me the most. But it has also given me the opportunity to tell you your story, and try to free you. For if you, Lord of the Race, turn Enemy toward your people, we are lost."

For an instant Michel saw in his mind's eye the image of Sybille upon the execution berm, crying out: *Luc de la Rose! I swear I shall find a way to free you!* He had told himself that she was calling out to the prisoner; but had not she been turned toward the platform—facing Michel?

And in that moment—why had he not recollected it before?—his heart responded with recognition and a love so intense he could not deny it. It swept over him, free-flowing and unchecked, and he *believed.*

The dreams of Luc—they had seemed so real because they had been his own memories returned to him by Sybille. Unshed tears stung his eyes; she had let herself be captured, had endured physical torment and now risked death, that she might save *him.*

At once, mental anguish seized him with nearly physical pain, the sensation of a hawk's talons gripping his scalp, and he clutched his head, whispering, "*Impossible.* Impossible. Chrétien and Charles raised me from a foundling. I lived a completely different life from Luc—"

"False memories, magically implanted once Chrétien seized control of your mind." Moved by his suffering, she leaned forward with difficulty and put a swollen hand atop his, as if to draw away the pain. "You have the memory of the cardinal lovingly holding your head when you were ill after the execution, do you not?"

Michel nodded, too overwhelmed to speak.

"Tell me, my love, how is this possible? During that time, Chrétien conducted a search of the papal palace for me. Directly afterward, he took off in pursuit of me on horseback. When did Chrétien provide this kindness? Before the search of the palace? Or earlier, when he stood with me before the pope? Before he left on horseback to follow me to Carcassonne?"

At once, he recalled Father Charles's eagerness to bar him from the interrogation: *She has bewitched you.*

Sybille's voice, countering: *Bewitched you are, Brother, but not by me.*

Michel moaned softly and let her tenderly draw his hands down, away from his troubled brain. He had no answer for her logic; indeed, he wanted nothing more than to rise and lead her from her cell, to fight the sentry, if need be, in order to help her escape . . .

. . . but a barrier existed in his mind—perhaps a religious one, he thought, born of his monk's training—which kept him seated, powerless to do what emotion bade him.

"He has taken your memories . . . and your power," Sybille continued gently, lightly clasping his hands in hers; at her touch, he again felt that electric yearning. "Your mother did not kill you, though the Enemy slew your mind. Even so, you still recognized me when you saw me in Avignon, and knew the healing was a holy act. That is why you do not scream with outrage when I accuse your own 'father' of being the Enemy.

"The truth is he is *not* your father. The truth is, you have been under his dominion in Avignon for over a year. Had you been raised in the Pope's Palace from an infant, son of the powerful Chrétien, you would have at the very least your own bishopric by now. But you are a scribe on only your second inquisition. How can that be?"

"I know not," Michel whispered, shuddering with the effort of forming the words. "But if you have told me the truth, why has my memory not returned?"

"Chrétien still keeps it from you." Sybille paused, and her once-calm expression began to waver with grief, with the passion and longing of the human woman. At last she said in a voice trembling with emotion: "Luc . . . Beloved. I have waited so long to find you, to tell you . . . If you can but trust me for a short while—"

She moved to embrace him, though it clearly caused her agony; he longed more than his very life to return that embrace, but again, an invisible barrier held him back, made him recoil from her.

She has bewitched you, my son. It is all a lie, a devilish seduction.

He countered Chrétien's silent voice with a desperate thought: *No, let me go to her. I have waited for her, have known her, my entire life. For a hundred lifetimes . . .* Yet he could not rise, could not reach for her.

Sybille withdrew her hands and lowered her face quickly, lest he see her weep.

Stricken, Michel said with a sudden burst of will, "I would do anything to save you from the stake."

Her face still hidden, she shook her head; and when she was enough recovered she said: "You *would* . . . but you cannot, for you are still under Chrétien's control. Your memories and powers must first be restored, if you are to help me."

"How?"

She looked up, her cheeks and eyes shining with tears. "Just as I was required to face my own fear directly, so must you face your own."

"My only fear is that you will not be given a fair hearing."

She shook her head. "That is Michel's fear. I am talking to *you,* Luc. You must surrender yourself to the Goddess and refuse to yield to your greatest fear. The Enemy feeds off terror; it adds to his power and makes us vulnerable. That is why I had to face my fear of encountering my Beloved as Enemy"—here she brushed his cheek with her crooked fingers, in comfort—"before I came to Avignon to find you. It is how Chrétien captured you—through that fear." She paused and leaned back against the stone wall. "Meditate on all that has been revealed to you as Luc. Confront your true fear, and freedom will come to you."

So it was Michel left her, mindful that less than a handful of hours remained for him to make his decision whether to help her escape, to go with her—or to deliver her confession to the cardinal. Both his mind and body ached, and his thoughts raced as if with feverish delirium.

I love her. . . . Whatever happens, I must help her escape. I cannot let her die. She is holy, a true saint.

She is a witch, and should be properly condemned. You are a pawn of the

Devil, Michel, to let yourself be so manipulated by a woman. Why do you think you burn with lust in her presence? It is a spell, a simple spell, and you the greatest fool. . . .

God help me. God help me. I have been bewitched, and I know not by whom.

On his rapid walk through the night back to the monastery, he saw at the end of the street the bishop's palace, built into the city ramparts; and as he watched, the gates swung wide, admitting the great, gilded *chariot* bearing the crest of the cardinal Chrétien.

He walked without knowing where or why he went; but at last he arrived at his mentor's bedside.

Barely alive, Father Charles still lay motionless upon the overstuffed bed, sounding barely capable of drawing another weak, hitching breath—the only sound in the room besides the crackle of the fire; in the nearby chair, Brother André slept, silent as stone.

Without a word, Michel gently shook the old monk's shoulder. André woke peacefully, heavy lids drawing slowly upward over aged, watery eyes. With a gesture, Michel bade him leave, which Brother André did as quietly as possible, as if there remained a chance of actually disturbing the patient. But as the old monk passed through the doorway, he paused, turned, and remarked in a low voice: "I have nursed many with pestilence; never have I seen one stave off death for so long, my friend. Keep up your prayers for him; God surely hears them."

When André had left, Michel stood over his beloved mentor, a palm resting on the priest's chest and the fever-heated linen there. Charles's lungs felt heavy with fluid; his parched lips were drawn back over yellowed teeth, his cheeks sunken and gray, his eyelids the shadowy purple of late sunset.

Pity and sorrow overwhelmed the young monk. He sank to his knees beside the bed, putting his other hand to rest beside the other on Charles's chest; and he wept.

At once an image came to Michel: that of the child Luc, stealing through the darkened castle to his sick father's bedchamber.

His father's thigh swollen hard to twice its normal size, beneath a poultice of mustard. The stink of rotting flesh. Sadness replaced suddenly by a sense of rightness, of warmth, of tingling beneath Luc's skin, inside his vitals, of a happiness he had never known. . . .

And a sense of direction, of purpose. Of his small hands upon his father's leg, and the buzzing warmth, the love that flowed out of him into his father, constantly renewing itself so Luc was always filled. . . .

"Goddess," Michel whispered, his tear-damp face pressed into the linens on the side of Charles's mattress. "Diana, Artemis, Hecate, by whatever name you are called, hear me: to you, I surrender. I surrender. I surrender, only restore to me the powers rightly mine at birth. Flow through me, as you did when I healed my father so long ago, and heal this poor man, Father Charles. He is a good man; and though he has killed many of the Race, when he understands his error, he will repent. Only help me, Goddess!"

Thus he prayed until his heart quieted somewhat; and when he had achieved a measure of calm, he stood, hands still upon Charles's breastbone.

A sensation of vibrating warmth, of bliss, began to descend. For an instant, Michel smiled, imagining the priest, his dark eyes wide with surprise and joy, saying: *Michel. Michel, dear nephew, you have saved me. . . .*

And as the young monk watched, Charles's eyes *did* slowly open, and his lips parted. A slow bloom of color appeared on his cheeks.

"Father?" Michel asked, his voice atremble with elation.

"Michel," the priest hissed slowly, his eyes looking blindly at the ceiling, at something beyond. So weak was Charles's voice that the young monk lowered his face until his ear almost touched the older man's lips. "Has she won you back?"

"Yes, Father. But you are healed now, by God, because of her—you are going to get better. Do you understand?"

Yes. The priest's lips formed the word, but no sound came. Then, with sudden strength, as if an external force expelled the words from him: "I pass now into the jaws of Hell." A sudden great rush of air escaped his lungs.

Charles's face went slack, and his open eyes became unfocused and utterly devoid of expression; a sudden stream of thick black bile oozed from the corner of his mouth onto his linen undershift.

"Father?" Michel asked again, and this time his voice held a note of panic. Sybille had warned him that he must not yield to fear, but she had said nothing about grief. At once he lifted his hands—now trembling—from the priest's chest, and instead pressed his ear there, and strained to listen.

For a long moment he remained thus; but Father Charles's rib cage never rose and fell again, nor did his heart beat once.

With the purest agony, Michel lifted his face to the ceiling and howled.

"I have killed him," Michel moaned, kneeling at Chrétien's feet and clutching the cardinal's skirts as an inconsolable child pulls at his mother's.

Frenzied, he had run from the monastery to Rigaud's palace, and shouted outside the gate until someone finally came to admit him. In the anteroom of one of the magnificently adorned chambers, Michel writhed on the floor at the startled cardinal's feet. "Dear Father, you must help me! I have sinned; I have let myself be bewitched, enticed and seduced by her magic—"

Chrétien, barefoot, bareheaded, clad in a lace-trimmed linen nightshirt partially covered by a red silk cape, reached out his hand and lifted the agitated young monk to his feet. "Michel, my son, whatever the problem is, we shall repair it. Only come, and sit, and calm yourself."

And he drew the monk further into his chamber, one that would well have housed thirty monks comfortably, and was filled with every luxury imaginable: beeswax tapers in golden candlesticks upon a bed-side table (apparently to encourage the unthinkable luxury of reading in bed), a chamber pot with a painted lid, a porcelain basin and silver pitcher full of water, soft furs that protected bare feet from the cold marble floor, a heavy brocade curtain about the bed that stopped prying eyes and prevented unwanted moonlight from streaming in from the canopied balcony. On the ceiling was painted a fresco of a heavy-lidded Eve, her blond pubis mostly hidden behind the spread feathers of a pea-cock, her round white breasts not quite covered by her golden hair as she seductively proffered a red apple to an uncertain Adam.

Chrétien led Michel to a pair of well-padded chairs, and made him sit in one while the cardinal fetched a goblet of wine for him. "Drink," Chrétien urged as he handed over the goblet and settled into the seat opposite Michel, near a small carved table. "Then speak."

Michel obliged, drinking deeply. And once he had swallowed and caught his breath, he said: "Your Eminence, I beg forgiveness. I have let myself be swayed by the sorceress Marie Françoise; she almost con-vinced me that I had always been her consort, and that you had cast a magical spell upon me to make me believe I was Michel, your son. She had convinced me to help her escape; and also made me believe that I had magical powers of my own." He tried but could not entirely sup-press a rasping sob. "God help me: I tried to use them to heal Father Charles, but instead caused his death."

"Poor Charles," Chrétien said solemnly; he seemed not at all sur-prised or emotionally unsettled. "But we should be happy for him, my son, not grief-ridden. He is with God now. And he served a great pur-pose in his life."

"But it is *my fault*," Michel said, pressing a palm across his eyes to hide shame and tears. "You must hear my confession, Eminence, and now." He leaned forward and set down the goblet upon the table, then knelt and crossed himself. "Bless me, Father, for I have sinned. I fell in love with the abbess and was so seduced by her story of magic and the worship of a goddess that I quite believed it, and lost my faith. Worse, I served as a conduit for her magic this very night; I laid my hands upon Father Charles because I believed myself capable of healing him; instead, she used me to kill him."

Chrétien had steepled his hands, pressed the tips of the index fingers to his lips, and created a deep furrow between his sparse gray eyebrows, listening with full, deliberate attention, the way he always did when considering matters of import. Once Michel had finished speaking and bowed his head, the cardinal said thoughtfully:

"You did not kill Father Charles."

Michel began to raise his head to protest, to say, *I know that* she *was behind his death; but I was the one who laid hands upon him, who made his death possible. . . .*

But ere he could voice the swift thought, Cardinal Chrétien said, in the same normal, deliberate tone: "'Twas I."

Michel could not find his voice. The cardinal's words were a joke, of course—though what a cruel one, considering that poor Charles had just died.

Yet with the passage of seconds, Chrétien's serious demeanor remained so; indeed, his brow furrowed even greater, and Michel told himself: *No, what he means is that he feels the most responsible for Father Charles's death, because he was not there to prevent it. Perhaps he feels he should have come to Carcassonne at the very beginning, to watch over the proceedings.*

But the young monk suddenly recalled the image of the newly ill and raving Father Charles:

This is my arrogance. . . . I trotted you around like a trained pony, showed you off as if to say, He's mine, all mine. . . .

Chrétien would as soon see you dead.

"Everything the criminal Sybille has told you is true," the cardinal said calmly. "Your true name is Luc de la Rose; you were born in Toulouse, not Avignon; and you have been with me not since your birth, but for the space of one year.

"But she is a pagan, a heretic, and the tale she tells underscores that fact. Her magic springs not from God, but the Devil, as does her Race. Yet she fancies herself holy, the representative of her Goddess."

With a great expulsion of air from his lungs, Michel sat back upon his heels: he felt like a lurching madman grasping vainly at sanity. Everything he had considered the true details of his life—his years at the monastery, his relationship with Father Charles and with the man standing before him, curling iron-gray hairs emerging from beneath the lace at his nightshirt collar—were merely dreams; and what he had considered mere dreams were in fact the reality of his life.

And the greatest truth of all was his love for Sybille, and hers for him; but he had rebuffed her embrace and turned away.

With pure revulsion, Michel looked upon the one he had esteemed as father, and knew that Chrétien saw him and Father Charles as naught but pawns in a game of power; he gazed into the cardinal's eyes and saw neither affection nor sorrow—only calculation and self-righteousness. All confusion, all doubt left Michel at that instant, and he knew Sybille's every word had been true.

But though Michel's thoughts grew focused and free, he felt Chrétien's crushing grip upon his will, as tangible as if the bearlike cardinal had seized him by the neck with a great claw.

Even so, he countered with barely contained hatred, "Then you are of the Devil, Cardinal. As am I, for she has said we are both of the Race."

An emotion between anger and urgency overtook Chrétien; he surged halfway from his chair.

"Fool! Do you not *see* what we are? We are a race of unholy monsters, the spawn of Lilith, she who obeyed neither God nor Adam. Our unnatural powers spring from a she-devil. Ask yourself: how could a woman ever be so holy as our Lord? God forbid we should ever embrace such vile magics—save to use them in God's cause, to destroy other monsters like ourselves.

"Do I evoke demons? Do I perform magic? I do—in the name of the Lord. Neither the flames nor the hell that follows are painful enough punishment for the vileness of the heretic's crimes."

"What crimes?" Michel interrupted. "Seeing the future? Healing the sick? Raising the dead?"

"If done without God's blessing, such are indeed crimes." The cardinal gathered his thoughts for a moment, then added: "Refusing to obey rules. Rebelling against order. This is the original sin: only by clinging fast to the laws, the regulations of the Church, are we redeemed. I have read every one of your wax tablets, Michel; I have Heard much of your conversations with her. Listen to the experience she describes of the Goddess! Wild, forbidden pleasure; ecstasy without rules, without limits. We men are craven creatures at best; and those of us of the Race, even worse. We must cling to Mother Church, follow her prescriptions, chant her liturgy, confess our sins, receive absolution. . . . This talk of free will is nonsense. Men cannot depend upon their own hearts to guide them. The will *must* be controlled, molded to God's—through coercion, if necessary."

Without acknowledging the cardinal's words, Michel interrupted with disgust, "Do not justify your crimes by speaking of how they will serve the Church. Sybille says that you eat the executed prisoners' souls, thus gaining more magical power."

"Why should I not, if it serves God?" Chrétien thundered. "I pray it is as purgatory to them, buying their slow redemption."

Michel closed his eyes in horror for those who had died at the cardinal's hands, including poor Charles. "And I suppose you will now kill me."

The cardinal's vehemence eased; a trace of affection crept into his tone. "Not at all, Michel. I will help you to fulfill your holy mission of becoming my successor, of being the most powerful inquisitor ever known. To you falls the honor of finding and destroying the Race, for your natural magical powers are far greater than mine."

"My name is Luc," he replied heatedly, "and I will answer to no other name, no other destiny." And he turned at once to leave, determined to go to his Beloved and free her.

"*Guards,*" Chrétien called, and at once two sentinels bearing drawn swords stepped swiftly inside the door, blocking Luc. "You are angry now and sympathetic to Sybille," Chrétien said behind him, "but by tomorrow all that will change. She will burn come morning, and any influence she had upon you will die with her. And you will be filled with a zealousness that will take you to the ends of the Earth in search of the Race."

Luc stared steadily at the blades of steel that threatened him. "You cannot harm me," he told Chrétien. "I know who I am now; I know what my powers are. Attack me with knives, Enemy; I cannot be cut. Cast me into flames; I will not burn."

A silent signal must have been given behind him, for he saw the answering nod on one guard's face and the silvery flash of the blade as it came toward him.

The steel, cold and hot at once, bit into the flesh of his shoulder; he cried out with surprise and pain as the weight of the blade brought him to one knee.

"*Enough,*" Chrétien thundered. "Bring linens at once."

Luc put a hand to his shoulder, drew it away, and stared in puzzlement at his bloodied palm. Belief in Sybille's story had not returned his powers to him; and here he had faced Chrétien without fear. With utter despair, he thought, *Then how shall I save her?*

"My son, forgive me," the cardinal said, approaching. "But I had to demonstrate forcefully that you are still a simple monk, not the magician you once were. You *can* be harmed, Michel, and to go to her now with thoughts of rescue would be sheer folly. Not all who anticipate her execution would be as lenient as I. You would be killed; and she would still go to her doom. Her death will come, and there is nothing you can do, physically or magically, to prevent it."

As Chrétien spoke, one of the sentinels returned with a thick wad of linen, which he used to bandage Luc's shoulder. The other stood guard until the work was complete; then the cardinal took up one of the empty wine goblets and disappeared into another chamber, only to reappear after a time with it half-filled.

The first sentinel helped Luc to his feet.

"Drink," Chrétien said.

Luc averted his face.

The cardinal's tone turned scornful. "*Drink*. It is only a medicinal draught to ease your pain and encourage sleep. Has she so convinced you that I am capable only of maliciousness? You are my *son*."

"I will not sleep while she dies."

"So you shall not," Chrétien agreed easily. "For until the deed is done, you will remain near me, lest anyone else attempt to do you further harm; thus, you will accompany me to her execution." And he raised the goblet to Luc's lips while the guards held him fast.

Yet Luc would not open his mouth. Finally the sentinels together pried it open, and the cardinal poured the wine mixture down the young man's throat. He tried to spit it out, and succeeded to some degree, but the guards thumped his back so that he ingested some of the draught despite all effort to resist.

"Take him," Chrétien ordered.

Before Luc was pulled away, he asked, "Why? Why did you let me interrogate Sybille?"

"Because she deserved to see you redeemed," the cardinal said with sudden heat. "Because she needed to know she was defeated before she died. There can never be enough punishment for the guilty, Michel— never enough. God was just in creating an eternal Hell."

Within the cardinal's great chamber was a closet just large enough to accommodate a mattress; Luc was locked inside. Although he fought against the effects of the sleeping draught by standing, he soon could only sit. Sooner still, he found himself lying down, the pain of his shoulder eased, his breath slowing. In the total darkness, his grief over Father Charles and terror over Sybille's approaching execution turned to numbness; and as he at last closed his eyes, his final mental image was that of the cardinal, holding the goblet, his round features slowly and unquestionably transforming into the sculpted ones of Edouard:

"Drink . . ."

PART VIII

XXII

"Michel, my son," Chrétien said, in his rich, officious bass. "It is time for her destiny, and yours, to be carried out." Uncharacteristically dressed in a plain robe and cloak, the cardinal leaned into the closet where Luc had slept. Behind him stood the same two sentinels who had prevented Luc from leaving the night before, and behind them stood Thomas, holding high a lamp in order to cast light upon the prisoner.

Luc pushed himself to a sitting position and promptly groaned at the pain of the blood-caked bandage tearing itself from his shoulder wound. Chrétien's draught had left him temporarily disoriented; palm to forehead, Luc gathered his thoughts slowly. Though the potion had caused him to forget most of his dreams, he knew that he had been struggling with them all night—terrible dreams of Chrétien, of Sybille at the stake, of Edouard—

Drink.

—and of Jacob.

Perfect union cannot occur in the presence of fear.

Chrétien turned to the guards. "Bring him."

Luc threw his legs over the edge of the cot and rose—too swiftly, for dizziness forced him immediately to sit again. One of the guards sheathed his sword and put a strong shoulder beneath Luc's good arm; with such help, the wounded monk was able to walk haltingly while the second guard flanked him, weapon at the ready.

As if I had any chance of fleeing, Luc thought with the numbed distraction induced by the drug.

And then, through the great, open window, he saw that the moonlight had been swallowed up by dark clouds, leaving the night utterly black. Dawn was hours away—and that apparently insignificant observation brought with it abrupt clarity and a rush of emotion.

They are taking me to watch her die, he realized. Chrétien was taking advantage of the early hour to avoid the wrath of the locals. By morning, when the public had assembled at the charred, deserted execution berm, the cardinal would no doubt be headed back to Avignon in his *chariot.*

Together the group of men departed the bishop's palace. Outside, the air was damp, scented with imminent rain, and cold enough to raise gooseflesh.

Desperate, Luc decided to test the extent of his ability. Abruptly, he pushed himself away from the guard, hoping for the impossible: that by sheer will he might run, might reach Sybille first, might somehow procure a weapon and free her.

Almost at once he fell gasping to his knees against the stone, barely managing with outthrust arms to keep himself from tumbling down the rest of the stairs.

Chrétien smiled faintly; Thomas, his eyes wide and somber in the lantern light, showed no reaction as Luc, too furious, too desperate to entertain such an insignificant emotion as embarrassment, let himself be picked up by the amused guard.

"Do not exhaust yourself, my son," the cardinal advised, "for you have much work ahead of you."

Pay attention, Luc told himself, trying to ignore the fresh blood that soaked his bandage. Another opportunity for escape would come—*had* to come, else this was the last hour of freedom for his mind and heart, the last hour of hope for the Race.

Out upon the city street, the sky was dark, without a hint of coming dawn. There was little to see—just shadowy forms marching in near-distant darkness, from the direction of the prison, and the occasional glimpse of a golden disc of moon, soon after occluded by black, swift-sailing clouds.

It seemed appropriate that his world, as it was, would not go on without her. His love was so fierce that his own fate seemed insignificant against the greater tragedy of his Beloved's.

The wind stirred, flinging sand. It blew into his eyes, and he stumbled, blinded, and was guided back onto the proper path by the guard's strong arms. For an interminable time he staggered on in agony, rubbing his eyes.

And when at last tears had cleared his vision, he saw that they had not gone to the city square and the berm that had been prepared for the executions; they were, as best he could tell in the darkness, in an alley behind the prison.

At a distance of several paces away, facing the three inquisitors, Sybille was kneeling at a stake. One papal gendarme was busy relocking the shackle that held the stake between her shins; two others had already begun to stack kindling and faggots around her feet and lower limbs. In the dim, wavering light cast by Thomas's lone lantern, Luc could not discern her features, but could make out only the dark outline of her head and shoulders, and the pale linen of her undershift.

Soon the guards had heaped the faggots to the level of her hip, and one took a long piece of the kindling and took it to Thomas, who opened the glass cover of his lantern.

Again the wind gusted, so strong that Luc shut his eyes against the stinging sand; when he opened them again, the lamp's flame had shrunk to a tiny sputter of blue tinged with gold, in danger of dying. Then the wind calmed abruptly, and the guard touched the tip of the fatwood to the fire; both lamp and kindling flared brightly as the latter caught.

Thomas's face was lit by the glow; with the astonishing clarity of a doomed man, Luc saw the look of fleeting but profound sorrow on the young priest's face. No one else saw: neither Chrétien nor the guards, but despite the darkness, Thomas gave a glance of acknowledgment in Luc's direction.

He is one of us; he has always been, Luc thought with sudden excitement.

But Thomas's expression immediately hardened, and he lowered the lamp to watch as the guard crouched down and touched the blazing kindling to the wood encircling Sybille's feet and legs.

Chrétien had already moved two paces away.

"Domenico!" Sybille cried in a voice fearless and strong.

> *You think your hate has finally won—*
> *Do you not see?*
> *It has only allowed Love to win again, to become*
> *Stronger than before.*

Luc understood at once: These were the same words her grandmother had uttered in the hour of her death. Sybille was now doing for him what Ana Magdalena had done for her: offering herself up in death that he might receive the supreme initiation—all of her powers, and a renewal of his, that he might defeat the Enemy.

"Beloved," Luc whispered, but could say no more; at the realization of the depth of Sybille's compassion, her courage, he felt love open his heart and spill forth, past the restraints of his body, even of the distance between them, and touch her.

The guard's flame caught the wind, and with a barely audible rushing sound—a rush of air, Luc imagined, much like the one that had entered Sybille's cottage on the night of her birth—set the abbess's kindling ablaze.

Until then, the darkness had been offset only by the tenuous glimmer of Thomas's lamp. Now, as the fire caught, it illumined her kneeling form so strikingly that there seemed naught else in the world but the night and her: her, face and flesh and linen incandescent against the blackness.

And beneath the wild surge of emotion, beneath the turbulence in Luc's mind, a Voice—small and barely audible, whispered . . .

Go to her.

Surely this was simply his own heart speaking; for he wanted nothing better than to do so—but it would be madness. He would be struck down at once, and the future of the Race destroyed.

Go to her, the Voice said again, and a sudden conviction seized him: this was not his own voice or that of the Enemy but one he had not heard in a long time.

With strength born of will, Luc tore himself from the sentinel's grasp and ran unevenly toward the flames. It mattered not to him whether he was impervious to fire or steel or the Enemy's attack; what mattered only was that he try to save her, try to ease her suffering, try to be with her.

As he reached for her, his hand brushing the blistering waves of heat, cold metal pierced his back, through ribs near the spine, and emerged from his chest, shattering the breastplate. Behind him, Chrétien screamed.

"Fool! You have killed him!" There came an electric-sharp jolt of pain as the sword was pulled from Luc's back, then the sound of another sword being unsheathed, of a melon-heavy object striking the ground.

Luc sank forward onto the earth, far hotter than the blood that rushed from his mortal wound, yet he felt no fear. Instead he looked up at the fiery spectacle of Sybille.

In the Dominican monastery at Avignon, he had often prayed at a small terra-cotta shrine to the Virgin Mary—Mary alone, without her husband, without her child. She stood in a narrow-fitting arched alcove, arms at her side, palms turned outward as if to welcome the world, a votive placed at her tiny, delicate feet. And when at night the wick was lit, the upcast light imbued her beatific and translucent features with an unearthly glow. Indeed, the glow seemed to radiate from within her, filling the alcove in the arched shape of a doorway, or a cathedral window. A miracle, the brothers had decided, and so the shrine was regularly graced with flowers, offerings, and prayers.

It seemed to Luc that Sybille's features possessed that same serenity, the same all-encompassing compassion, the same golden radiance that surrounded her in the shape of an arch; and were her arms not pulled back cruelly by the chains, they would be spread in welcome—even to her Enemy, Chrétien. And though he, Luc, lay in darkness, and she was no doubt momentarily blinded by the sudden strong light, she looked at him—directly into his eyes—and smiled dazzlingly.

"Hail, Mary," he called out to her, not with the humility of a sinner but with the jubilation of a believer, "full of grace! The Lord is with thee! Blessed art thou. . . ."

The wind howled as if grieving, and swirled through the alley with the fury of a whirlwind. The fire flared upward, consuming kindling and twigs with violent appetite.

With the wind had come a sparse sprinkling of rain; one cold drop stung Luc's cheek.

But the drops remained few and scattered; and the wind, penetrating Luc's body with cold so that his teeth chattered unceasing, swept the fire from the logs to Sybille's linen undershift, which caught and was consumed swiftly, orange flames feeding along the linen's edge, leaving floating black ash in its wake.

He struggled to hold his head aloft, to stay alive so that her dreadful sacrifice for the Race would not be in vain; yet he could not. Sighing, he closed his eyes and lowered his cheek to the ground.

"Hear me, Enemy!" Sybille demanded in a voice greater than her own—and Luc forced himself to look.

Sybille's features were fierce, transcendent, and her eyes, otherworldly, beheld something far greater than an alleyway or stone prison.

Chrétien had moved closer to the flames and was watching, too, so entranced he could see nothing else; on his face was a morbid joy, a hunger, a greed. He was waiting, Luc realized, to feed upon the most powerful of souls, that he might in turn become so.

She turned her face toward the cardinal and called out strongly, "You think you have won, Domenico! But here is the magic: the victory is ours!"

And then she gazed down at Luc, this time her voice breaking in small part because of the pain, but in greater part because of an urgent love, a Divine love that reached directly from her heart to his. "Luc de la Rose, remember!"

And he remembered.

Edouard saying: *"Drink . . ."*

Suckling at his mother's breast—the bliss, the joy . . .

All of it dashed as Beatrice hurled him to the ground, her mouth hideously twisted as she howled, the maternal affection in her eyes replaced by something feral, predatory . . .

The girl on the wagon's edge, shrieking at the very sight of him.

The Enemy's voice, a subtle whisper: *As you destroyed your mother, so shall you destroy her . . .*

He had lied to himself all these years, had convinced himself his deepest fear was that his mother would die a madwoman. But it had been Sybille, always Sybille, for whom he had been terrified. He had always known—had he not?—that he would hasten her doom. And so it was: she was forced now to die because of him, because of his inability to face the truth. He had refused to confront his fear when Edouard had given him the potion; had refused to remember that terrible moment when the Enemy had first seized control of his mind, by showing him the most unbearable sight, the same fearful image Sybille had fought so hard to overcome:

Himself, as Michel the inquisitor. The inquisitor whose testimony would bring about the death of his Beloved.

Forgive me, he prayed—silently, for he had grown too weak to utter words aloud. *Forgive me, for I am he no more, but Luc.*

And with the clarity brought by imminent death, he knew the choices before him: to retain the fear, and die before his Beloved did, thus abandoning the Race and dooming her to a meaningless sacrifice; or to surrender utterly.

He surrendered.

And the Presence came fully to him, with a sweetness he had not known for many years, not since his teacher Jacob had laid hands upon his shoulders. Luc pushed himself up on his elbows, oblivious to his fatal wound, and laughed aloud.

Union. Radiance. Bliss.

He remembered: Papa, Maman, Nana—all of them became real figures in his mind and heart; and he felt for each a real love and longing. Luc sobbed aloud, not with sorrow but sheer joy; for with the restoration of his memory had come the knowledge that Sybille had always been aware she might have to endure death to achieve his initiation; that she had surrendered willingly to Chrétien in order to do so. In his heart there was no fear, no grief, no shadow, only boundless love and knowledge.

And the Voice spoke mightily, not just through him but *with* him as though they were One, with all the passion and conviction in his heart.

"Hear me! Look upon the face of her whom you kill. 'Tis not the fire's reflection there, but the very radiance of God—of the Holy Mother Herself. Throw down your weapons and kneel before her, for you are in the Presence of a true saint."

Suddenly Luc found himself standing, facing away from the fire toward those who had guarded it and him; all four guards had indeed thrown down their swords and now knelt facedown in an attitude of reverence. Only Thomas and Chrétien still stood—Thomas with his expression one of triumph. But Chrétien, features contorted by vengeful hate, seized a dagger hidden beneath his cape and rushed at Luc.

Luc neither moved nor flinched, merely opened his arms in a gesture of welcome; Chrétien threw himself against his erstwhile son, roaring with fury as he brought the dagger down into Luc's chest again, again, again . . .

This time, the blade left no mark, and Chrétien fell sobbing to his knees. Calmly, Luc turned away and stepped into the hip-high flames without fear. With a smile—one he imagined as sweet as the one that had graced Sybille's lips when she had touched his cloven heart—he bent down and loosed her red-hot shackles with ease, his flesh sensing the heat but refusing to accept it.

She fell forward, eyes dimming, and he lifted her up in his arms. The skin on her legs and lower arms was charred black, sloughing off in places to reveal blood-red skin beneath; her poor face had been blistered beyond recognition, and the golden Solomon's Seal lay half-molten upon her heart.

An errant drop of rain struck it and turned immediately to steam; yet Luc did not weep. Instead he carried her from the flames, feeling no grief, only a bliss so profound that there was no Evil, no Enemy, no time or separation or waiting, only himself and his Beloved, here, in this eternal moment . . .

And slowly, gently, the gold beneath his palms cooled and re-formed into its original shape; blisters healed; charred skin turned pink once more, knit itself together, and became covered, impossibly, with linen.

As he watched, laughing, the rain began to fall, delicate and sparse at first, then hard, and harder . . . and his love caught his hands and sat up, laughing, her face, her hair, unmarred and beautiful, shining wet through the haze of steam that rose from the sizzling remnants of the fire.

They rose then, garments soaked through, and pressed lips to lips as they embraced each other in the darkness for a moment, for a time, forever. . . .

EPILOGUE

Sybille

XXIII

To the east we ride, my Beloved and I; ride beside those who have faithfully served us, who have worked for years by astral and physical means—even in the Enemy's camp, as has our faithful servant Thomas—to bring us at long last together, and safe. Geraldine is here, garbed and cloaked like a man, as is Luc's mother, the Lady Beatrice, and the surprisingly sturdy, ageless Bishop Rigaud. Luc's beloved uncle rides with us too, his face a constant wreath of joy. Edouard suffered much grief over many years, but now he has regained his nephew and sister.

True, there are times when destiny is hard and bitter; but there are times, too, when it is infinitely sweet.

Even so, there is much to be done. Chrétien has yet to be defeated, and there are others beside him, in different cities and different lands, who would see us and our kind destroyed. The souls remain trapped in the vile magical chamber hidden in the Palais des Papes, in Avignon.

Knowing this, I turn and look over my shoulder at my Beloved, who holds the stallion's reins. His face is flushed, and his eyes—pale green, flecked with gold, infused with the Divine—shine at me with utter love and happiness . . . and recognition. Together we laugh with unspeakable joy: he knows me, my Beloved, he knows me, and at that very instant, the horse's hooves crush rosemary, and I revel in its sharp fragrance.

Rosemary brings memories.

The first challenge has been met. Ah, but much remains to be done. . . .

ABOUT THE AUTHOR

A Florida native, JEANNE KALOGRIDIS began her career at American University teaching English as a second language. In 1982, she sold her first book under a pseudonym, and by 1988 quit teaching to write full-time. *The Burning Times* is her fourth book under the name Jeanne Kalogridis; her previous books include a historical trilogy about Vlad the Impaler, *The Diaries of the Family Dracul.* Visit her on the web at: *www.jeannekalogridis.com.*

The Burning Times

Discussion Points

1. Michel says of Sybille, "Heretic or no, there was much that was good in her; and even if there were not, she deserved, as did all God's children, the opportunity to come to know Him before her death." Do you believe that Michel wanted to convert Sybille to Christianity? How does Michel's experience with Sybille challenge and change Michel's faith throughout the story?

2. Discuss how the book differentiates between religion and morality. The characters identify themselves either as Christians or members of the Race. Which traits most distinguished the Christians from the Knights of the Race?

3. Is it necessary for the reader to believe in magic for this book to be effective? What symbolic meaning could the magical healings in this book have?

4. At what point did you suspect that Michel's role in the story went far beyond that of a mere scribe? When he was visited by Luc's dreams? Or earlier, when he first sensed Sybille's essential compassion and saintliness? What did you guess about his involvement before it was revealed to you?

5. Put yourself in Michel's position when Sybille reveals his true identity. Would you believe her declaration? Or would you distrust her on the basis of the teachings of your superiors? What events or details leading up to her revelation played a role in Michel's reaction?

6. What is the ultimate lesson Sybille learns from her extraordinary trials? Is the lesson religious in nature, or does it transcend spiritual definition? If so, how? How does she put this lesson into practice, and how does it help her achieve her goals?

7. Many of the book's central characters are misunderstood or mistreated women who nevertheless battle against forces of injustice. Do you see Sybille and her grandmother as forerunners of modern feminists? When female characters did seize power, how did they go about it? Besides women, what other groups were targeted by the Inquisition, and why?

8. Do Luc and Sybille remind you of any other notable historical or

mythical couples? In what ways? Now that they are reunited, what do you think will become of Sybille and Luc?

9. Kalogridis is unsparing in the description of pain and injury her characters suffer in their adventures. How did the stark realism of these descriptions affect you? Did they aid your understanding of what was at stake for the characters? Would the book have been less successful if Kalogridis spared us this vivid suffering?

10. Re-creating fourteenth-century Europe for current-day readers is a painstaking enterprise. Which details were most effective in evoking the book's setting? How much did you know about this time period before you read the novel? Did this affect your perception of it in any way?